The Fires of Lilliput

Michael Martin

ACKNOWLEDGMENTS

The Fires of Lilliput is fiction, but its story owes tremendously to the memoirs, diaries, and testimony of real people who survived the savage onslaught of the Second World War in Poland. No fiction could imagine the story presented in these pages. No imagination could conjure such a tale.

I read two powerful and moving memoirs during five years of research: *Why, Oh God, Why? A Daily Diary of Life Inside the Warsaw Ghetto* by Halina Gorcewicz; and *Bellum Vobiscum: War Memoirs,* by Zygmunt Skarbek-Kruszewski.

Neither Gorcewicz nor Skarbek-Kruszewski appear in this novel. But many chapters and passages owe much to their recollections of daily events, from which a central theme emerges.

Articulated so well by Langdon Gilkey and Viktor Frankl, it is that under tense circumstance, we are neither Christian nor Jew, rich nor poor, but man and woman, essential and exposed. The naked reality of suffering strips evil of its subterfuge; reveals good in simple glory; and finds people striving and struggling for some worthy goal.

In *The Fires of Lilliput*, that goal is life. – **Michael Martin**

For my wife and children.
For Bob Freedman and Selma Luttinger,
who encouraged me to write this story.

6   The Fires of Lilliput

"THIS INTERNMENT CAMP REDUCED SOCIETY, ordinarily large and complex, to viewable sizes, and by subjecting life to greatly increased tension, laid bare its essential structures."

–Christian philosopher and concentration camp survivor **Langdon Gilkey**, *Shantung Compound: The Story of Men and Women Under Pressure*

"WHAT MAN ACTUALLY NEEDS is not a tension-less state but rather the striving and struggling for some goal worthy of him. What he needs is not the discharge of tension at any cost, but the call of a potential meaning waiting to be fulfilled by him."

–Jewish philosopher and concentration camp survivor **Viktor Frankl**, *Man's Search for Meaning*

"DESTINY DECIDED THAT I SHOULD FIND adventure in the awful mess of a Europe swept by war." **–Primo Levi**, *survivor*

BOROUGH

One

The monsignor appeared with a young novitiate at her door on a cold Brooklyn day in November 1973. He had an address but no telephone number. He would not have called anyway.

A teenage girl answered the knock. She stayed behind a screen door.

"Is this the home of Shosha Price?"

"Are you looking for donations?" the girl asked.

"No. We came to talk to your mother."

"She isn't here."

"It's urgent."

The girl looked at the men. She looked at their black shirts and wide, white collars. They both wore black overcoats.

"She'll be home later," the girl said. "Can you come back?"

"Do you know when?"

"Maybe an hour."

The men looked at one another and nodded to the girl. She watched them raise their umbrellas and walk down the steps. Then she opened the screen. "Why don't you wait inside?" she said. The men turned and looked at her. "I can make coffee," she said. They walked back up the steps.

"Thank you," the monsignor said.

They spent little over an hour making small conversation. When the girl heard her mother coming in the back door, she stood and went to her. The monsignor and the novitiate heard them exchange words in another room. A well-kept woman in her early fifties came into the front room. The two men stood.

"Shosha Price?"

"Who is asking?" she said. She had a Polish accent, thicker than the monsignor's. He shook her hand gently.

"We are here on behalf of the Vatican," he said. "Jaruslaw Bachleda."

The woman looked at them.

"We're here for something good," the novitiate said. "From the Holy Father in Rome." He smiled and took her hand and her face relaxed.

"My daughter says you've come to speak with me."

"We have," the monsignor said. "We need to speak about Jakub Chelzak, a Servant of God."

The woman stepped back and raised her hand to her mouth. She almost tripped. "My G-d—Jakub." Her voice cracked and she felt her legs weaken. Her daughter took her by the shoulders and felt her trembling.

"Then you are Shosha Mordechai?" the novitiate said.

She looked at him. She was crying without sound.

"Yes," she said. "I am.

GHETTO

Two

Up close, Shosha Mordechai had never seen a soldier. She had only seen them passing in the streets and waving. The war had been a safely distant thing until a young Polish officer in uniform, Pavel Worcek, arrived with a flier advertising a vacancy in one of the Mordechai buildings. Shosha answered the door with a broom in her hand.

"Good day panna," he said. "Is your master here?"

"My papa?" She saw the flier. "You've come about the flat."

"Your papa?"

"I'll get the key."

He followed her across the street and down a block through an alley. They went upstairs to the second floor and she opened the door to a small, clean three-room flat overlooking Pawia Street.

"Fine," the soldier said. "It's fine."

"You should look around a little," Shosha said. "Over here—look at this view."

They looked down through an X-shaped paper strip on the window and saw a man with sidelocks and a beard sweeping the front of a haberdasher's shop.

"Well, if I need a tailor," Pavel Worcek said.

The soldier turned away, but three young men walking up the sidewalk caught Shosha's eye. They crossed the street to the haberdasher. Then she turned away.

"If you like it, my father requires a cash deposit of a month's rent."

"I have that—no problem." He took an envelope from his pocket, counted out the bills, and handed them to Shosha.

A scream from outside stopped her from recounting the money and she rushed to the window. "They're cutting him!" She ran out of the flat, down the stairs, and into the street.

"*Gevalt! Gevalt!*" The old man was on his knees crying—the thugs were shearing his locks with long scissors. People looked out windows and screamed "police!" but only Shosha approached. She turned and ran back and grabbed Pavel Worcek, who stood on the stoop outside the apartment.

"C'mon—you're a soldier," she said and she tugged him, but he resisted. She dropped his arm and went toward the men on her own. The small one held up the scissors when he saw her. She stopped and screamed. She eyed the men and picked up a rock and threw it through a window over the haberdasher's shop. Glass crashed onto the street.

"Spierdalaj ty glupia pizda," said one of the hooligans and they threw the scissors at Shosha and ran. She went to Meziel, the tailor, and bent down. He was bawling and she took his head in her arms. She looked up as a shadow crossed and saw the soldier Worcek. She jammed her hand into her pocket and held up the bills. She could not see the soldier's face for the glare of the sun.

"Keep your money," she said, and threw it at his feet.

Three

At first, it seemed anti-Semitism had suddenly gripped a whole generation of young Polish men, who wandered Warsaw's streets in gangs of six or eight, smashing windows or slashing the cheeks of boys wearing yarmulkes. But gradually the attacks took on a planned character, orchestrated on holy days, more frequent during the Jewish seasons.

"These thugs are Hitler's men," Lev Mordechai said. "Anybody who doesn't see it now, and refuses to fight the way armies fight —well, they will see it soon and more painfully."

Before he left for a two-week service on the wartime planning committee, Lev Mordechai told his seventeen-year-old daughter Shosha "remember, you are a Pole and a Jew. No one is a better Pole because he is Catholic, Lutheran, atheist, or a Russian who settled here turn of the century."

"I don't think about it, Papa."

"You will."

The Germans surrounded Warsaw in a fiery cannonade on Friday, the 1st of September 1939. Radio announcers said bombs fell at dawn on the outskirts of the city. Air raid alarms blared across Warsaw. People fled to basements and cellars. Tenants and homeowners glued X-shaped paper strips on windows to stop pounding vibrations from shattering panes. Shopkeepers secured mannequins and shelves. Children wearing gas masks played stickball in the street.

The people were ignorant and brave.

When the children organized parades, Shosha marched with them wearing a Red Cross satchel on her arm and a gas mask around her neck. When the sirens whined, she ran with the men and older boys to the attics, screaming and cheering and raising a toast with a fantasy glass whenever a German *Stuka* fell out of the sky. When her mother Rebekah found her in a loft, she dragged Shosha to the basement.

"You should know better," Rebekah said.

"No one was shooting at us."

"Your father hasn't told you about shrapnel? Or stray bullets?"

"All the time," Shosha said.

The women hid clothes, fabric, furs, and jewels in trunks and crates and suitcases, secret rooms and cellars. They laughed uncomfortably when Warsaw's president, Stefan Starzynski, lost his voice on the radio pleading for order and calm. Rebekah Mordechai stood over a fortress of food in the hallway, the stairwell, and the back rooms in her house.

"Leiozia, we need to divide this," she said to her housemaid. "Part to the cellar, part to the kitchen."

The Mordechai women set up a community pantry in a vacant ground-floor flat. Rebekah, Shosha, and Leiozia spent the mornings cooking and giving hot food to anyone who was hungry. The conflict crept and lines formed at the pantry—lines that grew daily, and then with every meal: Refugees who lost homes to bombs; soldiers from platoons and brigades that fighting had reduced to a wounded few; Jews mobs had marked for injury before war reached them. The Mordechais brought beds out of storage and from vacant furnished flats. They bandaged the injured—soldiers and civilians.

Polish propaganda director Colonel Roman urged Varsovians to build fortifications and all able men to leave Warsaw for the eastern front. A week into the conflict, the Polish government left the city. A stray bomb hit one of the Mordechai rental flats, killing an old widower, a Jewish classics professor forced to relinquish his emeritus status in a university purge.

"We have to leave—at least for a while," Rebekah said.

"Leave our home?" Shosha said. "What will we come back to?"

"They're saying this is temporary—until the Red Army comes. We can wait it out at the farm."

The farm was a summer home in Lev Mordechai's family for years, about twenty four kilometers (fifteen miles) north of the city. It was always stocked with provisions. The family took some belongings but left most of their food to people who couldn't leave the city. The army commandeered taxis and buses so at first they walked, over barricades and past soldiers who jammed the streets, and past other refugees.

"Shosha—don't try that," Rebekah said.

Shosha stood poised to jump at the edge of an anti-tank ditch that ran the entire width of the deserted street, stopping at two brick buildings. The women couldn't walk around it. The only other way was back and down another street. The ditch had water in it, and maybe explosives.

"Mama—how wide do you think this is?"

"You can't jump it," Rebekah said. "And even if you could, what about us?"

Shosha saw an open door in an abandoned building and a pile of broken bricks. She picked through them, running her hands along the edges. She took the brick with the flattest edge, walked up the steps to the door, and used it to knock out the metal posts that held the door to its hinges.

"Shosha. That's not ours," her mother said.

"I'll need help," Shosha said. "When the door comes out from the last hinge."

The women hesitated, but Leiozia went up the steps and held the door. Rebekah watched, but when the door was about to unhinge, she stepped up. Shosha popped the last hinge post and the women lowered the door. Farther off, they heard explosions and voices through bullhorns: screams and commands. They dragged the door, raised and positioned it, and let it drop over the ditch. They set it securely. Then they crossed, one by one.

"Shosha—my little saint," Rebekah said.

THE GERMANS BOMBED ALL night. The women passed the darkness in a drainage tunnel. They started out early next morning. They got out of the city by afternoon. They paid a carriage driver and traveled with a load of scavenged furniture to the farm. In a few days, after the curtains parted and fire lighted the house, Polish soldiers came.

"Have you seen Lev Mordechai?" Shosha asked every man. "He's a captain, he's tall, about two meters, dark hair—he has all of it, and he's very handsome."

Some soldiers thought they had seen him; some had seen men who looked like him. But in each case, the man they had seen had disappeared, together with men and munitions weaving a tattered web of advance and retreat across the countryside. Rebekah never had the nerve to ask about her husband. The man who vanishes from his family for too long has either taken up with a mistress or died.

LEV AND REBEKAH MORDECHAI met after the First World War, Lev a Jew from a prominent family, Rebekah a Lutheran. Though neither family blessed it, the Mordechai union thrived, free from the whims of bickering siblings and the will of parents from disparate faiths. With no dowry, Lev Mordechai made himself a wealthy man, collecting rents and rental properties, a summer estate, and land inside and beyond Polish borders. To honor her husband, Rebecca took the more Hebraic "Rebekah" shortly after their marriage.

Shosha grew up around the unmarried Poles and Jews who rented her family's two and three-room flats. They were young and sometimes beautiful, intelligent, questioners, writers, and skeptics. Shosha's friends included a bookish homosexual with a stack of unpublished novels, and a lovely researcher with three suitors who won a prestigious mathematics prize in Russia. A few of these open-minded intellectuals considered the Mordechai marriage a sign. The Jews, in particular, considered the union a philosophical bridge.

Some people associated Rebekah's faith with Hitler—even saying Lutheranism was the official church of the Nazi party (Hitler was baptized Roman Catholic and never named an official state church). Lev Mordechai was a member of the House of Ger, a great rabbinical line. He could trace his lineage to his great great great uncle, the Gerrer Rebbe Yitzchak Meir, the first Rabbi of Ger, a village in Poland. Lev Mordechai's great uncle, the Rabbi Yehudah Aryeh Leib of Ger, completed a work of monumental Talmudic scholarship, the Sefat Emet al Ha Torah, a commentary on the Torah in five volumes. Lev Mordechai's uncle, Rabbi Avraham Mordechai Alter, expanded the Hassidic community of Ger, to more than one hundred thousand people. He lived to see the Nazis annihilate most of them and lived to escape, to rebuild the Gerrer Chasidut from Jerusalem.

REBEKAH SAW THE FIRST Germans before sunrise: columns of men and machines on the other side of the fence and the pines and the bushes around the house. The tanks shook the windows and their tracks ripped the hard dirt and armored transports ground along in the dust. The women closed the drapes and built a fire at night. Warsaw fell a few days later.

In October, Polish soldiers brought word to the Mordechai farm that all former inhabitants of Warsaw could return—and should return, to help fight in the coming insurrection.

"If we go back, what can we expect?" Leiozia asked.

"Papa," Rebekah said. "Our best hope for him is in Warsaw." She sat near a cracked window.

"What's left?" Leiozia asked. "What can possibly be left?"

"I don't know," Rebekah said. "But I would like to."

They walked away from the estate, traveling at night across rough countryside to avoid Germans. Here and there, they hitched rides from friendly strangers. They stayed clear of lanes and roads they had used the first time. They saw villages burning, and they walked across deep ruts from tank treads and over mortar holes blasted into the Earth. Rubble, corpses, and tangled barbed wire outlined the edge of the city. Rebekah stopped and stood, stiff and still.

"Mama—keep going," Shosha said.

Her mother's eyes were dry and wide, her cheeks ashen. They walked to their house on Pawia Street. It took direct fire but the walls stood. Rebekah cried.

"We can rebuild the roof," Shosha said. "We can put in floors, ceilings, plaster and paint—the house would be good as new."

They didn't hear from Lev Mordechai, but the novelist on the third floor had heard a house in London would publish his latest book. The manuscript had saved him from a bullet. He stuffed it into the wall after the worst night of shelling.

"Look," he told Shosha, opening it to almost the end, where a bullet had burrowed into its thick pages.

"I think it's a sign," Shosha said. "The book will be a great success!"

But first things first. "Now I need to get another clean copy," he said.

AS LONG AS THE occupiers circulated the same currency, the Mordechai family had means to rebuild. They hired villagers— for hard cash and bricks—from the area around their summer estate. A pungent brew of char and decay dictated their first task. They exhumed bodies from heaps of brick and glass. Shosha helped cover the dead.

"You're enthusiastic in your work," Rebekah told her.

"Enthusiastic?" Shosha asked.

"This is the first war for you—how can you help but be excited by it? I was, in my first war."

"It's fear," Shosha said. "My stomach won't stay down. I just want to hurry up and get it done."

"This is the second war for me and fear is all I feel," Rebekah said. "My L-rd, where is Papa?" She sat but didn't cry.

Rumors circulated the Germans were planning a separate district for Jews, to halt the spread of typhus, they said. The occupiers closed all schools in Warsaw, forcing most Jews into clandestine academies called *komplety*. Shosha taught mathematics in a *komplety* for three weeks when the first hard frost coated the windows. Lines formed for coal.

"It's freezing!" She slapped her mittens against her legs.

Leiozia picked up the near-empty coal bucket next to the front door. "The furnace still needs work," she told Shosha. "They installed the wrong-sized flue. I think they'll never finish."

"At least we can live here."

"Barely."

Leiozia opened the door but before she could walk out, Shosha took the bucket from her. She wrapped the compulsory Star of David band around her arm.

"They owe me," Shosha said. "I've been teaching their children for free."

The fuel store proprietors took Shosha out of the line and around back. They filled her bucket with coal, extra full, past the top. She dragged the bucket through the alley and into the street, where she saw German *SS* troops standing a small man against the remains of a brick wall. She pulled her coal bucket behind a corner. She took off the blue star and stuffed it into her coat pocket.

"I am a Pole and will die a Pole," she heard the small man say.

"I am a German," one of the *SS* men yelled in broken Polish. "Say it."

"I am a Pole. I was born in Poland," the man said again.

"I am a German and I swear allegiance to *mein Führer* and the Reich," said the *SS* officer.

"I am a Pole," the man said. "A Pole I will die."

"*Ja*, apparently." The other *SS* turned the man around. He shook but stood fast. The soldiers laughed. Shosha thought she heard gunfire, but she couldn't be sure because shots echoed from other parts of the city. She ran as fast as her load would allow.

ENTRANCE FORBIDDEN TO POLES AND JEWS.
Nur Für Deutsche.
The Germans divided the city with signs like these on restaurants, museums, parks, and other public places. The cold —it reached minus fifteen degrees centigrade—gave the occupiers another way to remove the occupied. They rationed food and coal so tightly fewer and fewer people could survive the winter. In February 1940, temperatures dropped to minus twenty five degrees centigrade.

"Oh L-rd—my L-rd child, where have you been? How did this happen?"

Rebekah rubbed paraffin oil on Shosha's feet, blue-black with early frostbite. "If you can't even walk to the *komplety* without the cold seeping in, then you can't go out at all," Rebekah said.

"I stood in line for coal," Shosha said. "It's in the bucket."

"You have stockings and thick shoes—how long did you stand?"

"Long. They're almost out."

Rebekah looked in the coal bucket. "For this?" she said. "How long?"

Shosha hesitated and stared at her feet.

"How long?" Rebekah raised her voice.

"Four hours," Shosha said. "Four hours. Tomorrow it will be six."

"How much more of this can we stand?" Rebekah said. She looked at her daughter and the coal. "Come on. We'll use it to warm some water."

"So I go out only to have the coal used up on me?" Shosha asked.

"Doesn't make sense, does it?" Rebekah said.

She took her daughter's arm and helped her upstairs. They were careful because the carpenters never completed the handrails.

"SHOSHA!"

The sun was rising. Shosha lay in bed. She felt Leiozia's hand on her shoulder.

"What is it?" Shosha mumbled.

"Shhh," Leiozia said. "Everyone's still asleep." She motioned Shosha to the window. "Look."

"What?"

"They're fencing us in."

"What? Who's doing this?"

Leiozia led Shosha to the back door. They each put on a wrap and walked out, in the cold through the alley. They heard loud voices and shouting.

"*Schnell, schnell, Schweine banditen!*"

At the end of the alley, they peered around the building.

"What is this?" Shosha asked. "What are they doing?"

Piles of bricks, cement, and broken glass squatted around a trench. A few *SS* and other uniformed Germans stood and smoked and spit chewing tobacco. Men in prison rags were digging.

"They're waiting for more prisoners to help," Leiozia said. "I heard them say so."

"How can you be sure this is a fence?" Shosha asked.

"We've all heard the talk—about the Jewish district," Leiozia said. She sighed and bit the nail on her forefinger. "What else could it be?"

Prison workers erected walls made of war waste, three stories high and remarkably similar, across Swietokrzyska, Zlota, Freta, and Smocza streets. The residents of Okopwa and Pawia streets called a meeting at the Mordechai house, where the rubble wall was meters high and growing.

"It's for security," Josek Lodr said. "For us."

"I don't think they care about our security," Rebekah Mordechai said. "Why should they?"

"It could be for the children," Mrs. Stryzinsckzi pointed out. "They play in areas that make the Germans nervous. Too close to the prison, sometimes, and the guard stations."

"We should ask them," Shosha said.

"Ask them? You're a crazy child," Mr. Piermanski said. "You don't just go up and ask these pigs anything."

But Shosha did, a few hours later.

"What are you putting up here?"

"*Weg, weg, Jude!*" the soldier barked at her.

"I'm only asking," Shosha said. "I'm not going to bite."

"No?" said the soldier. "I hear you do."

Shosha was a woman of notable features—clean and open. The young soldier liked what he saw. He grinned.

"Little rat—*ee ee ee ee ee.*" He shriveled his nose and nibbled the air.

"And you're a pig," Shosha said.

The soldier raised his rifle. "What did you call me?"

"A pig," she coughed.

He aimed. "I could splatter your brains all over this nice wall," he said, in a mix of German and mispronounced Polish. He touched the barrel to her chin. She thought he must be about eighteen or nineteen. The Germans didn't waste the seasoned soldiers here.

"Better for me to die than live with a pig," Shosha said.

"You're brave," he said. He lowered the rifle. "Now go play with the other rats—*ee ee ee ee ee.*"

She walked away. She looked back once and the pig was laughing, biting the air and hissing, like a rat.

"I'm not such a pig," he said in Polish, slowly and with less stammer. "I didn't shoot you. You're a very pretty rat."

SHOSHA HEARD SOMETHING AND went out the back door to the alley. She never used the front door—no one used front doors anymore. She peered around the street and saw a man in uniform digging near the bottom of the wall. He cast a silhouette against the street in the moon. He loosened some bricks and stood straight. Shosha couldn't tell what uniform he wore, but could see it was not Polish. It looked disheveled in the poor light. The Germans wore their uniforms in the spit and polish fashion. The man turned and wiped his forehead.

"Hello," he called out.

She ducked back. He turned and went back to his digging. She slipped her head around the building again.

"If you want to watch," he said, "you certainly may."

Shosha looked around the deserted street. She stepped from behind the wall and walked toward the man.

"If we take out enough of these bricks, you can get to your schools without going round the guards," the man said. "And you won't have to put on that stupid arm band."

Shosha closed the gap between them and saw a stack of bricks and a hole near the bottom of the wall. "You could be shot for this," she said.

The man turned to her. He wore an armband with a swastika and an officer's cap with a dull iron eagle. His belt buckle needed polish and his shoes were muddy and scuffed. Shosha frowned.

"I'm afraid I'm not much of a soldier," he said. He took off the cap and she saw in the dim light his sidelocks, tied behind his head.

"Azar Gimelman." He extended his hand to her. "I'm from Krakow and your tata sent me."

Shosha's legs went limp.

"Papa?" her voice quivered.

"He thought you could use the services of a resourceful rabbi."

"He's alive? Where?"

"In Krakow. He is fighting, but they have not called up the rabbis—yet."

Shosha collapsed and the rabbi moved to her and took her in his arms.

"It's all right," he whispered. "You'll see him again. But we have to make arrangements."

"What are you doing here?" Shosha asked. "Why didn't you come to the house?"

"I was killing time," the rabbi said. "I found your house faster than I expected. Lev told me to wait until the wee hours of the morning, when no soldiers were around."

Shosha swept her hair from her face and looked at him through an uncomfortable smile and tears.

"And this ridiculous uniform?" she asked.

"I got it from a villager selling rags," the rabbi said. "I don't want to think where he got it."

"Killing time tearing down our wall," Shosha chuckled. "Papa sent us a brave man or a fool."

"A bored man," the rabbi said. "I was sitting there, on those steps, tucked away, just staring. I kept staring at the bricks. I couldn't help it when I saw so many loose—such poor craftsmanship these days."

"We should get out of the street," Shosha said.

"Let me finish."

The rabbi loosely put back the dislodged bricks. They looked around before they stepped out of the shadow of the wall and Shosha led the rabbi to the alley and onto her home.

After sunrise, the rabbi introduced himself to the other members of the household and presented Rebekah a handwritten letter from her husband. She looked at it and her hands shook and she became so dizzy she had to sit. The letter told her to stay safe and obey the rabbi, a man of the highest integrity whom Lev Mordechai had saved from a bullet. She stared at the words but couldn't focus her eyes enough to read them.

A FRAGMENTED MOSAIC OF leaden-glass shards that changed color in the sun spiked the top of the wall around the Jewish district. Gray and red and brown and orange bricks meandered twelve kilometers, like stooping shoulders three meters high. Impatience and fear weakened the wall in places, where mortar gave way to handfuls of sand, tamped in haste to avoid a beating or a bullet in the jaw. Barbed wire strands hung like a clothesline, strung between wooden crosses and V-shaped posts along the wall. A Christian artist from the Aryan side painted a mural on a section of the wall that imagined a crown of thorns surrounding the district. The artist named the entrance gates *Gethsemane*. The official German name for the enclosed area was *Seuchegefahrgebiet*, or "district threatened by typhoid." The German authorities declared the word *ghetto* strictly *verboten*.

Why a medical quarantine required a government separate from the rest of the city puzzled its residents. Governor Ludwig Fischer appointed Adam Czerniakow—president of the Jewish Council of Elders or *Judenrat*—"district burgomaster." The Judenrat was a hollow body "in charge" of the health department, food supplies, employment, and the Jewish police.

The district pulsed with a weak but functional heart of cafes, clubs, classes, seminars, and liquor. Shosha attended a lecture about the new science of quantum physics which involved so-called "imaginary numbers" that seemed as unreal as Warsaw. An "uncertainty principle" applied to quantum objects, where even a researcher with the latest and best technology couldn't tell the precise whereabouts of a particle. The lecture became popular, with demands for several encores.

Shosha helped collect money for covert shopping expeditions into the Aryan section. Children slipped across the wall through Azar Gimelman's "rabbi hole" under the word "L'Chaim" someone scratched across the bricks over the narrow passage. A first team of little bodies distracted the guards, or bribed them if enough time had passed since their last military payday. Children from Aryan-Jewish marriages worked best for the first team because they looked less Jewish. When Jewish children from the second team slipped under the wall, they sometimes had to wait in the shadows of gateways and porches of the homes of sympathetic Poles until the guards turned away or changed shifts.

The same sympathetic Poles dropped food by the edge of the rabbi hole and left notes describing changes in the guard routine for their streets. The children sent signs to one another calling the way clear. They visited the Aryan shops and sometimes bought more than they could carry back alone. It was common to see ragged children in the company of a shopkeeper's helper walking toward the wall and slipping along it, then disappearing and leaving the helper to return alone.

On the Jewish side, Shosha and Rabbi Gimelman had to teach the little Fagins to suppress their hunger until they could get the food across the wall. The elders planned to inventory the food and distribute it while the children stood and drooled, clasping a bundle of greens or a loaf of bread or a sack of potatoes with visible roots, their legs quivering and their stomachs audibly rumbling. They cried when Shosha took the bundles and some fell to the ground in a tantrum of delirious longing.

"For a starving person to see, touch, and smell food and not be able to eat it—could there be a faster route to insanity?" the rabbi asked. They modified the distribution plan so the children ate immediately.

RABBI GIMELMAN CALLED ON wealthy friends outside the Ghetto to open an entertainment center that would feature famous singers and musicians from the outside.

With investments from the Ghetto's elite and the rabbi's friends, Sztuka opened on Nalewki Street. Most of the performers were Jews, a few from London, and some from New York—Manhattan and the comedy clubs in Upstate. They slipped in and out of the Ghetto with bribes and subterfuge, and the power of American fame. Their entourages generated enough noise and activity to cover the transfer of money and valuables and contraband. A pipeline of contraband—coffee from South America, caviar from Russia, newspapers from New York—kept wealthy patrons coming back. A black market flourished, headquartered in other noisy nightclubs with names such as Palac Melodia and Casa Nova.

On the day comedian Morris Schwartzman—stage name Augie Pasquale—arrived, the rabbi wrote a letter in his office at Sztuka for Lev Mordechai. Things were better, he said. Life in Warsaw and the Jewish district settled down and food was not so short. He made sure Rebekah saw the letter before he sent it out.

"Azar."

Augie Pasquale was between sets and stood at Sztuka's bar. The house was full. An intermission band tuned up on stage. Rabbi Gimelman pardoned himself and walked away from a young man dressed in a faded silk suit and a young woman in a fur.

The rabbi sat next to the comedian at the bar.

"So how are you?"

"I'm well," Augie said.

"We've barely been able to talk," the rabbi said.

"And we must," Augie said. "I have something for you." Augie directed both their eyes to his clenched fist below the bar. He opened it to five large diamonds. The smoky light made them glimmer blue.

"Vodka, neat," Augie said to the bartender.

Augie took the drink from the top of the glass and dropped the diamonds into it. "Meant to say on the rocks." The rabbi grasped Augie's shoulder and took his hand and hugged him.

"L'Chaim!" Augie said.

"L'Chaim!"

"THIS WAR WOULD BE ONLY a partial success if the whole lot of Jewry survived it, while we shed our best blood to save Europe," the German Governor General of occupied Poland, Hans Frank, lectured his soldiers in 1941. "My attitude toward the Jews will therefore be based solely on the expectation that they must disappear. They must be done away with. Gentlemen, I must ask you to rid yourself of all feeling of pity. We must annihilate the Jews wherever we find them and wherever it is possible."

Two men in black overcoats handed Shosha a letter from Governor General Frank ordering "disinfection" for all persons in the Jewish district and their homes. Typhus remained an enormous threat, the letter claimed, and so this action was necessary for the health and well being of the children.

"Mama—look at this," Shosha said. "Under penalty of law," she read, "you must report not later than April 15 to the sanitary station in your district. They're the old mykwas on Spokojna and Dzielna."

"It's crap," Rebekah said. "What are they up to?"

"Houses in the district must be left open and unlocked at all times during the sanitation process," Shosha continued. "Teams will be on the premises to disinfect against all organisms capable of transmitting typhus and other communicable diseases."

"Another way to degrade and insult us," Rebekah said. "So this is what they've been up to—concocting this shitty idea."

On their assigned day, German and Polish "sanitary personnel" loaded Shosha and Leiozia into a stinking produce truck crammed with people. Everyone stood. The truck bumped and hobbled to the mykwa—a bathhouse—where sanitary personnel opened the trucks and soldiers used leather riding crops to force everyone into two lines—one for men and one for women—that wound around the building and down two blocks. Women dressed as nurses walked down either side of each line.

"Strip," they barked in Polish and German. "Strip naked, strip naked, strip, strip."

Clothes fell from one person after another and the sanitary personnel gathered garments and emptied pockets and confiscated jewelry. One man resisted so the soldiers took him into the street and they took a woman, though she wasn't resisting but standing silently and shivering. The soldiers yelled at the others in the line and raised their crops and beat the man and the woman in the face and the backs of the legs. After enough screaming, the soldiers pushed the man and woman back with the others.

Shosha looked up and down the lines, at the old women with stretch marks and birthing scars and atrophied muscles grasping at round flabby bellies that overhung thin, shaky legs. She looked at the young women, the muscles of labor, the firm, tight skin, and the marks of the sun and little scars on arms and legs, and breasts that were still high. She looked at the surgical scars, the marks, the moles, the bruises and the malformations. She looked at all the things once covered, now bare, all the things strangers were never supposed to see. Young propped up old and everyone looked away from the soldiers, who were laughing and ogling, spitting on the ground, sated and bored after a few eyefuls.

Shosha heard screams and cries coming from the mykwa. She looked at Leiozia as they rounded the corner and entered through the large double doors. The soldiers herded the lines toward the screams, into showers. They pushed Shosha in, then Leiozia, and the freezing water stung them until their bodies went stiff and their ears went deaf to the screaming and the stumbling crowd pushed them out and they stood, dripping and numb.

The wet, stark bodies moved toward more women dressed as nurses. The nurse's gloved hands opened the mouth, pried the nose and ears. She ran her fingers through the hair. She folded back the eyelids and probed the belly button. She slapped apart the legs and directed a lamp and spread the anus and fingered any hemorrhoids until she felt a wince. She turned the body around, into the light, then spread the vagina, first with two fingers, then four. Everyone—men and women—could see. The nurse spread each toe. Then she stood and yelled.

"Clean!"

Shosha stepped up. She stood bare with a ready fist. The nurse opened Shosha's mouth, pried her nose and her ears. The gloved fingers spread through her hair. The nurse moved down Shosha's body and her fist tightened and she looked at the guards at both doors. The nurse moved her hand down but Shosha grabbed it by the wrist before it could touch her vagina. The nurse looked up. Shosha narrowed her eyes and held the wrist. The nurse looked at the guard, then at Shosha, who looked down at her other hand, the fist. The nurse looked at the fist too and watched it open to a wad of cash, wet and crumpled. The nurse tugged at her wrist and Shosha's fist snapped shut. The nurse looked at Shosha. She placed her free hand on Shosha's fist and tugged her probing hand. But Shosha held firm. She partly opened her fist and the nurse opened her hand and wrapped her fingers around the cash. Shosha grabbed the nurse's fingers and the cash. She motioned to Leiozia with her eyes.

"Her too," Shosha said.

The nurse stood.

"Clean," she announced.

Shosha's hand snapped open and released the nurse's wrist. Another woman dressed in white pulled Shosha away, toward a pile of wet clothes that stunk with disinfectant. Shosha pulled out her damp shrunken sweater and searched the pile and watched the nurse's hands stop at Leiozia's belly.

"Clean," the nurse said.

Leoizia and Shosha searched through the clothes and pulled out what they could find. The whites were so discolored and the woolens so shrunken they couldn't be certain which clothes belonged to them. In twenty minutes of standing naked on the cold tile floor rummaging with the others and listening to screams and loud voices, they finally had enough to wear so they hurried out, past the guard at the side door and into the fading brightness of the late afternoon.

"I just want to be warm," Shosha told Leiozia. They ran through alleys. When they approached their house at 38 Pawia Street, they saw the front door open. Shosha ran up the steps and saw the inside and stiffened. Leiozia came up beside her, out of breath.

"My L-rd in Heaven," Leiozia said.

The sickening-sweet reek of carbolic acid permeated the clothes from drawers and closets piled in the center of each room. The "sanitary staff" had torn down curtains and drapes and drenched the beds and rugs in the dilute yet pungent disinfectant. Shosha picked up a feather pillow, but the down was so saturated that quills poked through the cloth and bit her fingers. She hurled the pillow at a mirror.

"Fuckers," she screamed. "Why did they do this?"

Shosha sat in a chair that sank and gurgled and she cried. Leiozia wrapped her arms around Shosha's neck and kissed her face.

"What will mother say?" Shosha asked. "What will she say when she sees this?"

Rebekah had already seen it and had cried for an hour. When she finally walked out of the house, she left the door open. She walked up the street without looking back and thought for a long time in the afternoon that she might never return.

EVEN NOW, NEAR THE end of spring, the smell of the disinfectant sometimes drove Shosha outside, where she stood on the stoop in the evening breeze in a cloud of her mother's French perfume. Leiozia stood with her and lit a thin cigarette and drew and watched the orange tip glow in the dim light of carbide lamps and candles in windows. The street lamp had been dead for a month.

"I swear to you on Talmud that I will someday kill as many of them as I can," Shosha said.

"Amen—but there is one good one."

Shosha took the cigarette and drew on it and handed it back.

"One of the blueys on Dzielna St.," Leiozia said. "For a pack of cigarettes and a hundred zlotys, he lets the boys pass under the wall."

"Tell them to get us more bread," Shosha said. "The *Judenrat* wants too much bribes for the ration cards."

Rebekah stepped onto the stoop carrying a tray of coffee and slices of a soft cake with a silky layer of crystalline sugar along its brown crust.

"That looks wonderful," Leiozia said. "Where did you get it?"

"Rabbi—he has a parcel of them," Rebekah said. "From the States."

Rebekah lay the tray on the stoop and sat. Shosha squeezed a perfume atomizer over her mother's head.

"Do I stink?" Rebekah said.

"No," Shosha said. "It's a sign of affection in these times."

Rebekah wrapped her hand around Shosha's neck and pulled her face close and kissed her on the forehead and kissed her hair.

"Rabbi wants to celebrate New Year," Rebekah said. "He's making plans."

"What about Tashlich?" Leiozia said. "How do we find enough water?"

Rebekah raised a china cup to her lips, careful to avoid a chip on its rim.

"I'll remind him," she sipped, "that we cannot cleanse our sins in the sewers."

"You'd better do it soon," Shosha said. "They're threatening to close the Ghetto."

"Just as papa's ready to come for a visit," Rebekah said.

"Papa?" Shosha said. "Where did you hear this?"

"Rabbi. The Home Army says they want to let him home for a respite."

"Rabbi, rabbi, rabbi," Shosha said. "Is there a miracle of which this man is not capable?"

"The miracle will be getting papa home," Rebekah said. "I think it's two pipes shy of a pipe dream."

"You know they beat Adam today," Leiozia said.

"Adam—our Adam, Czerniakow?"

"They want his loyalty," Shosha said.

"Fine way to get it," Rebekah said.

"They're cramming too many people in here," Leiozia said. "They can't afford even a peep of dissent." She drew on her cigarette. "It makes me sick—they fractured Adam's jaw."

"Rabbi has mentioned a revolt," Rebekah said. "The idea has many supporters."

Leiozia smoked the last centimeter of her cigarette then flicked the ashes into the street, where they flared and fell like Lilliputian firecrackers. She slipped another cigarette out of her pocket and lit it.

"You're living luxuriously over there, woman," Shosha said. She motioned with two fingers and Leiozia passed the cigarette. Shosha drew on it and watched the thin sleeve burn back from the glowing tobacco embers. She flicked them off and they fluttered to the street in another tiny pyrotechnic display.

"Live free or die," Shosha said, and she handed the cigarette back to Leiozia.

A HUMID SUMMER YIELDED to fall and the high holy season of Tishri. The rabbi spent September making plans for Rosh Hashanah and Yom Kippur and the Festival of Sukkot right after.

"I'm fretting about all this," he told Rebekah. "The logistics are impossible."

Rosh Hashanah—the Jewish New Year and the beginning of Tishri—fell on the third and fourth days of October 1940. Although Leviticus 23:24-25 institutes the New Year, the Bible never uses the name Rosh Hashanah, but instead refers to the holiday as Yom Ha-Zikkaron—the Day of Remembrance—or Yom Teruah—the Day of the Sounding of the Shofar, a ram's horn blown like a trumpet. Hearing its four distinct notes, each lasting for different intervals, is an essential observance of Tishri's commencement. On each day of the New Year, one hundred shofar notes sound, in what some say is a call to repent.

No Jew labored on Rosh Hashanah and because the Germans had closed the synagogues, Rabbi held traveling services in basements and empty buildings. But he didn't have a shofar and no one knew anyone who did. On the warm early evening of October 4th, the rabbi returned from his ministry and knocked at the back door of the Mordechai house.

"We're ready?" he asked Leiozia. He was carrying a bag.

"Yes," she said. "I'm getting goose bumps."

Leiozia, Shosha and Rebekah stepped down the back steps and followed the rabbi through the alley. He led them to the wall.

"Put these on," he said. He passed around wigs from the bag.

They each crawled through an opening in the wall and on the Aryan side they walked in the dark. They saw only one Nazi gendarme, but he was talking to a girl. They made it down to the Wisła.

"I don't know why," Rebekah said. "But when Leiozia brought this up, I hadn't thought of the river."

Poland's longest river, the Wisła—also known as the River Vistula—flowed through Warsaw on its way to the Baltic Sea, separating the city from its neighboring suburb, Praga. It carried water through several cities, including Gdansk, Krakow, and Oswiecim, otherwise known as the city of Auschwitz.

At the river's edge, Rabbi said a quiet prayer and they took what they had in their pockets and cast it into the water. "L'shanah tovah tikatevi v'taihatemi," the rabbi prayed. "May you be inscribed and sealed for a good year."

This was Tashlich, the "casting off," and Leiozia Strazinski was so moved she cried.

ON YOM KIPPUR—The Day of Atonement—Warsaw's Nazi occupiers officially created the largest Jewish ghetto in the world and published a map with the boundaries. Soldiers forced out 113,000 non-Jewish Poles to make way for 138,000 Jews, cramming thirty percent of the city's population into two percent of the city's area.

Augie Pasquale saw irony in the ritual restrictions of Yom Kippur. He joked to his Sztuka audience about fasting for twenty five hours ("I don't know about you, but most people here have been doing this for twenty five months."); washing and bathing ("Bath? Since when?"); wearing leather shoes (he took a tattered shoe from a man in the audience and held it up and examined it. "Yep—it's leather—I think.")

The audience roared.

In a makeshift synagogue, where an open cabinet displayed the scrolls of a Torah, Rabbi Gimelman concluded Yom Kippur. Everyone stood for this hour-long service.

"This is the closing of the gates," the rabbi told them. "We go into the next day cleansed and renewed."

The Holy Season's final festival, "Sukkot seems misplaced now," the rabbi said to Shosha. "It's not a particular celebration anymore. It's a way of life, but without much joy."

The Festival of Sukkot (Sue-coat) began that year on October 17, the fifth day after Yom Kippur. It is supposed to be a time of joy, but seemed like a return to the wandering it commemorated, in a desert without sand.

"Sukkot" means "booths," or the temporary, makeshift dwellings G-d commanded the Israelites to inhabit during their wandering. "You will dwell in booths for seven days; all natives of Israel shall dwell in booths." Leviticus 23:42

Before, the Mordechais built a makeshift celebratory sukkah (the singular noun) in their home, taking their meals in it for a week. Now "any reasonably sound dwelling in this forsaken wilderness will qualify," the rabbi instructed. When Shosha was younger, she used to sleep in the sukkah, and make a big deal about its careful construction. A sukkah must have precisely two and a half walls because one of the Hebraic letters in the word "sukkah" has two and a half sides. The walls may be of any size or any material—except the pillows Shosha tried to use one year, because wind can cast away pillows, and the walls of a sukkah must be solid. The roof of the sukkah must be made of a plant cut from the ground. Tree branches, corn stalks, bamboo reeds, sticks, or planed two-by-fours will work. It must be loose enough to let in rain and stars, but tight enough that there is never more light than shade.

The Mordechai family always decorated their Sukkot—with artwork, paper cutouts, unique ornaments, or pictures. To her Christian friends who sometimes helped, Shosha likened it to decorating a Christmas tree.

Neighbors gathered for this year's festival created a community sukkah from a damaged building seven doors from the Mordechais.

"Seven dwellings away," the rabbi said. "I like that."

Rabbi closed Sukkot with a prayer that the Messiah would come within the next year, at which time prophecy said Jews would slay a Leviathan and build next year's sukkah from the skin of the beast.

"Y'hi ratzon mil'fanekha Adonai Eloheinu vei'lohei avoteinu"
May it be Your will, L-rd, our G-d and G-d of our ancestors

"k'sheim shekiyam'ti v'yashav'ti basukah zu"

that just as I have stood up and dwelled in this sukkah

"kein ez'keh l'shanah haba'ah leisheiv b'sukat oro shel liv'yatan"
so may I merit next year to dwell in the sukkah of the hide of the Leviathan.

"l'shanah haba'ah birushalayim."
Next year in Jerusalem!

After Sukkot, Rabbi closed the Holy Season with Shemini Atzeret and Simchat Torah. Of the holy days, Rabbi best liked Shemini Atzeret —"the assembly of the eighth day"—because at this time G-d was inviting him and his people not to leave just yet, not to say goodbye, but to stay just one more day. For Simchat Torah—"Rejoicing in the Torah"—Rabbi read from the scrolls. The people carried on this quiet celebration, muted but elegant. The day ended as the season had begun—with distant gunfire and hope nearby.

Four

The Germans closed the Ghetto on November 14th and halted food supplies. Prices rose while currency fell and black marketeers refused paper cash, insisting on gold or silver coins or diamonds. The occupiers ordered death for persons who aided Jews. For Jews crossing the wall: fines, arrest, and imprisonment at the Jewish prison on Gesia Street.

Shosha inventoried the coal in the cellar. Leiozia went from street to street looking for bread. Rebekah stayed late in bed, staring at the ceiling. Frost came that night and stayed into the next day.

Shosha was the first to hear three knocks at the door to the back alley, followed by a pause, then two knocks, then three again. She ran up from the cellar and opened the door and swept Rabbi Gimelman into the house in her arms.

"Rabbi! Is it good to see you."

He kissed her cheek and held her face in both his hands, cold in leather gloves.

"How is the loveliest young woman in Warsaw?"

"I wouldn't say that."

"I was talking about your mother." He pressed her face.

"Rabbi."

He kissed Shosha's forehead and walked to Rebekah, standing in the entrance way.

"Are you trying to flatter me out of my funk?" Rebekah asked.

"What's to be in a funk about?" He pulled a cloth bag from his coat pocket and handed it to her. Rebekah peered into it.

"Rabbi—there must be a fortune here."

"Help me with the boxes," he said, and he led them to the back stoop. They carried in thick, corrugated cardboard boxes filled with potatoes, bread, and sausages.

"You can feed an army with this, for a little while," the rabbi said. He was short of breath and he set a bag of wheat flour on a shelf. "They've changed the boundaries again," he said. "I paid hell and a large bribe to get this here. I went by one of my usual routes, thinking, of course, I'm still in the district. Turns out I wasn't."

"They're adding more people, I heard," Leiozia said. She opened the door to the cellar and took hold of a bag of potatoes.

"Shrinking the place and adding more people," Rebekah said. "Tell me the logic in that?"

Leiozia descended the cellar stairs with the potatoes. "It's a logical way to torment," she said. "You want to hear something else?" She was in the cellar now. She stepped up the stairs. "Apparently Lichtenbaum and his sons made a fortune building that wall."

"What's that?" Shosha said.

"The wall—they helped build it."

"Our wall?" Rebekah asked. "Our *cage*?"

"They got a contract from the Germans and free labor from the prison."

"You're kidding," Shosha said. "Where did you hear this?"

"It's around," the rabbi interrupted. "It's old news."

"Old news that Jews helped imprison us for money?" Shosha asked.

"It's outrageous if it's true," Rebekah said.

"It's true all right," Leiozia said. "I've seen the paperwork—with Lichtenbaum's signatures."

"How did you see that?" Shosha asked.

"They'll show anyone who wants to see—especially Jews," Leiozia said. "Just go to the governor's office—they're quite proud of it. A Jewish traitor who sold out to them for a few zlotys."

"It's terrible—terrible," Shosha said. She slammed the side of her fist on a cabinet door. "How could the Lichtenbaums do a thing like that?"

"Money," Rebekah said.

"Not entirely," the rabbi said. He let the words settle.

"What do you mean?" Shosha asked.

The rabbi lifted the bag of gold and silver coins from a table.

"I mean, not entirely," he said.

Shosha breathed in a deep, frustrated way.

"Are you saying our anger is misplaced?" she asked. "Did Lichtenbaum give you the money?"

The rabbi said nothing.

"Did you take it?"

"A little of both," he said finally. "I was persuasive and Lichtenbaum was persuaded."

Rebekah saw her daughter about to speak again.

"You'll stay with us tonight, I hope?" Rebekah said.

The rabbi, so animated before, now hesitated. "The imposition," he said.

"How?" Shosha interjected.

"You don't need to be feeding me—" the rabbi said.

"No—how did you persuade Lichtenbaum?"

"You will stay with us?" Rebekah asked again.

"We need another warm body," said Leiozia, coming up the cellar stairs again.

"You don't need me taking up space," the rabbi said.

"So you won't answer me," Shosha said.

"You won't be imposing," Rebekah said. She was helping Leiozia up the stairs.

"I know things," the rabbi said to Shosha.

"You blackmailed him?" Shosha asked.

"We'll even feed you," Rebekah called from the stairs.

"Black and white mail," the rabbi quipped.

"What?"

"It's all in black and white, and I intended to mail it."

"Mail what? Mail it where?"

"Shosha," Rebekah said, breathless on the stairs. "Enough questions already."

"Photos," Shosha blurted. "You have photos of Lichtenbaum doing something he shouldn't."

"You are a devil, rabbi," Leiozia said.

"That depends on your perspective."

THEY LAY IN ONE bed together, six of them, including two boarders and the rabbi. The coal fire warmed the room into the dark, but the warmth faded. The awful cold from the river winds dropped the temperature to twenty-four below zero centigrade, enough to freeze a fully-clothed man wrapped in underwear and a coat and heavy socks and boots.

The rabbi and the others burrowed under four layers of blankets and long woolen underwear, and two of them wore coats, and still they felt ripples of cold with every flick of an eyelid or turn of a cheek.

"I'm worried for her." Rebekah spoke softly to the rabbi. Next to him on the other side, Leiozia slept. "How can a young person not emerge from something like this warped, if they live?"

"Shosha's too straight and strong to be bent by the likes of this," the rabbi said.

"And Lev?" Rebekah asked. The rabbi turned and faced her.

"He's coming back," the rabbi said.

"When?"

The rabbi lifted his hand from beneath the blankets and cupped Rebekah's cheek in his palm, warm from the heat they shared. She circled his wrist in her fingers and brought his palm to her lips and kissed it after a hesitation. She kissed it again and pressed it harder to her lips and her nose. The rabbi didn't draw away, but let his hand stay with her, pliable until she choked on tears. He pulled her close to him, her hair under his chin and her lips on his neck where her fractured sobs settled into a low weeping, muffled in this tumble-down arrangement of the living, a muted bereavement.

Someone pounded on the Mordechai's door. Rebekah sat up and wiped the frost from a window in the upstairs bedroom. She looked down at the empty street and then up, toward the sky. A cold haze over the city made the sun pale and small. Rebekah heard the knocking again. She crawled over the others, out of bed. She slipped on a robe that had an orange stain running along its side where carbolic splashed it during the last "sanitary inspection." She hurried down the stairs and opened the door to a man with a rifle butt poised to knock with it again. He lurched in with two other men and pushed her aside.

"Where is Lev Mordechai?" the man said. He wore a black suit with markings on his lapel.

"Not here," she said.

"You're his wife?" another man said.

"Yes."

"Wives lie for their husbands."

"I'm not lying," Rebekah said. "He's away in the war."

"*Kennkarte.*" The man put his hand out for her "Reich Identification Card."

"I don't—"

"Right here, *Herr Obersturmführer.*" Rabbi Gimelman strode down the stairs. He handed the twenty-something man a sheaf of papers. The man held them up to the light and Rebekah saw the German eagle stamp on each sheet.

"What do you want with my husband?"

"These papers appear to be in order." He returned them to the rabbi. "We have orders to search this house."

"Certainly," the rabbi said. He looked at Rebekah.

"Where is his room?"

"Whose room?" Rebekah asked.

"Lev Mordechai! His room or study—any place he kept a desk."

The rabbi encouraged Rebekah with his eyes.

"This way," Rebekah told the men. She led them up the stairs and opened a door to a room with a shabby desk and a bed barren of linens. The men went to the desk and opened the drawers.

"Shosha?" Rebekah whispered to the rabbi.

"In bed—I told them all to stay put."

The men pulled out papers, crinkled and blotched, and threw them on the mattress. One man went to the door, another sat on the mattress, and the third sat in a chair. They held the papers up to the dim light that glowed through the sleet on the window.

"Ledgers, it looks like—I can't tell."

"Shit."

"What happened here?"

"Lev did his bookwork, sometimes his—"

"*Nein, nein*—the ink's marred."

"You don't know what happened?"

"That's why I'm asking."

"They disinfected us," Rebekah said.

The agents looked at one another.

"I've never heard of such a thing," the second man said. "Did they disinfect the papers?"

"Yes."

"With what?"

"Carbolic," the rabbi said.

"Fucking idiots."

The men looked under the bed and in the closet. They found a small strong box and burst it open with the rifle butt. They flipped it over and water-diluted carbolic acid dripped out with bills, a few coins, and papers ringed with ink that used to form words.

"Who gave this order?"

"The Governor General gives all the orders," the rabbi said.

"Fuck!"

"Who else lives here?"

"Only us," Rebekah said.

"And if we search?"

"You waste more time," the rabbi said. "If, instead, you leave the house and go to the wall at the end of the street and remove the third stone from the curb along the bottom-most layer, there you will find something that will have made your trip here worthwhile."

"And if we search anyway and I shoot you in the head?"

"Then the wall stops giving," the rabbi said.

The men looked at one another. They moved past Rebekah and the rabbi and tramped down the stairs.

"*Heil Hitler,*" one of them said at the door.

"When Hell freezes," the rabbi said under his breath. He watched the men cross the street toward the wall.

Rebekah saw her breath in the cold air. "It already has," she said. She locked the door and wrapped herself in the robe. "What's in the wall?" she asked.

"Chocolate and cigarettes," the rabbi said. "And a little schnapps—put hair on their chests. They need it."

THE HEALTH DEPARTMENT ASSIGNED Shosha and Rabbi Gimelman for typhus and typhoid inoculations (to protect the occupiers from transmission) at the same time, a little trick of the rabbi's bribery purse. His presence in the Ghetto was not officially documented and he was not on any assignment lists, so with money he could control a bit of destiny. They stood together on Leszno Street and the rabbi watched a horse drawing a wobbly carriage from stop to stop. When it first appeared a few blocks down, the carriage absorbed entire passengers. But as it moved closer, feet, then hands, then heads and bags and coattails and finally entire bodies hung from the rails on the side. The carriage stumbled and halted. The rabbi held Shosha's hand as he pushed their way on board.

"One way, sixty groszy," the driver said.

"Raw capitalism alive and well," the rabbi said. He handed coins to the driver.

They created a space to stand and a place to grip and held each other and fell backward whenever the carriage lurched. It moved up the block then stopped for a white van with a red cross. Shosha watched men in white smocks and soldiers carry bodies down the steps of a three-story building. The carriage pulled around the van and rambled on. A stench penetrated the cold. The carriage stopped. The man next to Shosha craned his head over the others.

"Don't stop here," he yelled to the driver. "Stupid fuck," he said to Shosha.

"What is it?" Shosha gasped. She couldn't see the other side of the street over all the heads.

"Somebody died," the man said.

"How do you know?" Shosha said.

"The body's in the street," the man said.

"They leave the bodies in the street?" Shosha said.

The man looked at her. "Where do you live?"

Shosha hesitated. "Pawia," she said.

"North or south?

Shosha hesitated again.

"Don't worry. I won't rob you."

"North."

"That explains it."

Shosha looked at him.

"They *clean* the streets up there," the man said.

"This is awful," said the woman next to Shosha as people held their noses and tried to turn toward better air.

"Get this heap moving," the man yelled.

"Get going!"

"Go, Go, Go, Go." The crowd chanted and stamped their feet, then cheered when the carriage crept forward.

The rabbi and Shosha stood in another long line inside a dark warehouse, next to rows of bodies stacked along a wall—the recently dead who smelled only a little. Two hours later they emerged in the chill air and the orange hue of the setting sun in the low clouds along the horizon.

"Five hundred zlotys," the rabbi said. "Who can afford this?"

"Did you get an assignment for mama? And Leiozia?"

"Oh yes—weeks ago. That took plenty of money, too. That's the idea. Keep the price of shots so high everybody dies."

"People aren't dying of typhus," Shosha said.

"The prices are ridiculous. Insane."

They walked toward a gate along the wall and children came begging. The rabbi gave one coin to each child. He kept his pocket filled, like bird feed in a park full of pigeons. A girl of about five held out her hands. Shosha considered the girl then stooped to pick her up.

"I wouldn't," the rabbi said.

Shosha picked up the girl anyway. Her clothes were dirty and she smelled. She clutched Shosha around the neck.

"Will you take me?" the girl asked.

"Take you? Where?" Shosha said, watching the rabbi turn his head from side to side.

"Home," the girl said.

"Where is your home? I don't know where it is."

"To your home," the girl chirped.

"I don't know. I'd have to ask my mama and you'd have to ask yours."

"I don't have a mama," the girl said.

While the gate sentry was turned away talking to an old man, two boys and another girl ran past Shosha and through the gate to the Aryan side. The children stopped on the far side of the street and held out their hands to passers by. The sentry turned away from the old man. He walked toward Shosha and the rabbi. The girl squirmed in Shosha's arms.

"*Kennkarte*," the sentry said to them.

"Papers, always papers," the rabbi said.

Shosha set the girl down. She ran off.

"Good thing," the rabbi said. He pulled a wad of papers from his jacket while Shosha produced a neat folder. The sentry looked at the rabbi's papers, signed and stamped by bribed and high-ranking members of the propaganda ministry who relied on foreign entertainers to produce stage shows in Berlin.

"Impressive," the sentry said. He handed the documents back to the rabbi and took Shosha's papers. "Wait here," he said to her and walked toward his station where he kept a list of Ghetto residents. A few steps from where he had turned and not seen the Jewish children on the Aryan side, he now saw them, darting in and out of foot traffic pleading for handouts.

"Little bastards." He undid the strap on his holster, pulled his pistol, aimed and fired.

"Oy vey! He's shooting at them," Shosha said. She started toward the sentry but the rabbi grabbed her arm.

"Don't," he said.

"He's shooting them," she cried, and the rabbi held her tight. He turned her eyes away and pressed her head against his shoulder.

The sentry shot the little beggars, one in the head, the other in the side and the last in the back. The children fell but no one stopped. The right foot and left arm of the one shot in the head twitched. The others were still. The sentry holstered his pistol.

"Did he kill them?" Shosha said. "Let me see. I need to see."

"You don't need to see," the rabbi said.

"Oh Lord why, why, why?"   Shosha cried through hyperventilated puffs. "Why did these have to be sacrificed?"

"It's not a sacrifice, not to G-d," the rabbi said.

"God, God—how can He sit up there and let this happen down here?"

The rabbi took her shoulders. "Don't blaspheme," he said.

She pushed away and he saw her face, red and streaked with tears. She looked up.

"Help us," she cried. "Help us," she yelled. "Help us, goddamn you, help us!"

The rabbi saw the sentry through the window of the hut.

"Shosha—stop it."

"Help us. Help us. Help us." She yelled at God. "You son of a bitch!"

"Stop it." The rabbi grabbed her face. "Shut up," he said.

"Oh, why, why," Her face dissolved in his hand. "Why, why, why." She heard the sentry's boots. "I'll kill him," she murmured. "I'll kill him. Let me go. Let me go!" She pushed against the rabbi, but he pulled her toward a bench, where they sat and where he held her close and turned her away from the street. The sentry stepped up to them and handed the papers to the rabbi.

"In order," he said.

"Son of a bitch." Shosha mumbled into the rabbi's chest, where he held her with particular vigor. He eased his grip after the sentry went away. Shosha cried for a while and then the rabbi didn't hear her. He looked down and saw her staring. He looked away and saw soldiers prodding prison laborers across the street to the Aryan side, where they picked up the bodies of the three children and threw them into the back of a wagon.

They sat until the streets were dark. The rabbi felt rhythmic breathing against his chest and knew Shosha was asleep. In the light from the sentry's hut, he watched the changing of the guard for the evening.

Five

The winter of 1942 brought snows that covered bodies in the street and froze them to the ground. Two brothers —Pinkiert—devised a better method to pry up more bodies faster than any one else. They heated picks and shovels in barrels of burning coal on a wagon drawn by two mules, then broke the ice and snow from around and under the corpses, sometimes burning the flesh. This method was better, their workers would explain to curious passersby, than cutting the clothes away and tearing the body from the ice, which could tear flesh from the body, making for double work and making identification more difficult if the body were lying face down. With bribes for the Governor General and funds for supplies and workers, the Pinkiert brothers supported construction of a wooden bridge over the wall to connect the Ghetto with Kirkut, the Jewish cemetery. In exchange, they became the Ghetto's preferred funeral providers.

Shosha and Rebekah sat near a window in their drawing room watching a Pinkiert crew bring a body down the stairs of the row house across the street.

"Mrs. Fein?" Shosha asked.

"Too big for Mrs. Fein," Rebekah said. "Probably a boarder." Rebekah's stomach rumbled. "Oh. Pardon me."

"Does it ache?"

"Sometimes."

Shosha looked at her mother.

"All right—all the time," Rebekah said.

"Mine aches all the time, too," Shosha said. "All I dream about is food. Last night I had the best dinner of latkes and a sausage papa made of fresh venison."

"Oh, don't say that. With the radishes and steamed tomatoes? Remember that? That was so good!"

"Thank the L-rd for the rabbi," Shosha said. "If it weren't for him, they'd be taking us."

Rebekah craned her head for a better look at the Pinkiert crew. "They're wearing masks and gloves," she said. "I didn't think the fever had reached here."

"Maybe it has."

"I'd hate to be them—doing that all day. What a depressing business."

"They're well paid," Shosha said.

"They're helping on the Kirkut bridge—for nothing."

"Don't kid yourself, mama. They've been well paid for that, too."

"How can you separate good deed from good business in these times?" Rebekah asked.

"I'm happy about Kirkut. That's all I will say."

The front door slammed.

"They're coming," Leiozia yelled.

Shosha stood and Leiozia appeared at the door of the drawing room.

"Greens," she said. Soldiers. "We're the first house."

"Go upstairs—tell the boarders," Rebekah said. "Get the furs."

Shosha ran down to the cellar and opened a trunk filled with furs. She lifted out a sealskin coat. She heard pounding on the front door and her hands shook. She fitted the furs inside dust coats and rain jackets. She heard pounding again and loud voices and pricked her index finger pinning the collars and sleeves of the coats together so they would appear as one. She came up from the cellar, weighted with coats in both arms. She motioned to her mother and a soldier saw her.

"No time for that. No time for that." the soldier cried as Shosha slipped a camouflaged fur on her mother. She gave the other coats to Leiozia and one of the male boarders, and she slipped one on herself. She took her mother's hand and slid off the wedding ring and stuck it in her bra.

"*Raus! Raus! Schnell! Schnell!*" The soldiers marched four boarders and Leiozia, Shosha, and Rebekah down the stairs and into a van crammed with people. Shosha saw sanitary personnel enter the house as the van started down the street. It stopped at the church of St. Augustan on Dzielna Street, in front of an iron-fenced square crowded with people. Two women opened the van's rear doors.

"Out! This way." They herded the twelve through a gate.

Children cried. The old and sick and the depressed and hopeless moaned. Those with hope and defiance—or mental illness—swore and shouted.

"So—we sit, we stand, what?" Leiozia said.

"Mama needs to sit," Shosha said. She led Rebekah where others sat along the fence. "Please, please—she needs to sit—she needs to sit," Shosha said. "Here, please."

People stepped aside and Shosha lowered Rebekah, who today looked faint and old. She sat, huddled and singular, crowded against an old man on one side squatting and smoking a cigarette and on the other side, a woman of about thirty with her skinny knees tucked under her chin. The woman held one arm around her daughter, who stood combing her mother's hair.

Shosha looked beyond the fence, at guards in green and blue. Her mother's stomach rumbled and whined. She squatted and touched Rebekah's cheek.

"It will be all right," Shosha said. "We'll be home soon, after they're finished."

Rebekah looked at her.

"How long can it take, right?" Rebekah asked. "We don't have anything left."

"Hey—spare a little?" Leiozia spoke to the man with the cigarette. He handed it to her and she dragged on it and handed it back.

"Ah—that was good," she said. "You're a good fella."

The man squinted and smiled. Snow fell, a flake here and there. He opened his mouth and let the flakes settle on his tongue and lips.

"Shosha." Leiozia said. She motioned with her head toward the corner of the square, at people beyond the fence. "They have food."

"So?"

"They're trading."

"For what?"

"What else—the coats."

Shosha recoiled. "How do you know?"

"I've heard about it," Leiozia said. "From the Aryan side. They bribe the guards. Everybody gets a cut."

Shosha looked at her coat. Leiozia wrapped her hands around her friend's shrunken waist. "You need food more than a coat," Leiozia said.

Shosha bent down to Rebekah. "I'm going with Leiozia," she said. "Just over there," she pointed, "and not for long."

Shosha and Leiozia pushed through the crowd, stepping over the heads of squatters and dodging obscenities.

"You have to take it off," Leiozia told Shosha. "The top coat."

"The guards will see."

"No they won't. I'll cover you. Just make sure the traders see you."

Leiozia stood between Shosha and the line of sight of the two nearest soldiers. Shosha took off the topcoat. She unpinned the raincoat sleeve and rolled it up to reveal the fur.

"Miss. You—in the brown coat," a man said. "I'll give you a kilo of chops for the fur—okay?" He stood next to two burlap bags tied shut.

Before Shosha could open her mouth, Leiozia interceded. "Not enough," she said. "The fur's worth more. Never worn and top quality."

"One and a half kilos and some sausage. I have to eat too. Agreed?"

"Agreed," Shosha said. She started pulling the fur off, but Leiozia stopped her.

"Let's see the meat," Leiozia said to the trader.

He approached the fence. "You have to look fast," he said, untying the bags. He opened them and Leiozia peered in.

"In the light more," she said.

The man directed the bags toward the faint, cold light in the sky. Shosha had the coat off. "Give me the sack and I'll throw it over," she said.

"I can't give you the sack," he said. "I'll need it for the coat." He pulled the meat out, wrapped in butcher's paper and the sausage in a clear casing.

"Open the paper," Leiozia said.

"The meat's good—I have to hurry," the man said.

"Open the paper or no coat."

"Leiozia!" Shosha said.

The man unwrapped the butcher paper and revealed lamb, red and turning brown at the edges.

"Slaughtered kosher," he said. "Satisfied?"

"Let me smell it," Leiozia said.

"You're crazy."

"And you're cold. You want the coats?"

The man held up the meat and the two women leaned down to sniff it. Shosha swooned. "Oh!"

"Shh!" Leiozia said.

"Satisfied?" the man snapped.

"No," Shosha interrupted.

"Shosha!"

"What's the sausage?" Shosha said.

"Venison," the man said. "Also Kashrut. Take it or leave it."

"Take it!" Leiozia said. She reached through the bars. The man re-wrapped the meat and placed it in her hands. Leiozia and Shosha wrapped it again in the dust coat. Shosha passed the fur through.

"What an ordeal," Shosha said.

"Now my coat," Leiozia said.

"We're going to freeze out here," Shosha said.

"Better to freeze on a full belly."

Leiozia slipped off her topcoat. "Cover me." With Shosha between her and the guards, she pranced by the fence.

"Nice coat—aren't you the fortunate one?" said a woman inside leaning against the bars.

"At least you still have that," said another woman. "You won't die, not like the rest of us."

"Shut up," Leiozia said.

"Miss—come over here."

Leiozia saw an old woman sprouting little whiskers outside the bars. "That fur—real or fake?" the woman said.

"Real seal," Leiozia said.

The woman put her hand through the bars. "Touch, please."

Leiozia extended her arm and the woman felt the fur. "Wonderful," she said.

"What do you offer for it?" Shosha asked.

"Butter and cheese, potatoes and yams, and beets—the reddest, freshest beets you've ever seen."

"This fur is new," Leiozia said. "It would be worth more food than we could carry back."

"I can deliver it," the old woman said. "When you get out of here, my sons can help bring it to wherever you're going."

"Thirty Eight Pawia Street," Shosha said.

"They get the coat then, and only then," Leiozia said.

"We'll see you there," the old woman said. "I watch this place to see when you leave."

They walked back toward Rebekah. One of their boarders, Henryk, came up to them carrying a plain topcoat in his arms. He unfolded it a little to reveal a pile of pletzlach (flat onion rolls); four round onions; two bunches of carrots; radishes; and two large, full beef sausages. Henryk was tall so Shosha stood on the tips of her toes to kiss his cheek.

The snow had fallen to an inch or so by three in the morning, when the guards opened the gates of the makeshift cage. "Out," they yelled. They entered with clubs and short ropes and herded the people into the street. "Out. Get out. Go on! Go home!"

Seven people from the Mordechai household came to the enclosure, but only six walked out together in the snow and darkness.

"Where's Rudi?" Rebekah asked. "Anyone seen Rudi?" Her voice was faint.

"He'll show up," Shosha said. "He probably took a detour."

"Oh." Rebekah stumbled and wailed.

"Mama—here—take some." Shosha held out a piece of bread.

"I told you before—no," Rebekah said. "I want to wait. I want to savor it."

They walked up the steps to the house. Shosha saw a crack and missing glass in a downstairs window in the moonlight. She opened the door and went in first. She lit oil lamps and candles and watched the light illuminate the latest work of vandals and thieves. She said nothing, only led everyone in and upstairs, to their rooms, where furniture lay overturned and blankets lay stripped from the mattresses on the floors.

Everyone dropped where they stood and slept. In the morning Shosha and Leiozia fried the sausage and onions and made a gravy with flour and laid it over the pletzlach.

"That is the most wonderful thing I've smelled since I last smelled your papa's cheeks," Rebekah told Shosha.

"Sit. We eat," Leiozia said.

The old woman and her sons didn't come with the food for the seal coat, which the household discussed and dismissed as probably expected. They wondered about Rudi, the missing boarder, but no one seemed worried because Rudi was sometimes gone for days. The Mordechais and their boarders were sitting and talking and luxuriating in fullness when they heard a knock at the door on the alley.

"I bet I know who that is," Leiozia said, and she stood and went to the back. The people at the table heard her greet the rabbi and she brought him into the room.

"Rabbi," Rebekah said. "Please, sit! You must eat—we have plenty left."

"I haven't come to eat, but I will join you," he said. He sat and the women laid food before him.

"Kashrut," Leiozia said. "Or so they told us."

"You know, I concern myself less about that these days," the rabbi said. "But it's good to know." He took a bite of the venison. "Oh," he said. "Oy, that's terrific!" He ate another bite and drank coffee. "I have something to say that must be kept quiet," he said. "I know I can trust you all."

"Certainly," Rebekah said.

The rabbi paused and sipped. "I've spoken of an armed rising," he said. "The time is near, according to everything I'm hearing."

"When?" Shosha said. "I've heard the same—from Frenkel, up the street. But he never knows when."

"In weeks," the rabbi said. "We have to dig tunnels, we have to build enclosures, we have to store food and get weapons."

"How can we help?" Henryk asked.

"We need as many people as possible," the rabbi said. "We keep losing people to the fever and the camps."

"I've heard," Shosha said. "Stutthof."

"That's where they make the soap from Jewish fat," Leiozia said.

"Leia," Rebekah said. "That's a rumor."

"Is not. Professor Spanner and his *Reines Judische Fett*." Pure Jewish fat. "It gets you clean because it's Kosher."

"Leia! Rabbi—it's a rumor. Tell her. And tell her not to be sacrilegious."

"Don't be sacrilegious," the rabbi said. "But it's probably true."

Six

The rabbi stood outside club Sztuka watching a strange scene. A man in dark glasses with hair that shined in the sun stood behind a large motion picture camera yelling at some locals. He started the camera and looked up from behind it and yelled again, setting uniformed police after the group. Then he yelled at the police and they stopped, while soldiers stopped the locals. He walked over and talked to the police.

"Positions," he commanded. He walked back to the camera, stood behind it and adjusted it. "Action!" He filmed the same scene, but this time the police raised batons and looked more menacing. "Cut!" the rabbi heard.

"You," one of the soldiers yelled. "You can help with this."

"With what?" the rabbi asked.

"With this—with the filming. We are making a movie—you want to be a movie star?" The soldier whistled at the young director and motioned him over. "Everyone wants to be a movie star," the soldier said.

The director waved off the soldier and looked behind his camera again.

"Hey," the soldier called.

The director didn't look up.

"Goddamn it."

The soldier huffed and walked toward the director and the rabbi turned and hurried into a maze of alleys, dodging uniforms and ducking away at any sound that indicated soldiers nearby. He emerged behind a kiosk in the marketplace, Kercely Square, where he saw Poles and Jews and a few guards.

"Rabbi!"

He jumped. The man behind him, selling leather hides from a kiosk, reached for his hand.

"You're a good omen today," the man said.

"A good omen?" the rabbi said.

"I keep the faith," the man said.

"You almost scared me out of what little faith I have left," the rabbi said.

The two men thought they heard firecrackers. Pop, pop, pop, pop. Then something zinged overhead and people in the front of the square ducked and someone screamed. The rabbi and the merchant crouched and the rabbi squirreled behind the kiosk. Another pop and a window broke over their heads, sending glass crashing near their hands.

"Who's shooting?" the rabbi said.

"Who else?" the merchant said.

They heard more screams and trucks growling and braking. The rabbi looked up and saw soldiers pushing men and women with their hands over their heads beyond the edge of the square and storming the narrow aisles between booths and stands.

The rabbi watched a soldier raise his rifle to a man who held his hands over his eyes. The soldier forced the man to his knees, out of the rabbi's sight. Pop. The rabbi saw the rifle kick. The soldier kicked at something twice, then walked down another aisle.

The rabbi looked at the entrance to the alley. He thought about running, but the soldiers would shoot. He thought about crawling, but he saw the soldiers watching the ground, looking for crawlers. He took hold of a leg of the kiosk and pulled it. It was light and had wheels but stones blocked the wheels so he reached over and pushed one away.

"What are you doing—stay put," the merchant said.

"Move the other rocks," the rabbi said. "Stay behind this."

The merchant pushed the rocks away. "What are you up to?" he said.

Pop. Pop. Pop. They heard a man's deep voice above the screaming crowd.

"Fuck them!" the voice cried.

The rabbi dragged the kiosk but the merchant grabbed his wrist.

"Fuck them," the rabbi said, and he yanked hard on the cart and moved it toward the alley. The merchant understood.

"Not all at once. Not all at once," the merchant said. "A little at a time."

"Okay—together," the rabbi said. They pulled the kiosk a little farther. "Again."

Again, a little farther. Again, and again, until they were almost in front of the alley.

"I hate to leave this," the merchant said. "How do I feed my family?"

"You leave here on foot or on your back," the rabbi said. "At least this way, you can feed them one more day."

They pulled the kiosk hard in the noise of gunfire and bullets hitting glass and ricocheting off the high brick walls around the square. Then the alley was behind them.

"Stay down and run," the rabbi said.

They stayed low and ran down the alley and turned at the first corner, a city block from the square. They stopped, bent forward, hands on their knees, panting.

"I'm this way," the merchant said and he grabbed the rabbi's hand and motioned toward the other side of the street. The rabbi saw a placard on a wooden post over the merchant's head.

Umrzeć z honorem. "Die With Honor."

The letters were red and outlined in black. The merchant looked up and saw the placard. He took it down and crumpled it in his fist.

"Not today," he said, and threw the wadded paper in the street.

REBEKAH *NEVER* OPENED THE back door to anyone but her household or the rabbi, especially now, at night. But here stood a boy with fat red cheeks, eleven or twelve, holding a burlap sack. Rebekah said the first words that entered her mind.

"You're a healthy looking one."

"Rabbi asked me to bring these." The boy held up the bag and Rebekah saw impressions in the bottom that resembled eggs. She reached for the bag but the boy withdrew it.

"Rabbi told me under no circumstances was I to open the bag anywhere but inside the house."

"Well—if that's what he said, come in with it and let's have a look."

The boy stepped inside. One of the boarders, a heavyset man who had lost three dozen pounds in two months and had leftover flesh hanging from his arms, sat in the downstairs drawing room reading an old newspaper in the dim light from the street. He saw the bag before he saw the boy.

"Eggs. Fresh eggs! By god, who's sent them?"

"Rabbi," the boy said.

"That rabbi," the man said. "Let's cook up a few."

"May I?" Rebekah asked the boy. He handed her the bag. Her arm dropped unprepared.

"Must have been some big chickens," she said. She untied it and looked in. Four or five, maybe half dozen white egg-shapes clicked against each other with a metallic knock. She reached in and felt one. It was cold. She lifted it out.

The man in the chair almost leapt out of it. "That's a grenade!"

"Oh!" Rebekah dropped it. The man cringed and shut his eyes. The boy picked it up.

"You have to handle these with great care, rabbi said." The boy put the grenade back in the bag.

"Whew." The boarder had lost his breath. "They're supposed to *look* like eggs I suppose," he said.

"What should we do with them?" Rebekah asked. "Rabbi's said nothing about this."

"It's not his plan—it's from the Underground," the boy said. "Each person carries one, and if they are beaten, they pull these." The boy indicated the firing pin and a lever.

"Suicide," the boarder said. "The hunger must be getting to Rebbe. It must be getting to all of you if you'd consider a thing like this."

Rebekah took the bag into the kitchen and stuffed it on a high shelf. "What I don't understand is why he gave these to a child," she said.

"The soldiers see me but don't suspect," the boy said. "And I can squeeze out of tight spots."

Rebekah returned with some carrots and radishes and offered them to the boy.

"Rabbi feeds me," he said.

"Then for the trip back," Rebekah said. The boy took one.

"I could do with one of those," the boarder said. Rebekah threw a carrot and it landed on his lap. He picked it up and munched. "Beats those eggs," he said.

Seven

*A*ll Jews in Warsaw are to be immediately deported.

On July 22, 1942, the Judenrat received this instruction from Heinrich Himmler, Hitler's second in command, and Governor General Hans Frank, demanding it round up some six thousand people per day for deportation from the *Umschlagplatz* or "transfer station," a rail spur north of the Ghetto. *Gross-Aktion Warsaw* had begun and on learning of its aim—the complete annihilation of his people in the city— Judenrat leader Adam Czerniakow swallowed cyanide.

Ghetto police chief Jozef Szerynski rounded up civilians for deportation with a logistical gusto that surprised even the Germans, who previously arrested and tortured him for fur smuggling. Szerynski implemented daily "house blockades," or what the occupiers termed "block aids" from 7 to 7:30 each morning. German, Ukrainian, and Jewish police left No. 17 Ogrodowa Street, heading toward the block selected for that day's "aid" and shooting any person looking out a window at the ensuing commotion.

"ALLE HUNTER!"

"Shosha—get away from there." Rebekah hissed from the door to the third-story bedroom, where her daughter sat near an open window shrouded in a tattered curtain looking out on the close, muggy street.

"*Alle Hunter!*" The voices outside tore through the heavy air. Shosha didn't move.

"You want to get shot?" Rebekah walked toward the window and stood to the side, out of sight of anyone on the street. Soldiers banged on houses on the next block with their rifles and batons.

"Look at this," Shosha said. A soldier dragged a woman down the front steps by her hair. "Adam died for *this!*"

People lined up and formed columns at the end of lashing tongues and rifles. Soldiers marched them away, toward trucks that blocked the streets.

"We're the next block, mama."

"They're going north, not west. They'll leave us for a while."

They heard knocking at the back door downstairs and Leiozia answer it.

"Bekka," Leiozia called up. "You have a visitor."

Rebekah walked back to the bedroom door. "We have air raid sirens for the purpose of loud alerts," she called down to Leiozia. She looked at Shosha, still at the window. "Come away from there before I tackle you," she said.

Downstairs, she greeted the rabbi cheek to cheek. "You grace us twice in a week," Rebekah said.

He kissed her forehead. "We're saying goodbye to Jerczek," he said.

"He's leaving?" Leiozia asked.

"He is," the rabbi said.

"He's said nothing about it," Leiozia said.

"Leiozia," Rebekah said.

"Well, I'll miss him," Leiozia said. "Who will take his place?"

"No one," the rabbi said. He smiled. "The children are being moved."

"Moved?" Rebekah said.

Shosha walked, step by slow step, down the stairs.

"I arranged it," the rabbi said. "Out of the Ghetto."

"Where are they going?" Leiozia asked.

"A new facility, nothing like a traditional orphanage," the rabbi said. "Being built as we speak with dollars, francs, pounds —and more than a few *Reichsmarks*."

"Where? Certainly not here, not in Poland?"

"In Austria," the rabbi said. "Near Vienna."

"This is wonderful," Rebekah said. "How did you manage it?"

"Connections," the rabbi said. "We're giving Jerczek a send off tomorrow night at Sztuka. At seven. I came to invite everyone in the house."

"When are they leaving?" Shosha asked.

"I didn't see you lurking there in the shadows," the rabbi said. He took her cheek and kissed it.

"When are they leaving?"

"Next week."

"The facility is finished?" Shosha asked.

"Not quite. The propaganda ministry—for the purposes of propaganda—will be housing the children in a temporary facility meanwhile."

Shosha lost her balance. "The Germans—"

Leiozia and the rabbi grabbed her arms. Shosha slipped toward the bottom of the stairs, faint but conscious. "You're letting the Germans take them?" Shosha asked.

"It's only for a short while," the rabbi said. "They will even be filming their departure and arrival at the new children's village."

"How can you do that?"

"It's all arranged."

Shosha grabbed the rabbi's shoulders. "How can you be so stupid?" she said.

"Shosha!" Rebekah said.

"You saw what they did," Shosha said to the rabbi. "You stood with me and you saw what they did."

Rebekah grabbed her daughter's arm. "How dare you disrespect this man in my house."

"I know what I'm doing," the rabbi said. He took Shosha's hands from his shoulders. "I know what I'm doing."

He lowered her hands and went for the door. Leiozia walked with him and they opened the door together. The rabbi avoided Shosha's eyes.

"See you all at seven," he said. "It should be fun."

SZTUKA HAD BECOME *THE* venue for the richest Jews and a few Catholic Poles who had ties with Rome and money. Low lights and smoke lent anonymity to recognizable faces the rabbi moved amid as an old friend. Shosha, Rebekah, and Leiozia arranged themselves and their boarders at a table near the stage. Uncorked wine, a bottle of old brandy, and cigarettes on a silver tray sat on the table.

"I can take one?" asked Henryk.

"I'm going to," Leiozia said.

Henryk picked up a cigarette and put it to his lips and picked out a long wooden match from a decorous arrangement in a squat brandy snifter. "This is fabulous," he said and lit the cigarette.

Shosha sat with her arms crossed. Leiozia smoked. Rebekah read the program, printed on paper made with rags and speckled with colored thread.

On a happy farewell for Dr. Janusz Jerczek
Founder of Our Children's Home

We welcome this evening
Distinguished Warsaw pianist Wladyslaw Szpilman
Singer Andrzej Wlast, aka our own Waclaw Tajtelbaum
Marja Ajzensztadt, "The Ghetto Nightingale"

Rebekah thumbed through the program, read the back two pages.

Janusz Jerczek dreamed of becoming a doctor from his boyhood. He lost his father to illness as a child, worked through his youth saving money, and enrolled in medical school at age 18. In 1909, he started working with children at the hospital on Sliska Street. Dr. Jerczek considered himself a "scribe, writing the details of love and life on the souls and hearts of the children." It was in this artistic frame of mind that he took control of the orphans' shelter on Franciszkanska Street.

A dry summary. Dr. Jerczek was a perfect clown, Rebekah thought, always throwing his hands around and exclaiming some new idea he had for the orphanage or "god damning" the occupiers and vowing never to die at their hands. He charted the progress of the most hopeless cases, the children with diseases or malformations that Rebekah just knew would never amount to any more than they already were. It made her sad sometimes, listening to the doctor's optimism. She wanted to tell him to shut up and stop creating false hope. But as the weight of it would start to bear down on her, he'd end it all with a joke or some other silliness that would lift her and create more false hope, a momentary diversion that helped her forget.

She read on.

A patriot, Dr. Jerczek served as a military doctor in the Russo-Japanese War, and in the war that engulfed the world in 1914. He wrote a book entitled "Love and Learn: The Way to Bring Up a Child." After he returned from the front, he lost his mother, with whom he was very close.

Well, he wasn't *that* close to her. After Jerczek's father died, some kind of rift developed between mother and son, but Rebekah didn't know the mother—Oza or Osa or Ocza (she tried to visualize the name in her mind). She would sometimes catch them arguing in the main hallway of Our Children's Home over matters that, under the circumstances, could only be minor. When Jerczek stood over his mother's body, Rebekah didn't see him cry. His eyes looked hollow, she thought, the eyes of a stoic in a city of loss. He did make sure, however, that his mother was buried in the Jewish cemetery, with bribes in Swiss francs and handshakes and promises he couldn't keep.

His bio continued.

Dr. Jerczek established two orphanages in Warsaw—one Jewish, Our Children's Home; and one Christian, The House of the Blessed Ones. With patience from Heaven, Dr. Jerczek did everything possible to ensure that his orphans' homes would house healthy and happy children. Dr. Jerczek welcomed children of every religion in Warsaw, and every capability—even mentally retarded or crippled in the legs. "We exist to give you the longing for a life which is not here, but will be one day," Dr. Jerczek wrote. "A life of truth and justice that will lead you to G-d, fatherland, and Love."

"Fatherland" sounded too German to Rebekah. She would take it out.

The house lights dimmed and a spotlight shown on the stage, a small round center for a few musicians, a piano, and a chanteuse. The rabbi walked through the audience and up two steps and took a microphone from a slender silver pole.

"I would like to present," the rabbi said, "the sweetest voice in all Warsaw, our own Marja Ajzensztadt, 'the Nightingale'."

Terrific applause lifted the little bird above the smoke and she sang and that is all anyone would remember about the evening. Yes, Dr. Jerczek bowed and walked to the stage to tell people what he thought of them and goodbye. Yes, he said he would always remember their support and the great efforts they undertook—especially the rabbi—to secure his passage and the passages of the children out of Poland and out of the war. And yes, he was revered here as something of a saint in minor vestments.

But the voice of this woman, this sweet, sweet voice, with its force and its purity and all the force that purity can exert in such a ruined and decimated place—this was a sound of beauty, this voice, this was the sound of truth.

THE NEXT DAY, IN the early morning, Shosha left her house by the back door and took a carriage to the Jewish orphanage. She stepped off at a corner and walked the rest of the way and when she arrived, she saw the double front doors open. She hiked her skirt and mounted the steep brick steps. At the top, she paused. She was hungry, she was always hungry, and every effort loosed wavelets of fatigue. She had lost twenty pounds and was not a large woman before. When she took off her top garments, she no longer had to contract her diaphragm to see her ribs, which lay bare and malnourished, embarrassing protrusions that forced her to wear heavy clothes, even on warm days.

She leaned against the railing and breathed. Fatigue roiled her stomach, like a grinding wheel sharpening a dull and chronic pain that wanted to waylay her. She rolled her head to stretch her neck. She looked around and noticed the windows on either side of the doors were open as high as they could be forced. She peered in.

"Hello?" Her voice jarred the air.

"Hello?" A hollow echo returned.

She looked at the wood floor down the long center hall and the dark lights hanging from ceilings eighteen feet high. She heard water, dripping in the cavern. She stepped in and heard her hard shoes echo on the black slate tiles in the entryway. She pushed a door and it stopped against the wall. She looked into a room.

She walked into it—tap, tap, tap—on a hard painted floor and saw a long row of windows that looked out on an alley, and beneath the windows, a row of radiators connected by a thick pipe and a thin pipe that stopped at valves and stopcocks then turned and dove through round, coarse holes in the floor.

She stared. She thought about how she had wanted to speak with Jerczek last night, after the show, maybe stand outside with him, away from the others. But well-wishers surrounded him and she may have missed an opportunity by spending too much time in the lavatory with Leiozia, who was drunk.

BY THE TIME LEIOZIA was able to walk on her own, Dr. Jerczek was outside, standing in the street talking with his hands to Rebekah. Before Shosha could speak, Rebekah cut her off with a loud introduction and the doctor and Shosha joined hands. The doctor recalled the first time he met Shosha and asked her why he hadn't seen her in such a long time.

"Oh, she's been very busy helping Rabbi," Rebekah said. She lowered her voice. "Keep this quiet, but the Jewish Combat Organization is working with the Underground on the other side of the wall and Shosha is a scout."

"Really?" the doctor said.

"Yes, by Jiminy Jehoshaphat," Leiozia grunted and laughed, her arms wrapped around Shosha's tiny waist.

"How long has Shosha been a scout?" Jerczek asked.

"Just got picked. While I—" Leiozia giggled. "Did not." She pouted.

"Leiozia—mind your self," Rebekah said.

"It's all right," the doctor said. "I'm glad to hear all this. I wish I could be with you, and I would be, in other circumstances."

"They're building a tunnel under the wall," Rebekah whispered.

"Mama—I wouldn't say so much out here," Shosha said. "Which train do you take?" she asked the doctor.

"Szelna Station. We load in the morning."

"I wish you weren't leaving," Shosha said.

"Trust Rabbi," Rebekah said.

"He is an amazing man," Dr. Jerczek said. "I don't know if he realizes the impact he has."

SHOSHA STOOD IN THE dust and shadows and the silence struck her because she hadn't heard true silence in a long time. She felt panicky, little strings of anxiety strummed in her belly. She couldn't believe they had left so early. She thought "sunrise" when the doctor said he and the children were leaving in the morning, but they must have left in the wee hours, in the dark, for cover so the soldiers wouldn't harass them.

"IT'S WONDERFUL," THE DOCTOR told them about the new orphanage. "Just outside Vienna."

"I've seen the drawings," Rebekah said. "Rabbi brought them by for my skeptical daughter."

"Skeptical?" the doctor said.

As her legs weakened and sleepiness settled her inebriated fog, Leiozia tugged on Shosha. "We need to get her home," Shosha said. She took the doctor's cheek in her hand and pressed her cheek to it. "Shalom," she said.

"Shalom!"

Rebekah took his hand. "Shalom beshaa muclachat." Goodbye and good luck.

The doctor kissed Leiozia's cheek and she opened her eyes and smiled.

SHOSHA WALKED OUT THE front doors of the orphanage but turned around for a last look. "Shalom beshaa muclachat!" The words sounded hollow but she didn't hear an echo this time.

Eight

Himmler repeated his demand all Jews be removed from Warsaw by year's end. The Judenrat stepped up the daily quota of deportees in an operation Berlin christened *Gross-Aktion Warsaw*. Over the next two months, the Gestapo shrunk the Ghetto by moving three major boundaries. A heinous stench squatted everywhere, and the fortunate few with perfume wrapped their faces with saturated scarves.

Soldiers fainted and dropped and lay with the dead until their conscious comrades revived them with smelling salts or a kick in the side. Lucky gendarmes kept busy marching Ghetto residents to the *Umschlagplatz*, where thousands waited for cattle cars in a plague of heat carried to the city by a thick, muggy swarm of degrees. Less fortunate soldiers stood around bored in hot buildings, hot courtyards, hot doorways, and on hot streets, smoking, swearing, spitting stale tobacco and gum, and kicking rocks, bottles, and mangy dogs. Another favorite practice of the bored soldier was to shoot a Ghetto resident—preferably in the head near a wall—then force other residents to clean up the mess.

Guards at Pawiak Prison with nothing to do urinated on the Alsatian hounds that guarded the yard, trying for their eyes. That routine got old so in an instance that reeked of the blind pathos that had befallen Europe, the guards took to starving the hounds then sicking them on a Franciscan priest charged with "issuing phony baptismal certificates to help disguise and save Jews."

This barbarity went on for a week, in the first mornings of early autumn, until the morning Leiozia walked by, on the other side of the street from the yard where the priest lay alone near the inside edge of the barbed wire, bitten and bleeding. Leiozia hurried because the rule on the street was to avoid the street, but if you had to be on it, to walk quickly, but not too quickly. Running brought soldiers, who were as likely to shoot you as stop you and ask for your papers. Leiozia walked without much attention to the dead because they lay everywhere and had become the second-most common obstacle to avoid, behind the soldiers. The dead were a nuisance because they stunk and brought flies and sanitary personnel, who would look around at the surrounding houses and remind themselves which ones they had yet to disinfect. The dead, as they always are, were a reminder—of things past and of things not done and of things yet to come.

The friar was not dead, but his small movements and whispered groans consigned him to the third class of obstacles to avoid—the dying—who also lay everywhere, moaning, begging, or in the semi-comatose sleep that precedes a quiet end, without pain, drama, or untoward event. This man of God —with his lacerated knuckle resting against the fence and his fingers opening and closing in slow, fruitless grasps—should never have caught Leiozia's eye. She had left the house before dawn and followed a circuitous path through alleys and side streets to the last place within walking distance that sold coal on the black market. She was coming back now without any coal, angry she had wasted valuable physical energy, angry she was hungry again, angry no one had told her the coal stores had not been replenished for a week. Rabbi should have known; we have an underground newspaper; someone is always talking and gossiping about the latest bad news, even competing over whose news is worse. Why wasn't this news reported? Thank G-d it was only autumn and coal was not as necessary, but stocking up for winter was on everybody's mind.

The sun crept over the tops of tall buildings and peered between spires and struck the priest, a singular figure. A brown robe cinched with a white rope (cincture) wrapped him below his white face and his white hands and his white hair. Leiozia stopped when she first saw him and stood with her fingers wrapped around the rough wooden handle of the empty coal basket. She had never seen a prisoner alone in the Pawiak yard before and hopeful thoughts presented: they're short staffed; they're planning to abandon the place; or they already have.

She was alarmed to see the priest move his head. She watched him and felt compelled. She looked up and down the street and when she saw it was clear, she walked across and stepped over the rust-colored water that trickled in the gutter. She was closer to the priest and saw blood in his hair. The torn robe stuck to his skin. Blood stained the three white knots in his cincture—one each for the Franciscan vows of poverty, chastity, and obedience, drooped outside the fence.

"Can you hear me?" Leiozia asked. She crouched along a brick-and-stone berm the length of the block. The prison fence ran along the top of the berm. She couldn't see the friar's face, but she heard a low sound that seemed to come from it. She thought about what to do.

"Can you move your finger if you hear me?"

He bent his index finger up and down.

"Where are the guards?"

The priest opened his entire hand.

"Are they still here? Move your finger if you mean *yes*."

The priest moved his index finger up and down again.

"Will they come back for you?"

She saw him move his arm. "They'll see you if you move much," she said. "Just move your finger." Leiozia examined him. "The soldiers did this?"

The priest hesitated. Then he moved his finger again.

Leiozia considered. "You're going to die," she said. "Do you want water?"

The priest moved his index finger.

Leiozia unwrapped her scarf from her head and dipped it in the gutter. She slid her hand through the fence and held the scarf against the priest's lips. She could feel him and had an uncharacteristic thought.

"Do you want revenge?" she asked. For a time that seemed long, the priest didn't move his finger. Then he moved it, up and down.

Leiozia withdrew her hand and opened her jacket. She dug her fingernails between the top threads that sewed her inside pocket shut. She tore open the top of the pocket and reached in and brought her fingers around the white grenade. She took the grenade out and loosened the safety clip and pin. She slipped it inside the fence and positioned it in the priest's hand.

"This is a grenade," she said. "Do you know how to work it?"

He raised his index finger. She slipped it into the loosened safety pin's pull ring.

"Can you do it?"

He grasped the egg-shaped bomb as though to separate the safety pin and release the detonating lever.

"When you see them coming," Leiozia said. "Take as many as you can."

Leiozia looked around and saw no one. She dipped the scarf into the water again and set it to the priest's lips. She pushed the cincture through the fence, setting it next to his leg. She looked around a second time and stood and walked to the other side of the street and away. She remembered later that she had left her scarf with the priest and panicked until she realized nothing would be left of it.

"A WONDERFUL THING HAS happened." The rabbi kissed Rebekah on both cheeks and threw up his hands. "A bomb went off inside the Pawiak."

"A bomb?" Rebekah said. "Who put it there? Was it an accident?"

The rabbi shut the back door. "Our enemies are tight lipped. Won't say anything. Running around like a gaggle of lost geese. Don't know who did it. Don't know why. Don't want to talk about it."

"They're usually out with the guns, lining people up anytime a thing like this happens."

"A thing like this has never happened," the rabbi said. "A stealth attack on their own turf. It's exhilarating."

Rebekah heard footsteps on the stairs.

"Leia?"

"Yes, ma'am?" Leiozia spoke from the drawing room, out of sight.

"Have you heard about this?"

"About what?"

"This bomb in the Pawiak."

Leiozia's heart leapt. Her mouth dried. A pang knotted her stomach.

"Leiozia?"

Leiozia grabbed her fleeting composure and stepped around the corner into the kitchen. "What a place for a bomb to go off." she said. "Do they know who put it there?"

"The only thing I've heard—and this is only a rumor—a friar," the rabbi said.

"A friar?"

"The only problem with the story is that it appears, from the people who were walking on the street before it happened, the friar was dead."

"He must have been very well connected," Leiozia said.

The rabbi laughed. Rebekah cast her eyes downward.

"What?" Leiozia said. "What's funny?"

The rabbi choked on his chuckle and bent over the counter.

"Oh, oh." He stopped and caught his breath and rubbed his eyes. "It's terrible to laugh at such a thing, I know. But—hah!" He took a deep breath again and smiled. "I haven't had a laugh like that in—I can't remember how long. Can you forgive me?"

"A priest, for heaven's sake," Rebekah said.

"Please—no more," the rabbi said. "Are these puns deliberate?" He sighed.

"Where does this leave us?" Rebekah said.

The rabbi lowered his voice. "I think it leaves us in a good position."

TERRIFYING REPRISALS SHOULD HAVE punctuated the story of Leiozia's grenade, but Leiozia Strazinski, a simple Jew, a peasant here, had executed the perfect crime. She had murdered three German soldiers in an explosive volley of shrapnel that looked like a suicide and destroyed any evidence that might suggest otherwise. She had employed a Roman Catholic trigger man who wore a belt attached to a virtual leash that led to all the way to Italy, and *Il Duce*—Mussolini—who was an important Nazi ally engaged in a precarious dance with the Vatican.

The first officers in Berlin to receive word of the incident—which became known as "the Pawiak Incendiary"—vowed it would never reach Hitler or any of the General staff and sent orders back quashing the "usual course of action." Retribution against the Poles would only draw attention to the sorry lapse of security that permitted the first successful surprise attack from within not one, but two walls. These were dual barricades, a fenced prison in a walled-off ghetto, a hell within a hell, where the flames of sadism were supposed to burn white-hot and untouchable.

The occupiers also realized the potent effect this story might have on the occupied, so they guarded what they knew of it—three gendarmes dead, two Alsatian hounds blown to bits, Nazi uniforms scattered on the barbed wire. Despite the cover up, ripples of gossip swelled into a tsunami of exaggeration, a twice-told tale of daring-do told twice again, each time with added bravado. The impetuous act of a housemaid and a doomed cleric became a planned assault orchestrated by the Underground in concert with the local Catholic authorities, a short but victorious preamble to a bitter battle yet to come.

Leiozia was as unsuspecting of the factors that conspired to protect her as she was unsuspected of any crimes. Fear lapped at her, dogging her movements through days and nights of secret panic, stalking, watching, waiting, but never pouncing, because perfect crimes toll like petty blackmailers. Although like everyone in the Ghetto, Leiozia suffered from chronic hunger, malnutrition and fatigue, she nonetheless lost what little appetite she had and forfeited her coveted ability to sleep through the loudest gunfire. Her purposeful street-smart stride became dazed and unbalanced, a fleeting, loopy heartbeat held her hostage to bouts of lightheadedness, and worry-driven surges of adrenaline churned her stomach, tossing what food she could keep down into a froth of anxiety. She fretted to the point of illness and she despaired, for she could tell no one.

THE FIRST ORDERS ISSUED post Pawiak Incendiary commanded the residents of Mila, Niska and Smocza streets to assemble on the *Umschlagplatz*, where two directors of a military uniform factory—Schultz and Toebbens—would select the strong for labor—and the right to live. Selected persons would have *Lebensnumern*—numbers of life—stitched to the backs of their shirts.

The bold rhetoric of the Underground and the success at Pawiak empowered the physically strong, who generally avoided selections, hiding instead as so-called "wild tenants" in cellars, lofts, basements, and secret rooms in houses that appeared deserted from the street. Those who stood on the *Umschlagplatz* during these, the Ghetto's latter days, were hungry, weak, impoverished, and resigned. The few selected for life hung their

Lebensnumern like medals around their necks and marched to the Sheds—barracks and workshops arranged in blocks behind yet more blockades. The others boarded trains for the camps.

Close contact in the Sheds yielded a harvest of sedition. Young lions of Zion once training to fight in Palestine formed the first resistance organization, the Zhydowski Zwiazek Wojskowy —Jewish Military Union—or ZZW. Thirty Jewish members of the Polish Workers Party, men and boys, also formed the Zhydowska Organizacja Bojowa—the Jewish Fighting Organization—or ZOB. They named as their leader Mordecai Anielewicz, a 24-year-old economics and history student who dreamed of being a scholar before the war.

The ZOB allied itself with Żydowska Samopomoc Społeczna (Jewish Self-Aid Division) and the American Jewish Joint Distribution Committee. Through the secretive and ethereal Waclaw—who had escaped the Ghetto over a year ago, but lingered in the shadows of the Reich—the ZOB passed appeals with diaries and photographs to allies in Western Europe, France, England, and the United States. Bewildered black-and-white faces looked wide-eyed from the snapshots' blurred lines: lines of the camp bound; lines of the newly disinfected; lines of the fallen and the falling, captured surreptitiously on film by Ghetto historians like Emanuel Ringelblum and his covert group of documentarians, Oyneg Shabbos.

With journalistic precision, Ringelblum, Oyneg Shabbos, and others detailed day-to-day desperation, but also questioned G-d and mused on meaning and tried to weave hopeful threads into the ropes of anguish that bound every person, some by the hands, some by the heart, some by the neck. In time, money came, and with money food, arms and munitions, smuggled into the Ghetto from the Aryan side through tunnels and passages and sewage canals. Courage followed supplies, the first inklings of it in an appeal from the ZOB.

"Stop! Defend! Fight!"

Stop surrendering to certain death, the ZOB urged. "Stop marching like lemmings to the *Umschlagplatz*. Hide, and if they find you, barricade yourself and if you have a gun, shoot them as they reach in to pull you out."

A smuggling operation took shape between the wild tenants, the workers in the Sheds, and Gentile allies who lived on the Aryan side. Outside the Jewish Council buildings, where corpses came for dispensation and Jewish guards stood watch while Jewish civilians stripped their deceased brethren, the living—young and slender boys—hid themselves beneath the dead. Under this cover, the boys traveled beyond the Ghetto to the *Skra*, a sports field on the Aryan side converted to a mass graveyard that replaced the Kirkut.

The dead went first into the open holes. The boys underneath stretched and smiled and raised their legs and arms to the pallbearers, who heaved them by their ankles and wrists into the graves with whistles and quips that made nearby guards ponder what happy occasion could have befallen these sorry souls. The boys waited in the open graves until night, sometimes hiding under bodies, then slipped out and ran a well-traveled route to the Jewish Aid Division with maps, notes, and memorized information. The guards shot only one boy, mistaking him for one of the dead who had not quite died. The rule was never fidget or move, but pull oneself out and run, always at dark during the wee morning hours.

THE UNDERGROUND REVOLT BEGAN overhead, where from all other sides, taller buildings obscured this roof. On this side, it overlooked the *Umschlagplatz*. Three men got up here this hot August night. They wore black vests, black gloves, heavy black pants and black shoes. Shosha and two other women spent half an hour rubbing the men's cheeks and foreheads with fine coal dust. They blended with the darkness.

This building of flats was almost abandoned so the men weren't quiet when they walked up the stairs. Wild tenants and an elderly man stepped out doors and when the old man saw the rifles, he raised his fist, big and white. A woman in tattered bedclothes whistled through bad teeth.

The men crawled on the roof to the narrow space that overlooked the *platz*. Christien and Mosze had the rifles. ZOB deputy commander Icchak Cukierman, known as "Antek," stood watch and chewed gum. Christien stretched his fingers, cracked his knuckles, and patted his hands on his legs. He brought the rifle scope to his eye. The lens steamed over, so he held it farther from his face. Mosze assembled his rifle.

"Sveet!" Christien whistled through his teeth. Antek slid over and looked through the scope. A figure in half a uniform walked toward a group of men and women on the train platform. Karl-Georg Brandt wore an *SS* coat but the dress slacks of a man about to enjoy the evening. He wore dress shoes that shone in the light from the overhead lamps around the *platz*.

Antek handed the rifle back to Christien, who held it up and focused himself through the scope. He watched Brandt, the so-called "Lord of the Ghetto" who with Hermann Höfle headed the *Befehlstelle*, the command team on Żeromskiego Street charged with liquidating the Ghetto. *Hauptsturmführer* Brandt stood on the platform with *Oberscharführer* Gerhardt Mende, who was always with him. Everyone talked about Brandt and Mende—the Germans, the Jews, and the Poles on the other side of the wall. The two men were always together.

Brandt smashed the butt of his gun into a woman's face.

"Oh! Fucking bastard," Christien said. Mosze took up his position. He looked at each of the lamps through his scope. "Oy."

Christien and Mosze watched Brandt drag the woman from the line, kick her, and pull her to her knees. Other soldiers grabbed an old man from the line who stood straight and had a short, groomed beard. The snipers were too far to hear much. They watched the noisy drama until they heard a faint but continuous chirp. They saw soldiers blowing whistles. A group of women in grubby uniforms took to the platform and started stripping each person in line.

"*Werterfassung*," Antek said. A special stripping team.

"Crazy bastards," Mosze said.

Christien nodded. "Hard to get a shot."

The woman on her knees turned and Mosze saw her face. "It's the Nightingale," he said. "She has her hands out."

"She's begging," Christien said.

"She sings like that."

"She's not singing—don't be a fool."

"She's begging and crying."

"You can't tell," Mosze said. "You can't see tears, can you?"

"I can tell from her face," Christien said.

"I thought she was protected," Antek said.

They heard a gunshot and Christien saw the bearded man fall. He moved his scope to see the soldier who held the pistol. Around the soldiers and the deportees, the *Werterfassung* piled shoes, coats, hats, socks, and undergarments. Antek pushed Christien aside and looked through the scope. Two women from the stripping crew descended on the fallen man.

"That's Nightingale's father—I'm almost sure," Antek said about the bearded man.

"It's not her father," Mosze said. "He used to come to the club."

"Rabbi knew him," Christien said. "Her father is on the train, I think."

"It looks like her father to me," Antek huffed.

Christien watched Brandt, who stood near the Nightingale. "I wish he'd move. I can't get a shot."

"Take out a light," Antek said.

Mosze took off his gloves. He raised his rifle and aimed at a lantern near the *platz* and squeezed the trigger. The rifle echoed and the lantern burst and the soldiers dropped on the platform. Antek and Mosze dropped at a second shot. Then they saw Christien had fired again.

"Missed," Christien said.

"Fuck!" Antek said. "You scared me to death."

Mosze scanned the platform for Brandt. "Fucker's hiding," he said.

"I've got Mende," who had left the platform and was running low toward the street. Christien squeezed off a shot and the bullet tore Mende's cheek and spun him around and dropped him. The snipers whooped and whistled. By now the platform was deserted except for about twenty deportees crouched and naked, with their hands over their heads and their bodies tucked together. The Nightingale stood and raised her arm and pointed. She looked up, toward the source of the gunshots. Christien and Mosze could see her mouth.

"She's singing now," Christien said. With the scope, he followed her pointing finger and saw Brandt, ducking below the platform. Something in Brandt's hand glimmered in the lantern light.

Christien lay down his rifle. "You see that?" he asked Mosze.

"Pistol."

"He can't get us from there," Antek said.

Christien picked up his rifle and refocused. The Nightingale was still standing, pointing and screaming. She started to walk, toward the edge of the platform where Brandt hid.

"Stupid girl," Mosze said. "He has a gun."

"I'm going to take him out before he can use it," Christien said. He watched the singer and the platform. "Stay away stupid girl, stay away," Christien said. "Let me get a shot, get a shot, get a shot." The rifle fired and kicked and the bullet burst through the wood on the platform. The Nightingale ducked and dropped and didn't move.

"Well?" Antek said.

"I think I got him," Christien said.

"I don't see anything," Mosze said. He scanned the edges of the platform.

"He was under where the bullet hit," Christien said. "I know I got him."

"What about the Nightingale?"

"She's staying down. She's okay. I didn't hit her."

Antek was the first to hear footsteps on the street. Many footsteps, in hard shoes, running. He stood and grabbed Christien by the shoulder. With their rifles the snipers ran down the stairway and didn't hear the last gunshot from the *Umschlagplatz*. The bullet came from the dark below the platform. It killed the Nightingale and she laid open-eyed and bleeding.

The Lord of the Ghetto waited until the sun's first faint rays to cautiously emerge from beneath the deportation platform.

The other prisoners had gathered their clothes and fled and the *platz* stayed deserted until after the sun fully rose, clear and bright in a cloudless morning sky. Near the street, skinny dogs lapped at blood congealing around Mende's neck and sniffed the Nightingale where she lay closer to the platform.

Brandt did not notice Mende as he left the courtyard.

Nine

The winter of 1943 settled over Warsaw with below-zero temperatures that slowed the Germans and stopped the death camp deportations. The enemy's pause energized the Underground, especially when word leaked a first-time visitor was coming to the Ghetto during the lull.

On January 9, Heinrich Himmler arrived. He wandered around for a few hours under heavy guard, waving his hands like a movie producer and saying things in the ears of henchmen who leaned forward and back and nodded and laughed. He stopped and looked into the gray sky and over the buildings. He walked within five feet of a camouflaged bunker, where two giddy boys watched him from the hole. Here Himmler himself stood, with *SS Oberführer* (Colonel) Ferdinand von Sammern-Frankenegg and the chief of the security police, Dr. Otto Hahn.

"Shh. Listen," the older boy said.

"By February 15, no later—we have about sixty six—tausend?"

"*Ja, Herr Reichsführer*," von Sammern-Frankenegg said.

"Labor and resettlement."

"*Ja, Herr Reichsführer*."

"No later than February 15th—you know what I'm telling you?"

"*Ja*."

"It's fully understood?"

"Absolutely."

On February 16, 1943, Himmler ordered Friedrich-Wilhelm Krüger, *SS Polizeiführer* of the General Government in Poland, to liquidate the Ghetto by April 19, the day before Hitler's birthday. "I expect it complete in three days and no more than three days," Himmler told Krüger. "What a birthday present the *Führer* shall have—a Warsaw clean of the Jews."

Krüger assigned Ferdinand von Sammern-Frankenegg and *SS Brigadeführer* (Brigadier General) Odilo Globocnik to carry out Himmler's orders.

"Three days is a ridiculously short time to do such a massive job," Globocnik told Krüger. "We would need no less than three weeks, at a minimum."

"Get Stroop" was Himmler's only reply when Krüger tried to complain.

A World War I veteran who conducted guerrilla warfare against Soviet partisans in the Ukraine, *SS Brigadeführer* Jürgen Stroop knew all about piss ant bandits who barricaded themselves behind makeshift fortifications and threw homemade bombs at legitimate troops. He knew only a massive offensive would shutter the Ghetto in the three days Himmler commanded. He trained *Trawnikimänner*—captured Ukrainians and Red Army prisoners of war—in brutal urban warfare at Trawniki, Poland. He assembled a hard scrabble lot of felons and murderers who would fight their way to freedom once he loosed them on the Jews.

FROM THE MIDDLE OF January and all through February, the siege continued, with morning street round-ups. The soldiers dragged people out of their homes and shops, by the hair, the hands, by any part of the body they could grasp.

The rabbi had bribed every member of the Judenrat and paid protection money to every ranking member of the governor's staff and the local *SS*, but the forces that pressed for eradication surged. Himmler's visit only confirmed the awful and inevitable.

Most of the boarders at the Mordechai house had fallen victim to death camp selection, and a few had died—one of typhus, two from hunger. Rudi was still missing and now presumed dead. The heavyset man was heavy no more, but "skinny as the rail line to the *platz*," he quipped. He was a man with the tastes of an epicure who loved to eat but now lived in a miserable empty shell that affected him worse than it affected the others. Henryk was still Henryk, tall, lean, quiet, unflappable.

The three women Rabbi Gimelman spent a fortune to protect had grown weak. Leiozia developed a cough, a first sign of tuberculosis. Shosha retained her ornery coloring but lost her appetite and wasted. Rebekah dressed in garments that hid her body, but her face was gaunt and distressed. They had food some days and clean water and warmth, but their appetite for comfort had waned and they found themselves victims of a paralysis of the spirit that made it difficult to move.

"**COME, COME, COME, COME**, come."

The rabbi's repetitive delivery of this simple word helped moved one foot on one woman down one stair. As he continued the cajoling cadence, Shosha stepped again, and again, until she was on the first floor. Three Underground fighters escorted Leiozia, Rebekah, and the last two boarders down from their rooms.

"Lev," Rebekah said. "What if he comes and we're gone?"

"He's been sent word," the rabbi said. "He knows where to find us."

"But what if the word doesn't reach him?"

"It already has," the rabbi lied. "He sends his love to everyone, you especially."

"You heard from him?" Shosha said. "Why didn't you say anything?"

"There wasn't time."

They went out the door to the alley and an awaiting carriage, a rickety contraption harnessed to a thinning ass. Rebekah grabbed her escort's hand and looked back, at the open door and the light inside. She looked up, at the windows and the moonlight on the glass, lackluster there, but brilliant in the sky. The rabbi and the other men loaded her family and their remaining boarders. But Rebekah stood. Her breath rose in the cold air.

"We have to go," her escort said. "We only have a little window."

"How can we leave?" Rebekah said. "Where else is there?"

"We have to go."

"Where?"

"Problem?" The rabbi stood with them now.

"She doesn't want to go," the man said.

Rebekah gripped the railing to the steps and looked at her feet. She felt warmth in her face and tried in her mind to push everything back. Her legs shook with the effort. The rabbi took her arm.

"We have to go," he said.

"Where?"

"Anywhere but here. This is death to stay here."

Rebekah held fast and the rabbi squeezed her arm.

"Mama. Come on," Shosha called from the carriage. "Time's wasting."

Rebekah looked at the rabbi.

"Was he joking?" she asked.

"Who?"

"Lev," she said. "In the letter, he said he saved you."

"He wasn't joking," the rabbi said. "He saved me."

Rebekah looked at the rabbi's hands. "How?" she asked.

The rabbi took her arm. "It's not important," he said.

"It is," she said.

"Mama!" Shosha, from the carriage.

The rabbi waved at her and gently tugged Rebekah.

"It's important to me," Rebekah said.

"There was fighting outside the city," the rabbi said. "We were near the river."

"The Wisła?" The Wisła runs through Krakow, too.

"Yes," the rabbi said. The carriage driver came up to them.

"We really need to go," he said.

"Lev may come back," Rebekah said. "I can't be gone then."

"Lev won't come here," the rabbi said.

"Where will he go then?" Rebekah said.

"Where we're going."

"Where? Where are we going?" Rebekah looked up at the shanty she once called her home. "The letter looked like his handwriting," she said. Her voice broke and tears trickled down her cheek. "Where are we going?"

The rabbi placed his hand along her shoulder and her neck. He squeezed her and moved his face close to her. "To life," he said.

THE TUNNELS LED UNDER the wall beyond the Ghetto and, it seemed, were always being dug out and extended. Short walkways led to bunkers that came off the main tunnels like pouches. Some bunkers sheltered weapons, some sheltered food, others sheltered people. From the bunkers, they could hear the shots on Mila Street. From the Aryan side, it looked like the entire Ghetto was burning.

Underground, everyone ate and worked. Rebekah joined three women filling glass bottles with a mixture of kerosene, gasoline and sulfuric acid. Shosha corked the bottles and glued a cloth strip soaked in a crude, diluted solution of nitroglycerin.

Leiozia rested on a straw bed over cold dirt near a little pool of fire. The damp in the tunnels aggravated her lungs and they seized with phlegm. Her face was hot in the afternoon and the heat crept into her arms and legs at dusk and into her hands and feet by night. Her eyes were hot and she couldn't sleep but she kept them closed until she saw irrational thoughts that forced her to open them and look into the dark. So long as the thoughts vanished, she knew she wasn't hallucinating and she took no more than lukewarm tea made from a packet of bitter root that came with a donation from Montana.

"They're filling the Pawiak again." Antek lit a thick cigarette in a fire pit. He stood with the other deputies in a large cellar— the command bunker.

"What about Schultzie?" asked one of the men, about Schultz the factory director at the Sheds.

"Not good," Antek said. "I stood across the street from the workshops. Idiots didn't see me. Too busy with the beatings."

"I thought they needed good workers."

"Not so much, apparently. The courtyard's full of people. We're cutting a hole in the fence—see who we can get out. Szymek got the money for the bribes."

"Kac?"

Antek dragged the cigarette and nodded his head: Szymek Kac.

"Get the bottles—we go tonight," said another deputy who stuck his head through the entry.

SHOSHA SAT BESIDE LEIOZIA and wiped her hot forehead with a damp towel and spoon-fed her thin cereal of mashed oats. The rabbi walked in and Leiozia looked up at him and smiled.

"How are you?" he said.

"Edelman was just in to see her," Shosha said. Marek Edelman, a medical doctor, was ZOB second in command.

"And?" the rabbi said.

Shosha fed Leiozia the rest of the cereal then kissed her forehead and stood and walked with the rabbi out of the bunker into the tunnel hallway where two men were stacking crates and bundles.

"Edelman can't do anything else," Shosha said. "He's given her antibiotics, but only time will tell on that."

"What does he think?" the rabbi said.

Shosha looked up and sighed. "Typhus, probably. Not contagious, but we have to make absolutely sure everything is absolutely clean. No fleas, no lice, nothing like that. And everyone has to bathe. Everyone has to stay clean."

"No small chore," the rabbi said.

"But we do it," Shosha said.

"Too bad we can't get her to Marienburg," said one of the men near the crates, about a town in East Prussia on a branch of the Wisła River known as the Nogat.

"Where?" Shosha said.

"To the Healer," the man said. "He lives near Marienburg."

"We have a doctor," Shosha said. "We have two doctors, in fact."

"The Healer is not a doctor," the man said.

"He's been verified," the other man said. "I've read two stories about him and no one can explain his gifts. Not even Szarzynski."

"Szarzynski?" the rabbi said. "The surgeon?"

"Yes."

"The Healer's name is Chelzak," the other man said. "First name of Jakub. He bleeds from his hands and feet. Szarzynski verified him for the Church."

Anatol Szarzynski was the top surgeon in Prussia and one of the top surgeons in all Europe. The public knew Szarzynski from his early days as an *enfant terrible* of the surgical suite and his later pronouncements on the fate of ailing politicians and other important persons. An astute self promoter with a sixth sense for the sensational, Szarzynski accepted a commission from Adolf Cardinal Bertram, the Archbishop of Breslau and leader of the German Catholic Church, to investigate claims surrounding Jakub Chelzak. An affirmation would boost Szarzynski's renown. A debunking would die in a day.

Szarzynski verified "the wounds on the wrists and palms are genuine, from the perspective, at least, of a medical examination. What is in this man, Jakub Chelzak's, heart—that is, whether or not he is saintly—is another matter best left to those who can ably judge such things."

"Waste of time," Shosha said. "Szarzynski's a very public asshole."

"It's not just Szarzynski," the man said. "Everyone knows about the Healer."

"I don't believe in such things," the rabbi said. "And the Church is not our friend."

"That's not true, Rebbe. Not for all. Look at Koplin, wandering our streets for alms, for us, til they took him to Oswiecim."

"He's a Capuchin friar, Rebbe," the other man said. "Like the one who bombed the Pawiak."

"Father Kolbe, too, Rebbe. Another Franciscan killed at Oswiecim. He took another man's place. They injected him with carbolic instead."

"I know the fathers do good deeds," Rabbi said. "I know that. I've seen it. But none of them could heal Leia."

"Jakub Chelzak heals the sick. It's documented."

"By whom? By Catholics?" Shosha said. "Who knows how true any of it is."

"He's healed some very tough cases," the first man said. "Hopeless ones."

"How does he feel about Jews?" the rabbi said.

"Why would he care?"

Shosha sighed. The rabbi looked at her. The men stacked more boxes.

"You should go see him," the second man said.

"Out of the question," Shosha said. "Too dangerous. And for what? To see a fake Jesus?"

The man stacking boxes shrugged. "There are ways to stay safe," he said. "If anyone knows those ways, it's Rebbe."

"It's always problematic," Rabbi Gimelman said. "Everything's problematic."

"You need to stay here," Shosha said. "We need you here. This man can do nothing for Leiozia."

The rabbi thought. "Does anyone else here know anything about him?"

"Antek has talked about him," said the first man.

THE WEATHER WAS COLD but calm. The fighting was worse.

"Mama," Shosha said. "Marian is here."

"Oh. Oh!" Rebekah stood and brushed flour from her dress. She looked at three loaves, rising on a wooden table. She smoothed the hair from her face and joined Shosha.

They walked down the tunnel and up some steps into the cellar of a house on Mila Street that had become an informal headquarters for the fighting groups. The cellar was large, its walls thick stone, lighted with candles on crates and hanging gas lamps. The flames were low and flickered on the men's dirty faces. Shosha, Rebekah, and a young woman grasping the arm of the man next to her were the only women. Marian—aka Colonel Mordecai Anielewicz—commanded the ZOB. He sat on a crate, talking and smoking with the other men. Shosha pointed him out. Leon Fajner, a lawyer who moved between the Ghetto and the Aryan side, stood.

"Please—all stand," Fajner said.

The twenty Underground leaders stood and each person placed a hand on a weapon.

"Repeat after me, please" Fajner said. "We fight this battle not only for victory, but for the dignity and honor of the Jewish Nation."

"We fight this battle not only for victory, but for the dignity and honor of the Jewish Nation," the group repeated.

"This meeting shall now be called to order."

They sat, on the ground, on flour-filled burlap sacks, on crates of ammunition, wherever they could.

"Progress?" Marian said.

"ZZW killed five traitors at the brush manufacturing workshops in Swietojerska Street."

"Floor rats?" Marian asked. The speaker nodded. Floor rats were Jew turncoats on the workshop floors who stood watch over the workers and beat them.

"ZOB?"

"We got Nossig," came the reply. Jewish intellectual Dr. Alfred Nossig was a once-ardent Zionist turned *Gestapo* agent who made a map of the Ghetto's underground bunkers for the occupiers.

"How?" Marian asked.

"Through the window."

"Through his big fucking head."

"At home?" Marian asked.

"Muranowska Street, right?"

"Yeah—forty-one, forty-two. Something like that."

"They're sure how?"

"Found his *Abwehr* card. Turncoat bastard."

"Who sent the stuff to Brühl?" Marian meant Brühl Palace, German Governor Ludwig Fischer's headquarters. The men looked at one another. "Mail bomb—exploded there," Marian said. Still no answer. "No one knows? Okay. What else?"

"We got the warehouses at Nalewki."

"Yes," Marian said. "I saw the flames—I wondered who did that." He turned and picked up a stack of papers. He looked at Shosha. "How is Leia?" he asked.

"Better," Shosha said. "A little, anyway. Rabbi was in to see her. He's worried."

"Rebbe always worries," Marian said. "He was worrying to me about *Pesach*. I was kidding him about the need to be more rabbinical."

"How can anybody worry about that now?" Rebekah asked.

"I haven't met you," Marian said to her. He reached over.

"This is my mother," Shosha said.

Rebekah smiled and extended her hand demurely. "Rebekah Mordechai," she said.

"You're husband's a legend. We all miss him, very much."

Before Rebekah could turn away in a blush, Marian took her to his cheek. "I was only kidding Rebbe," he said. "I promised to get him some matzo if he promised to cook it."

"He blessed the food," Rebekah said. "He always does."

Marian turned to the group. "Let's see if we can't finally get this fucker Brandt," he said. He looked at the women. "Sorry," he said. "It's the only word I know for him."

ANTEK HAD BEEN IN the streets for days, but finally returned one night late. The rabbi was in the bunker and still awake. He asked Antek about Jakub Chelzak from Marienburg.

"I have family near there," Antek said. "Everyone knows about him."

"What have you heard?"

"Same as the others," Antek said. "Sick people come to him."

"What kind of sick people?"

"Any kind."

"Jews?"

"Why not? Jews get sick too."

"I don't mean that," the rabbi said. "This man is Catholic. Are his gifts reserved for Christians, or are they Christian wishful thinking?"

Antek lit a cigarette. "You're making too much of it," he said. "Sick is sick."

"We can't afford a wild goose hunt," the rabbi said.

"Who can't afford?" Antek said. "You or Leia?"

THE RABBI DIDN'T SLEEP. He thought and prayed during the night. Leiozia's hoarse hacking carried in the tunnels and shook the women out of their sleep. Her face was gray, her eyes dull. She slept most days. She ate almost nothing.

"L-rd," Rabbi said. "Why do you present such difficulty? How can I know what to do?" He stared at the darkness. Why was he even considering this? The way the thing was presented—by strangers stacking boxes in a tunnel—struck him. As the men were talking, he felt an intuition. That was all. But that was all sometimes one had. Who could say, his father used to tell him, that feelings weren't answers to prayers?

Marienburg was in the Zulawy region, fertile lowlands at the mouth of the Wisła not far from where it emptied into the Baltic Sea. Trains went there from Aryan Warsaw. Glowny Station, Antek told him, had a late express with no stops until Marienburg, then north to Gdansk. It left at 2:17 in the morning. But what was he thinking? What a choice. Walk in harm's way to find a Christian myth based on the grassroots sentiments of a few scruffy Jews. Or not. Leiozia probably dies with the first option. Leiozia certainly dies with the second. Ridiculous. They needed him here. Shosha, Rebekah—the other men, the other women. Lev.

Lev.

The light of even the faintest hopeful glimmer attracted Lev Mordechai like a moth. It was one reason the two men had been friends like brothers.

"I'm an impractical pragmatist," Lev had once told him. "You're a pragmatic dreamer."

So as to encounter no resistance nor second-guessing, Azar Gimelman left a short note and quietly departed after midnight. To get on the train, he bribed a woman he had given money over the past year. With a mock passport, and simple disguise, leaving the Ghetto was not as hard as he expected. The trip took a few hours over about three hundred kilometers. On this two-day journey, he would be gone a week.

TOWN

Ten

Gray cold gripped Marienburg, East Prussia in the winter of 1941. It was the only other thing people in the area would say they remembered about that time. The first thing was the situation of Jakub Chelzak, who one afternoon fell prostrate, pierced and bleeding. Scratches and punctures sweat blood from his temple and matted his hair into clumped strands that dried stiff in the heat from the coal fire in the stove downstairs. Nails made of flesh, twisted and misshapen, erupted from his wrists.

"Jakub!"

Kazimiera—Mia, his mother—ran into her son's bedroom. "Dear God," she said. She took him and dabbed his face with her apron and looked at his eyes. "What's happened to you?"

Jakub reached for her face, and pressed his hand over her cheek. She took his fingers. "Where's Karl?" he asked.

"In the village," Mia said.

"I can't move," Jakub said. "When's he coming back?"

"He shouldn't be long," Mia said. "But I need someone now."

"Stay with me," Jakub said. "Don't leave."

When Jakub's brother Karl returned, Jakub and his mother were sleeping on the floor under blankets. The bleeding had stopped, but the wounds were visible. A doctor visited the area weekly. When he examined Jakub, the wounds were faint and faded.

"I don't know what it is," the doctor told them. "You lost a lot of blood. You should be dead."

Word got around the village and the following Sunday Monsignor Starska stopped Jakub after mass. He took Jakub's hands and his fingers trembled as he probed the flesh around the faint outlines of the wounds.

"Why you?" he said.

WARMER DAYS BROUGHT THE poor, the infirm, the wealthy and the well to the Chelzak farm, situated in the verdant lower Wisła river valley known as *Zulawy Wisłane* (Wisła Lagoon). The town took its name from Marienburg (now Malbork) Castle, which F. Scott Fitzgerald wrote was "the largest pile of bricks north of the Alps, a magnificent mountain of lore." It was visible from the Chelzak farm on a clear day.

On this clear day, Mia stared while a woman presented Jakub with a basket of fruit and her daughter on a porch overlooking the valley. Jakub took the girl, who had a cleft lip, spoke to her, placed his hand over her lip, and prayed. His body slumped.

"Enough," Mia said. The woman looked at her daughter's lip. She tried to kneel. "I said enough." Mother Chelzak raised her voice.

The girl's mother fixed her whole body on Jakub, who was still. Her daughter slipped back into her arms. Mia came to them.

"What should I do if someone offers even a little hope?" the woman said to Mia.

"I'm—"

"You're selfish," the woman said. "Your son has a great gift. Is it for you to say how he shares it?"

"Time for you to go," Mia said.

Jakub strained to right his neck and refocus his eyes. The woman took the girl, whose lip was not changed, and they stepped down from the porch. Mia returned the woman's basket. She looked at her son. "Why give these poor souls hope they shouldn't have?"

Jakub looked at the ground and ran his hands through his hair. "What am I supposed to do?" he said.

Mia watched the woman and the girl on the edge of the farm now, turning toward the road. "I'm sorry," she said. She kissed her son on the forehead. "I love you." She stretched and stood. She went inside and Jakub heard the door slap against the jamb.

MEN IN GRAY UNIFORMS traveled in a black car down the narrow road past the Chelzak farm. The words *Org. Todt* hovered

over Reich insignias on each door. Named for *Oberführer* Fritz
Todt, *Organisation Todt* was the Third Reich's construction arm.
The black car slowed and stopped near workers laying rail near a
barren edge of the Chelzak farm. Karl Chelzak pulled weeds in a
nearby potato field. He stood and leaned on a rake and rested his
back. His hands were cramped. He saw the men, and beyond
them, the castle in a low haze. Rustling in the crops startled
Karl. He turned and saw a slight man with thin black hair
squinting at him through fogged spectacles.

"Chelzak?" The man removed his specs and wiped them on
the tail of his shirt. He put them back on and looked at Karl
again. "Karl Chelzak?" He waded like a greenhorn through the
tilled soil. Karl saw the man's long face and sad clothes. A train
whistle receded with a melancholy whine.

"Chelzak," the man croaked. "Chelzak—you are not
permitted to work in this field..." The man stumbled and
brushed off his pants. "...between the hours of thirteen hundred
and sixteen hundred."

Karl bent and pulled a sweet-smelling, flowering weed.

"Did you hear me, Chelzak?" The man stopped. "I said stop
working."

"Are you a soldier?" Karl asked the ground.

"No," the man said. He walked toward Karl and handed him
an *Organisation Todt* identification card. With a hand that could
grasp a watermelon, Karl gripped a large stalk and ripped it out.
Black soil rained between them.

"Why should I stop working?" Karl asked.

"That's not for you to ask," the man said.

Karl straightened his back. "They're laying track over there," he said. "Where to?"

"I'm not a planner," the man said. "My orders are for you to stop work. You can finish later."

"You're too small to make me stop work and you don't have a gun," Karl said. He bent over and started loading weeds into a satchel.

"I'm a *kapo*," the man said. "We aren't allowed guns."

Kapos were Jew traitors if Karl believed what he heard in town. "You do what they tell you?" Karl asked.

The man brushed dirt from his hair and shirt. "They kill my family if you don't leave this field," the man said.

"And mine starve if I do," Karl said. He kept working, then wiped his forehead. He looked at his farmhouse. "Who kills you?"

"Soldiers," the *kapo* said. He took his glasses off.

Karl reached over and grabbed the satchel. He spat in the dirt. "So you owe me," Karl said. He slung the satchel over his shoulder. "For saving your family." He turned and walked toward the farmhouse.

"I don't owe you anything," the *kapo* yelled after Karl was far enough away.

MONSIGNOR STARSKA SIPPED WEAK coffee in the Chelzak's downstairs room. The morning was cool. Mrs. Chelzak stepped down the wooden stairs. "All night, Father," she said. She ran her hands through her disheveled hair, blinked the fatigue from her eyes. "Go see him."

The priest walked upstairs. He ducked into a cramped room. Jakub lay in bed with his head propped on a pillow. His eyes were closed. The priest reached down to the bloodied sheets piled on a chair. He touched them, slipped their folds between his fingers. They were brittle and dark. He stood absent-mindedly until he heard voices downstairs.

"The Bishop," he overheard Karl say.

"I don't care," Mia said. "I don't want soldiers in my home."

Monsignor Starska looked through the window and saw black cars and deacons. Maximilian Kaller, Bishop of Ermland, stood with soldiers and they were talking. The German Kaller—a staunch anti-Nazi who opposed Hitler's embrace of mysticism—knew of Archbishop Bertram's interest in Chelzak and was visiting to see for himself and run interference if necessary. A German nationalist who refused to ruffle the Nazi hierarchy for fear it would disrupt the Church's enviable status quo, Archbishop Bertram promoted appeasement. He went so far as to send the Führer congratulatory birthday greetings on behalf of all German Catholics each year. Kaller hated him for it.

"The soldiers can force their way in," Karl said.

"Let them try."

"They only come to keep order," Starska said.

"Order?" Mia said. "What's out of order here?"

Monsignor Starska crept downstairs to Mia, standing near the open front door.

"Let them in," the priest told her. Mia looked at him. "They've come to see your son," he said.

She moved away. "*You* let them in," she said. "But the soldiers stay down here."

"He is ready," Monsignor Starska said to the men. Bishop Kaller stepped into the cottage and Monsignor Starska genuflected and kissed the prelate's ring.

"God be with you," said the Bishop, and he placed his hand on the priest's head and walked upstairs. Two soldiers followed and Karl stepped forward to intervene. Monsignor Starska caught his arm.

"Mama doesn't want them," Karl said.

"Why?" Starska purred. "What does she really know about them?" He poured another cup of coffee from the pot on the round stove. "I like to think what your papa would want," he said. "He would want you alive and unmolested."

"He should have taken his own advice," Karl said.

"For his sake and yours," Starska said. "Once a man joins the Resistance, his household falls under permanent suspicion." He sipped his coffee. "But your brother has kept this household out of trouble." He stared out the window at a crowd gathering for a chance to see the bishop.

Mia Chelzak stomped downstairs. "I can't stand them," she said. "They stink—they don't bathe. Why didn't you keep them down here?"

"Shh!" Karl said.

About a half-hour later, Bishop Kaller and his entourage reappeared.

"Thank you for inviting us," the Bishop said.

"Oh!" Monsignor Starska said. He genuflected. "It is a great honor."

"Yes," Kaller said. "It was."

Eleven

Bishop Kaller informed Archbishop Bertram he had visited Jakub Chelzak, did not personally witness the stigmata, and could therefore not speak to its authenticity. Though Nazi troops had been using nearby Castle Marienburg for youth training camps, the occupying force appeared unaware of Chelzak or his unusual "gifts," which suggested they were little more than small-town rumor and field-hand gossip.

The two Church leaders exchanged more letters, Bertram attempting to portray Chelzak as a mystical presence with preternatural powers, Kaller diplomatically resisting. Even if the stigmata did appear, they could be evidence of a skin disorder, emotional hysteria, psychological injury, or some other natural cause, Kaller explained. He also found no evidence of any healings or otherworldly interventions.

"Though people of faith do visit Chelzak seeking his intercession on matters of sickness and sin, I have found no one for whom he has done any more than provide common-sense counsel," Kaller wrote the Archbishop.

"I understand your position, but I still believe the situation warrants further investigation," Bertram replied. He directed his subordinates to prepare a report for two offices: the Secretariat of State for the Vatican in Rome; and the Reich Ministry of Public Enlightenment and Propaganda in Berlin. Bertram understood the Reich's appetite for propaganda. In Jakub Chelzak, he might have found an appeasing tidbit: a person whose unusual condition would, as Hitler required in *Mein Kampf*, "appeal to mass emotion" while representing a "single point that could be repeated like a slogan until even the very last man is able to understand."

The point: that Jews killed Jesus and Jakub Chelzak was a living reminder of the brutal way they did it.

EXCERPTS FROM REPORT OF the Archbishopric of Breslau on the Case of Jakub Chelzak of Marienburg

I.   Introduction
II. Archdiocesan Imprimatur
III. Statement of the Case
IV. Historical Precedence of the Stigmata: Latter Day Manifestations of the Crucifixion Wounds of Our Lord, Jesus Christ in Persons of Pious Repute

IV. Historical Precedence of the Stigmata

A. Earliest Cases

Perhaps the first reference to a person other than Jesus bearing His crucifixion wounds—stigmata—came from St. Paul, who wrote, "I bear on my body the marks of the Lord Jesus." *Galatians 6:17.*

When we speak of stigmata, we generally speak of five wounds: nail entry wounds in the palms of each hand or each wrist; nail entry wounds in the feet; and, in select cases, a lance wound through either side of the torso. Only rarely have the marks of the crown of thorns around the forehead and temple been reported, as they have in the case of Jakub Chelzak.

Following St. Paul, the next recorded case of stigmata occurred with the Italian founder of the Order of Friars Minor, St. Francis of Assisi (1182–1226). St. Francis and his disciples prayed and fasted on Mount Alverno in the Apennines for forty days, after which time Francis had a vision of Jesus Our Lord on the cross, and received the four nail wounds and lanced side.

Oddly, St. Francis exhibited stigmata a mere two years after authorities arrested a man from Oxford, England for impersonating our Lord by self-inflicting the five wounds.

Within a century of St. Francis's death, some twenty cases of stigmata were reported, several unfortunately false. Despite many true and ecumenically verified cases, a general skepticism about stigmatics has persisted that we believe the Church has a duty to either dispel or confirm with each new case.

B. Common Demographic Features

By 1908, 321 stigmatics were of record who shared certain characteristics.

1) All were Roman Catholic
2) One third from Italy
3) Two thirds from France, Spain, and Portugal
4) 87.5% women
5) 66% from religious orders
6) 100% devout in their religious faith

The case of Jakub Chelzak presents three unusual demographic characteristics:

a) Chelzak is Polish and hails from East Prussia
b) Chelzak is not a member of any religious order
c) Chelzak is male

While we would not characterize Jakub Chelzak as devout, he is pious; baptized in the Roman Catholic faith; and regularly attends mass under the ecclesiastical auspices of Monsignor Jarus Starska, diocese of Ermland, archdiocese of Breslau. Chelzak prays the rosary and takes the sacraments of confession and communion.

C. The Form of the Wounds

The form of stigmata wounds vary. St. Francis did not bleed. His wounds included impressions of round black nails, made of flesh distinct from that covering his wrist and feet. Wounds reported in other stigmatics include small slits, crosses, slash marks, or indentations. In the case of hysterics or false events, the wounds have been known to change from round to rectangular over time, presumably as the subjects learn the true shape of Roman nails.

The side wound, from the Roman soldier's lance noted in *John 19:34*, has exhibited a variety of manifestations:

1) Appeared on the right or left side of the body
2) Varying shapes, e.g. lateral slit or crescent

Whip marks on the back and shoulder and cuts or gashes from carrying the cross also appeared in a few cases.

Letters on the skin bearing the names of Joseph, Mary, and Jesus were reported on the left hand of the nun Jeanne des Anges (1602–1665), who toured France displaying her hand. The letters proved a hoax.

The Capuchin friar Padre Pio da Pietrelcina (Francesco Forgione) of San Giovanni Rotondo, Italy exhibits wounds whose supposed painfulness and the thick crusts of blood that cover them have stymied their examination. A pathologist sent by the Pontiff noted that beyond the scabs was a lack of "any sign of edema, of penetration, or of redness, even when examined with a good magnifying glass." He concluded that the side lance wound had not penetrated the skin. Padre Pio keeps his "wounds" concealed with finger-less gloves on each hand. Other investigations yielded mixed findings (see Appendix, re: Bignami, Festa, Gimelli examinations). Pio's case awaits further review.

Jakub Chelzak exhibits swelling, redness, and marked puncture depressions in the areas of his wounds. He also exhibits fleshy protrusions that resemble nails.

D. Personal Traits of Stigmatics

1. Worldliness

Many stigmatics were men and women of the world, enamoured of money, possessions, high society, and worldly pleasures. We provide two examples.

St. Francis was the son of a wealthy merchant, at one time a hedonist preoccupied with extravagant parties, beautiful women, rich foods, wine, and gaiety. Only Our Lord's voice persuaded him to relinquish these pursuits.

Blessed Angela of Foligno (1248–1309) lived a worldly life before her conversion. A married woman with children, she renounced her sinful existence at age 37. Her family did not support her conversion, and each member died shortly thereafter. Following their deaths, Angela sold her country villa and distributed the proceeds from the sale of her worldly possessions to the poor. Angela was permitted to join the Third Order of St. Francis at age 43.

By no means is our subject, Jakub Chelzak, a worldly or wealthy man. He is not a convert to the faith, nor has he renounced any part of his life or circumstance. He is, by all appearances, a peasant farmer.

2. Illness and Hysteria

Many stigmatics suffer from a host of illnesses, and dozens were bedridden for much of their lives. St. Lidwina (circa 1410) was reported to have suffered every illness imaginable.

Hysteria is also reported. Marguerite Parigot of the Blessed Sacrament (1619–1648) suffered from attacks so terrible they were attributed to demons. Anna-Maria Castreca (1670–1736) threw herself violently around rooms and fell into childish speech and mannerisms.

Ecstatic states and religious trances were reported in St. Veronica Giuliani (1640–1727), Victoire Claire (1808–1883), St. Francis, and Passitea Crogi, who fell into a rapturous vision of Christ bruised and bleeding on Palm Sunday, the year of our Lord 1589.

It must be noted that our subject, Jakub Chelzak, age 26, is neither sickly nor hysterical. In fact, he remains vigorous and completely lucid by all reports. His mother, Kazimiera Chelzak, reports ignominious suffering whenever the wounds make their appearance, but this pain subsides in hours. Jakub Chelzak is reported to bleed, sometimes profusely, during these periods. He is not reported to have had rapturous visions or other potentially delusional incidents.

3. Preternatural Powers

Reports of prophecy, healing, levitation, bilocation (the ability to be in two places at once) and the ability to fast for long periods are common among stigmatics. Angela of Foligno may have gone without food for over a decade. The corpses of some stigmatics may withstand decay. Vials of dried blood preserved from the stigmata of Passitea Crogi reportedly become liquid periodically.

Subject Jakub Chelzak is said to have exhibited curative powers on several occasions. Various eyewitnesses report that he has healed paralysis, heart ailments, mental disturbances, gout, and in one unusual instance, homosexuality (*the subject of this case lives in Zakopane*). No third party medical verification exists for any of these reports, however. As previously documented, Dr. Szarzynski has verified only Chelzak's wounds. The sick and their families cannot be considered sound witnesses for any healings or other miracles in his name. Until such time as proper Church process takes its course, such witness testimony remains hopeful rumor.

4. Frauds

History suggests most stigmatic frauds are either exposed or confess. Fake stigmatics include Magdalena de la Cruz, who confessed in 1543, fearful of dying with the stain of such an unholy deception on her soul. A sister nun observed Maria de la

Visitacion, the "holy nun of Lisbon," painting a fake wound onto her hand and reported the incident. Maria de la Visitacion was brought before the Inquisition. Her wounds were scrubbed and the coloration removed, revealing normal skin.

Fraudulent stigmatics often engage in questionable activities. The British stigmatic Teresa Helena Higginson (1844–1905), a teacher, was dismissed for thievery and drunkenness. Belgian Berthe Mrazek, a circus performer turned stigmatic, was arrested for fraud and committed to an asylum for the mentally deranged. Other stigmatics self-mutilate too much to distinguish the mutilations from genuine stigmata. Lukardis of Oberweimar (c. 1300) regularly drove her fingernails into her palms before receiving the stigmata.

The natural question—is Jakub Chelzak a fraud—may not yet be substantially determined. However, he is a simple man; he has not confessed to fraud; nor has any person stepped forward to condemn him. As for healing the sick, though he makes no claims on this point, he does not turn away those who seek his counsel or intercession.

5. Profiteering as a Motive for the Stigmata

Padre Pio was once thought to have been put on display by his friary in order to make money. A following both credible and dubious has grown up around Pio. Con men sell his supposed relics, including pieces of cloth spotted with chicken blood. His stigmata wounds may be real or result from ongoing application of corrosive substances.

Our subject, Jakub Chelzak, hails from a family of limited means. The question arises, then: are his wounds motivated by profit that would induce him to fake them? On first examination, the answer appears to be "no," as Chelzak does not take money for his visitations, nor did Dr. Szarzynski find evidence of fraudulent self-infliction.

V. Summary Biographies of Board Investigators

1. The Reverend Woitla Lankewicz
2. The Reverend Lanid Cherusz
3. The Most Reverend Monsignor Viktor Tladeusz, presiding

VI. Imprimatur

VII. Conclusions

We conclude that Jakub Chelzak of Marienburg exhibits a convincing form of stigmata. His situation is devoid of indications of fraud, hysteria, hypochondria, or illness that may otherwise mimic false wounds. His character appears to be simple and pious. His mental state is sound. His wounds appear real. If the phenomenon is indeed an act of God, Jakub Chelzak appears to be a legitimate bearer of the crucifixion wounds of Our Lord Jesus Christ.

Twelve

A single-engine locomotive pulled aging passenger cars past the outskirts of the Chelzak farm after crews completed the new rail spur late that summer. From where he stood against orders at 1400 hours, Karl saw a few heads—well-dressed men with slicked-back hair; women with gloves and hats; children peering over high, scratched windows. A child waved and Karl waved back. The train disappeared over a curve on the horizon.

In the house, Jakub sat on his bed.

"Body of Christ," Monsignor Starska said. The priest took a thin white wafer from a silver pyx and placed it on Jakub's tongue. They heard a door open and shut downstairs.

"I'm going into town today," Karl called up. "Can you handle things?"

"Of course," Jakub said. "I'm not an invalid."

"Not today."

Jakub looked at the priest.

"He resents you," Starska said. "What were we just talking about?"

"He's a good brother," Jakub said.

"Not today."

Karl was eating a potato and cabbage when they came downstairs. "Father." Karl spoke with his mouth full. He stood up. "I didn't know you were here."

"Not a problem," Starska said. "Jakub was just telling me what a good brother you are."

Jakub rubbed his hands through his hair and drank a glass of water.

"Mother's in Elbing at the loom," Karl said. "You're on your own—unless the Monsignor is staying."

"No," the priest said. "I have to be getting back." But he made no move to leave.

Karl stepped around Jakub and wiped his face. He took Jakub's head in his big hands and pulled him close and kissed him on his hair.

"Good brother," he whispered. "Be careful with Father."

Jakub looked at his brother. Karl smiled and went out the door down the path toward the road into town.

The priest splashed a cup of coffee with whiskey from a silver flask. He pushed it across the table toward Jakub. "You'll feel better," Starska said.

Jakub sat and stared. "I have lots to do," he said.

The priest looked at him.

"You shouldn't do anything," the priest said. "You've been sick. You need rest."

"I'm rested," Jakub said. "Karl's been doing everything. Mama says we need money. She's gone all the time now, at the loom."

"At the loom, at the loom," Monsignor Starska said. "Listen to you." He reached across the table and moved his fingers across Jakub's wrist. "You shouldn't worry about such things."

Jakub moved his hand away and sipped the coffee.

"Do you understand how special you are?"

Jakub put the cup down.

"You are." the priest said. "Very special." He stood and put his hands on the younger man's shoulders. "I can't even be around you without feeling it." He leaned down to Jakub and whispered. "Don't you understand?"

"I've been sick, like you say."

"It doesn't matter," the priest said. "You're on the mend and we're safe."

"Karl says no one's safe," Jakub said. "Papa used to say it all the time."

"I thought your papa was a quiet man."

"Not about war."

"Well—it doesn't matter," the priest said. "Not to you and me."

"I'll rest now," Jakub said.

"You want your bed? Let me help you."

"No," Jakub said. "I can rest here."

The priest was about to speak.

"Alone," Jakub said.

Monsignor Starska gathered his hat and walking stick. Jakub walked him to the door. The priest took Jakub's hand and raised it until the wrist was visible beyond the sleeve. He lowered his head and set his lips on the faded wound. He genuflected in a kind of shallow curtsy. "Your grace," he said.

Goose bumps needled Jakub's neck. He watched the priest walk up the path, carrying his walking stick like the staff of Moses. He was drained, but not from the wounds.

THE TRAINS PASSED AT the same time every day on their way to the Stutthof concentration camps outside Elbing. The rail cars, Karl thought, needed paint. Spider web fractures covered their windows and blotted out their passengers. Karl saw a man on yesterday's train kicking at the glass with both feet. The window popped out and smashed beyond the tracks in the field. The man pushed himself through the opening, which was too small and wedged him in. Karl walked toward the broken glass and watched the car move on with the man stuck halfway out the window.

The trains left a wake of litter in the fields—papers, books, photographs, hats, scarves, stockings, even lingerie and razors. At first, the litter only attracted children. Then Pavel Cherienk found a denture with gold teeth. After two days of chasing away adult treasure hunters trampling his crops, Karl started picking up the litter as soon as the trains passed. On days when Jakub was well, he policed the tracks while Karl sold produce in town. Trespassers were afraid to anger Jakub, and fled when they saw him. They assumed that one who could make well could also make sick, or withhold grace in time of need.

Today, Jakub's wrists and feet bore no wounds and no inflammation. His temple was red and stung when he touched it and he had a headache, so he sat on a bench outside the house looking toward the river. He sipped coffee splashed with his mother's sour mash from the stashed bottle she started to keep after Wojciech Chelzak—the sixteen-year-old boy she married— died fighting the Soviet Red Army when they invaded in late 1939. The mash was powerful and seeped into his conscience like an insidious fume. As his daydreams devolved, slurred, self-pitying questions slithered past his better nature. He let his head hang and closed his eyes.

Why should an innocent man receive an atrocious punishment? Why should pressures require that man to keep his head up and his mouth distorted in a smile? Were the wounds a gift, as Monsignor Starska and the Archbishop had said, or were they a scourge, which was how they felt? If they were a gift, from whom? God? Satan? There he was—Jakub Chelzak, a young man, saddled with his own pain and the unjust obligation to relieve it in others.

When he looked up, Jakub saw children running in the field and a man following them. By now the mash was clouding his vision. He rubbed his eyes and his hair to the back of his head. He stared at the field and saw children gathering. Green plants shivered in the river breeze. Jakub stood and let the wobble drain from his legs. The cool air coaxed his face.

"Hey," he yelled. "Hey!"

The man turned toward Jakub's voice, then ran to the children. Jakub stumbled up the path through the trees. He reached for a walking stick resting against one of the big, wide oaks that hid his house from the town road.

"You're trespassing," he yelled. "This is our land."

The man didn't look at him. The children looked down. The smaller of two girls danced around and flailed her arms. Jakub moved closer. The man grabbed the smaller girl, yelled back, and left the field with her. Jakub approached the railroad tracks worn shiny by the grinding wheels of the overloaded cars. He shaded his eyes from the glare. The children bent over something, going through it with their fingers. Jakub came up to them. He raised the stick and yelled and brought it down near the oldest boy. The boy screamed and stumbled back. The other children ran.

Jakub shadowed a man. His pants lay over the tracks and his wallet lay open and empty. His bloody shirt clung to his crushed ribs. The body was fresh and Jakub saw flies, gorged and listless in a red pool. He shook himself and ran back to the house. He grabbed a shovel. He ran to the track and saw a dog tugging the body.

"Ha! Hey! Hey!" He yelled and shook the shovel and stumbled. The scrawny dog pulled the bloody cloth. "Go! Get! Go!" The dog growled. "Go on!"

Jakub lunged at the dog. It bared its teeth and barked. "Go on!" Jakub threw the shovel. The dog backed away then grabbed the shirt in its teeth again. Jakub raised the shovel.

"Get off him!" Jakub struck the dog over its snout and it jerked back.

He looked at the man—his black, thick hair, young eyes, blue and open. The dog lurked near a tree, walking in a little circle and sneezing. Jakub thought about how deep he would have to bury the body to keep animals from digging it up. He bent down and grabbed the shirttails and dragged the body off the track.

"Burn it."

Jakub turned and saw Karl, walking through the field. "You want to dig six feet of hole?" Karl asked.

"If it burns it will stink."

"It won't," Karl said. He looked at the body. "He's the talk of the town."

They built a pyre of wood and straw and set the body on it. Karl went to the house and returned with a jug of sour mash and splashed it on the body and the straw. Jakub sparked it with a flint and they stood back. Flames and smoke took off. The fire reached the man's hair and the stench became terrific so the brothers backed away. Jakub blessed himself—in the name of the Father, the Son, and the Holy Ghost. He said a prayer for the dead man's soul. "Amen," he said and opened his eyes. He saw the smoke, but not his brother. He looked toward the house, through the fields and toward the track.

"Karl?" He called. "Karl!" His brother was not there.

KARL WALKED INTO THE house much later. "You won't believe what I got for the fall crop." he told his brother. "Did you handle everything?"

"What?" Jakub said.

"Did everything go all right?"

"After you helped me," Jakub said.

"Helped you?"

"In the field."

"I was in town all day."

After the war, Monsignor Starska told this story to a beatification board of five Cardinals. He said the corpse on the tracks was a Jew. Only later did the board learn the man was a Russian atheist the Germans had labeled a spy.

Thirteen

"This is not something you need be concerned with," Monsignor Starska said. "Not in the least."

"He's asking for my help," Jakub said.

The priest brought his palms over Jakub's shoulders and moved his hands up and down Jakub's arms, where the hairs stiffened like quills.

"They will look into everything," Starska whispered. "Everything you've ever done. Everything you've written or spoken. Every person who says you healed them."

"I didn't promise to heal him," Jakub said. "I'm not even sure why he came to me."

"Because of that man from Zakopane."

"I didn't do anything for him."

"It doesn't matter. The story's taken on a life of its own." The priest sighed. "This man Lutz wants you to change what he is, a part of him, like an eye. He wants you to rip it out."

"I agreed to talk with him."

Jakub turned and walked toward the porch. The priest called after him.

"You're going to be a saint someday," he said. "But you have to play it right."

SAINTHOOD MEANT NOTHING TO Jakub nor did the money he could have received from Karol Lutz, a prosperous publisher whose Vatican testimony on behalf of the candidate proved among the most valuable, for what it suggested about Chelzak's moral compass. Lutz determined to introduce the decadent capitalist world of F. Scott Fitzgerald to German and Polish readers, partly as a literary swipe at the statism creeping across Europe, but mostly to make money. He was a good businessperson who saw profit in the punch line. He was also homosexual. Scott did not approve.

"Scott." Zelda, his wife, drew out the "awe" in the middle of his name and slid her forearms along both sides of her husband's neck. He was sitting on a balcony overlooking the Wisła drinking scotch, neat and straight.

"We need the money," Zelda said. She kissed him.

"Badly enough to wreck my reputation?"

"It's only over here. It's not like you're changing publishers back home."

"No one but you will see it that way," Scott said.

Lutz succeeded in a niche other publishers avoided—bringing contemporary American and western European thought to the darker half of Europe—the East. He also published in India, parts of Asia, and the Soviet Union, where capricious regulations restricted merchants to selling Fitzgerald on Tuesdays, W.E.B. Dubois on Fridays and Dickens in March. Lutz had so mastered the circumnavigation of bureaucratic whims that Soviet regulators approved, for exclusive distribution in Moscow and Stalingrad, *Mein Kampf,* their mortal enemy's life story. Lutz had made a deal with Hitler. He became the European publisher of the Führer's autobiography and so was permitted to operate unmolested in Berlin and other Nazi strongholds.

These feats in the absurd gymnastics of 20th-century Euro-politics impressed Zelda Fitzgerald. When she and Scott received Lutz's invitation to visit Poland, they went without hesitation. Scott the ebullient optimist only started hurling words like "queer" and "faggot" after they had round-trip tickets Lutz purchased and an innkeeper's bill Lutz paid.

"If you didn't want Lutz to publish you, why did we accept this trip?" Zelda asked. "You knew about him."

"Sober," Scott said. "I knew about him sober. Now I'm drunk." He wheeled his face around to hers. "And more than a little pissed." He threw himself into a plush chair.

"Stupid," she said.

"He published fucking *Hitler,*" Scott said. "How fucked up is that?"

"Fucking *attention getting,*" Zelda said.

"You're either fucking naïve or a fucking idealist," Scott said.

"Or fucking a naïve idealist," Zelda said.

"Or fucking an ideal naïve," Scott said.

Zelda slithered onto her husband's lap and curled her head around to his ear. "That's 'knave,'" she whispered.

Scott looked her in the eyes. "Traitor," he said. Then he looked over her, through the bay doors toward the river. "Be fag, be queer—but don't be-tray." He sipped his scotch. "I won't be sullied by a turncoat."

"What's traitorous about publishing Hitler?" Zelda asked. "He's just another nut with a book."

"Oh. And is that what I am, Miss Zeldy? Just another kook with a book?" He grinned and licked her nose. She bit his lip. He pushed her off and stood.

"Goofo." She took his drink away. "I said 'nut.' You're a terrible cook."

He grabbed for the drink, but she held it at bay. "Sober up. He's bringing the galleys by."

"How is it you know these things before I do?"

"Clairvoyance," Zelda said.

"Witchcraft."

"He knows you don't like him—*now*, after everything's paid for," Zelda said. She set his drink on an end table. "Why do you have to be so *obvious*?"

"Bitchcraft." Scott picked up his glass, licked the rim, aimed unsteadily, and hurled it at a tree off the balcony. It hit the ground intact.

"You throw like a girl, Goofo," Zelda said.

"Good. I have something in common with the queers."

"You should pity them," Zelda said. "They have a sickness."

"Then they can be cured," Scott pronounced. "They can be healed."

YEARS LATER, KAROL LUTZ sat with Jakub Chelzak on his porch.

"You speak to me as though you are not sure you can help me," Lutz said.

"Maybe you need a priest," Jakub said.

"I have nothing to confess," Lutz said.

"You've lived with this all your life?"

"Yes," Lutz said.

Jakub considered. "You don't look sick to me."

"I'll be clear with you, Mr. Chelzak," Lutz said. "My life is in danger if I continue to live this way."

"I don't see how I can help you." Jakub stood. "I don't think you're sick."

"I can pay you handsomely, if that's an issue," Lutz said. "Very handsomely."

"My family always needs money," Jakub said. "But for honest work."

"So leave me to the beast," Lutz said. "It's what I deserve, right?"

Jakub stepped from the porch and Lutz grabbed his arm.

"I am compelled, Mr. Chelzak. Compelled. Do you understand me?"

Jakub took away Lutz's hand. "You're not sick," Jakub said. "There's nothing wrong with you."

Lutz looked across the field. He heard a train in the distance. "Maybe not according to you."

"Do you have family?"

"Not here," Lutz said. "I cleaned him, you know—after he threw up," Lutz said. "*Their* Führer. At a party." He looked toward the waning daylight and shaded his eyes. "Puked all over himself," he said. "If you're not going to help me, I need to be going. It's getting dark."

Lutz walked down the little road past Monsignor Starska's walking stick, leaning against the thick oak where he had forgotten it a day or two before. The glare obscured the walking man but Jakub saw his shadow until it became the shadow of the tree.

KAROL LUTZ LEFT THE continent a few months later. He lived in London for nine months and moved to Florida. From 1945 to 1950 he republished and revived the literary legacy of a writer he had long admired but who had died failed, broke and alone, consigned to obscurity by a flurry of sordid and belittling obituaries. By 1960, Lutz had secured F. Scott Fitzgerald a lasting place among the giants of literary fiction.

Mein Kampf, meanwhile, fell out of print and Lutz sent his own copy, by request, to General George Patton, who read it and passed it around to his other generals. Avidly literate, Patton returned the favor by providing Lutz the book jacket quote that would cement Fitzgerald's posthumous reputation.

"The closest thing we have or may ever have to the Great American Novel," Patton wrote of *The Great Gatsby*. "What

American doesn't now understand the tragedy of a man whose reach so vastly exceeds his grasp?"

Rumors of Lutz's homosexuality dogged him until the gay lifestyle became vogue. Long at peace with himself, Lutz broke his lifetime silence after reading a New York Times story about the Vatican's efforts to identify Holocaust saints. Chelzak's prominent mention prompted a flood of memories. He wrote the Vatican, requesting an audience with Church lawyers. Jakub's steadfast refusal to regard him as either sick or sinner, despite the chance to profit from a man weakened by fear and stress, singularly encouraged him to flee the insanity of the Nazi occupation, he testified, leaving everything and everyone he knew and loved behind.

Karol Lutz died in St. Petersburg, Florida in 1988, at the age of 82, after a profitable affair of whispers and innuendo involving the writer Truman Capote. Capote may have been the first to gossip that Zelda Fitzgerald had ghostwritten a number of her husband's stories, which had the effect of selling more books, paying the rent, and enhancing the Fitzgerald mystique Lutz had so carefully cultivated.

Fourteen

Corporal Stadt and Corporal Kessler, both nineteen and recently promoted to *SS-Rottenführer*, arrived on a train that passed Marienburg and the Chelzak's fields before it reached the Stutthof concentration camp. They smiled and waved from the train at girls with baskets of produce and flowers in their hair. At the camp, they checked in with the other enlisted men. The officer on duty—harried with unfinished assignments—screwed-up their orders and in the chaos of too many men with nothing to do, released the two corporals on a weekend pass.

They were both from small Bavarian towns populated by a few rich merchants who worked the markets and many poor families who worked the land. Stadt's father raised dairy animals —goats and cows, and chickens after milk prices plunged in the waning years of the Weimar Republic.

"Hitler rescued milk," Stadt's father told him. "He has my vote."

Kessler's mother, a widow, worked for a textile merchant who sold expensive Bavarian wool in America and the Orient. She lost her job when Hitler ordered Jews out of businesses and her employer fled the country to join family in Manhattan. Jews taught her how to read in a town of mostly illiterates, and she made another job reading crop reports and war news to farmers, storekeepers, and landowners for a fee. She charged extra to read German re-tellings of the exploits of Al Capone, John Dillinger, and other American gangsters.

"Hitler is a fool who will fuck us all," she told her son. "He's nothing but a gangster robbing a very big bank." At least the Americans, she said, did not allow their country to be taken over by thieves and murderers. "Look at them—Goering and Himmler. They look like child molesters." She also taught her son to read.

Stadt leaned against the wall of a shop in Marienburg, looking at contraband—a copy of *Der Stuermer*, a pulp magazine he picked up from a bench at the camp.

"What does this say?" he asked Kessler and pointed.

Kessler slapped him playfully on the side of his head. "Stupid baby can't read."

Young women wandered past wearing perfumes that smelled exotic and dresses unlike anything Stadt or Kessler had ever seen. They looked at the reflection of their own uniforms in the shop windows.

"We look good," Kessler said. "We could have any of them."

Stadt nudged Kessler and pointed at Karl Chelzak emerging from a shop with a bag and a bouquet. "You have any money?" Stadt asked.

Kessler shook his head. Stadt strolled across the street toward Karl. "Pretty flowers," he called out. "Are those for your girl?"

Karl ignored the boy soldiers who hung around in corners and crevices, eyeing the girls, picking fights, and trying to be noticed. Stadt came right up to him and stood.

"I'm speaking to you," Stadt said.

"So what."

"What did you say?"

"Fuck off," Karl said.

He was a much larger man but Stadt kneed him in the balls. Karl bent over and dropped his flowers.

"Fucking Pole-lock," Stadt said.

Kessler watched and stood. Men walked out of shops toward Karl and Stadt.

"Hey—what are you doing there?" a man said. Stadt looked at him. "You!" the man pointed.

Kessler saw other townsfolk and ran to Stadt and took his shoulder. "We should go," Kessler said.

"He needs to stand and look me in the eye and tell me to fuck off again," Stadt said. Stadt bent down and picked up Karl's flowers, but one of the locals ran up and whacked him across the ear with a stick and he stumbled. The other men grabbed him and Kessler, and dragged them toward the side of a building.

"Take your clothes off," one of the men said. His Germanic accent suggested Prussian heritage. He had a gun and he raised it to Stadt's face.

"You'll die for this old man," Stadt said.

"You're a disgrace to your uniform. Take it off!"

"What do you know about my uniform?"

"Defense of the Fatherland. *Entkleiden*."

Kessler and Stadt took off their coats, shirts and pants.

"Now underwear," the man said.

"You're crazy," Kessler said.

"*Schnell!*" The man with the gun fired into the air. "*Strippen!*"

The young soldiers took off their underwear and stood naked.

"Now march," the man with the gun said. "Back to your company."

"You're crazy," Stadt screamed. Kessler was crying.

"March or I shoot you both."

They marched and the townsmen hurled rocks and sticks. They marched into the street and other townspeople picked up anything they could find and threw it at them. The soldiers started to run, but the gun fired again.

"Slow down," one of the men yelled. "March only."

Others jeered and screamed and followed them, throwing stones and sand. When the two soldiers were far enough from the edge of town, the people turned back.

"They're going to get the fucking wrath of God for this," Stadt said.

"You shouldn't have done that," Kessler cried. "Why the fuck did you have to do that?"

Stadt turned when he felt something hit his back. His uniform lay at his feet. Karl threw his shoes and belt and Kessler's uniform too. The three men stood alone on a dirt road that ran past the castle. Kessler bent down to pick up his shirt but Stadt grabbed him.

"What are you doing?" he yelled to Karl. "Are you trying to humiliate us?"

Karl turned with his flowers and walked toward the town.

"We won't be humiliated. You hear me? No fucking Pole lock is going to humiliate us!"

Kessler pushed Stadt away and gathered his uniform.

"Fuck you," Stadt screamed at Karl. "Just fuck you!"

Kessler put on his uniform under a tree. Stadt gathered his uniform and walked with it under his arms, naked in the sun.

MIA CHELZAK CAST FEED to the chickens from a weathered wicker basket. An autumn wind swept through the aspens that lined the road. She looked toward the trees and saw Jakub, standing in the leaves.

"How are you feeling?" she asked.

"I ache all over."

"You taking what the doctor gave you?"

"Yes, but I still feel useless."

Mia took her son. "You're not useless," she said.

"You and Karl are working all the time. What am I doing?"

"You help people," Mia said. "They leave us food and other things. It's what the Lord wants for now."

They heard a train that looked like a snake weaving through brown winter grass.

"Did Karl tell you what happened?"

"What? No."

"Good—I told him I would."

"Well?"

"There was a body on the tracks."

"A body? A dog?"

"A man," Jakub said.

"That's terrible," Mia said. "Why didn't you tell me sooner?"

"Karl told Monsignor."

"But no one told me," Mia said. "Just like your father. Never talk. Keep everything inside." She spread more seed and set the basket down. "Do you remember where you saw it?"

"We burned it."

"You burned it? Who burned it?"

"Karl. Me. But Karl wasn't there. He was in town all day."

"You're not making sense." Mia moved away. "Show me. I want to see."

They walked into the fields. A few meters from the rail, Mia gasped. "It's burned," she said. Jakub walked to the charred ground. He saw pieces of cloth and leather. "There's blood," Mia said. She took her son. "What was it doing here?"

"He fell off the train," Jakub said.

"How?" Mia said. "I've never heard of such a thing."

"He jumped. Ask Karl. People try to get off these trains."

"Why?" Mia said. "Where on Earth are they going?"

THEY ATE DINNER AT a large table in a small room. The running of the trains had ended for the day and they were returning to the monotony of a winter wane. The leaves were trying to bud in places.

"They're worse off than we are," Jakub said. "I feel sorry for them."

"I'd be careful who I sympathized with," Mia said.

Karl drew in a deep, tired breath. "What do you know about them?"

"Enough."

"Enough? Enough what?"

"They're devious and greedy," Mia said.

Jakub looked at his food. "They don't look rich to me," he said.

"They come in to a place and they close it off to everyone but their own," Mia said. "They demand freedom, then cry about bigotry and tell everyone else how to live. They are the most bigoted people I know. If you aren't one of them, you're nothing."

"If you aren't a German, you're a nothing," Karl said.

"That's different," Mia said.

Karl looked at his mother and chewed his food. "How?" he asked.

"The war makes it different."

"What do you know about Jews," Karl said, "other than papa slept with one?"

Mia looked at her son and her jaw tightened.

"What did you say?"

"Nothing," Karl said.

"Say it again. What did you say?"

Karl kept chewing. Mia slammed her hand on the table. "Don't ever talk to me like that." She pushed her chair away and stood. "You disrespectful prick." She stomped up the stairs.

"You shouldn't have said that," Jakub said. He drank some water. "She's going to hate you for a week."

"She'll get over it."

Jakub looked at the stairs. "She hasn't yet," he said.

"GOOD MORNING."

Jakub saw Monsignor Starska coming down the narrow road toward the house. He felt a pang in his stomach. The day was bright and the priest was ready for it. He wore an oversize hat like a nun's cornette except it was black. The floppy brim waved up and down as he walked, like two dark wings. The priest rested his walking stick against the oak. He carried a leather tobacco pouch.

"I came to see how you were," Starska said. He wiped his forehead. The morning air was humid but cool. "You weren't at Ash Wednesday mass."

"Mama wasn't well," Jakub said.

"Don't tell him that." Jakub turned and saw his mother. "Monsignor," she said. She smiled and took the priest's hand.

"I'm sorry to hear you were sick," the priest said.

"I wasn't sick," Mia said. "It was my son who wasn't well. We didn't want to leave him."

"I understand," the priest said. He looked at Jakub. "I've brought the mountain to Muhammad," he said. He placed his thumb in the tobacco sack and brought it to Jakub's forehead. He drew a cross with fine gray ash.

"Thou art dust and unto dust thou shalt return."

"Amen," Mia said. Jakub whispered a refrain.

The priest repeated the ritual with Mia. "Is Karl about?"

"I haven't seen him," she said.

He closed the tobacco sack. "Some other time, then. The Archbishop would like to meet with you."

"The Archbishop?" Mia asked.

He placed the sack in his vest pocket. "Yes. In Breslau."

"Oh," Mia said. She looked at her son.

"They're very interested," the priest said to Jakub. "It's a good sign."

"Breslau is very far away," Mia said.

"We can't afford it," Jakub said.

"You won't have to pay," the priest said.

"I'm needed here for spring planting."

"I can get help for the planting," Starska said.

"I've never been that far," Jakub said. "I'd be lost."

"You won't be lost," Monsignor Starska said. "I'll be with you."

"It would be so much closer in Danzig," Mia said. "Why isn't the archbishop *there* interested?"

Monsignor Starska shrugged. "Politics," he said.

Jakub looked at his mother. "It's still a wonderful opportunity," she said.

"I have to think," Jakub said.

"About what?"

"Archbishop Bertram was planning for next month, before Easter," the priest said.

"Well—I think the answer can only be yes," Mia said.

JAKUB SPENT THE NEXT few weeks moping and anxious. He never told his mother, but he did tell Karl, who liked Monsignor Starska even less than he did. When the day came, the Monsignor arrived. Mia was outside feeding the chickens.

"Monsignor," she said.

He set his walking stick against the oak. Mia took his hand.

"Is Jakub ready?" he asked.

"He is. I'll get him."

She went toward the house. "Would you like to come in?" she called to the priest. But he waved her on. She came out of the house with Jakub, who carried a suitcase.

"Wonderful," the priest said.

Mia turned to her son and wiped her brow. She saw gray streaks on her hand. She ran her fingers across her forehead and her fingertips turned black.

"Mama?"

"What is this?" she said. They looked around and saw fine white dust falling in the air.

Jakub felt urgent. "Go inside," he said. "Go!"

He pushed his mother and Monsignor Starska followed. They hurried up the steps and Jakub pulled the door shut. "Sheets—quick!" Jakub said. Mia rushed upstairs and brought down a handful of sheets. "Stuff them," Jakub said. "Around the door and the windows."

They watched through the glass. The dust thickened and swirled.

"Where's Karl?" Mia asked.

"Buying a belt for the tractor," Jakub said.

"When's he coming back? Did he tell you—he never says anything to me."

"Tonight," Jakub answered.

Mia stared out the window. "Tonight? Are you sure tonight?"

"I'm sure," Jakub answered. "Yes—tonight."

"Then who is this?" Mia said. She saw the outline of a person walking in the dust. She pulled the sheet away and opened the door. A lone man emerged from the storm holding a royal purple handkerchief over his mouth and nose. He was small and wore a hat.

"Jakub," Mia said. They went down the steps together and took the man's arms and led him inside. He took off his hat, wiped his face, and looked at his handkerchief.

"Ash," the man said.

MIA TOOK RABBI GIMELMAN'S hat. She looked at the ash on it. "Where did this come from?"

"I'm sure I don't want to know," the rabbi said. "This is the home of Jakub Chelzak?"

Mia looked at him. "May I know who I'm talking to?"

"Azar Gimelman," the man said. "I've traveled a long way to see Jakub Chelzak."

The monsignor intervened. "What's your business with him?"

"I've come to ask for help," the rabbi said. "His reputation reaches us in Warsaw."

"Warsaw?" Mia asked.

"Frankly, the stories seem exaggerated."

"You should sit down," Mia said.

"Perhaps even grossly," said the rabbi. He followed Mia to a chair.

"The stories are not exaggerated," the monsignor said. "But Mr. Chelzak has other business."

"My situation is dire," the rabbi said. "We have a very sick family member."

Jakub stepped forward and extended his hand. "I'm Jakub Chelzak," he said.

The rabbi immediately stood. "Azar Gimelman," he said. "Rabbi."

"Oh good Lord," Mia said.

"You flatter me, madam," the rabbi said.

"A rabbi?" the priest said. "How did you get out of Warsaw?"

"Something—some tea, something to drink?" Mia asked.

"Water. Cold water." The rabbi looked toward the window, at the chickens in the winnowing ash. Mia handed the rabbi water. Jakub sat.

"They haven't killed us all," the rabbi said. He sipped the water.

"Are you Orthodox?" the priest asked.

"No one who knows me would call me that," the rabbi said. "But I apologize. I've lost my manners." He extended his hand to Monsignor Starska. They shook.

"Jarus Starska," he said. "Monsignor."

When the rabbi extended his hand to Mia, she hesitated. "I'm Jakub's mother," she said. He took her hand in both of his.

"A member of my synagogue is very ill—far too sick to travel."

Mia and Jakub looked at the rabbi.

"I realize we don't believe the same things about certain matters of faith," the rabbi said. "But I've heard the L-rd is a mysterious mover."

"That may be," the monsignor said. "But right now, the Lord is moving us toward a more pressing engagement."

"What could be more pressing than a life?" the rabbi asked.

Jakub looked at the monsignor, then at his mother. "What am I to be paid?" he asked.

"Jakub?" his mother said. She whispered into his ear. "You've never asked for pay." He grasped her hand.

"I don't think pay will be an issue," the rabbi said.

"He doesn't work for free." Mia looked at her son.

"I wasn't suggesting you did," the rabbi said to Jakub. "I mean to say, money is not an issue with this family."

"Then what were you thinking?"

The rabbi pulled some money from his coat. "I was thinking in the range of two hundred zlotys per day, against an advance of one thousand."

"A thousand." Mia gasped. "That's five hundred *Reichsmarks*."

"You may be away for some time," the rabbi said. "Once we get into Warsaw, leaving will not be so easy. It will take a lot of time. There's a high level of danger."

"Mama?" Jakub said. Mia looked at her son.

"Your expenses will be paid," the rabbi said. "We can get the rest home to your family."

Mia brought her hand to Jakub's cheek. His eyes pleaded.

"Mr. Chelzak and I are going to Krakow," the priest said.

"The Ghetto there?" the rabbi asked.

"No. The cathedral."

"What are *you* offering?" Mia asked the Monsignor.

Jakub smiled.

"The rabbi is offering two hundred zlotys a day; one hundred *Reichsmarks*."

"Advanced against one thousand," the rabbi added.

"The archdiocese is paying our expenses," the priest said.

"But nothing additional?" Mia said. "We need additional."

"I can inquire," Starska said. "But I doubt they will pay anything more."

Mia looked at her son. "What do you think?"

Jakub stood up. "The Archbishop is not ill. The young woman is." He felt relieved.

"He's already committed," Starska said.

"And the money," Jakub said. "If I'm gone and you need to replace me."

"We can meet the Archbishop another time," Mia said. She kissed her son's cheek and looked at the rabbi.

"This gift of yours," the rabbi asked. "How long have you had it?"

Jakub looked at him. "Gift?"

The rabbi smiled. "You knew I was speaking about a young woman, but I never said so," the rabbi said. "It is a young woman who is ill."

Mia was about to say something but Jakub stopped her. "It's money," he said. "A lot."

Mia took his hand. "Rabbi—you write down what he tells you and you post it to me? We have no phone here."

"I have a phone," Monsignor Starska interjected.

"But you never let anyone use it," Mia said.

The rabbi looked at Jakub.

"He reads but doesn't write," Mia said. "I've known some rabbis, and they could always do both."

"We can leave after Karl returns," Jakub said.

BATTLEFIELD

Fifteen

On a rooftop perch higher than where they killed Mende on the *Umschlagplatz*, Christien and Antek watched a black car moving between the lights along Okopowa Street, outside the Ghetto walls.

"I'll tell the others," Antek said.

The building was empty but the stairs were unsafe. Antek crawled along the tiled roof and lowered himself down a pipe over the side of the brick wall and into the alley. He ran out of sight of the gendarmes, toward ZOB headquarters in the dark. Air raid sirens stayed with him part of the way, then moved as he moved, far then close again, an auditory illusion amplified between the walls. Christien stayed atop the roof. He saw the black car he recognized as *SS* stop at the Chlodna Street gate. The car surprised him by turning in his direction.

JAKUB CHELZAK HAD ENTERED the Ghetto. The rabbi took a folded stack of bills from a pocket sewn inside the lining of his pants and leaned forward and tapped the driver with it.

"You're pushing your luck, excellency," the driver said. "But I appreciate your pushing it my way."

"We'll be out of here before long—maybe before you," the rabbi said. He spoke over the sirens.

"You've paid me well enough to desert," the driver said. "I'm seriously considering it."

The car pulled tight with the opening of an alley. The rabbi reached across Jakub and opened the door.

"You know, you're the only Jew I think who's ever sat there," the driver said.

The rabbi swooshed his hands toward the open door motioning Jakub, who slipped out. The rabbi stuck his leg out the door and the driver caught his arm. The rabbi could only see the driver's left cheek and his chin in the faint light. He squeezed the driver's arm and slid out, into the alley.

"That man was a soldier?" Jakub asked.

"In a manner of speaking," the rabbi said.

They moved along alleys in air that betrayed death. The rabbi kept Jakub close. The lights were out in the buildings and only the sirens moved. Jakub saw open doors and broken windowpanes and a corpse, white and stiff in the street.

"They'll bury him," the rabbi said.

They entered a basement door off Gesia Street and walked through blackness.

"Watch your head here," the rabbi said. He patted a stone overhang and ducked under it. They crawled for several meters and the rabbi stuck his head through a larger opening and immediately felt two cold rifle barrels against his temple.

"L'Chaim!" he said.

"Rabbi!" One of the men bent to help him up. He stood and Jakub stuck his head through. The men aimed their rifles.

"It's all right," the rabbi said. "Where is Leia—have they moved her?"

"Leia?"

"Leiozia Starzinski, of the Mordechai house."

The men looked at one another.

"Well?"

"Leiozia is dead, Rebbe."

Rabbi Gimelman staggered and caught himself. "Dead? Oh, G-d—may I speak your name. How long?"

"Two days."

"Oh L-rd, L-rd, L-rd."

Jakub laid his hand on the rabbi's shoulder.

"Our journey is wasted," the rabbi said.

When Rebekah saw Rabbi Gimelman, she dropped to her knees and threw her arms around his waist. She had cried two days but didn't cry now. "She's dead," Rebekah said softly.

"I'm so terribly sorry," the rabbi said. "We meant that she would live." He didn't look at Jakub. "Where is she?"

"At the far end," Rebekah said. "Where it's coolest."

"We have to bury her," the rabbi said.

"It's too risky."

"*Shiva*?" the rabbi said.

"Not until we bury her." Shosha emerged from a shadowy place and her voice carried in the catacomb. "It has to be Kirkut, not the *Skra*."

"That's not realistic," Rebekah said. "We've discussed this."

Shosha looked at Jakub. "Is this the man you left us for?"

Before the rabbi could answer, "Leiozia asked for you," Shosha said.

"You can't imagine my grief," the rabbi said. "You can't imagine it." His voice broke. Rebekah stood and he hugged her. He felt bones through her flesh.

"I can help you bury her," Jakub said. "I've got a strong back and I've eaten."

"That would almost be appropriate," Shosha said. "The man who came to save our Leia's life now puts her in a grave."

"Shosha—your tongue," Rebekah said. "I think it's a crazy idea to take her out there. We can bury her here, cover her with lime. Marian has said so and I think he wants it done soon."

"She should be buried with Jews in the right place," Shosha said. "Can you consecrate this ground?" she asked the rabbi.

"I could pray over it," the rabbi said. "But how sure we would be, I cannot say."

"I insist you do not go out there," Rebekah said.

"What about typhus, mother? Having a dead body in here with typhus."

"How far is the cemetery?" Jakub asked.

"Less than a kilo, but through the fighting," Shosha said. "I can go with you." She squeezed Jakub's arm. "He's right—it's solid."

"To go out there to bury the dead—what if you end up dead?" the rabbi asked.

"This is Leiozia!" Shosha said. "You've hired this man already —have you been paid?" she asked Jakub.

"I wasn't expecting it until my work was finished," he said.

"If anyone has to go, I'll go," the rabbi said.

"Even more out of the question," Rebekah said.

"They know me," the rabbi said. "Every German here has received a gift or three from me."

"And they kill you now because the gifts have stopped," Shosha said.

"The gifts never stop," the rabbi said. "They know that after the war, those who helped will have means."

"Yes? And how are they so sure of this?" Shosha asked.

"What other hope do they have?"

"A lot more hope than we have." Shosha turned away and started to walk. "We have to do this soon," she said. "Antek says the gendarmes have left Kirkut. But they can always return."

REBEKAH CAPITULATED AFTER A night-long battle with her daughter that ended with the inarguable need to reduce the threat of typhus. They wrapped Leiozia's body in burlap. It wasn't hard to move because she was dehydrated and had starved to under one hundred pounds—a full twenty pounds, at least, less than her normal weight. She was stiff with rigor and her body didn't sag much when Jakub lifted her with the rabbi's help.

"Marian would spit if he knew about this," Rebekah said.

"He has enough problems," Shosha said. "This is one problem he won't have."

They lowered Leiozia and slid her through the narrow opening to the tunnels, into the blackness, where there was no light and the eyes never adjusted. The rabbi moved with Shosha and Jakub toward an opening on the alley. They tied Leozia's body with ropes to a makeshift gurney pieced together from wooden crates and burlap sacks.

"Lech Shalom!" Rabbi Gimelman said to each of them and they kissed, cheek to cheek, and he hugged them. He took Shosha's head in his hands and looked at her, and looked at her eyes.

"Come back," he said.

They lifted the gurney and walked out. These early hours of Monday were still. Soldiers and circumstance had driven anyone still living underground, to cellars, caves, catacombs, sewers, and tunnels. The Underground had constructed strategic bunkers around the Ghetto and behind these fortresses fighters hid, waiting for the sun.

Shosha walked behind Jakub supporting Leiozia's bound feet. They walked in the alleys and side streets. Shosha saw

Gesiowka Prison, dark and empty. She walked up to a locked gate.

"We have to go around," she said.

They went up steps to open doors, passing through empty buildings to back doors and out again. They walked over broken glass and crumbled bricks, and paper everywhere—newspapers, notes, letters, books, magazines, propaganda, waving in the rubble. Jakub stopped and gasped and heaved, but never let Leiozia down.

"The smell?" Shosha said.

"Terrible."

"I must be used to it." Then around a corner, "Bread!"

Shosha saw something she had seen many times—a cage on a baker's table imprisoning a loaf. But this time no one was around demanding too much for it.

"Can we set her down?"

"Yes," Jakub said.

"Can we set her down?" she gasped louder.

"Yes," Jakub said again.

Shosha looked in all directions. She ran to the table, leaning against a wall on the narrow street. She took the loaf out. It was large, with a hard crust, a little stale, perfect. She bit into the bread without a thought of her companion, bit in and swallowed whole and let the hard crust slide into her stomach. She was not so hungry that food would make her sick, but eating too quickly could cause her to throw it up and she remembered this and looked at Jakub leaning against the bricks with Leiozia lying on the walkway in front of him.

"Oh!" She went back to him. "I'm so sorry."

"Good time to rest," Jakub said.

She held the loaf up to Jakub and he took a small piece. She took another piece and started to chew it, then instead let it sit in her mouth. She took another bite, and another, slowly. With each piece, she chewed a little more. She leaned against the wall and let her eyes roll with the slow, savoring up-and-down movements of her tongue and the moist insides of her cheeks.

"A mekhaye! Mekhaye!" she said. She looked at Jakub. "You don't know how good this tastes. You just don't know."

Jakub moved along the wall, creeping on his feet. At the edge of the alley, he saw men running with their hands in the air.

"The police." Shosha spoke from behind him. "Our police, the Jewish police."

Four uniformed *SS* officers in long dark coats followed. They lined up the Jewish police and the *SS* men raised pistols and fired until the pistols emptied and the police fell. A few twitched then stopped. Men with guns in heavy, dirty uniforms wearing heavy boots stepped from the backs of trucks. These fighters were Trawniki men the soldiers called *Askaris*, from the *SS* training camp near Lublin, recruited from the prisons of the conquered Eastern territories. The German commander Stroop was turning them loose with weapons and rounds. Marian said the arrival of the *Askaris* would be the first sign of the end, the final fight to clear the Ghetto and its evidence so the Germans could move men and weapons from here to the Russian front.

Two Trawniki men lugged large metal cans across the street. They set the cans down and unscrewed them and poured fluid over the bodies. The SS men laughed and talked, leaning and smoking and moving their hands and swaying their backs, tapping their feet and snapping orders at the Trawniki men and laughing again. With a monotonous sweep of their hands, the Trawniki men lit matches and flicked them one by one onto the bodies. The flames barked and crackled, and warmed the air as far as the alley where Shosha and Jakub stood with Leiozia.

The SS men stepped back from the heat. Through the fire, Shosha and Jakub saw their faces—their smiles, laughs, frowns, and furrowed brows in ordinary conversation.

They waited until the flames died and the soldiers dispersed. They raised Leiozia and walked. Before they reached the cemetery gates at the corner of Gesia and Okopowa, Shosha brought her scarf to her nose. She held another one to Jakub, who waved it away. An armed gendarme usually stood at the gate, but not now.

"Just like I thought," Shosha said.

Vandals had toppled tombstones and shattered statues. Graves lay open and heaped with the dead and the stench was unbearable. The air was warmer here, and in the morning, the place buzzed with flies and farther away, the noise sounded like a low hum.

They walked past tent-like tombs, the ohel reserved for the rabbis. Jakub felt his hands and feet aching but he kept walking with Shosha behind him, supporting Leiozia's feet and legs.

"We're close," Shosha said.

They turned right and followed the road to the back three plots. Shosha lowered Leiozia's feet and Jakub turned to let her head down. He leaned and stretched his back.

"We need to find an empty grave," Shosha said. "They were opening more back here." Shosha walked the maze of paths at the end of the yard. She found open graves, but with occupants in various stages of dress and decay. If not for the dark, she would have recognized someone. She came finally to holes and dirt piles on either side of the path. The larger grave comfortably cradled five bodies and the smaller grave was overfilled with two. She went back to Jakub who was sitting against a tree with the tail of his shirt over his nose.

"We have to move two bodies," she said.

They walked to the open graves. A breeze fluttered the early spring leaves and punctuated the smell. Shosha raised her chin and closed her eyes and let the cool air drift across her cheeks.

"There's another cemetery called the *Skra* but it's not really a cemetery, just a grave," Shosha said. "I didn't want Leiozia at the *Skra*."

They stepped into the smaller grave and lifted the bodies, Jakub at the shoulders and Shosha at the feet. The bodies were decayed and lightweight and they swung them up and onto the path. They stepped out of the grave and lifted the bodies again. They lowered each body into the larger grave.

"May your souls return to G-d and your bodies rest in peace," Shosha said.

Jakub blessed himself in the manner of the Catholic Church, in the name of the Father, of the Son, and of the Holy Ghost. They went back for Leiozia and together carried her to the small open grave. They lowered her into it and Shosha stood over the body.

"Your soul return to G-d and your body rest in peace," she said. While Jakub blessed himself, Shosha saw blood on his hand in the faint light of the rising sun.

She put her hand on her blouse and cried out, and tore the right side of it.

"Leiozia, Leiozia, Leiozia, you were my friend, my loyal friend and I will miss you with every part of my being!" She cried but gathered herself. "We need to bury her," she said. She looked at Jakub's hands. "I can do it," she said. "Your hands are bleeding raw."

"I'm okay," Jakub said.

Shosha got behind the dirt pile and began pushing it into the hole with her hands. "I don't need it all. Just enough to cover her —and them." She nodded toward the larger grave.

Jakub moved to help.

"No—the soil must be free of blood," Shosha said. "I can do it."

She squatted and pushed more dirt into the hole. Then she stopped and sat back. Perspiration covered her face.

"Free of blood? Did you hear what I just said? The soil here free of blood?" She pushed more of it into the hole. Then she rested again and pushed her wet hair out of her face. She looked at Jakub's hands. "Is that what Rabbi was talking about?"

"What?" Jakub said.

"The bleeding." Shosha looked at his face. "May I see it?"

Jakub sat next to her. She took his hands and turned his palms into the light. She saw blood, dry at the edges, and felt his palms.

"Not there," he said.

He pulled back his sleeve. Near the top of his wrist, where it joined arm to hand, she saw a fleshy, wet protrusion. On the other wrist the protrusion was in a different place, off center, smaller, as though the nail had gone in from the side, carelessly, and not all the way through.

"Does it hurt?" she asked.

"Sometimes."

"It looks terribly painful. How do you bear it?"

"I'm used to it."

Shosha lowered his hand and looked at his head—there was no blood there—and his feet, also dry. "Do you get all the wounds?" she asked.

"Sometimes," Jakub said.

Shosha placed her index finger on his wrist. "Am I hurting you?" she asked.

"No."

She traced the wound, careful to avoid touching any blood. "So what do you think of this?" she asked.

Jakub coughed and raised the shirt to his nose again. "The wounds?"

"No." Shosha looked around. "This," she said.

Jakub lowered the shirt. "It's the most terrible thing I've ever seen," he said. "How do you bear it?"

Shosha thought about this question, which no one had ever asked. "I don't," she said. She rolled away from Jakub and pushed more dirt over Leiozia and covered her, but barely. She was too tired to do more.

"We need to get back," she said.

"SHOSHA!"

She and Jakub had walked from the cemetery, hiding in the usual places, and now they crouched in a doorway on an alley. Shosha heard her name, but didn't recognize the urgent, hushed voice.

"Shosha." She stood and bent around the edge of the doorway. "Up here!"

She looked up. From a building across the street, a man waved in a window without glass.

"Antek?" she said.

"Yes. Who's with you?"

"A friend."

"Who is he?" Jakub asked.

"Icchak," Shosha said. "But he's called Antek. He's our best shooter, but he hates to kill. The women are all in love with him."

"Come up," Antek said. "It's not safe down there."

"We have to get back," Shosha said.

"Not now."

"Yes now!"

"Wait up here," Antek said. "Till the fighting dies down."

Shosha looked at Jakub.

"Why not?" he said. They hurried out of the alley and across the street.

"Come up the stairs," Antek said.

Shosha and Jakub went into the building and up four flights of stairs. Antek walked into the hallway. "Shosha." Antek had gun oil on his chin and oily strands of hair hung across his forehead. They hugged. "What were you doing out there?"

"We buried Leia," she said.

"At Kirkut?" Antek said. "You took Leia to Kirkut?"

"Yes."

"How?"

"With Jakub."

"Chelzak? You're Chelzak?"

"He came with back with Rabbi."

"Unbelievable." Antek extended his hand to Jakub. "Welcome to Hell," he said. "What a devil Rebbe is. He actually brought you."

They entered a flat overlooking the street. Shosha saw a typhus quarantine sign on the door. Overturned furniture and papers littered the room.

"We should be in here?" Shosha asked.

"You mean the sign?" Antek said. "Just more bullshit. This family didn't go to any sanitarium." Antek picked up his rifle. "You have a good arm?" he asked Jakub. "They gave me these and I have no use for them." He pointed to women's stockings bulging with grenades. "I'm a shooter," he said.

"I'm not trained," Jakub said. "I wouldn't be much help."

"Friends who won't fight for friends are cowards," Antek said. "Are you a friend?"

"Friend or not, I don't think Jakub would be much good at throwing anything," Shosha said. She held up one of his hands. "He's rubbed his hands raw helping me carry Leiozia."

"Leiozia," Antek said. He took Shosha's hand and squeezed and kissed her forehead. He looked at Jakub. "Too late," Antek said.

"I can throw those things," Shosha said. "But we're hungry. Any food?"

"In the cabinets," Antek said and pointed. "Some flour, some old potatoes. They're starting to grow."

Shosha gathered the potatoes and a dwindling sack of flour and brought the feast to a place near the window and they sat.

"It's quiet now," Antek said. He sliced the sprouting roots off a potato and chewed it. "It wasn't earlier."

"We need to rest," Shosha said. "We've been walking forever."

AN EXPLODING MINE WOKE Shosha. Jakub sat against the wall chewing a potato. Antek stood to the side of the pane-less window.

"Somebody's fighting," Antek said. He peered out. "Will you look at this, will you look at this." A Trawniki man emerged from under a building. "Dumb bastard."

Shosha peeped above the window and yawned. Antek raised his rifle.

"Do I shoot him in the face or in the back?" He looked at Shosha and grinned. He turned to Jakub. "Which is it?" Antek said. "In the face or in the back?"

"Why ask me?" Jakub said.

Antek returned to the Trawniki man in his gun sight.

"Do you know how ugly it is? What it looks like when a bullet rips through a neck? What it feels like for that split second, or longer if you bleed?" he said.

"I've seen people shot," Jakub said.

"But have you ever shot?"

"He's getting away."

"Maybe."

"Just shoot him and get it over."

"Ah—you're a tough guy," Antek said. "In the face or in the back? Top of the head or smack in the ass? Maybe the knee. Excruciating."

"In the back," Jakub said. Shosha looked at him. "In the back, so he won't know what hit him."

"Listen to your friend," Antek said. "In the back, just like a coward." He narrowed his eyes and glared at Shosha. "What do you say?" He looked back through the rifle site.

She watched Antek's fingers move on the trigger. Buds of perspiration sprouted on his brow. He turned to her again and she watched his other hand come to her face and she flinched when she felt it, hot and rough.

"Live or die," he said.

She saw his dirty fingernails move toward her temple and she flinched and pulled her head back when his fingers touched her hair. She moved her hand.

"In the back," Jakub said and on "back," his hand landed on the rifle and he snatched it from Antek and brought the scope to his eye. He fired through the window and the Trawniki man turned and ran. Antek scrambled while Jakub fired again, but the Trawniki man was gone. He shoved the gun at Antek.

"Out of range," Jakub said. He gathered Shosha and they walked out of the flat.

SHOSHA AND JAKUB ARRIVED at Resistance headquarters within the hour. The rabbi threw his hands around Jakub and kissed Shosha. Rebekah hugged them and cried. They had buried Leiozia in the Kirkut, they said, and she was not lying in an uncovered grave like so many others, though the layer of dirt that covered her was thin.

"Did you say Kaddish?" Rabbi asked Shosha.

"No," Shosha said. "Mama?"

"Rebbe should say Kaddish," Rebekah said.

The rabbi nodded and led them into one of the storerooms where candles burned and Rebekah had covered a broken piece of mirror. He stood Rebekah and Shosha side by side and whispered to Jakub that unless he wished otherwise, his participation, as a person who never knew the deceased, was not necessary. Jakub nodded and took his place next to the women.

"Then may we begin," rabbi said. The women turned and faced him. He stepped up to Rebekah and grabbed her blouse and tore it. Shosha had already torn her blouse so the rabbi took it in both of his hands and tore it only a little.

"Yeetgadal v' yeetkadash sh'mey rabbah," the rabbi began in Hebrew. "May His great Name grow exalted and sanctified."

After the prayers, "Amein," the women said.

"Amen," Jakub followed.

Shosha had taken extra potatoes from the flat. She pulled two from her pocket and handed them to the rabbi. It was custom at the first meal after the funeral for mourners to eat something round to indicate that life is like a circle.

"Do you know Kaddish?" the rabbi asked Jakub.

"No, but I prayed on my own."

"Leiozia has a friend in you," the rabbi said. "As do we."

Sixteen

Monday of Holy Week, First day of Pesach
19 April 1943

"Why are you doing this?" Rebekah entered a bunker and saw the rabbi and Jakub. It was early Sunday morning before the first day of Pesach, or Passover and the rabbi was on his knees cleaning the underside of the baking table. Jakub wiped down a shelf with a moist cloth.

"Chametz," the rabbi said.

"We cleaned it two days ago," Rebekah said.

"Just to be safe."

The rabbi was cleaning away chametz, or leaven—any unbaked thing made from the five major grains—wheat, rye, barley, oats and spelt—used to make bread rise. He had to be thorough. Cleaning away the leaven commemorates Jews who did not have time to let their bread rise because they had to flee Egypt. It could take a day to clean a house of chametz, but in this house only one room would be prepared for the holiday.

The rabbi stood and looked at Rebekah. She smiled. "If you'd like to help," he said. "I promised our friend here I would help him get a letter to his mother."

JEWISH FIGHTERS SAW GERMAN gendarmes and Polish police circling the outer Ghetto walls around two in the morning the following Monday. All Underground fighter groups were ready. Alerts went out, and most Ghetto inhabitants moved to shelters and cellars and attics. When dawn broke, German tanks and armored cars rumbled and pounded Mila and Zamenhofa streets. Behind walls, windows and doors, from the top stories of the row houses to the makeshift bunkers beneath basement stairwells, Jewish fighters watched. The ground stilled and the motors idled and each man and boy—there were many boys— waited. The Germans laughed and cheered. No one was here to fight them. "Fucking cowards," they cried. They looked around in the empty silence.

Michal Klepfisz, who engineered bridges across uncross-able rivers, looked at his positions through binoculars. He watched the street and whistled twice. He heard footsteps and echoes. The Jewish fighters looked out from their perches, eyeing Trawniki men on foot-borne reconnaissance with radios and telephones and binoculars, darting into alleys and up stairways and through open doors of empty buildings.

Five minutes passed then ten, then twenty, a waiting, waiting, waiting. The fighters heard screeching gears and motors, hissing and roaring. They felt the ground tremble. They saw the long gun on the first turret turn onto Nalewki Street. Still they waited, for the fleshy part, the belly—the foot soldiers, swaying under arms. When they heard the *click clack click clack click clack* of marching boots, the fighters raised their weapons and before the diesel beasts could roar, the first whistle blew.

Then another and another and another, until whistles blew from every position and bullets pelted the enemy like sudden hail. The soldiers thought insects were stinging them at first, and swatted the air until they saw blood and scorches on their threads. Some fell and the whistles and the gunfire confused the others and they panicked and ran, but some ran into Underground positions and saw the barrels and the smoke before they, too, fell.

Bottles hit the first tank and flames spread and the beast stood still. No one came out. The tank burned. The other armor stopped. A truck turned around. The fighters threw grenades and fired. The foot soldiers retreated. The morning was explosions and machine gun fire and soldiers falling and bleeding with their dead eyes open in surprise. They tried to pull back but the fighters cut them off.

JÜRGEN STROOP WASHED SHAVING cream off his face when his aide, a young lieutenant, answered a pounding at the door of the general's suite at the Hotel Bristol on the Aryan side. Sammern-Frankenegg rushed past the lieutenant and looked in every room until he found his commander.

"We've sustained losses, *Herr* Stroop."

Stroop was staring at himself in the mirror over the sink.

"To be expected," Stroop said.

"Serious losses."

"How serious?"

"I ordered a retreat."

Stroop lit a cigarette.

"We need aircraft," Sammern-Frankenegg said. "We could get them from Krakow in under an hour."

"Bullshit." Stroop spoke through his cigarette. "How long can these sewer rats resist?"

"A much shorter time if we had aircraft."

"And how would that look?" Stroop drew on his smoke. "There are Reds across that fucking river. Reds looking for planes. I don't want them here. The only red I want to see is the blood of these sewer rats." He looked at Sammern-Frankenegg. "I'll take charge from here, *Herr Oberführer.*"

"I can handle this, *Herr Brigadeführer.*"

Stroop looked at Sammern-Frankenegg through cigarette smoke and the sun that streamed into the room.

STROOP WENT INTO THE Ghetto later that morning under heavy guard and set his paper work and makeshift battle plan on a bench outside the Judenrat office. "I want your men to take the corner of Nalewki and Gesia," he told Sammern-Frankenegg. "Commence at noon. Hit and run." He lit another cigarette and looked at the sky. "We included some artillery support at Muranowska Place," he said.

Resistance fighters assaulted the Germans with an air attack of their own, dropping or throwing grenades from rooftops, then hopping across the narrow alleys that separated one roof from another. Stroop relented on his previous order and permitted Sammern-Frankenegg to call up light aircraft, but "only one or two. They give us no choice," the general said.

The bombers approached from the east, and the fighters torched the German warehouse at 31 Nalewki Street and retreated to Rabbi Maisels Street to let the aircraft waste ammunition on a deserted battlefield.

Back at the Hotel Bristol, Stroop wrote his first report to Himmler and Krüger.

"At our first penetration into the Ghetto, the Jews and Polish bandits succeeded, with arms in hand, in repulsing our forces, including the tank and armored vehicles. The losses during the first attack were: 12 men." Stroop ordered bombers to hit the Ghetto hospital in retaliation for the warehouse fire. He sent *Askaris* and a few German troops to start "checking the patients out permanently."

IN THE MAIN HALL of the hospital, battalion sergeant Hans Streger conceived a stunt to please Stroop and demoralize the Resistance. He rounded up an eighteen-year-old private and his sixteen-year-old sidekick who had lied about his age to join the defense of the Fatherland and two days later received orders from Berlin to Warsaw by way of Trawniki for urban warfare training. The older boy, Ludwig—Luddy—and the younger boy, Wolferle—Wolf (who had lost part of his hand in a factory accident)—had been together since they first met in Berlin. Luddy came from a farm and Wolf from a depressed section of a German industrial town. They both taught themselves the rudiments of reading, and they both looked forward to a proper education paid for by the Reich at the end of their service.

Ludwig's father had cattle and sheep and he ran a small slaughtering operation. Wolf's family sold produce in a market they owned. He and his mother went to work in an armament factory shortly after Germany started declaring war on her neighbors. Some day—they told each other and everyone who would listen—they would leave Germany and see the world, maybe even come to America. Neither boy knew exactly why they were in Warsaw.

"I want you to go down to the rooms where they have the pregnant women," Streger told the boys. "Do some damage."

"Shoot the women?" Ludwig asked.

"You have bayonets," Streger said. "Use your imagination."

The boys hesitated.

"Go," Streger said. "*Raus!*" He looked around at the burning hospital. "She's not going to last forever."

The boys went through the smoke down the hall. The maternity wards were on the other side of the hospital, and they were lost at first. They went upstairs. They went down hallways toward deserted wards and saw other soldiers. When they found the rooms with the cribs and bassinets, they entered awkwardly.

Two nurses were dressing three women—all with child—and when they saw the baby-faced soldiers, they stiffened.

"What do you want?" said one of the nurses. She spoke broken German. "You come to kill us?"

The boys looked at each other. "We have orders," Ludwig said.

"Just let us go," said a patient. "We're going to die anyway, don't you suppose?"

Ludwig raised his bayonet and the nurse grabbed his arm but he stabbed the woman and she grabbed herself and fell. The other nurse jumped him and grabbed his neck and he tried to throw her back.

"Wolf," Ludwig yelled. "We have orders!"

The patients screamed and cried and the nurses shouted profane things and smoke crept under the door. Wolferle grabbed a nurse and dug his fingers into her arm and tried to pull her away. Ludwig stomped toward the fallen woman and stabbed her again and cut her. He turned with his rifle and shot a patient and turned and shot a nurse. The other nurse ran for the door and Ludwig fired at her, but an explosion jolted him and he missed and dropped the gun. The nurse pushed through the door and ran into the smoke. Wolferle looked at the fallen woman, whose stomach heaved and was big.

"Cut it out," Ludwig said to him.

Wolferle hesitated.

"Cut it out!" Ludwig grabbed Wolferle's rifle and positioned the bayonet over the woman's stomach. He cut her superficially and her blood streamed.

"See," Ludwig said. "We have orders."

Wolferle moved back.

"Okay then," Ludwig said. "I'll do it." He aimed for the woman's stomach near the side and cut it again.

"Fuck you!" Wolferle said.

Ludwig heard a sidearm cock and looked up.

"Fuck you," Wolferle said. "Get away from her!"

"You're crazy," Ludwig said. "You'll be hanged. We both will."

"Get away!"

"I won't."

"I will shoot you if you don't."

They heard a muffled cry. It was the woman, not the baby, but it sounded like a baby.

"Oh God," Wolferle said. "Oh God." His hands shook and he was losing his grip. Ludwig stepped forward and Wolferle snapped the pistol taut again and stepped back. They heard sirens and aircraft engines. They heard crying sounds, loudest of all. Wolferle stepped back. He lowered his pistol and fired it into the woman's head. He fired again. The crying stopped.

"You'll be hung for this," Ludwig said. "They may not even court martial you first."

Wolferle raised the pistol to Ludwig again. "How will they know?" he asked. "Who's the witnesses? Who's going to tell them? Who's going to tell them I wouldn't help you tear a baby out of its mama?"

"You going to shoot me?" Ludwig said.

"We don't deserve to live," Wolferle said.

"We won't live if we don't get out now," Ludwig said.

"That's right," Wolferle said. He walked over and sat on a bed, keeping the pistol on Ludwig. More bombs dropped. They heard walls collapsing and flames roaring and sucking out the air.

"You crazy enough to kill us both?" Ludwig said.

Wolferle looked at him, blank and rigid.

Ludwig marched forward and said in cadence "Well I won't let you," and reached for the pistol and thought he heard the closest burst yet, until pain struck him and he touched his stomach and felt wetness and warmth. He pulled his hand away and looked at the blood. He looked at Wolferle. "You fuck."

Wolferle undid the strap on his side arm and pulled it out and aimed the barrel at his temple.

"No," Ludwig said, but it happened with a loud pop.

Ludwig stood stunned. But the heat moved him and he stepped over Wolferle's body to the wall and stumbled under the weight of his wound and saw smoke around his ankles. He tried to right himself by pushing off the wall. He moved toward the door. He pushed it open and stumbled into the hall. Flames closed one side but the other side was clear. He gathered himself and tried to breathe and leaned against the wall and moved his feet along the tile floor, sideways, toward the door at the end of the hall. He slid along the wall and choked. The smoke thickened and swirled, lapped his legs and hugged his waist. It rose and caressed his neck. He pushed himself forward and gasped and heard the flames behind him roar. He looked up and saw fire along the ceiling, creeping and fluid. He lost his thoughts in the swirls, white and yellow wheels churning overhead, and smoke all around. He caught himself and looked toward the door. A few more steps. A few more sideways passes along the wall.

He was finally to it. He raised his hand but the heat wouldn't let him touch the metal door. He leaned into the handle but the heat pressed through his uniform and he backed away. He gathered himself and leaned again and pushed the door. It opened and light flooded in but the fire sucked the air and pulled the door. He felt flames lick his neck and his back and the backs of his legs and the door shut. He pushed again, against the air, against the fire that pulled the door back. He pushed and felt cool air and he pushed and pushed but the fire leaped out, snarling and roaring, and pulled him back.

From outside, Hans Streger saw fingers of flame wrapping the door. Two Trawniki men saw the opening door and the sleeve of a soldier and ran toward the door, but Streger saw the General's finely shaved cheeks. He called the men back.

"But *Herr Oberscharführer*," they protested.

Stroop's finely shaved cheeks and his gray-green eyes.

"Too dangerous," Streger said.

The door stopped opening soon enough.

AT 3 P. M., STROOP TOOK personal charge of three hundred *SS* troops and they assaulted Marek Edelman's area. Edelman was twenty four years old, and he always fought at the head. He commanded the Resistance at Swietojerska, Walowa, Franciszkanska and Bonifraterska streets. Short on bullets, the fighters set mines along drainage pipes and threw grenades. A mine exploded in the right place and a tank rolling unstoppably jolted to a stop and burned. Flames swept out of the turret, and the fighters thought they heard the men inside, and maybe screams, but they couldn't be sure. The turret never opened. The thing just sat in the street and burned.

In the late afternoon, trucks with anti-aircraft guns blasted fighters on Muranowska Street. Soldiers stormed the Jewish positions and in hand-to-hand fighting, the Germans took eighty prisoners and the Jews killed a senior *SS* officer. Stroop ordered a hundred Jewish prisoners executed—unarmed women and children, and a few old men.

Captain Jozef Pszenny and Polish Armia Krajowa (AK) forces arrived at night outside a desolate part of the Ghetto wall that faced Bonifraterska Street. Early in the revolt, the AK hesitated to get too involved with the Jews, and only smuggled a few guns and a little ammunition. After the terror bombing of the hospital and the early successes of Michal Klepfisz and his men, Pszenny urged his comrades to support the Resistance. He planned to establish a supply line between the Ghetto and the outside. He alerted the ZZW and the ZOB that he would blast a hole in part of the wall across Bonifraterska Street that was poorly lit and ignored by the Germans. Pszenny's men would stand ready with crates of rifles and ammunition and food.

Resistance leaders were skeptical. The sudden solidarity of the Roman Catholic Armia Krajowa—Europe's largest Nazi resistance group—with the Jewish fighters struck some leaders as too little, too late. The ZOB sent only half a dozen men to Bonifraterska Street that night. Pszenny arrived as planned, but the land mine his team exploded didn't pierce the wall. Polish police, sympathetic to the Germans out of necessity, reported the incident. German troops showed up and fired on Pszenny's squad, forcing them to abandon the smuggling operation and leave behind a food and supply cargo of such significance that Marian and Klepfisz described the incident as "heartbreaking."

The German advance for the day ended in late evening at the gate to Wolowa 6. Marian watched from across the street as the German detachment positioned an anti-aircraft gun and aimed it at a building. They were preparing to fire when Marian pushed a button and a mine planted in the gate exploded. Twenty-two Germans fell and the others retreated behind a resistance volley of bullets and grenades.

RABBI ANNOUNCED TO JAKUB and the women and the fighters in the bunker that they would celebrate Seder—the traditional Passover meal—in two parts. To eat the entire meal at once, though it was meager, seemed disrespectful to the fallen. They reclined in candle light on mats and straw bedding. Rabbi blessed the wine by reciting Kiddush and adding "this day of the Festival of Matzos, the time of our liberation."

Marian raised his eyes from the table. They each drank a small portion of wine. The rabbi washed his hands in a bowl that was never used to mix bread dough. He dried his hands and took a different bowl of water and dipped a radish into it twice. He bit the radish, a bitter vegetable called here "maror."

"There is no salt, Rebbe," Marian said. Normally the water would be salted to symbolize the tears of Egypt's Jewish slaves.

"From *our* tears, then," Rabbi said, passing the bowl to Rebekah. The fifteen people in the bunker took turns dipping radishes twice and eating them. The rabbi next broke one of three unleavened bread lumps—matzos—on the table. He set half the broken matzo back with the other two. "Shosha," he said. "Mah Nishtanah."

Shosha looked at Jakub and smiled. She was the youngest and she began to sing in Hebrew. Her song answered Four Questions.

"Mah nishtanah ha-lahylah ha-zeh mi-kol ha-layloht, mi-kol ha-layloht?"

Why is this night different from all other nights, from all other nights?

"She-b'khol ha-layloht anu okhlin chameytz u-matzah, chameytz u-matzah. Ha-lahylah hazeh, ha-lahylah ha-zeh, kooloh matzah."

On all other nights, we may eat chametz and matzo, chametz and matzo. On this night, on this night, only matzo.

"She-b'khol ha-layloht anu okhlin sh'ar y'rakot, sh'ar y'rakot. Ha-lahylah ha-zeh, ha-lahylah ha-zeh, maror."

On all other nights, we eat many vegetables, many vegetables. On this night, on this night, maror.

"She-b'khol ha-layloht ayn anu mat'bilin afilu pa'am echat, afilu pa'am echat. Ha-lahylah hazeh, ha-lahylah ha-zeh, sh'tay p'amim."

On all other nights, we do not dip even once. On this night, on this night, twice.

"She-b'khol ha-layloht anu okhlin bayn yosh'bin u'vayn m'soobin, bayn yosh'bin u'vayn m'soobin. Ha-lahylah ha-zeh, ha-lahylah ha-zeh, koolanu m'soobin."

On all other nights, we eat either sitting or reclining, either sitting or reclining. On this night, on this night, we all recline.

The rabbi turned to Jakub. "You are welcome to pray with us," the rabbi said.

Jakub looked at him. "I don't know your prayers."

"Pray in your own way."

Jakub bowed his head and he was silent.

"Out loud," the rabbi said.

"Rebbe?" Marian said.

"Out loud," the rabbi said again.

"Our Father," Jakub began. "Who art in Heaven, Hallowed be Thy name."

They listened to the L-rd's Prayer and the rabbi blessed the wine again in his own way.

"I've always thought it was a beautiful prayer," the rabbi told Jakub that night. "You should hear it in Hebrew."

"Like your prayers?" Jakub said.

"Yes."

"You know it?"

"Yes," the rabbi said. He recited the prayer.

"avînu shèbaShamayim"
Our Father who is in Heaven,

"yitqaDash shemèkha"
Let be hallowed Your name.

"Tavo malkhutèkha"
Let come Your Kingdom;

"yé'asèh retsonkha"
Let be done Your will,

"kemo vaShamayim"
As in Heaven,

"kén ba'aréts"
So on Earth.

"èt - lèhèm huQénu Tèn - lanu"
Our appointed bread give us

"haYom"
this day,

"uçlah - lanu èt - hovotênu"
And forgive us our debts,

"ka'ashèr çalahnu Gam - anahnu"
Even as we ourselves forgive

"lehaYavênu"
our debtors.

"ve'al - Tevî'énu lîdê niÇayon"
And do not bring us into trial,

"kî 'im - haLtsénu min - hara"
But deliver us from the Evil One –

"kî lekha haMamlakha"
For Yours is the Kingdom,
"vehaGvurah"

And the power,

"vehaTif'èrèt"
And the glory,

"le'olmê 'olamîm"
To the ages of the ages.

Jakub said "Amein."

They saved the second part of Seder for the following evening.

Seventeen

Tuesday of Holy Week
20 April 1943

On this, Hitler's birthday, the Germans issued an ultimatum to the Resistance: lay down your arms or face annihilation. At 7 am, a detachment under Stroop blasted Jewish fighters at Zamenhofa Street and took houses along Zamenhofa, Gesia, and Nalewki streets, driving the Resistance from roofs and attics.

The fighters drove Stroop back and he withdrew his troops beyond the Ghetto wall. Armia Krajowa troops under Captain Henryk Wojskowy met ZZW fighters with smuggled arms and ammunition on Muranowski Square. The Germans returned with flamethrowers later in the day and burned houses along Leszno, Nowolipie, Nowolipki and Smocza streets and retook the Schultz and Toebbens workshops. This day the fighters lost, by some counts ten, by other counts twenty-five men.

AFTER SUNSET, RABBI CELEBRATED the second half of Seder with twelve people—three fighters had not returned. He poured water from a jug three times over each hand. He held his cleansed hands together and said, "Blessed are you, O L-rd our

G-d, King of the universe, Who has commanded us about washing the hands." He blessed the matzo and more radishes and passed the food around. The people dipped the maror in a peanut butter-like concoction, a makeshift "charoses."

"In the manner taught to us by the great Rebbe Hillel," the rabbi said, placing maror and charoses and matzo together into a sandwich-like "korech" and with the others eating it with soup. Near the end of the meal, the rabbi broke the second half of the previous night's matzo and gave it to the others. It was called "afikoman," the last part of the Seder meal. They talked and ate the sparse feast and then Rabbi addressed them to say Birkat Ha-Mazon —the after meal grace.

"Chavarei n'vareich."
Friends, let us bless.

Marian responded:

"Yihi shem Adonai m'vorach mei-atah v'ad olam."
May G-d be praised from this moment through eternity.

The others said:

"Barukh ata Adonai bone v'rachamav Yerushalayim. Amein."
Blessed are You, Adonai, in compassion You build Jerusalem. Amen.

They poured a third cup of wine and stood aside from the door to let the spirit of Elijah enter. Shosha raised her face and closed her eyes. When she opened her eyes she looked at Jakub and saw his hair waving, though the room was still and down here, there was never a breeze. She took her mother's hand and directed Rebekah to look at Jakub. He looked calm. He moved his hair out of his eyes.

The rabbi spoke of the great punishments that would be meted to their oppressors and the wrath of G-d as it was in the time of Pharoah. He led them in Hallel, the Psalms of Praise. He blessed and they drank a fourth cup of wine—now barely more than a drop—and the rabbi concluded Seder. "Next Year in Jerusalem," he proclaimed. He was exhausted and retired early.

Before sunrise, the rabbi woke Jakub and handed him a purse that bulged softly. The morning was cold and they sat around a pool of hot coals in the bunker.

"Open it," the rabbi said.

Jakub slipped his fingers in and spread the purse and saw four currencies: Polish zlotys, Swiss francs, American dollars, German *Reichsmarks*.

"In case one goes bad," the rabbi said. "That's how I get them, from our friends."

"Thank you," Jakub said. "My family and I are grateful."

"Your work here was finished some time ago," the rabbi said. "I can get you back. You should go and go now."

Jakub considered. "I know," he said. But the rabbi heard hesitation.

"This isn't your fight," the rabbi said.

"A friend who won't fight for a friend is a coward," Jakub said. He stared at the glowing coals in the dirt pit. "It's not safe to leave now," he said.

"I can get you out," the rabbi said. "It's as safe as it will ever be."

"What about the others?" Jakub said. "Shosha, Rebekah, all the others?"

"They won't go," the rabbi said. "Rebekah is waiting for her husband and honor forbids the rest."

"Can you write to mama? Send her this money?"

The rabbi looked at Jakub, at his face and hair, at his shoulders and hands.

"Yes," the rabbi said. "I can get the money out."

"You have to do it soon—I need to let her and Karl know I'm all right."

The rabbi put his hand around Jakub's knee. "You're all right," the rabbi said. "Your family will know. You can be sure of it."

Eighteen

Ash Wednesday
21 April 1943

Rebekah and Shosha spent the morning carrying grenades and petrol bottles to the first set of bunkers outside Resistance headquarters. Shosha told the story of the rifle and Antek, how Jakub had snatched the rifle and aimed it proficiently and fired but how the Trawniki man was out of range. Michal Klepfisz heard the story. He was cleaning a rifle on a table and he asked to speak with Jakub.

"Can you hold a rifle for a long time?" Klepfisz asked Jakub.

"Yes," Jakub said.

"I've heard about your wounds."

"My wounds only hurt when they bleed, and they only bleed sometimes," Jakub said.

"You have an unusual condition," Klepfisz said. "Rabbi explained some of it." Klepfisz held up the rifle and looked through the site. "Could you stand guard? At the entrance, but you'd be inside and not the first defense."

"I could do that," Jakub said. "Am I paid?"

"If Rabbi made no arrangement, I'll talk to him about it."

"I'd have to be paid," Jakub said. "The money's not for me—I send it to my family."

"It sounds like we have an adept ally in this fellow Chelzak," Klepfisz told his group at the evening meal. "Not like some."

The men chuckled. "You mean Pszenny," one of them said.

"No. I meant me. I meant us. Pszenny tried."

"He should have tried earlier," one of the men said. "Who can trust those AK bastards?"

"I trust Wojskowy," someone said.

"Wojskowy's all right," Klepfisz agreed. "I know his family and him since a little boy."

HAND-TO-HAND COMBAT broke out across the Ghetto in the afternoon. The fighters ran up to tanks and armored vehicles and dropped grenades into whatever crevices or openings they could find and ran for cover. A few men took bullets in the back and legs, and toward late afternoon, Klepfisz, known as Tadeusz Metzner outside the Ghetto, took a bullet near his heart. He fell against a wall and another fighter, Zygmunt Fridrich, ran to him.

"Go back to the bunker and get Marek," Marek Edelman the doctor, Klepfisz told Zygmunt. "I can't die now."

"It's too dangerous."

Klepfisz grabbed the man's shirt. "I can't die now."

"I'll be shot if I try to get there now," Zygmunt said. "I have to wait."

"If you wait, I'll die."

"You should stop talking," Zygmunt said. "You need your breath."

Klepfisz tugged at Zygmunt's shirt. "Get him," Klepfisz said.

Klepfisz relaxed his grip. Zygmunt looked up the street and saw the wall curl around to an alley. He heard explosions and gunshots. He crept along the wall toward the alley. Klepfisz watched him. Zygmunt turned into the alley and saw smoke ahead. He looked back at Klepfisz and sank along the wall. He rested his arms across his knees and lowered his head into his arms where light punctuated darkness under his legs. He looked around the corner again at Klepfisz, who was still. He looked up the alley, toward smoke and noise. He leaned and laid his head in his arms again and closed his eyes.

Klepfisz died with his eyes open. He looked surprised, Zygmunt thought, and like he was trying to say something. Zygmunt told everyone Klepfisz must have been hopeful because he had his fist clenched. Klepfisz had no family here so each person prayed in their own way. The evening meal was cooked potatoes and greens scrounged from deserted buildings, and a little bread. People gathered and bowed their heads. Rabbi lit a candle and led them in saying, "Honor to his heroic death. Honor to his holy memory. Honor to all that died a hero's death today on the field of glory." Rebekah and Shosha stood together and Shosha's hands shook.

"What do we do about shiva, Rebbe?" one of the men asked.

"We keep this candle lit, and when it dies, we light another for seven days," the rabbi said. "We are not able to bury Michal. We have no other practical way."

"Michal Klepfisz was a man of great honor," Rebekah told her daughter. "He was a man I wish Lev Mordechai could have known." Rebekah cried that night because she was remembering why Lev Mordechai did not know Michal Klepfisz.

A RAGGED ZZW FIGHTER named Sturlan came in from the streets late that night and went to the first authority he could find: Rabbi Gimelman.

"Rebbe—Moryc is injured." Moryc Zydowski was commander of the ZZW unit at Muranowski Square.

"How so—how badly?" the rabbi asked.

"Bad but not dire, but we're stuck for now and we need supplies—ammunition especially."

"We're low too," rabbi said. "Who's been supplying you?"

"Captain Wojskowy," Sturlan said. "From the AK unit on the other side."

"Can you get to him?"

"Not with our men. We need someone fresh, not injured. That's why I came."

"We can't spare any," the rabbi said. "We lost three last night, one tonight."

"I was thinking of Chelzak," Sturlan said.

"Chelzak?" the rabbi said.

"He's not one of us."

"So put him in harm's way?" the rabbi asked.

"No," Sturlan said. "They're afraid of him."

"Who's afraid of him?"

"The Germans and their helpers from the East."

"How do you know this? Who said so?"

"They all talk of it," Sturlan said.

"Why in this weird, strange, screwed up world of ours would the Germans be afraid of Chelzak?"

"Moryc says it's because of the wounds. He says the soldiers won't bother him. He says that's why they let you come back unharmed."

"That's crap," the rabbi said. "I paid the right people."

"Sammern-Frankenegg knows about him," Sturlan said. "He's been hiding it from Stroop, but the men say Stroop has heard, but only a little."

The rabbi ran his hand through his hair.

"The Germans would be happy to get him out of here, and he could contact Captain Wojskowy," Sturlan said.

"I'll talk to him," the rabbi said.

"I hear they're afraid of you," the rabbi told Jakub later. Wojskowy was Catholic, he explained. The Germans were mostly Lutherans, and among the Trawniki men, many Muslims. They were all, apparently, superstitious. "Maybe we Jews are immune to you."

"I'll go," Jakub said. "Give me a message and I'll deliver it."

"I think it's a terrible idea," the rabbi said. "The only way it makes any sense is if once you're beyond the wall, you keep going."

"Will you send another letter to my mother?"

"I will," the rabbi said.

"Telling her I'm safe and sending her the money."

"Yes."

Rabbi explained the particulars and where to find Wojskowy. He explained which train to take back to Marienburg and when it departed.

"After you see Wojskowy, you go and you keep going," the rabbi said. "I don't want you coming back. I want you home."

"How do I get out?" Jakub said.

"With me," the rabbi said.

JAKUB CHELZAK AND AZAR Gimelman walked past soldiers who knew Jakub from descriptions and gendarmes who had received cash from the rabbi. The soldiers—mostly boys—stepped away, walked to the other side of the street, and gawked, but no one said anything to either man, nor laid any hand upon them. Three men prepping artillery stopped and looked at Jakub. Other men said things under their breath, but when the rabbi looked at them, their faces and mouths looked reverent, not obscene. The rabbi stopped at the Leszno gate and brought his palms together on Jakub's cheeks.

"You understand what to tell Wojskowy?" the rabbi whispered.

"Yes," Jakub said.

"Then go with Him."

The men hugged and the rabbi turned back. Jakub waited until his friend disappeared through an alley. Outside the gate, a handful of *SS* stationed on the Aryan side stopped Jakub but German soldiers on the Jewish side whistled and yelled and waved them back. One of these soldiers ran up to Jakub, grabbed his hand and pulled up his sleeve to expose the remnants of the wound.

"*Sehen Sie!*" the Ghetto soldier said.

"*Er ist nicht ein Jude,*" said one of the *SS*. "*Wie heisst du?*"

"Jakub Chelzak," the Ghetto soldier interrupted.

One of the *SS* men lifted his side firearm to Jakub's cheek.

"*Verboten,*" the Ghetto soldier said, and put his hand on the barrel.

"*Verboten?* Naa!"

"*Es ist verboten, um Jakub Chelzak zu beschädigen!*" the soldier said. "*Es ist verboten, um mit er sogar zu beeinflussen oder zu sprechen!*"

"*Auf wessen Aufträgen?*" said a second SS man.

"Sammern-Frankenegg," the soldier said.

Without telling Stroop, Sammern-Frankenegg forbid offensive activity near ZOB headquarters. He assumed Chelzak would be leaving soon because he knew—the entire Ghetto knew—that Chelzak had come to save a dead woman. The boy soldiers wrote home about it—the whole strange situation. Sammern-Frankenegg was not superstitious, but many of his men were getting letters and notes in care packages from worried mothers and grandmothers and aunts warning their kin not to harm this man. Sammern-Frankenegg saw it spelled out in one typewritten letter.

"I don't know anything about him, but from what you've written, it's probably best to avoid him." An uncle agreed, advising in long hand—"just do what she tells you. We want you back in one piece."

That Chelzak was permitted to bottleneck the Ghetto offensive would have infuriated Stroop, an atheist, but the situation was convoluted. Many of Sammern-Frankenegg's men relied on the rabbi for income to supplement meager Army pay and regretted how mutual survival in the bowels of Hell had devolved into Final Liquidation. Himmler could come in here and wave his hands around and act important, but in the end Berlin was far from this god-awful, filthy, and demoralizing place. Even hard core *SS* who refused bribes looked away from the other men, many of them young with families, who took money from the Jews in return for life and liberty at critical moments.

Not every German was an anti-Semite, either. In fact, the rapacious hatred of the Jews that drove the liquidation seemed ill advised and strategically suspect to many in the *Wehrmacht*. The closest ideological link between many Germans and anti-Semitism was the idea that Jews killed Christ, a tired dogma reinvigorated with obscene illustrations and jingoistic diatribes in pulp German fiction. Now, a man who bore the wounds of Christ walked among them. To the Christian anti-Semites, to harm this man would be to emulate the Jews who had harmed

Christ. To the superstitious, Jakub Chelzak was a mystical presence who might command unearthly powers. To skeptics and pragmatists, Chelzak was of no consequence. To Sammern-Frankenegg, Chelzak was a problem that would resolve itself quickest by departing the Ghetto unmolested.

The *SS* man standing with Jakub whistled and waved at a young corporal mulling beside a staff car parked down Leszno Street on the Aryan side. The corporal got in and drove the car to them.

"*Nehmen Sie dem Glowny diesen Mann*," the officer said to the corporal as he showed Jakub into the car. Jakub hesitated until the soldier smiled.

The corporal let Jakub out at Glowny Station and after he drove away, Jakub walked a mile to the Lutheran cemetery, which bordered the Jewish cemetery on the Aryan side. At the gate, he passed a chapel and a little way in he saw a stone mausoleum with a granite angel sculpted over the entrance. Men with rifles emerged from the trees.

"What's your business?" one said.

"I have a message for Captain Wojskowy," Jakub said. "From Moryc."

"Moryc sent you? What message? How did you get here?"

"The fighters on Muranowski need food and ammunition," Jakub said. "Moryc is injured."

The men looked at one another then pushed Jakub toward the mausoleum. He ducked in and saw other men sitting on the dirt floor and on crypts of stone and marble. Squat, malformed candles cast scattered shadows on the walls. The men passed around a bottle and threw their heads back when they drank. The men from outside stood.

"This man has a message from Moryc."

"Moryc?" said another man who was sitting in a far corner.

They pushed Jakub. "Tell."

"The rabbi asked me to come," Jakub said. "Moryc is wounded."

The man from the corner stood and came into the light. This was Captain Wojskowy.

"Wounded?" Wojskowy said. "How badly?"

"I don't know," Jakub said. "My message is that his fighters on Muranowski need ammunition and food."

Wojskowy turned to the other men. He looked at Jakub. "How did you get out?"

"The rabbi."

"Figures."

Wojskowy motioned toward the other men. Jakub sat. They passed him the bottle. "This is my brother Waclaw and these are my sons," Wojskowy said. "Alojzy, Roman," he pointed. "I am Henryk Wojskowy."

They extended their hands. When Jakub reached out to Roman, the young man gasped.

"What is that?" Roman saw the wound in Jakub's wrist. "Did they do that?"

"No," Jakub said and he drank from the bottle. "It's an old injury."

Waclaw took Jakub's hand and slipped the sleeve above his wrist. "It looks new," Waclaw said. "You know Rabbi but you're not a Jew, are you?"

Jakub shook his head. "Catholic, like you."

"From here?" Wojskowy asked. "How come I don't know you?"

"Not from here," Jakub said. "From Marienburg."

"Marienburg," Waclaw said. "You know the castle?"

"Yes," Jakub said.

"It's a good Catholic place," Wojskowy said. He took a drink. "I've known Moryc a long time. He's a good fellow."

"Why are you here?" Roman asked. "You'd be better off in Marienburg."

"The rabbi hired me," Jakub said, and he drank a little more.

"For what?"

"They call this the Jerusalem of the Dead," Wojskowy interrupted.

Jakub looked at him.

"Here, Lutherans; next door, Catholics; a little ways away, Muslims; on the other side, Jews," Wojskowy said.

"They're all dead and they still can't get along," Waclaw said.

"Why the rabbi hires you?" Roman asked again. He frowned at his father.

"Maybe it's not our business," Uncle Waclaw said.

"For this," Jakub said.

"To bring a message?" Roman asked. "Rabbi hired a messenger all the way from Marienburg." The men laughed.

"Other things too," Jakub said.

"What other things?" Wojskowy asked. "What could be so important that a man must be brought from Marienburg?"

"The rabbi hired me to cheat death," Jakub said.

Waclaw grabbed the bottle from Wojskowy.

"What are you talking about?"

Wojskowy considered Jakub's face above the flames. He took back the bottle from his son. "No more drink," he said.

Nineteen

Maundy Thursday
22 April 1943

Henryk Wojskowy and his men left the cemetery around 2 a.m. Jakub forgot the rabbi's admonition against returning to the Ghetto. He wanted to come with them.

"You're in no condition to cheat death now," Henryk said.

Jakub gripped the side of the mausoleum entrance. "I can stand," he said. "And walk." He stumbled and Henryk grabbed him.

"Sober up," Henryk said.

Wojskowy took eighteen men, including his sons and brother, and rendezvoused with an underground supply station on the Aryan side. They entered the Ghetto through a tunnel that went from the cellar of 6 Muranowska Street on the Aryan side to Moryc Zydowski's position, the cellar of 7 Muranowska Street, behind the Ghetto wall. They carried supplies in their hands and on their backs.

"Henryk." Moryc limped over to his friend on makeshift crutches and hugged him. "What angel has sent you?"

"A drunk one."

Henryk turned to Waclaw. "Have them unload everything and stack it there. What do you need topside?" he asked Moryc.

"Food—desperately. Bullets and incendiaries, desperately."

Henryk motioned to his men, who headed up to the street through a door that opened onto the first floor of an empty row house.

"My men are scattered along Nalewki, and some on this street," Moryc said. "But we can signal them for chow once it's ready."

"They beating you up, are they?" Waclaw asked.

"Pounding us," Moryc said. He limped over and rested against the cellar's cold rock wall. "I feel like such a limp dick," he said.

"Where'd they hit you?" Roman asked. He set a box down.

"Left leg. I was bleeding like a mother fucker but they tied me up pretty good."

"We'll get you out," Henryk said.

"I can't leave," Moryc said.

"After we're finished," Henryk said. "You can leave then, right?"

"Finished? When might that be?"

"Alo—we're finishing right?"

Alojzy, who rarely spoke for a speech impediment, nodded his head.

"Cocky fuck," Moryc said to Henryk. "How come I wasn't born Catholic? You need a multi-syllabic faith to survive in this world."

"A what?" Henryk said.

"Episcopalian, Presbyterian, Anglican, Lutheran, Catholic, Christian, Muslim. Jew. You can't tell?"

"Convert," Henryk said. "I could pull some strings."

"Ahhh." Moryc waved his hand. "Pius is a chicken shit."

"Keep saying that and they'll never let you in."

Three men carried in a wounded fighter from the street.

"There's a hospital on the other side," Moryc said.

"How far?"

"It's walkable."

"Okay—we need four men on evacuations," Henryk said. "Roman, Alojzy—I want you with me. Mosze and Kosta—get two more men to carry the wounded through the tunnel."

"What about a stretcher?" Roman asked.

"How much wood is outside?" Henryk gently slapped his son's head. "I haven't taught you how to use this?"

"We have hammer and nails," Moryc said. He pointed. "In that crate."

Roman and Waclaw went topside to the empty house and dragged down scrap lumber from the debris. Alojzy nailed together a makeshift stretcher from two-by-fours and long flat planks. The first team of four men loaded the wounded fighter and entered the tunnel. Waclaw went up to the street. Roman finished the second stretcher.

"Here." Henryk motioned to his son. They picked up the stretcher and set it next to Zydowski.

"You cocksuckers," Moryc said. "I told you I'm not going."

"When I tell you, hit him over the head," Henryk said to Roman.

"You hit me and I'll shoot you," Moryc said. He raised his shotgun a little.

"All right," Henryk said. "We need more wood." Roman and Alojzy went back up to the empty house.

"Calling the Pope a chicken shit," Henryk said. "My Pope."

"He is a chicken shit."

"He gets courage and we get more dead Jews," Henryk said.

"Bullshit," Moryc said. "He could call up the fires of hell on all our enemies."

"Which would singe your delicate little toes." Henryk gently kicked Moryc's good foot.

"That's my bad leg, you cruel fuck."

"I thought it was this one." Henryk raised his foot as though to kick Moryc again but an explosion outside toppled him. Dust and rocks broke loose from the cellar wall. Roman ran down from the street.

"Alo's hurt," Roman said.

"Shit," Henryk said.

"Waclaw's with him." Both men headed topside.

"Be careful," Moryc yelled.

Moryc listened to the gunfire and blasts from the street. "Limp dick, limp dick, limp dick," he said to himself.

Waclaw, Roman and his father carried Alojzy into the cellar. He was unconscious.

"Put him over here. Over here."

They laid him on the stretcher. Moryc took a knife from his belt and started cutting away the bloody cloth from Alojzy's thigh.

"Is he hurt bad?" Roman asked.

"He's bleeding like I was," Moryc said. "Maybe an artery." Henryk stood pale and still. Moryc handed his knife to Roman. "Light some scraps and heat this," Moryc said. "Over there— where the smoke will vent." He looked at Henryk. "What's it like up there?"

"Terrible," said a man coming in from the street. Two other fighters followed him. Dirt and mud covered their clothes and boots. "You have food?"

Moryc nodded toward the open crates. The men unwrapped old newspapers that covered potatoes, radishes, sausage and bread, and ate without thinking. Roman held the knife over a small fire.

"What's happened to him?" one of the fighters said.

"Shot," Moryc said.

"He took shrapnel," Henryk said. "Hurry with that fucking knife. What are you going to do with it?"

"Stop the bleeding," Moryc said. Roman handed him the hot knife. Moryc touched Alojzy's leg and his whole body jerked and he awoke and screamed.

Wojskowy knelt next to his injured son and took his hand and wrapped his arm around him and kissed his head. "It'll be all right," he whispered.

"Drink." Moryc threw his head toward a whiskey bottle. Henryk took it to his son's lips. Moryc handed Roman a piece of burlap. "Into his mouth," Moryc said. Roman stuffed it into his brother's mouth. "Bite down," Moryc said.

Henryk nodded to Moryc, who cut away the shredded flesh between Alojzy's screams while wiping blood with another piece of burlap.

"We can get him to the hospital if we can stop the bleeding." Moryc saw the thin cut in Alojzy's artery and a metal shard. "I forgot to ask," Moryc said. "How is Renata?"

Henryk considered. "Dry," he said.

"Come on."

"Been like that for years."

"Then I need to teach you a few things," Moryc said. "A few techniques."

"You?" Henryk said.

"I need Roman to heat some water on that fire," Moryc said. "And I need a man to wash his hands in hot water and hold this artery."

"I'll do it," Henryk said.

"No—you're his father," Moryc said. "Waclaw—wash up then come here."

Waclaw scrubbed his hands in the bowl of hot water and knelt next to Moryc, who moved Waclaw's fingers toward the artery. Henryk watched Waclaw squeeze his fingers in the damaged thigh until the bleeding stopped. Alojzy passed out. Moryc removed the metal shard.

"Jesus," Henryk said.

"Don't look," Moryc said. He looked at Alojzy. "He'll be in a lot of pain when he wakes up."

"We brought morphine," Henryk said.

"Good. I've drained ours," Moryc said. "The hospital has morphine." He wrapped the leg with a makeshift tourniquet. Mosze and Kosta and the two other men came back from the tunnel.

"Give him some morphine then load him," Moryc said. "You know how to inject?"

Henryk nodded. He took the morphine from a back pack and administered it. They lifted the stretcher and Henryk kissed his unconscious son. "Be careful," he said. Mosze and Waclaw left with the stretcher through the tunnel.

"I'm going up," Henryk said.

"I don't have to tell you," Moryc said. "Be careful."

On their way to the street, Henryk and Roman passed two other men coming into the cellar.

RAIN PATTERED AROUND ARTILLERY fire. A chill stilled the air. Moryc pulled a blanket around his waist and shoulders and watched two men eating and they exchanged small talk. Voices outside rose above the rain—a scream nearby or a hollered command a little way off. The men in the cellar heard the "whoosh" of a flamethrower and fire crashing against windows and heat cracking wooden frames set in brick. They heard thunder, too. The two men eating each took a slug of water.

"Up we go," said one of them. When they opened the door Moryc felt cold air. He heard the weather and the fighting. He stared at the fire, vented to an old coal furnace flue. The rain fell in sheets when three men entered with mud on their pants and grime on their faces. Moryc didn't recognize them. Two of the men wore sodden woolen hats.

"Eats!" one of them said. The man spoke Polish but Moryc thought the word sounded funny. The men tore off hunks of hard bread and wrapped it around sausage. They were not starving, Moryc thought, like other men who rushed the food and stuffed it into their mouths without thinking to make a sandwich. Two men turned and Moryc saw their faces in the light from the fire. They wore side arms and one had a knife.

"Manna!" one of the men said. "You know about manna?" he asked Moryc. He slid down with his back against the rock wall and stretched his legs and crossed them. "Bread from Heaven," the man said. He rested against the wall. "But this is not Heaven."

The other men ate and watched.

"You injured?"

"No," Moryc said. He knew the men were fighters from somewhere else now because all the men here knew he was injured. "Resting," he said.

The man against the wall smiled and moved his hand toward his sidearm. Moryc watched the man's hand and pulled the blanket back from the shotgun by his left leg. The man saw the shotgun. He pulled a flask from the inside pocket of his coat.

"I saw a war in Warsaw," the man said. He drank. "To it, I was sent." He passed the flask to Moryc. "In the darkness, in the light, to fight with all my might."

Moryc took a swig from the flask.

"I never knew my enemy," the man said. "Only heard his name. Have you heard this?"

"No," Moryc said, hearing an accent he had not heard before, either.

"From the politicians, who thought it all a game," said one of the other men. He took off his hat. "It's a song, I think. Or a poem."

"On the battlefield, where we played, I finally saw mine enemy," said the man against the wall. "How does it end?"

"I don't know," the other man said.

"You have children?" the man against the wall asked Moryc.

"Yes," Moryc said. "Two."

"Did they get out?"

"No," Moryc said.

"Are they alive?"

"No," Moryc said.

The man against the wall swigged his vodka again. "Russian," he said. "Good stuff." They listened to the rain. "Sounds like a banshee," he said.

"Sounds like my wife," said the third man.

"Did she get out?" Moryc asked. The man against the wall frowned at his married companion and slowly shook his head.

"No," the married man stammered. "She didn't get out."

Moryc placed his hand on his shotgun. The second man turned to the food. He unsnapped his sidearm. They heard rain pelting streets and metal roofs and wind moaning as it blew across chimneys and holes made by shells.

"It's nice in here," said the man against the wall. "When you going up?"

"Soon," Moryc said.

"When the others come back?"

"Before that," Moryc said.

"They not coming back for a while?"

"They'll be back to eat," Moryc said. "There wasn't food before. Now there is."

The man against the wall turned and nodded to his two companions. Moryc leaned forward and pulled the shotgun onto his lap.

"You a good aim?"

"Don't have to be," Moryc said.

The man against the wall raised himself to his feet and motioned to the others. Moryc lifted the shotgun.

"We should go now," the man said.

They turned for the dark exit and each man heard a cock.

"Leave your weapons."

They stopped and the man who had been against the wall turned and saw Moryc aiming the shotgun.

"We'll be killed without them," the man said.

"You'll be killed with them," Moryc said.

The men hesitated. Moryc looked through the gun-sight. "You're in a good line," Moryc said. "One shot here, three shot there."

The third man unsnapped his sidearm and drew it.

"Put it down," Moryc said.

The men tossed their pistols in the dirt.

"And the knife," Moryc said.

The third man drew his knife and threw it down with the pistols.

"Get out," Moryc said.

"You going to shoot us?"

"Then I'd have to drag you out of the doorway," Moryc said.

The men turned and Moryc heard them open the cellar door and walk on the wood floors in the empty rooms overhead. He heard their voices and then he heard nothing.

MORYC HEARD VOICES AGAIN and raised the shotgun. The cellar door opened.

"We can't leave them out there—we have to get them."

Moryc recognized Henryk's voice. He heard another low voice.

"How can I worry about that?" Henryk said.

Moryc saw Henryk bowed and limping in the arms of another man he didn't recognize.

"It's all right," Henryk said. "This is the angel I told you about."

Moryc lowered the shotgun and raised himself on his crutches and helped Jakub lower Henryk to a chair.

"What the fuck happened?" Moryc asked.

"How about some water," Henryk said. Moryc pointed Jakub to the jugs. Henryk took the water from Jakub and splashed it into his mouth and over his face.

"They set up artillery—outside a house about four blocks down," Henryk said. "Three Krauts—I needed to get into the house. I had an opportunity and I ran."

"How'd you get out?" Moryc asked.

"I never got in. Chelzak tackled me. Right before the cannon fired. Took out the whole fucking wall."

"What was in the house?" Moryc asked.

Henryk looked away. He rubbed his face, rubbed away dirt, tears, and snot. "My boy."

"Roman?" Moryc asked.

"Yes," Henryk said. His voice and hands shook.

Moryc put his hand around Henryk's shoulder. "Did you see him?"

"No," Henryk said.

Moryc extended his other hand to Jakub. "You're to be thanked," Moryc said. "How did you find him?"

"This is Chelzak," Henryk said. "He was drunk when we left him. It's a miracle he found anything."

"He wasn't hard to find," Jakub said.

"Where's Mosze and them?" Henryk asked.

"Not back yet, but they know they can't leave Alo 'til they get a doc."

They listened to the rain outside. "The famous Chelzak," Moryc said, extending his hand. "We have to get out of here."

"How can I leave?" Henryk asked.

"We can't stay," Moryc said. "They know we're here."

"How do you know?"

"I had visitors."

Jakub looked around. "We can go up—find another place," he said.

"There's no other place," Moryc said. "There's through that tunnel and that's the only place there is."

"How badly are you hurt?" Jakub asked Henryk.

"I can walk," Henryk said. "But I can't leave. Not without my Roman."

Moryc leaned down to his friend. "Listen to me," he said. "We have to go." Moryc open a backpack and pulled out two large white cloth patches. He handed them to Jakub. "Take these upstairs and put them where they'll be seen," Moryc said.

When Jakub returned, Moryc motioned him toward Henryk. Jakub leaned down to help Henryk to his feet. Henryk glared.

"We can't help Alo if we stay here," Moryc said.

Henryk wanted to push Jakub away but needed his help to get through the tunnel. He stopped midway through and looked back with Jakub's arms around him. He stood for a while and looked at the lamplight in the cellar. Jakub tugged him and he turned and they went to the other side. Jakub came back for Moryc and carried him through the tunnel, setting him down three times to rest. It was quiet on the Aryan side and with a few more fighters they got Moryc to the hospital in little over two hours.

The Germans never came to the cellar at 7 Muranowska and during the night and the next morning, thirty four men saw the white cloth that meant evacuation and entered the tunnel and went to the Aryan side.

Two days after a doctor stitched Alojzy's wound with a needle he was unable to sterilize, Alojzy died of bacterial sepsis. Henryk fantasized for a long time about killing the doctor but never saw him again. Henryk didn't see Roman again, either, and for weeks he cried when he was awake. For many more weeks, he consoled himself by thinking his son would turn up. This thought grew harder to endure and Henryk had to become more determined in the thinking of it.

When he rejoined Renata and his brother Waclaw in the Aryan district, they sheltered and hid Jews and other refugees. To every person, Henryk Wojskowy showed photos and asked the same questions. No one had seen Roman, although two young women said he was extremely handsome from his photo. These same women talked together for an hour about how much they missed gentleness, how much they missed making love or just having sex, how much they missed being kissed or held, and how before, they never could have imagined that hunger for food could so kill hunger for everything else.

A few years after the war, the Polish Ambassador to Israel decorated Henryk and Renata Wojskowy. After the ceremony, over his wife's gentle protests, Henryk asked the ambassador if he had ever seen Roman Wojskowy.

Moryc Zydowski had no family to return to. A few years later, he remembered the unfinished poem about the war in Warsaw and tried to finish it but never did.

Twenty

Good Friday
23 April 1943

O n this holy day, the occupiers burned houses before sunrise. Searching for fighters, soldiers rushed stairs, beat doors, splashed kerosene, and threw long streams of fire from dark nozzles. They smoked out women and children and a few old men, living skinny and depraved in empty buildings. These were the Ghetto's walking dead. Every place the occupiers infected had walking dead—the death camps, the prison camps, the villages, and the cities. Non-combatants who stayed in the Ghetto as Easter 1943 approached were so starved and bowed they could barely move. Fire and smoke pushed them out and soldiers shot them.

Some soldiers shot straight—aim, fire. Some soldiers shot crooked, piercing legs or blowing off fingers—even their own. Some soldiers pretended they were gunslingers in the old west, shooting Indians like John Wayne, a hero except when he was fighting them. In the movies, all the Indians fought valiantly. Here, the valiant ones leaped off balconies and rooftops onto the hard stone streets or into the flames. That suicide under these circumstances—the only act of self-determination left—was as honorable as fighting never occurred to the boy soldiers.

Dust and smoke squatted over the Ghetto by dawn and the air reeked of burning hair and feathers. Stroop sat at the desk in his hotel room. His hand slowly moved a pen. He read his words aloud to himself, stumbling on pronunciations.

"*Die jüdische haupsächlichgrupe,*" he wrote, "*mit einige polnische banditen gemischt innen, zog zurück.*"

"The main Jewish group, with some Polish bandits mixed in, withdrew."

He looked at "*haupsächlichgrupe*" and re-read it aloud. He crossed it out with a clean line and replaced it with "*hauptsächlichgruppe.*"

"*Zum sogenannten Mura—*" he read—and stopped writing again. "Fuck."

He looked out the window and saw the smoke on the other side of the wall. It was white, like smoke from a crematorium or the smoke of surrender, or the smoke that announces a new Pope. This smoke was heavy too, and of the kinds of smoke Stroop knew about, only crematoria smoke was as heavy. He let his thoughts wander and at first, he didn't hear the knock. "Come," he said finally.

Stroop's aide opened the door. "*Polizeiführer* Krüger, sir."

"Show him."

Krüger strutted in with papers.

"Himmler wants an acceleration," he told Stroop.

"Acceleration? We're not moving fast enough?"

"Not for him. He expected this done days ago."

"Rome wasn't built in a day," Stroop said.

"We're not building Rome, *Herr Brigadeführer*."

"No," Stroop said. "We never *build* anything." He looked at his report. "How do you spell Mura—Muran—?"

"Muranowski?" Krüger replied.

"Fucking Pole words," Stroop said.

Krüger looked at the report. He took the pen and completed the word. "What do I tell *Herr* Himmler?"

Stroop thought. "Tell him the action will be completed this very day," he said.

Alone in the room again, Stroop wrote a few more words, but the letters didn't look right so he straightened curves and made an "s" into a "z." The words still didn't look right. He stopped and thought about dictating the report to his aide. Then he remembered his aide couldn't read.

Twenty One

Holy Saturday (Shabbat)
24 April 1943

The rabbi saw Jakub Chelzak for the first time in two days, on the Sabbath during a ten-hour break in the fighting. He threw his arms around Jakub at the door to the ZOB bunker on Mila and Zamenhofa Streets and they spoke about the fighting in Muranowski Square. It was 3:47 in the morning.

"Amazing," the rabbi said. "It's amazing that you ignored me and didn't get the hell out of here when you had the chance."

"We can get through the tunnel," Jakub said. "It's still open. The Germans don't know about it."

"How do you know?"

"No one followed us through."

The rabbi thought. "I'd like to get Rebekah out," he said. "But she's frail."

"I can help, but we should go now, before light."

The rabbi thought again. "We get her out, where do we go?"

"The Aryan side."

"For how long?"

"Do you know of a boat? To go down the river?"

"To cross the river, maybe," the rabbi said. "I have friends in Praga," a suburb of Warsaw across the Wisła.

"I don't know Praga," Jakub said.

"The Russians are there."

"We would be safe?"

"The Germans are also there," the rabbi said. "Not as many as here, but still."

"Any place is better than here."

"I don't think Shosha will go," the rabbi said. "And Rebekah won't leave her."

"I'll talk to her," Jakub said. He remembered Moryc and Henryk. "It's hopeless here. We have to get out."

The rabbi leaned against the wall and rubbed his forehead. He looked at the ceiling and sighed. "We could get a boat. I'd have to pay a few guards," he said. "That would take some doing."

"How long?" Jakub asked.

"A few days," the rabbi said. "I don't want to risk getting stuck on the Aryan side. Everything has to be arranged—boom, boom, boom."

"Did you get the letter to my mother?" Jakub asked.

"Yes. Which reminds me." The rabbi pulled an open envelope from this jacket and handed it to Jakub. "I didn't know if you were coming back and I thought I'd better see what it said," the rabbi explained. "She's been getting the money and she thanks you for it, but she and your brother want you back."

STROOP TRIPLED THE NUMBER of flamethrowers. "Every man on foot needs to be behind one of these," he told Krüger.

The soldiers marched and turned in unison and fired streams of flame at every standing thing. Burning walls thundered down and black smoke seared lungs, stung eyes, and choked breath. The heat forced people from the deepest hideaways and radiated from the tight pores of every stone thing —bricks and blocks and even marble stairs. Along every street, buildings burned. Wild tenants climbed to higher floors but flames dogged them and they threw themselves out windows or off roofs. Their clothes were sometimes on fire and their faces filthy and sooty and as they fell, their bodies twisted like burning debris.

By early evening the sun was setting, but darkness would not come here for three days. With the rising sun on Easter Sunday, the descent into Hell was complete. The resurrection seemed further away than ever.

"WE HAVE TO MOVE."

This daily refrain dogged Rabbi Gimelman and his charges. Rebekah grew weaker, and Shosha thinner. Though he lost weight, Jakub was all muscle to begin with, and he changed only a little.

The first bunker they moved from had been their home for months—18 Mila Street, the former nightclub and headquarters of the Jewish Combat Organization. They left Marian, his best friend Jurek, and a dwindling number of ZOB friends. They moved to bunkers at Nos. 5 and 7 Mila Street and then to bunkers on Wolynska, Szczesliwa, Niska, Zamenhofa, and Nowolipki streets. At 29 Ogrodowa Street, the occupiers killed every fighter. 36 Siwetojerska St. fell and with it, ZOB leader Szymek Kac.

THE GERMANS CORNERED THE ZOB leadership in a bunker on Leszno Street the night of April 27. ZOB leaders met into the early hours of April 28, calling on Regina Fudin, a courier with a photographic memory who knew the situation above ground better than any one else. Fudin would gather the remaining fighters in the factory area and lead them out. They would leave the severely wounded behind in the bunker with the Ghetto's fiercest fighter, a woman, Lea Korn.

Late night April 29, Fudin and Lieutenant Wladyslaw Gaik of the Gwardia Ludowa (People's Guard) led forty Jewish fighters through the sewers to the Aryan side. A Pole, Riszard Trifon, sheltered them for the rest of the night in several attics. The next day, Gwardia Ludowa trucks transported the group to the forest in Lomianka, about seven kilometers from Warsaw. The Nazis learned of the escape and with a few Trawniki men attacked the remaining fighters. Lea Korn held them off for hours. Indeed, as Stroop would later write, the women fighters in the Ghetto were among the most valiant and courageous.

"The women belonging to the fighting groups were armed in the same way as the men," Stroop wrote. "Sometimes these women fired pistols from each hand at once. It happened time and again that they kept their pistols and hand grenades hidden in their bloomers till the last minute, and then used them against the armed *SS*, police and *Wehrmacht*."

The soldiers killed Lea Korn and everyone else in her bunker.

"TWO DAYS," THE RABBI said. "I can't believe it's been two whole days since we last moved."

Men sat along the walls of a cellar stocked with barrels and bags. In candlelight, Shosha saw her mother, pale and tired, lying on a lumpy mat with her head on a sack of grain.

"Our next move needs to be away from here," one of the men said. "Far away."

"Where?"

"Anywhere but here."

"It's too late for us," Shosha said. "We waited too long."

"Others get out," Jakub said. "I'm sure the tunnel at Muranowska is still open."

Shosha looked at Jakub's eyes. "Mama couldn't make it," she said.

"She could," Jakub said. "We all could."

Shosha took his hand. "I can't believe you stayed with us," she said. She traced the area near his wrists where the wounds appeared. "I don't see them," she said.

"I don't have them all the time," Jakub said. "If I did, I couldn't live."

Shosha looked at her mother, at her wane eyes and sallow cheeks. She took Jakub's hand to her face and held it there, against her skin. He felt her tears and squeezed her fingers.

"I'm crying," she said. "I didn't think I still could."

Twenty Two

The 23-year-old man who would lead the first major Jewish revolt against an oppressor since the Masada staved off the Romans in the year 135 AD, Marian—Mordecai Anielewicz—was born in Wyszkow, Poland to a working-class family in a poor neighborhood. He was a member of Betar, the Zionist youth group. When war erupted and he heard about Jewish mass murder, Marian led HaShomer HaZair, Poland's first Jewish youth movement. "We must fight and we must never, never give up," he said to anyone who would listen. He single-handedly took charge of the Jewish Combat Organization, the ZOB.

Marian sent a communication to ZOB contacts outside the Ghetto in late April 1943. "This is the eighth day of our life-and-death struggle," he wrote. "The Germans suffered tremendous losses. In the first two days, they were forced to withdraw. Then they brought in reinforcements in the form of tanks, armor, artillery, even airplanes, and began a systematic siege.

"Our losses, that is, the victims of the executions and fires in which men, women and children were burned, were terribly high. We are nearing our last days, but so long as we have weapons in our hands, we shall continue to fight and resist.

"Sensing the end, we demand this from you: remember how we were betrayed. There will come a time of reckoning for our spilled, innocent blood. Send help to those who, in the last hour, may elude the enemy—in order that the fight may continue."

On May 8, 1943, the soldiers came to one of the last houses in the Ghetto that still stood—the main ZOB bunker at 18 Mila Street. They covered the five entrances. They screamed and threatened. They fired their rifles. Some of the men standing around pissed on the side of the building. Three hundred civilians surrendered. But eighty armed fighters—including Marian and many boys—fought for every floor, every window, every square centimeter and inch of that building's ground. They fought through grenades and gas bombs. They fought through smoke and dust. They fought hand to hand. They used knives against bullets, sticks and pipes against bombs.

"While it was at first possible to catch the Jews, who are by nature cowards, in great numbers, this became increasingly difficult as the action went on," Stroop reported. "Fighting groups of twenty to thirty or more Jewish youths, aged 18-25, kept turning up, sometimes with a corresponding number of women who kindled fresh resistance. These fighting groups had been ordered to defend themselves to the last and, if need be, to escape capture by suicide."

Marian committed suicide. Thirty four fighters who could have died, by chance discovered an exit through tunnels that led to the city sewer system. After thirty hours in the sewers, they emerged outside the Ghetto. Gwardia Ludowa troops drove them to join their fellows in the Lomianki forest.

Eight days later, Stroop wrote his last report to Berlin. "The action was completed on May 16, 1943 with the blowing up of the Warsaw Synagogue at 8:15 p.m. All the Ghetto buildings have been destroyed." He praised his troops. "The longer the resistance lasted," Stroop wrote, "the more implacable became the men of the *SS*, the police and the *Wehrmacht*, who continued untiringly in the fulfillment of their duties in the true comradeship in arms."

But his was in truth a partial victory with ten times the casualties he claimed. Stroop's war took twenty eight days when Himmler demanded three. The Nazi *Blitzkrieg* that conquered Poland had taken only two days longer. Resistance fighters continued to attack the occupiers for a year, in isolated pockets, all over the Ghetto.

"ALLE GLEICH! ALLE GLEICH!"

Shosha opened her eyes the morning of May 17.

"*Die kleine schweine Verfluchen Jude! Alle gleich, alle gleich, banditen Jude! Kaput!*"

The voices came from the street somewhere. Shosha pushed herself up. She leaned on her hands. The darkness in the cellar was complete so she sat and stared into it and listened to the rhythmic breathing of sleeping men in cool air. She flinched and caught her breath when she heard a match strike and before she could speak, the flame lit a candle and she saw the rabbi's face.

"We have to get the fuck out of here," he whispered.

Her stomach seized and she did the first thing that came to her mind—she tore her skirt and wrapped her hair with shaky hands. She grasped the end of the skirt near her ankles and tore it down the middle, back and front, and tied the sides into loose-fitting pants around each leg. She leaned over Jakub and shook him awake. She crawled to her mother and kissed her forehead and stroked her cheek. The other men were rousing.

"Mama—time to get up."

Rebekah opened her eyes. "What? What is it?"

"Time to go."

"Scout," someone whispered.

Shosha helped her mother and held a small metal cup half full of water to her lips.

"Hey—Scout!"

Shosha felt a hand on her arm. "We need a scout," the fighter named Wladislaw—Vladi—said to her. "Aren't you a scout?"

"Not for a long time," Shosha said.

"Once a scout, always a scout."

"That's not a woman's job," said another man. "There's plenty of us."

"Rabbi," Shosha said, "can you help mama?" To Vladi: "What do you want me to do?"

"Go up—tell us what you see."

Shosha stood.

"I'll go with you," Jakub said. He walked behind her, stooping.

"Whew—you stink," Shosha said. "I hope they don't smell you."

They pushed open the cellar door. Through holes in the walls above the floor, they saw a line of naked men, captured resistance fighters. They saw a soldier pull a clothed man by his hair from a bunker.

"*Jetzt! Gehen Sie!*"

The soldier threw him forward and kicked him. The man stumbled.

"They're going to shoot them," Shosha said. "Then they'll be here."

Jakub watched the clothed man struggle to his feet. "I count three," he said.

"Soldiers?"

"Yes."

"*Kleider ausziehen!*"

With unsteady hands, the man unbuttoned his shirt. The soldier slapped the man's hands and tore the shirt open.

"Stay here," Shosha said.

She ducked into the cellar. Jakub watched the man strip.

"Here." Shosha pushed up an old bolt-action rifle and bullets. "It's loaded," she said.

He took the rifle and tried to aim it. "I can't get a good shot," Jakub said.

"Try anyway."

He slid the rifle on the floor and slipped out of the cellar. Shosha hovered beneath the cellar door.

"Can you do it through the holes?"

"Maybe," Jakub said. He crawled toward a wall. He tried lining the sight through one of the holes, but both barrel and scope wouldn't fit.

"Too small," he said.

"Try the window."

Jakub crawled over and peaked through smoke-scarred glass. He rubbed away soot and dirt and could see the soldiers. "It's good," he said. He lined up the sight and aimed.

"Can you kill them?" Shosha asked.

"Shhhh."

Shosha watched the soldier push the last naked fighter into the line.

"There's three," she whispered. "Can you kill three at once?"

"Shut up, please."

Jakub saw his chance through the sight when one soldier stepped behind another. He fired and glass shattered and the bullet went through the heart of the first soldier. It hit the second soldier in the arm and he stumbled. Jakub cocked the rifle and fired again. The bullet went through the soldier's shoulder and he hit dirt and didn't move. Some of the Jewish fighters dropped to the ground. The third soldier took cover behind the fighters who stood. He looked up, across the street, around.

"*Möchten mich, Judeschwein schießen?*" the soldier shouted. "*Möchten mich schießen?*"

"Only one more," Jakub said.

"Can't you get him? Can't you shoot?"

"Hush." Jakub aimed but he couldn't shoot the soldier without shooting a fighter. Then one by one, the fighters who stood lowered themselves and stretched across the ground.

"*Stehen Sie oben.*" The soldier aimed his pistol at the head of a fighter. "*Bleiben Sie Stellung.*"

"*Schießen Sie mich!*" the fighter said. "*Schießen Sie mich! Warum sollte ich mich interessieren?*"

A gunshot echoed and the German slumped. The fighters peered up. They waited for more shots. One man stood on shaky feet. He ran to his clothes. He raised his fist. The others watched him and stood. Jakub kept his eyes on them.

"Did you get him?" Shosha asked.

"Yes."

"Then let's get the fuck out of here."

THEY MOVED OVER HOLES, craters, embers, and bodies beneath rubble. The rabbi and Jakub helped Rebekah. She was the only one among them who ate this morning and her strength was a little improved. Shosha, Vladi and another fighter scouted ahead. Two men from another bunker joined them and stayed at the rear. Burning beams and timbers crashed nearby and roofs wheezed and groaned or slammed to the ground. It sounded like thunder, clapping around the Ghetto. Smoke was everywhere and heavy. They had to pause many times to get a breath. The rabbi stopped them near a burned-out church.

"Here," he said. He pointed to an area that, in all the debris, looked artificially covered. The wood was not burned; the stones not scorched or hot. Jakub pulled the cover away to a tunnel.

"How did you know this was here?" Rebekah asked. The rabbi seemed surprised: Rebekah didn't talk much anymore.

"They planned these tunnels months ago," the rabbi said. "There are a few around."

Shosha lowered herself after the first fighter. "Oh! Cover your noses."

The nine refugees moved through a narrow passage.

"Are you sure we're going the right way?" a fighter asked.

"They told me it was here," the rabbi said. "I don't know any more than that."

A ways farther and Rebekah stopped.

"Go ahead," the rabbi told them. "She needs rest."

"We're not leaving you," Shosha said. "We'll wait."

"We can't wait," said a fighter at the rear.

"We wait," Shosha yelled back.

In a few minutes, they went a little farther and saw light. It came through a small, square opening. They heard fire smoldering on the other side. Vladi tried to pull himself up to reach the opening but the bricks around it were too hot to touch.

"This can't be it," the rabbi said. "Keep going."

They crawled farther in darkness.

"There's a hole here, in the wall," Vladi said. "Do we go straight or through?"

"One person through," the rabbi said.

"I'll go," Jakub said. He slipped head first into the hole.

"You'll feel built up walls," the rabbi said. "It will be obvious if it's right."

Jakub could only crawl and he pushed himself snakelike with his hands, elbows, and toes. He only went a few feet before he felt wooden reinforcements. The slender tunnel emptied into an antechamber. At its mouth, Jakub felt something hanging in the darkness. "A ladder," he called back. "This must be it."

"Go up it," the rabbi called back. His voice didn't travel in the narrow passage. "Tell him to go up it," he said to Vladi. "Then tell him at the top to say the word 'Hannibal' loudly."

When Jakub did this, a round wooden door opened.

"Mordechai?" a man's voice asked softly.

Jakub relayed the question. It traveled person by person, back to the rabbi.

"Yes," the rabbi said. "Mordechai." The word traveled back.

"Yes," Jakub said. "Mordechai."

Two hands reached down and took hold of Jakub's forearms. He swayed unsteadily on the rope ladder but the hands helped pull him up.

"Merciful God in Heaven." A friar in a hooded black tunic with a rosary hanging from his cincture looked at Jakub. "Jakub Chelzak, from Marienburg," Fr. Fredric continued. He took Jakub's hand. "How on Earth did you come to be here?"

"With the rabbi," Jakub said.

The rest went through the hole. The rabbi went in front of Rebekah and a fighter went behind. They pushed her when she needed extra strength. Shosha's head popped up from the antechamber. Jakub and Fr. Fredric bent to help her. "Mama's next," she said.

The seven men and two women entered the small chamber one by one. A crucifix hung above an altar. Statues of St. Francis, St. Peter, St. Michael the Archangel, and St. Jude book-ended a library along the walls. An oversize velvet chair relaxed inconveniently in the center of the room.

"Father Fredric." The rabbi shook the priest's hand and they glanced cheek to cheek. "My thanks—our thanks."

"Not at all," Fredric said. "Father Stanislaw told me about you, how much you've helped us in the past."

"Where is he?"

"In Praga—with another group. He'll take you when he returns."

Fr. Fredric led them down another tunnel to a lower chamber with mattresses and blankets, a basin with water, soap, a wash cloth and clothing on a chair in the corner. Vladi set the clothing on the mattresses and the rabbi and Shosha lowered Rebekah into the chair. The rabbi looked at the basin. "Is that steam?" he asked.

Fr. Fredric opened his hand toward the basin. The rabbi put his hand in and scooped up a little water. "It's warm," he said. He held the water up. "Forgive me please, but L-rd in Heaven it's downright hot." He opened his fingers and the water dripped on his hair. "Ay-yay-yay." It went down his forehead, and onto his cheeks. "I haven't felt anything like that in—I can't remember how long." He scooped another palm full of water and again let it trickle through his hair.

They cleaned with warm water and ate a meal of hard biscuits and coffee. They changed clothes and lay on the mattresses.

"God stay with you," Fr. Fredric said to them before they slept, and all but one had as deep and fine a sleep as they had ever had.

JAKUB WOKE WITH INTENSE throbbing in his ankles shortly after 3 a. m. He sat up on the mattress and looked over the sleeping bodies of the other men. The bunker was pitch black, but he remembered where he lay. Jakub crawled, all he could do when the pain started. He crawled on his elbows and knees around the men and out, along the narrow passage toward the chapel. He envisioned reclining in the chair and letting his hands and feet bleed over the stone floor in private. He would clean the blood with a mop he had seen in the passage.

Jakub crawled into the chapel and felt around for the chair in the dark. He pulled himself onto it and leaned forward. He pulled off his new socks and pulled back the legs of his new pants. He knew when he felt the four first bruises—three on one leg, one on the other—that tonight he would endure the full compliment of wounds and injuries. Bruises and welts would cover him, an intermittent quality of his stigmata the clerics paid little attention. Nails would pierce his feet. He might—or might not—sweat blood from his forehead, an unusual but painless phenomena Church historians wrongly attributed to a crown of thorns.

He pried the buttons of his shirt from their holes—painful in this condition—and slipped the shirt off. He tucked it behind his head. He stretched his feet out from the chair and laid his hands over the armrests, supporting his forearms there to reduce the throbbing. He lay in darkness repeating the Lord's Prayer, a habit his mother emphasized, hoping it would reduce the pain. He clenched his jaw and uttered a restrained cry, then short staccato gasps like a woman in labor. The nails pierced him, first through the side of his left ankle, then the right, in front of the Achilles tendon. He felt the hammer miss and slam his thumb pad. He felt the nail shatter his wrist bones. He passed out before the pain reached its crescendo.

Jakub woke ninety-minutes later to a male voice saying a rosary. He opened his eyes but the throbbing had moved to his head and though candles now lit the room, he couldn't make out the hunched, robed figure that knelt somewhere near his legs. He brought his hand to his forehead and Fr. Fredric looked up from his prayers.

"Bless me," the priest said. "My last confession was so long ago I can't remember. Is it important that I remember?"

Jakub rubbed his head. "Remember what?" he asked.

"Remember how long ago I last confessed my sins."

"Why are you asking me?"

"Because I know I have offended you and I am sorry."

"You haven't offended me," Jakub said. "You've been as kind as anyone I know."

"That isn't true."

"Of course it is," Jakub said. "Look at everything you've done."

The priest thought for a moment. "That's only now," he said. "I'm talking about before."

"Before when?" Jakub asked. "We just met."

"How can you say that? I've known you all my life."

Jakub looked at the floor. He tried to stand but the pain was too great in his ankles. The blood was dry on his flesh but wet where it pooled on the floor. The priest must be kneeling in it, he thought.

"I'm the one who should be apologizing to you," Jakub said. "I've messed up your floor."

"The floor?"

"I meant to clean it."

Fr. Fredric stood. "This floor will never be cleaned again," he said. He walked to the other side of the chair and knelt again, but on one knee. He bowed his head. "Lord, I am heartily sorry for having offended thee. I detest all my sins because I dread the loss of Heaven and the fires of Hell. But most of all because they offend thee, my God, who art all good and deserving of all my love."

Jakub put his hand on the priest's wrist.

"I am asking for penance," Fr. Fredric said. "Forgiveness."

Jakub took a deep breath. "I don't have that power," he said.

The priest looked at him. "Everything is in your power."

Jakub looked away.

"Why won't you hear my confession?" the priest asked.

"I'm tired."

The priest considered. "Why are you toying with me?"

"I can't take your confession," Jakub said.

"You have the power to loose my sins and you won't? Why?"

"I don't have that power."

"Are you saying you're a fraud?"

"No."

The priest stood again. "If you're not a fraud and you can't give penance, then you must be the Devil."

"I didn't ask for this," Jakub said. "I've done nothing to deserve it."

Fr. Fredric bent down and touched his finger to the blood on the floor. He brought it to his lips. "I know blood," he said. "Only God and the Devil could spill so much of it and live."

Jakub looked at St. Jude in the candlelight.

"I want you out," the priest said. "Now, tonight."

"I can't move," Jakub said.

Fr. Fredric grabbed both arms of the chair. "Then I should drag you out of that chair and throw you down that hole."

"Get away from me," Jakub said.

Fr. Fredric stood up. He looked away. "You've tempted and humiliated me," the priest said. He walked over to the opening in the stone floor and slid back the rug.

"I told you I didn't ask for this," Jakub said.

"Quiet, Satan. Your voice offends."

The priest grasped the handle and pulled back on the round wooden door. He lifted it aside, exposing the hole and the ten-foot drop into the antechamber. Rung by rung he pulled up the rope ladder and set it aside. He walked back to Jakub and seized his leg and pulled. Jakub gripped both sides of the chair. Fr. Fredric muttered as he pulled Jakub and the chair toward the hole.

"Down to Hell, down to Hell, back where you belong."

Jakub tried to kick the priest off, but his feet were in too much pain.

"Shosha," he cried. "Shosha!"

The priest kept pulling.

"Rabbi!"

The ruckus woke several people. Candles and oil lamps cast shadows along the stone walls of the passage. Shosha appeared first at the entrance to the chapel. "What are you doing?" she said. "What's going on?"

The priest ignored her.

"He wants to throw me down that hole," Jakub said.

"What?" She grabbed Fr. Fredric's arm and tried to pull him off. He pushed her back. She stumbled into the rabbi, who steadied her then took hold of the priest.

"Stop it," the rabbi said. "Stop it now."

Two fighters came in and held the priest. The rabbi pried Fr. Fredric's fingers from around Jakub's legs.

"What's wrong with you?" the rabbi said.

"That." The priest pointed at Jakub.

"Jakub?" Shosha said. "What are you talking about?"

"I want it out of here," Fr. Fredric said.

"He'll leave when we leave," the rabbi said.

"It leaves now."

"Go back to your chamber," the rabbi said.

"Not before this defilement is gone."

"We can't leave now," the rabbi said.

The fighters restrained the priest and the rabbi leaned close to him. "This man is a friend," the rabbi said. "Do I tell Fr. Stan the war's made you a lunatic?" the rabbi asked.

"Don't insult me," Fr. Fredric said.

"You insult yourself," the rabbi said. "Go back to your room." The rabbi looked at the two fighters. They relinquished their grip.

"Clean my floor," the priest said. He pushed past the men and disappeared without a candle down the passage.

FATHER STANISLAW RETURNED FROM Praga to escort the rabbi's group across the Wisła. "Where is Fr. Fredric?" he asked the rabbi. No one knew, and no one said anything about the incident in the chapel.

"Did he give you your papers?" Fr. Stan asked.

"No—only clothes and food."

"They must be in the office." Fr. Stan returned shortly with a handful of envelopes with names on them. "Papers first," he said. "Please—everyone here."

The eight-person group lined up along the passageway wall. "Fr. Fredric put these together last night." Fr. Stan passed out envelopes to each person. "They appear in order, but please check them."

Those who couldn't read—or couldn't read well, including Jakub—opened the envelopes and glanced at the papers then put the packets into their shirts or coats.

"Now—let me see you all." Fr. Stan stepped back from the line. "You," he pointed to one of the fighters. "Shave, different hat. You—different shirt, this one stands out. Rabbi—no more beard."

"Shave my beard?"

"You have to look like average Poles."

"Who's knowing? We pay the gendarmes, we get down to the boat."

"No boat," Fr. Stan said. "I couldn't get a boat."

"Then how are we going?" Shosha asked.

"Tram—to Szeroka Street."

"That's crazy—we'll be spotted the minute we step on."

"Not if you pay attention," Fr. Stan told the rabbi. "Now go shave."

THE GROUP LOOKED SUFFICIENTLY drab and left the bunker for the tram station at the bridge to Praga about half a mile away. They were on foot and two men helped Rebekah.

"We're finally getting out of here," she said.

"Mama—you don't speak three words in a week and now you say this." Shosha said. "You've never wanted to leave."

"Lev knows where we're going," she told her daughter. "I just hope I make it."

"You'll make it," Shosha said. She turned to Jakub. "She'll make it, won't she?"

He nodded.

"See? He says you'll make it."

"Maybe he has connections we don't, eh?" Rebekah said.

The river and the bridge across it came into view. Fr. Stanislaw stopped them. "The tram is that way," he said. "Remember—average Poles. The more Poles they can get out of Warsaw without having to waste valuable camp space reserved for Jews, the better they like it."

They saw gendarmes, standing and talking. They saw average Poles with chickens in cages and fresh produce from G-d knew where. They saw women and men with sacks of potatoes and newspapers and an occasional cigar. One woman had a rooster in a crudely-fashioned cage.

The river breeze blew across their faces and swept smoke from the Ghetto to the sky. It rose and thinned over the river, resettling in an acrid haze over Praga on the other side. Shosha breathed the fresher air. She looked toward the sun, rising and orange in the haze. She turned again and saw Fr. Fredric. She felt sick. "Don't look," she whispered to Jakub. The cleric approached them.

"Fred—we were looking for you," Fr. Stanislaw said.

"I went for money," Fr. Fredric said. "In case we have to pay anyone." The rabbi looked at him. "I want to apologize." Fr. Fredric took Jakub's hand. He glanced at three gendarmes. "You must accept my apology," he said. "I misunderstood."

Jakub noticed the priest's hands were cold.

"Apology for what?" Fr. Stan said.

"An earlier misunderstanding," Fr. Fredric said. He withdrew his hands.

"Rabbi?"

"That's right," the rabbi told Fr. Stan. "A minor thing."

The tram was boarding now. "Well," Fr. Fredric said. "Goodbye and may the Lord bless and keep you." He looked at Nazi gendarmes walking toward the group. They pushed through the crowd and came to Jakub.

"*Jude,*" they said. "*Jude.*"

"What? This man is not a Jew," Fr. Stan said. "He's Catholic, from Marienburg."

"*Kennkarte.*"

The gendarmes opened the envelopes person-by-person. Jakub handed over his packet. A gendarme opened it, laughed, and held up the papers. Meaningless letters covered the pages. "Gibberish," he said and let the papers fall into the street. The other gendarmes seized Jakub.

"No," Shosha cried. The rabbi pushed toward her. "He's with us," she said. "He's not a Jew."

The rabbi grabbed her arm, but before he could speak, the gendarme was upon her.

"You know this man?"

The rabbi tightened his grip on Shosha's arm. He looked the gendarme in the eyes.

"I'm not with them," Jakub interrupted.

"What?" Shosha said.

"Shut up," the rabbi whispered to her.

"I'm not with them," Jakub said again.

"You're lying," the gendarme said. He looked at the rabbi and the priest. "You're sneaking this Jew across."

"For what purpose?" Father Stan said.

"What else?" the gendarme said. "Money."

The rabbi intervened. "He already told you—he's not with us."

"The Father said he was Catholic, from Marienburg," the gendarme said.

"I told them that just now," Jakub said. "Here in the line."

"That's not true," Shosha said. "Why are you lying?"

The gendarme turned to Jakub. "Are you lying?" he said.

"Tell them the truth," Shosha said.

"Well?" the gendarme asked Jakub.

"I told you twice. I'm not with them."

"No," Shosha screamed.

The rabbi pulled her close. "Shut up." he said.

"I think that settles it," the gendarme said. He took his sidearm from its holster and raised it to Jakub's head.

"No," Shosha cried again. She dropped. "No—please, you can't kill him. You can't." She grabbed the gendarme's legs.

"I don't understand," the gendarme said. "How can this woman care so much for a stranger?" The gendarme knelt down to Shosha. He took her face and held it up.

"Please don't kill him," she said.

The gendarme swept the hair from her face. He looked at her eyes, glistening and black. "God, you're beautiful," he said. He looked at his men, and the gawking crowd. "I suppose we'll have to sort this out," he said. He waved off his cohorts, who took Jakub by either arm and started leading him away. "The rest of you board the tram," the gendarme said.

"Where are you taking him?"

"Shosha," her mother said. "Keep quiet and get on."

"You can't take him." She ran toward Jakub. "You can't take him." She took hold of the first gendarme's arm.

"Let go of me," he said. "Let go." He raised his hand to her face but hesitated. The rabbi and Fr. Stan pulled her back.

"You," she cried, but the rabbi grabbed her mouth and the two men pulled her back and forced her into a doorway out of the crowd. They waited until the gendarmes were gone to let her speak.

"Get off me!" she said.

"Shosha, please," the rabbi said.

"After all he did for us, you turn him over to those jackals."

"He turned himself over," the rabbi said.

"They'll find out his true identity and let him go," Fr. Stan said. "He's not a Jew. He has nothing to worry about. Come with us, come aboard the tram."

"I'm going with him." She tried to get away but the two men held her.

"This is foolishness, woman," the rabbi said.

Shosha's face was flustered and heavy.

"You have a choice now. A choice," the rabbi said. "Follow him and die. Follow us, and you have a chance to live. When was the last time you had that kind of choice?"

"Shosha," Rebekah called. "We have to get on." A conductor herded people aboard the tram.

"Come with us," the rabbi said. "You can't find him anyway. Not now."

He brought his hand to her arm again. She shook it off.

"You," she said to the rabbi. "You enable them. You give them money and comfort. *Our enemy.*" She stood straight. "Don't touch me," she said.

She looked in the direction opposite the tram.

"If you don't get on, we carry you," the rabbi said. "Kicking and screaming if you wish."

"All aboard. All aboard now."

Shosha looked at the rabbi.

"Final call—all aboard."

She looked in the direction Jakub had taken.

"All aboard."

She heard her mother.

"Shosha."

She looked at the rabbi.

"Why do you care what I do?" Shosha said. "You're not family. Why do you care so much?"

She heard her mother again and saw her boarding the tram.

"Shosha—please."

Her shoulders slumped. The three of them walked together toward the tram.

SUBURB

Twenty Three

On October 6, 1939, the provocateur of the greatest war humankind has ever endured addressed his people in this way.

"It was a fateful hour" when on September 1, "I had to inform you of serious decisions, which had been forced upon us as a result of the intransigent and provocative action of a certain state."

"A state," the leader said, "of no less than thirty-six million inhabitants, with an army of almost fifty infantry and cavalry divisions." A state that "took up arms against us," with a "confidence in their ability to crush Germany" that "knew no bounds."

The leader told his people about his moral code on the battlefield.

"That the last remnants of the Polish Army were able to hold out in Warsaw, Modlin, and on Hela Peninsula until October 1 was not due to their prowess in arms, but only to our cool thinking and our sense of responsibility."

The leader told his people that he was merciful.

"I forbade the sacrifice of more human lives than was absolutely necessary."

He explained how the enemy tried his patience and tested his restraint.

"I still clung to the hope, misdirected though it was that the Polish side might for once be guided by responsible common sense instead of by irresponsible lunacy."

The leader insisted he was a compassionate man, even to his enemies.

"Sheer sympathy for women and children caused me to make an offer to those in command of Warsaw at least to let civilian inhabitants leave the city. I declared a temporary armistice and safeguards necessary for evacuation—"

But the lunacy of his enemies stood in the way.

"The proud Polish commander of the city did not even condescend to reply."

The leader persevered. "I extended the time limit and ordered bombers and heavy artillery to attack only military objectives, repeating my proposal in vain."

He even offered the enemy sanctuary. "I thereupon made an offer that the whole suburb of Praga would not be bombarded at all, but should be reserved for the civilian population in order to make it possible for them to take refuge there."

The enemy—such madness (the leader brought his fists together, over his heart and raised his closed eyes toward the sky)—such absolute madness—refused.

"Praga was bombarded very heavily," said Praga native Leah Hammerstein Silverstein. "My father had a brother living on the left side of the River Wisła. So, he collected us children and we ran from Praga to Warsaw, hoping that Warsaw is not bombarded so heavily as Praga is."

So like the enemy's lunacy and stubbornness—to flee their own sanctuary.

"The flight from Praga to Warsaw, you know, we had to cross the bridge, and the bridge was one of the main targets of these planes. You know, I don't have exactly the right words to describe the panic that existed among these running people. The screams and, you know, the cries of the children, the women, the, the, the, the terrible panic that seized the population. And, and the planes coming down on you. It was a miracle that we made it through that bridge, but we did. And we came to Warsaw, to my uncle."

So, was Warsaw, defiant Warsaw, fortress Warsaw still whole?

"Warsaw was even worse bombarded than Praga," Silverstein said. "For the first time in my life, I felt the smell of burning domiciles. This was the invitation to the terrible five years that came later on."

Having crushed the Polish threat, the leader explained his "aims."

"First, the creation of a Reich frontier.

"Second, the disposition of the entire living space according to the various nationalities; that is to say, the solution of the problems affecting the minorities.

"Third, in this connection: an attempt to reach a solution and settlement of the Jewish problem.

"Fourth, reconstruction of transport facilities and economic life in the interest of all those living in this area.

"Fifth, a guarantee for the security of this entire territory and sixth, formation of a Polish State so constituted and governed as to prevent its becoming once again either a hotbed of anti-German activity or a center of intrigue against Germany and Russia."

Then the leader told his people that "if Europe is really sincere in her desire for peace, the States in Europe ought to be grateful that Russia and Germany are prepared to transform this hotbed into a zone of peaceful development—" He reminded that "neither force of arms nor lapse of time will conquer Germany. There never will be another November 1918 in German history." He declared it "infantile to hope for the disintegration of our people," and warned "Mr. Churchill" about who might be the eventual victor. "I do not doubt for a single moment that Germany will be victorious. Destiny will decide who is right."

The leader concluded by raising his fists to his heart again and turning his eyes toward Heaven. "As *Führer* of the German people and Chancellor of the Reich, I can thank God at this moment that he has so wonderfully blessed us in our hard struggle for what is our right, and beg Him that we and all other nations may find the right way, so that not only the German people but all Europe may once more be granted the blessing of peace."

SHOSHA STOOD AT AN open door watching steam rise from a white clawfoot tub. Water—warm water and this much of it. She had not seen this much water in over two years and it was all hers. The steam from the tub looked like it was rising from a cloud. She closed the door and slipped off her robe. She tried not to look at her body, but she saw her face in the mirror. She turned away—she had not looked in a mirror for months and when she caught herself touching her cheeks or mouth she would stop and lower her hands. She placed her foot in the tub then pulled it out. She put her hand down and felt the water.

She put her foot back in. She watched it penetrate the surface and descend until it touched bottom. She put in her other foot. With both feet touching the white metal bottom, she brought herself around and bent down to sit, but it was hot and she stood instead. She stood and looked at her feet in the water and watched the steam rise around her. She brought her arms up to cover her ribs. She clasped her hands under her chin. She stared, down at her feet and the water. She closed her eyes. The rising steam warmed her and she felt sleep.

THE MORDECHAI'S "NEW" HOME, off Targowa Street in Praga, had two stories, three bedrooms, a kitchen, a bath, and a cramped sitting area off the front door. It was in a "good" neighborhood, close to the Wilenska Railway Directorate, near the park, zoo, and shops. When they first stepped across the threshold, Shosha sighed. Plaster lay crumbled on the floor;

paint peeled from the walls; rust ran from the taps; and an acrid odor of fuel and fire lingered. Rebekah was more sanguine as she went from room to room.

"We can fix this up. I'm sure Madame Krushenski's sons will help."

"You're in no shape to be renovating an old house," Shosha told her mother.

"But I will be," Rebekah said. "And so will you."

They rented the home with an option to buy it and with time, they started work—on themselves and the building. Both women gained weight. The walls gained plaster. The color returned to Rebekah's face. Shosha's bones receded and coloring returned to her cheeks. They painted the walls, inside and out. They painted rouge on their lips, laughed, and wiped it off. They brought things together.

Shosha looked better outside but felt worse inside. She took no pleasure in eating, a luxury long denied her. She ate so she would live to see her father. She worked on the house to please her mother. She slept more than usual. She thought about Jakub.

"I'VE TWISTED MY ANKLE." The rabbi stood rubbing his ankle at the door of the Mordechai home.

Shosha looked at him.

"May I?"

She stepped aside and he hobbled in.

The rabbi sat on a faded divan with fabric armrests worn to the wood. "Is your mama about?"

"No."

The rabbi waited. "Sleeping?" he asked.

"Mama—no."

"Shopping?"

"No."

"Well—how many guesses do I get?"

"She's at Madame Krushenski's."

"Everything all right?" he asked.

"Yes."

"Sure?"

Shosha looked at him.

"I know—it's a dumb question," he said.

"Have you heard from Jakub?" Shosha asked.

"I was going to ask you," the rabbi said. "I thought he might have written."

Shosha turned away and leaned against the wall. She shook her head. "What do you take me for?" she asked.

"What?"

She turned to Rabbi Gimelman. "You let the soldiers have him," she said. "Just when does he write?"

"To me or to you?" the rabbi said.

"To either of us."

"You asked me if I'd heard from him."

"You have your ways. You might have at least heard *about* him."

"No," the rabbi said.

"When do you think you will?"

"I told you—I explained that."

"You didn't explain anything," Shosha said.

"I did."

"Just like you explained Jerczek," she said.

The rabbi rubbed his ankle then sat back and looked up at her. "If I could stand up, I'd slap you."

"You'd slap me?" Shosha said. She walked to him and knelt down before him. "Then why don't you?"

The rabbi looked at her. "You want that we should sacrifice all of us—you, your mother, the good fathers, the fighters, me—for one man?"

"Good fathers?" Shosha stood up. "One of them was a lunatic."

The rabbi looked away.

"What do you know about sacrifice?" Shosha asked. "You've spent this war fed and fat."

"And keeping you alive."

"Well," Shosha said. "If this is life."

She went toward the stairs to the second floor.

"I made a choice," the rabbi said. "Whether you like it or not, this *is* life and I chose it for all of us."

Shosha turned to him. "Who asked you to make choices for us?"

The rabbi rubbed his ankle. "Whom do you think?" he said.

"Whatever debt you owed my father, you've long ago repaid."

The rabbi stopped rubbing and lowered his foot to the floor. "How do you know?" he said.

Shosha went up the stairs. Then she stopped. "What could you possibly owe him by now?" She walked the rest of the way and the rabbi heard the bedroom door close behind her.

WITH REST AND NOURISHMENT, Shosha was able to work and she did—as an assistant at a clinic on Grochowska Street run by Dr. Jablonski, who was active in the AK. He re-introduced her to the Underground and set her up with his AK cell. Each cell had five to eight members who knew one another, but only by aliases. Shosha became "Sheba," from Bathsheba, wife of David and mother of Solomon.

AK fighters took a Christian oath. "In the sight of Almighty God and the Holiest Virgin Mary, Queen of the Polish Crown, I place my hands on this Holy Cross, symbol of suffering and salvation, and swear that faithful and unbending, I will guard the honor of Poland. I will fight for its liberation from bondage with all my strength, including the sacrifice of my life. I will obey without question all orders of the Armia Krajowa and will preserve its secret come what may. So help me God."

For Shosha, the oath became, "In the sight of the Almighty L-rd, I place my hands on the hands of my fellows, and swear that, faithful and unbending, I will guard the honor of Poland. I will fight for her liberation from bondage with all my strength, including the sacrifice of my life. I will obey without question all orders of the Armia Krajowa and will preserve its secret come what may. So help me, G-d."

The month was September 1943, and preparations were under way for a general revolt that would involve not only the remaining Jews but all Warsaw. Handguns, bullets, newspapers, drawings, plans and maps circulated around Praga within and beneath loaves of a simple but delicious potato bread Shosha and Rebekah baked every few days. After making a large batch one afternoon, Rebekah leaned back from the cutting board. She placed her open hands in the small of her back and stretched backward and blew the hair from her eyes. She looked at her daughter.

"Look at us," Rebekah said. "We're a mess."

Shosha rolled a slab of dough.

"I heard you last night," Rebekah said.

"Heard me what?" Shosha said.

"Crying."

"I wasn't crying."

"I cry too. I cried last night, a little."

Shosha shaped three loaves and placed them on a tray.

"It's all right to cry," Rebekah said.

Shosha set the loaves into the warm oven. The heat poured over her face.

"I miss them, too," Rebekah said.

"Miss who?"

"Leiozia. Papa especially. Jakub."

"I wouldn't have guessed it," Shosha said. "You haven't let on."

Rebekah looked at her daughter. "I don't know how you can say that," she said. She took off her apron. "I talk about papa all the time."

"I wasn't speaking of papa," Shosha said. "Leiozia either."

Rebekah thought. "I miss Jakub as much as you do," she said.

"Really?" Shosha said.

She undid her apron, laid it aside, and walked past her mother on her way out.

Rebekah followed. "I don't like your disrespect," she said. "It's not fair, not to any of us."

"Tell that to Jakub," Shosha said. "Tell him about respect."

"He knew the risks," Rebekah said. "He stayed willingly. Rabbi told him to leave, begged him to leave. But he didn't."

Shosha looked at her mother. "You're right," she said. "He knew the risks. He wouldn't listen. He was well paid for his services." Shosha went out the front door, into the street. Her mother watched her pass the window.

Twenty Four

Word of plans for a revolt on the Aryan side of the Ghetto wall reached the enemy and by fall, the occupiers stepped up their attacks on the Polish population, with open-air executions on both sides of the Wisła. Hundreds of Poles, lined up and shot in Warsaw proper, at the Plac Teatralny; on Pius XI Street; and on the corner of Senatorska and Miodowa Streets. Gunfire and soldiers also provoked constant anxiety in Praga.

"I was out the other day walking when I heard shots around the corner," the rabbi told Shosha and her mother.

"You shouldn't be out," Rebekah said.

"I have to—just to get fresh air."

"They taking good care of you?" Rebekah asked.

The rabbi shrugged. "As good as can be expected."

Since their arrival in Praga, Rabbi Gimelman had become a scarce and mysterious character, moving from house to house and cellar to cellar with help from the AK. Everyone knew the enemy wanted him. The Ghetto had fallen like skin from bone, revealing the skeletal remains of the rabbi's network of financiers, informants, spies, suppliers, and functionaries. The razing of Sztuka was itself informative, like beheading a Medusa at the right spot and watching the Resistance crumble. The enemy considered Rabbi Gimelman a key "behind-the-scenes" player, an arranger of alliances with a sharp, pragmatic mind willing to resort to any strategy, creative or simple, planned or momentous, that circumvented death or trumped the other side. Rabbi Gimelman had become an elusive adversary the more thoughtful commanders regarded with the care of chess players.

He may have played the game with cold intent, but the rabbi was affected. He happened on scenes of heinous devastation, where the smell of rifles still lingered and blood ran in streams on the street. He prayed in quiet and often wept. Sometimes when he was alone, he started to pray and ended up raising his voice to G-d and asking over and over, "Why?" Lately, he spent entire days in bed, hearing shots and voices in the street, wallowing in darkness until night, then rising with pangs in his stomach. When he slept, it was only for a few hours and the deeper the sleep, the worse the awakening, the greater the panic, the more rapid his breathing and the wetter his perspiration-soaked clothes. He lost more weight in Praga than he had in the Ghetto. He kept his hair short and his beard shaved. Unlike his anxiety, he couldn't keep his thinning frame and sinking cheeks from the people who knew him.

"Rabbi worries me," Rebekah said to her daughter. "I've never seen him like this."

"He's feeling the weight," Shosha said. "Of all his choices."

TWO DAYS LATER THEY saw Rabbi Gimelman at an outdoor farmers market.

"We're walking to Jagiellonska later." Rebekah stood with a bag, from which peeked the top of a wreath made of sticks and fallen leaves. "Come with?" she asked the rabbi.

Rebekah and Shosha were going to pay respects at 36 Jagiellonska Street in Praga, where an earlier massacre had defied even the twisted logic of war. Thirty or so twenty-somethings gathered for a friend's wedding reception at the bride's third-story apartment. Someone informed the local *SS*. Large groups were *verboten*. Four *SS* officers showed up at the reception. The bride and her father answered the door of the apartment. The *SS* could see the people, dressed in tuxedos and fine clothes, standing inside and out on the balcony. Some stood in the hallway.

"You know this is not allowed," one of the men told the bride's father.

"It's only a wedding," he said. "My daughter was just married." He kissed her head.

The *SS* didn't know anything about the groom—that he was Christian, or his Germanic ancestry. They only saw people, drinking and celebrating.

"We have to come in," the uniformed men told the bride.

"What's wrong?" Her new husband stood at the door.

"These men say we can't have our friends here."

"Why?"

"It's a rule," one of the *SS* said.

"It's my wedding," the groom said. "See?" He flashed his lapel.

"That's not an issue."

"Then you're not invited," the groom said. He pushed past his wife and father-in-law and shut the door.

The *SS* shot the door and kicked it in. People screamed. The soldiers invaded the room and fired into the crowd. People fell and screamed and blood soaked white clothes.

Some people jumped off the balcony. The soldiers stormed the hallway and the bathroom and the bedrooms. They fired at everyone. When the room was clear, they went back to the door. One of the men saw a cushion moving on the couch. He walked to it and pulled it away. A four-year-old child peered up at him. The soldier shot the child and left the room with the other men.

REBEKAH, SHOSHA AND RABBI Gimelman stood outside the apartment a week later. Rebekah laid a wreath where others lay, with flowers and candles that burned with jittery flames. Women knelt and crossed themselves or clenched their fists and prayed. Men wept and children stood and looked, at places where blood stained the pavement under the balcony. Somewhere distant, the rabbi heard boots, motors, and the hum of war. He sidled up to Rebekah. She stood with Shosha and their heads were bowed.

"Listen," he said. He tugged on Shosha's arm. She turned and the rabbi whispered in nearby ears. "Soldiers," he said. "Pass it on and go—quickly."

They looked up the street. In one direction, the nearest cross street was far. Toward the other direction, they listened.

"That's where they are," Shosha said.

They crossed the street and walked away. They saw the mourners dispersing as the rabbi's refrain passed from person to person. They stepped into a hat shop and closed the double door as the first soldiers rounded the corner a ways off. Two cars followed the soldiers, who fired into the fractured crowd. Some people panicked and ran toward the soldiers and fell. Others ran toward shops and pushed past shopkeepers who hurried to lock their doors. Shosha watched people run up to the door of the hat shop. She went to open it and the hat maker grabbed her hand.

"You crazy?" he said. He pushed her back.

People fell in the street. The hat maker stayed low and crept from window to window pulling down the blinds.

"Shosha—get away from there," the rabbi said. "Stay down."

They heard shots and screams and feet, marching and running, fleeing and halting. They heard bodies crash against the door and hands and heads strike the glass. The shades over the windows were thin and the sun shone through them and they could see from the back of the shop blood running thinly down the leaden panes. The hat maker peered out the window at the soldiers.

"Sons a bitches," he said. He saw the rabbi whispering prayers on the other side of the room. "Where you from?" the hat maker asked.

"Targowa Street," Shosha said.

"I haven't seen you before," the hat maker said. "I know everyone there. You know Cetkowski?"

"No," Shosha said.

"Hmm. Well, I see you're saying your prayers. Say a few Hail Marys for me."

The shooting stopped but they still heard voices and cries, soldiers yelling, engines idling, and a sound that kept repeating, like latches locking or shutters closing. The sound came closer and they heard boots on the sidewalk. Latch—boots—latch—boots—latch—boots. The hat maker crept to another window and peered out.

"What are they doing?" Shosha asked.

"I can't tell," he said. Then the boots were in front of his shop.

The hat maker crouched. The others saw a shadow through the blinds and they heard hands fumbling with the doors. The bottom half of each door was solid but the top halves had three small windowpanes covered by a single blind. The person outside pushed and shook the doors, then called to someone up the street. He spoke German and his voice sounded young. More boots ran to the door and they saw another shadow and heard a second voice that was older. The older shadow stepped back and the butt of a rifle smashed the lowest pane in the first door, blowing the curtain forward and spitting glass on the floor. The rifle withdrew and smashed the bottom pane of the other door. They heard a third pair of boots and something metal hit the sidewalk. Gloved hands thrust a chain through the first broken window and looped it through the second. The chain pulled tight and they heard its links lock. The gloved hand pushed back the blind and a soldier peered in. The rabbi and the women saw the face of a boy but they were huddled far back in the shop where it was too dark for him to see them. The shadows withdrew. They heard rope scraping across wood and then they heard nothing.

Shosha stirred behind some boxes. "Are they gone?" she asked the hat maker. He didn't reply. "Are they gone?" Nothing. "Hey—you there?"

Shosha crouched and moved toward the front of the shop.

"What are you doing?" Rebekah asked.

"They're planning something bad," Shosha said. "We can't stay here."

"I'll look—you stay back," the rabbi said.

"I'm already here." Shosha lifted the curtain and looked out. She saw three bodies but no soldiers. She looked up the street as far as she could. She looked at the heavy locked chain that shackled the doors. The breeze stroked her cheek and the temperature was perfect. In a month of rain and clouds, this was a perfect day. "No soldiers." Shosha saw the hat maker from the corner of her eye. She crawled to him.

"Where's the shopkeeper?" Rebekah asked.

Shosha looked at the hat maker's open eyes. "Here," she said. She lifted his hand and felt his pulse.

"Is he hurt?"

"No," Shosha said.

"Is he shot?" the rabbi said.

Shosha took his chin and turned his head from side to side. She looked at his clothes. "Not that I can see," she said. "But he's not living."

"Oh," Rebekah said. "Poor man. We have to get home."

"We can't go out the front," Shosha said. "Not without breaking down the door."

"The windows are too small," the rabbi said. They were thick panes about six inches square, nine to a window, glazed into iron frames. The rabbi stretched his legs. He looked around the shop. "There's a door," he said. He crawled to it and turned the handle. "Not locked," he said. He opened the door and saw a staircase. "I'm going up."

"Are you sure?" Rebekah said. "Is it safe?"

They heard the rabbi climb the stairs and heard him walking around overhead. They heard him walk back and down the stairs.

"There's a balcony up here."

The women followed him upstairs to a room filled with boxes and hats. In another room where the hat maker lived alone, Shosha opened the door to the balcony.

"How do we get down?" Rebekah asked.

The rabbi found quilts but they were too thick to tie or wind.

"There are ropes out here," Shosha said.

They walked on to the balcony. Rebekah gasped and covered her mouth.

Hanging from the balconies of neighboring buildings, people swayed in a gentle wind. They hung from hands where necks were too slender or feet where arms were too weak. They were young men and boys, old women, girls, gray clothes, dark clothes, and clothes with colors that twirled like piñatas in the bright afternoon sun. The rabbi held Rebekah's hair and pressed her head under his chin. Shosha ran her hands through her own hair and looked up the street, at doors barricaded with ropes or chains. She reached across to the balcony on the building next-door and went across to a third building's balcony.

"I'll go first," she called back.

"What—go where?" the rabbi asked.

Shosha climbed over the balcony railings.

"You can't jump," the rabbi said. "You'll break your neck."

"I'm not jumping."

"What are you doing?" Rebekah said.

"Escaping."

"Shosha!"

Shosha looked at the ropes and slipped over to one on which a man hung from his ankles. He was young and she thought he would hold so she grabbed the rope and let her self down.

"Shosha—this is madness," the rabbi said.

Past the hemp, she wrapped her legs around the dead man's legs and hugged herself to his body. She felt him give but she was light and he did not give. She lowered her feet a meter or so above the street, positioned herself, looked down, gritted her teeth, closed her eyes, and let go. She dropped and hit the street, but before she could gather herself, she heard a whistle. She looked up and saw another man above a different gallows looking down at her. She stood and felt her ankle give. She limped to her feet and looked up at the rabbi and her mother.

"I'm all right," she said. "Mama next."

"I don't like this," the rabbi said. "It's completely disrespectful."

"You're the practical one," Shosha called back. She looked over to see the man on the other balcony descending the same way and more people coming out. "It's the only way," she said.

The man from the other balcony dropped to the street and joined Shosha. "Come on," he called to Rebekah. "I did it."

Rebekah looked over the railing. "I can't," she said. "I'd rather jump."

"You can't jump," the rabbi said.

"Then I'll die. I don't care."

The rabbi looked down and thought. "I'll go," he said.

Rebekah looked at him. "What about me?" she said.

"That's up to you," he said. "I figure if you see both of us made it, you'll come down the same way."

"What if you don't make it? What if the rope breaks? Or the body?"

"That could happen," the rabbi said, "but what's the alternative?"

"The doors?"

"None of us is strong enough to break them," the rabbi said.

The rabbi let Rebekah go and climbed the balcony railings to the third building.

"I don't want to be here alone," Rebekah said. She followed him, slowly and warily.

He reached for one of the ropes. Rebekah grabbed his arm as she topped the side railing. "No, no. I'll go. Let me go before you."

"Sure?" he asked.

"No, but what's the alternative?"

Rebekah went over the front railing. She climbed down the same rope Shosha used. "I hate this," she said. "I hate it."

The body gave. Rebekah stopped.

"Come on mama," Shosha called. "You can't stop now."

Rebekah froze.

"Lower your feet," said the man with Shosha. "Just a little more."

Soon there were other people in the street.

"Come on—you can do it," Rebekah heard.

"I did it, and I'm an old woman."

The body gave again and Rebekah started to drop. Shosha and two men reached up and took her feet and lowered her to the street. The rabbi prayed to himself as he descended a different gallows. Others reached up to help him and more people joined them in the street. Near the end of the rabbi's descent, the rope gave way and the body fell with him and just missed hitting him on the street.

"Oh, what have we done? What have we done?" the rabbi said.

Rebekah looked at him. "We've survived," she said.

Twenty Five

P ushed back by Soviet forces, the Germans retreated from the East and overwhelmed the streets of Warsaw. Cars and trucks congested narrow byways. Foot soldiers pushed wounded comrades in stolen farm carts. Deserters in mangy tattered uniforms drove plunder from surrounding villages—cows and goats, chickens and pigs. The chaos provided cover to AK and resistance operations, and made it easier to transport contraband.

On February 1, 1944, a 20 year-old AK scout, Lieutenant Bronek "Lot" Pietruszkiewicz, led an attack on Warsaw's *SS* commander, Franz Kutschera. This third attempt on Kutschera's life succeeded. The *Gestapo* arrested General "Grot" (Stefan Rowecki)—founder of the Armia Krajowa—in a Warsaw apartment after an AK reconnaissance officer betrayed him, then defected to the German side. The *Gestapo* took Grot to camp Sachsenhausen and murdered him there on Himmler's orders. General Tadeusz Bor-Komorowski took Grot's position as leader of the AK.

General Bor had heard of Shosha Mordechai's courage after the Jagiellonska Street massacre in Praga. In early May 1944, the Resistance assigned her a delivery—of false identification cards, maps, and messages—to a Polish family in Skierniewice, about seventy kilometers southwest of Warsaw. This family—

Warnickz, an old name in Polish industry—operated warehouses the Germans had appropriated. Family members stayed on to run the operations, siphoning off goods to resistance fighters around Warsaw. They used their influence and contacts to help people escape from trains going to the camps. They hid people in warehouses when supplies were low and they had extra room. They provided papers—proof of employment, identity, and passports.

"I don't want you to go—not at all," Rebekah told her daughter. "I don't know why you would ask me. You know how I feel."

"I'm asking you because if you really don't want me to go, I won't."

"Rabbi?"

"I'm staying out of this," the rabbi said.

"What would papa want?" Shosha asked.

"Papa would want you safe," Rebekah said. "He would say we've done our part."

"I don't believe that" Shosha said.

"Rabbi—you know Lev."

The rabbi looked at Rebekah. "Yes," he said.

"What would he say?"

The rabbi thought.

"Well?" Shosha said.

"What do you think he would say?"

With some food packed in a bag and her mother's reluctant blessing, Shosha used false identification to board the tram back to Warsaw and a train to Skierniewice, which she reached in the late afternoon. The Warnickzs warned her to be alert for gendarmes. She made her way to their house, where they received her warmly and invited her to stay the night.

THE SUN WOKE SHOSHA the next morning and she dressed and went into the family's courtyard in back of the house. The day was clear and blue and the nighttime chill was fading. No one else was up and Shosha stood with a mug of coffee in crisp, quiet solitude until she heard faint yelling and barking dogs. Gendarmes might be coming. If they saw her, they could arrest her and the family. The barking came closer. She heard familiar words.

"*Raus! Schnell! Banditen!*"

Her stomach tightened. She tossed the coffee. She looked through knot holes in a fence toward the street, where German soldiers were going house by house. She hurried out of the courtyard into the back alley where after walking a ways, she found a hole in a brick wall. She tucked herself into it. She heard footsteps and panting. She closed her eyes and her stomach seized. A dog stuck its snout in the shadows where she hid. Shosha opened her eyes and saw it—an enormous Alsatian on a leash.

"Man or woman?" she heard a voice say in Polish.

The dog breathed and drooled.

"Man or woman? Answer me or I'll shoot you."

Shosha hesitated. "Woman."

"Armed or unarmed?"

"Unarmed."

"Pole or Jew?"

She hesitated again.

"Pole or Jew?"

"Both," Shosha said.

She saw a large hand reach in and pull the dog back by its collar.

"Come out," she heard the voice say. Everything inside of her dropped. "Come out!"

She stuck her head out. She stood, bending down to massage a cramp under her thigh. The dog barked and jumped. She felt her knees shake. She saw the big hands holding the leash and her eyes traveled up a Reich uniform too large for its wearer. The soldier was a slender boy. He had big hands but without his gun, she felt sure she could take him.

"You're very pretty," he said. "Skinny, but pretty."

She felt sick but fought the feeling. To overpower this boy and escape, she had to stand firm and not faint. The boy relaxed the leash and the dog ran to Shosha and sniffed her. She stood, with her hands at her sides, squinting in the sun that peeked over the buildings. The dog licked her hand.

"He likes you," the boy said. "He doesn't usually. He doesn't like Polacks."

Shosha gathered her courage and knelt. The dog licked her cheek.

"He really likes you," the boy said.

"He's very friendly," Shosha said.

"Not to Polacks," the boy said.

Shosha looked at him. "Where did you learn to speak my language?" she asked.

"I grew up on the border," the boy said. "Near Kostrzyn."

"Oh," Shosha blurted. "I have an uncle in Debno and cousins around Sulecin."

"Really?" the boy said. He tugged at the dog. "You know Chesmykin?"

"The dairy?"

"Yes!"

Shosha cautiously stood. "My family knows them from way back."

"I used to work there," the boy said. "Before all this. My father was Chezzie's best friend."

"You have to be kidding," Shosha said. "Chezzie. I haven't seen him since I was a girl."

"I saw him at Christmas," the boy said.

"Is he still fat?"

"Not since Hitler," the boy said.

Shosha looked at him. He looked at his dog and then at her. He petted the dog and his hands shook. "I'm supposed to take you," he said. "Or shoot you."

Shosha felt a terrible, sinking hollowness in her gut, but she didn't flinch or tremble.

The boy tugged on the dog. "This dog," he said. The dog barked. He pulled it back. He looked at Shosha.

"You taking me?" she said. "Or shooting me."

The boy loosened the leash and the dog went to Shosha again. She stiffened.

"This dog," the boy said. "He's hungry."

The soldier pulled the dog away. He looked at Shosha, and she thought he looked at her for a long time. Then he turned away. "He's hungry," the boy said. He started up the street. "He gets cranky, like a baby."

Shosha was still until dog and soldier were far enough away. She stepped back, one step at a time. She thought if she turned and ran he might draw his sidearm and shoot her in the back. She stepped backwards until she came to a street. She kept her eyes on the boy then slid around a building, gathered her breath, looked around, and hurried out of sight.

Identified now, she couldn't return to the Warnickz house, not even to gather her things. If the boy happened to be around, to see her again, to see her with the family or in town with anyone else, he could make a lot of trouble, he could round them all up with his Nazi friends and have them deported to some camp. Or he could just shoot them. Shosha went to the train station and used her return ticket. She would tell the Warnickz what happened after her return, and the Underground would have to send someone else. She traveled back to Warsaw but without her papers, crossing the Wisła to Praga would have to wait.

CAMP

Twenty Six

J akub Chelzak spoke little during his interrogation and the
gendarmes determined that the circumstances surrounding
his activities in Warsaw were not clear. To clarify his
situation, they sent their reticent captive to a new resettlement
facility erected to finish emptying the country's Jewish ghettos.
During the journey, Jakub thought about his family and the
Mordechais, but tried to put them out of his mind. Whenever he
thought about Shosha, his stomach knotted. He considered
forcing himself out a window as the train drifted past empty
fields, then remembered the trains that crossed his own fields.
Besides, several armed German soldiers sat in the car ahead.

The train passed the village of Melinka, a clean hamlet
nestled in a picturesque valley called the Dolina Koscieliska in
the Tatra Mountains of southern Poland. The train slowed as it
approached the resettlement camp, named for the village. It
stopped near a row of wooden ramps. Jakub stepped off the car
with the rest of the "resettled." A letter regarding his
dispensation had not yet arrived, so the guards left him at the
ramps, where the camp's chief physician, Dr. Joachim Hehl, had

months ago instituted an orderly regimen. Two stocky women herded the groups into an open area.

"*Kleider ausziehen!*" they yelled.

People unbuttoned their shirts with shaky hands, slipped off their shoes and dropped skirts and trousers. Guards whipped the modest, or the slow, or the ones who stopped at their underwear. Jakub stood naked, no sign of his wounds. The women stopped barking while the newest doctor, Fiddler, wove through the group. His face was red and his nose speckled with petechiae and his breath smelled like old rum. He brought his thumb up and for each person he passed, he twisted his wrist, sometimes right—a soldier and a kapo pulled this person aside—sometimes left, lazily, with a drunken, disinterested gaze.

Doctor Fiddler came to an old man who could barely stand on his knotty legs. Fiddler looked at the kapo and turned his thumb to the right. "By truck," the doctor said. The kapo and a guard took the man's arms and he stumbled and muttered as they dragged him away.

Fiddler came to a boy. "Can you shine these?" the doctor asked, and looked at his dirty shoes.

"Oh yes," the boy said. "Oh yes! Those and a hundred more."

The doctor motioned the boy to fall in behind the kapo. They continued the awkward trek through the ranks and the kapo stood behind the doctor, motioning the new arrivals to keep their heads up, stand straight, chests out, shoulders high. Other uniformed women entered the crowd and gathered clothes and purses and wallets and watches that squatted at each person's side. The guards ordered the new arrivals to bend and lean. They took jewelry. They tore pierced ears if taking earrings took too long or the new arrival didn't bend low enough. The women rammed their fingers into mouths looking for fillings, and wrote on a clipboard for each gold tooth they found. They spread anuses with gloved fingers and looked up noses and in ears with lights and swabs and rough wooden probes. They watched the doctor, which way his thumb would turn—left for life, right for death.

Fiddler thinned the group by half with his languid hitchhiking. The selected ones formed two lines by two trucks marked with red crosses. Each truck filled with people, drove away, and returned for another load. An unselected woman became selected by asking, "Where are they taking them?" and receiving the polite and logical answer, "Why don't you find out?"

Fiddler came to Jakub. "What can you do?"

"I live in Marienburg," Jakub said in Polish. "I was sent here to get papers."

"Really?" Fiddler said. He understood barely a word. He turned his thumb to the right.

"But *Herr Doktor*," a kapo said. "This one looks strong."

"Fine," Fiddler said. The kapo waved off the guard approaching Jakub.

"You're being too conservative." Fiddler turned to the *Arbeitsführer*, a Reich Labor Service major walking toward them. "By the looks of the size of this crowd," the *Arbeitsführer* added.

Fiddler signaled a stout woman.

"Ausrichten," she yelled to the unselected group. *"Auf eine Linie bringen." Line up!* And keep order.

The women guards led the group to a row of outdoor showers. They turned on the water and pushed each person under it and held them there for exactly ninety seconds by stopwatch, per Dr. Hehl's written instructions. Next, they shaved every head, exposed every bump and scar. Women with long hair fought or wept. They beat the women who fought. To the women who wept, they handed their hair, in ironic piles. The other hair they carted to a repository at the northern end of the camp.

"Anordnung!" Order!

The women handed a standard uniform to each arrival—a thin shirt with a serial number sewn on the back, thin pants, a pair of wooden clogs—and led them to the blocks. Each block had an entry, washroom, and sleeping quarters. Two-tiered bunk beds three rows deep lined the sleeping quarters. The beds were narrow boxes filled with wood shavings and waste paper where inmates slept, four to a bunk with one blanket for two people. The women yanked the arrivals to their bunks.

"Achtung. Achtung!" The group stood at attention. Kapos passed out a paper to each person.

"Diese sind Ihre Aufgabenanweisungen," the lead woman yelled. *These are your duty assignments.* Serial number 166097 was assigned to the infirmary. This serial number belonged to Jakub Chelzak.

Twenty Seven

When Heinrich Himmler visited the Dolina Koscieliska, he saw the beating heart of *Lebensraum,* the "living space" Hitler ordained in *Mein Kampf* for his master race of blue-eyed Aryans. The Death Camps, the Polish *Blitzkrieg, Operation Barbarossa*—Germany's disastrous attack on the Soviet Union: all bricks on the road to *Lebensraum.*

Before Himmler, colorful travel guides attracted American tourists, calling the Dolina Koscieliska "Eden in Poland." At the urging of Karol Lutz, who described the valley and the village of Melinka as a "perfect little paradise," Scott and Zelda Fitzgerald visited and wrote bantering, chatty travel notes about sitting in the soft fall sun sipping cheap burgundy in their Sunday best. They positively charmed their Long Island readers.

"I think the spirits must pool crimson in her cheeks," Scott wrote of his wife. "The way she giggles while we toast the valley tempts me to make love to her right here, to hell with the villagers, to hell with the friars in their cassocks mouthing their beads."

"Zeldy, how do I describe this pretty morning?"

His wife was on the balcony of their room.

"These lovely mornings glisten in the dust," she said.

"What dust?"

"Who's been sneezing, goofo? Pollen. 'The early fall pollens that float in the dying circumstance of another drunken summer.'"

"Dying circumstance," Scott said. "Very good."

That afternoon, Scott finished his thoughts with a bourbon and a view of the valley in the late September sun. "These days make me feel all the man, the Adam," he wrote. "At my highest, I can't help but think it is here our damnation began."

FIFTEEN YEARS LATER, THIS arose in the valley: eight guard towers; rows of plain, wooden barracks; a triple layer barbed-wire fence; three brick buildings with chimneys; a large stone manse; a glass greenhouse; and ground cleared bare to dirt. In normal times, one to three trains a week passed through Melinka village. For construction of the resettlement facility, *Organisation Todt* needed seven: one train per day bringing trucks and tools, soldiers and slaves—Jews mostly, from Krakow, and homosexuals.

The manuals were explicit about which person was best suited to which job. The lowest Jews—the merchants, who would otherwise be sucking the economic blood of the German people—and the mentals—made the best diggers: ditches, latrines, graves. The mentals had to be controllable, no violent paranoids or Mongoloids who shit all the time. A large Jew mental with a strong, wide back: now there was one in great demand. You always found them in the holes. Jew lesbians made the best supervisors. Educated Jews who worked with figures could go two ways. If the figures had to do with the way the Earth moved around the sun or the grand design of God for the positions of the stars, the educated Jew worked on blueprints for barracks or showers and ramps. If the figures had to do with money, the educated Jew went into the holes. Young German recruits found the manuals—bound, printed on coarse paper, with no title or other marking on the cover—especially helpful for their black-and-white clarity.

"The Jew is the most versatile laborer," began the untitled chapter on the ethnicity, sexuality, and psychology of work. "The lesbians—Jew dykes in particular—are tough and angry and not afraid to use a whip, while the smallest Jew child can play the violin like a master." The chief value of a violin playing lovely music over a loudspeaker would "become apparent and obvious in due time," the manual informed.

This afternoon, waves of heat poured off the metal roofs of the barracks. Laborers with heavy gloves pounded nails and wrapped barbed wire around fence posts. The camp rose with prodded speed—"*Schnell! Schnell! Los! Los!*" The guards shot anyone who couldn't keep up. They met those who had kept up, but were now exhausted, on a case-by-case basis. I argued with my girl today, so I shoot you; I get transferred to the front next week, so I shoot you; Lieutenant von Kempt is watching, so I shoot you; the Commandant visits, so I let you live.

After a week of rain, workers finished the Melinka Resettlement Facility (MRF) enlisted men's club, a barracks with long tables and a rough pine floor. In a corner under dim lights one night, a sergeant was talking to a recruit who had lied about his age and enlisted at fifteen.

"You look a little wide-eyed to be a veteran," the sergeant said.

The boy looked at him. "*Herr Unterscharführer*?"

"No '*Herr Unterscharführer*' here. Just call me 'sir.'" The sergeant chuckled. "What's your name?"

"Johann Walkenburg."

"That sounds like a proper name. Good family." The sergeant sipped his beer. "How do you like it here?"

"I haven't thought about it," the boy said.

"Why not?"

"I don't understand it."

The sergeant lit a cigar. "What's not to understand?" He puffed. "We have a duty to perform. We perform it." He blew out his smoke. "When the duty gets a little hard, I just look at myself in the mirror and ask, 'What is better for the prisoner—whether he croaks in his own shit or goes to Heaven in a cloud of gas?'"

The sergeant laughed. He slipped his hand over Walkenburg's crotch. The boy jerked away.

"What are you doing?"

The sergeant blew smoke. "Enjoying the evening." He put his hand on the recruit's leg and squeezed.

"Go fuck yourself," Walkenburg said. He stood and walked away.

"I like to suck cock," the sergeant yelled after him. "Nice and hard—get it nice and hard for me tonight."

Walkenburg went outside. His face felt flushed. He looked at the men in the guard towers. Humid air shrouded the lights along the fence in haze.

SS-STURMBANNFÜHRER (**MAJOR**) Heinrich Petersdorf, MRF's second in command, crossed the grounds with *Wehrmacht Unterfeldwebel* (Sergeant) Schmidt, who had grown old without promotion.

"The trains arrive whether we're on schedule or not," Petersdorf said.

"The *Kommandant* and *Frau* Strauss—when do we expect them?"

"Don't know—they're in Austria on holiday."

"You served under the *Kommandant* before," Schmidt said.

"In Berlin."

"What's he like?"

"He delegates," Petersdorf said.

Oberleutnant (First Lieutenant) Klaus von Kempt, third in the camp's command chain outside the medical corps, tailed a labor squad that passed Petersdorf and the sergeant. Von Kempt did not salute.

"You let him walk by like that once and you've lost," Schmidt said.

"He limps," Petersdorf said.

"Yes, but he's a good German," Schmidt said.

"*Herr Oberleutnant,*" Petersdorf yelled.

Schmidt hurried to the lieutenant, stopped him, and pointed to the major. The two men walked back together.

"*Heil Hitler!*" Von Kempt saluted. Petersdorf returned the courtesy.

"I see you know how," Petersdorf said. "You're not *SS.*"

Von Kempt looked at the major. "No," he said.

Von Kempt was *Wehrmacht*, regular German army.

"Not out in the field?"

"Injury," von Kempt lied. The army had little use for a man born with a short leg who couldn't march. "What unfortunate circumstance brings *you* here, *Herr Sturmbannführer?*" von Kempt asked.

But Petersdorf and Schmidt walked away.

THEY DISEMBARKED AND STOOD, clean and well dressed: suits, hats, black shoes, ties, fashionable coats, gloves, purses, gold teeth and jewels. The new ramp smelled of fresh pine. The band on the platform played a polka. The man walking in front of them was a doctor. The man next to him wore a well-tailored suit. There were no soldiers, only uniformed kapos attired like bellmen in the better hotels. Dr. Fiddler took a flask from the knee-deep pocket of his white coat and turned away.

"You have to start so early?" said the man in the suit, the *Arbeitsführer*.

"Try doing this shit sober."

The *Arbeitsführer* waved his hand. The band stopped playing. He stepped on the platform. He smiled and looked at the line of railcars idling behind the crowd.

"Everyone—everyone please should be smiling," he said into a megaphone. "We are at the dawn of an important era in Europe and it is my pleasure to welcome you to an important part of that era—the Melinka Resettlement Facility."

Gray trucks marked with red crosses crept up and parked.

"We welcome you here with our warmest regards," the *Arbeitsführer* said.

Fiddler took another swig and scratched the side of his unshaven face with the flask. A hum of uncertainty drifted across the crowd.

"Warmest regards—hah!" an older man said. "I've heard people are killed in places like this."

"Killed?"

"Yes. Killed. Murdered! By poison."

"By accident?"

"Shhh." This from a tiny woman grasping a doll.

"As many of you know, Melinka is a *temporary* relocation center," the *Arbeitsführer* said. "A place for you and your families to live with warm food and a nice bed while our troops rout the Communist forces, who are attacking under the orders of Stalin, a monster who has murdered thousands of his own people."

"Can you believe this?" Fiddler whispered to himself.

"At this very moment, our *Führer* is deciding what best to do with you—where, that is, he would like to relocate you—so that you are out of the way of the Communist advance and the suffering it will inflict upon innocent people."

"If the *Führer* needs soldiers, why not us?" a man yelled from the crowd. "There are plenty of young men here."

The hum rose again.

"Is it true what I've heard?" a woman spoke up. "That people are murdered in a place like this?"

The *Arbeitsführer* motioned guards into the crowd. "Are there any questions?" he asked through the megaphone.

"Is that true?" said another woman. "Is that true?"

The hum intensified.

"Is it true what she said? That people die here?"

The hum roared.

"*Sehr gut.*" The *Arbeitsführer* passed Dr. Fiddler. "Begin."

"Shit." Fiddler took a swig. The *Arbeitsführer* motioned to the band. A tuba bellowed and the doctor walked up the wooden stairs to the platform. The *Arbeitsführer* grabbed his arm. "Remember—save the best-looking ones for tonight."

"Who among you is sick?" Fiddler droned. Several stepped forward, some young, some old. "Is that all? We are offering treatment." A few more stepped out. "Yes—that's better. Step up." He raised his finger. "You," he pointed. "You by truck. You—you walk. You—by truck. You, you, you—walk. You," he paused. "You stay."

"But my hand—my hand is infected," said the one who would stay, holding it up for the doctor.

"Hmm," Fiddler said. He held out his hand to a kapo, who passed a syringe, needle, and rubber-stoppered bottle. The doctor stuck the needle in the bottle and drew up a clear liquid.

"An injection?" said the one who would stay.

Fiddler squirted it through the needle. "Antibiotic," he said. He thrust the needle into the woman's heart and plunged the syringe. Her eyes widened. Fiddler pushed her off the needle into the arms of a soldier, who dragged her toward a red cross van.

RUDOLF HÖSS COMMANDED THE Auschwitz-Birkenau death camp for most of its existence.

"The mass extermination, with all its attendant circumstances, did not, as I know, fail to affect those who took part in it," he wrote in his autobiography. "With very few exceptions, nearly all those detailed to do this monstrous 'work,' and who, like myself, have given sufficient thought to the matter, have been deeply marked by these events.

"Many of the men involved approached me as I went my rounds through the extermination buildings, and poured out their anxieties and impressions to me, in the hope that I could allay them.

"Again and again during these confidential conversations I was asked: Is it necessary that we do this? Is it necessary that hundreds of thousands of women and children be destroyed? And I, who in my innermost being had on countless occasions asked myself exactly this question, could only fob them off and attempt to console them by repeating that it was done on Hitler's order. I had to tell them that this extermination of Jews had to be, so that Germany and our posterity might be freed forever from their relentless adversaries.

"There was no doubt in the mind of any of us that Hitler's order had to be obeyed regardless, and that it was the duty of the SS to carry it out. Nevertheless, we were all tormented by secret doubts."

Himmler also understood the difficult but essential task ahead, as he explained to the *SS-Leibstandarte* Adolf Hitler Regiment.

"Gentlemen, it is much easier in many cases to go into combat with a company than to suppress an obstructive population of low cultural level, or to carry out executions or to haul away people or to evict crying and hysterical women."

Major Petersdorf was dealing with such issues in the Commandant's office.

"I can't permit you to take leave from selections duty tonight," he told Dr. Fiddler. "We don't have the personnel."

"Three times last week and four times this week," Fiddler said. "I'm drinking too much and having too many nightmares. Let Hehl do it."

"I don't have time to reassign anyone," Petersdorf said.

"Problems?" The camp's Commandant, Franz Strauss, walked in. Petersdorf stiffened. Fiddler slouched.

"*Heil Hitler*," Strauss said. He took Petersdorf's hand. "Good to see you, Heinrich."

"*Danke*. Same, *Kommandant*."

"Franz. You know that." Strauss picked up some papers on his desk. "But as I was asking, problems?" he said.

"One of our men—a corporal, apparently—at least, as best we can tell—"

"He's suffering from ramp-duty hysteria." Fiddler jumped in. "Like I will be if I don't get some leave."

"Ramp-duty hysteria." Strauss didn't look up from the papers. "What's being done about it?"

"The corporal is in the infirmary," Petersdorf said.

"The infirmary? Is he infirm?"

"He tried to take his own life," Petersdorf said.

"We need more doctors, *Herr Kommandant*," Fiddler said. "The Third Reich can't expect men trained to heal to soil their hands killing more than a few times a month."

"Certainly not," Strauss said.

A group of prisoners carried in a large painting.

"Franny?" Greta Strauss, his wife, called from the other room.

"Here."

"Franny."

"Here," Strauss called back. "For god's sake—deaf at twenty six. Excuse me." He walked past Fiddler and Petersdorf and pushed through the cluttered house, through the flowers—acres of flowers—and paintings, and furnishings heaped, and piles of boxes.

He found his wife directing a piano.

"Is this all right?" she asked.

"Fine," he said.

She smiled and motioned the men to set the piano down.

Strauss kissed her cheek. "We are going out my dear—the major and I," he said.

"Don't step in any shit," she said.

STRAUSS WALKED WITH PETERSDORF around the Commandant's greenhouse.

"They are the hardest in the world, the cruelest, the most predatory, and the most attractive, and their men have softened or gone to pieces nervously as they have hardened," Strauss said.

"I've read that somewhere," Petersdorf said.

"I always forget what Gretty can be like when we've been separated."

They looked up at three prisoners and two guards installing a large pane of glass near the angled top of the east wing of the greenhouse.

"How is morale?" Strauss asked.

"Morale?" Petersdorf asked. He looked down.

"You have to think about it?" Strauss said.

"Morale is—so-so. We can't expect happiness."

"No," Strauss said. "Sadness is a part of war."

"No one is particularly sad."

"You're baiting me," Strauss said. "Not happy, not sad. Which is it?"

Petersdorf thought. But before he could answer, they heard yelling from the greenhouse. They looked up as the glass slipped and crashed.

"IS HE THE ENEMY?" Major Petersdorf read a letter that asked this question.

The mail arrived late in his office. A young private, Höfstaller, sorted it and opened anything not marked "personal" or "private." He set the letter on the major's desk and returned to his own desk in the front reception area.

1943/6/22

Forward Command
Warsaw District
Office of Logistics
Division of Inquiry

Kommandant
Melinka Resettlement Facility
Melinka, Poland

We have forwarded to your charge a man who claims to go by the name Jakub Chelzak. He was discovered attempting to board a tram to the district of Praga with falsified papers and no identity card. We are uncertain as to the nature of his business in Warsaw or how long he was in the area.

As you may be aware, resistance and treason here have cost the lives of many heroic German soldiers in recent months. For this reason, we ask that you investigate this man's claims and any potential involvement he may have had with any resistance groups.

You are under orders to forward any information you may learn to this office.

Heil Hitler!
Beruge Stain
Chief

"*Schütze!*" Petersdorf called.

Hofstaller returned. "Ja, *Herr Sturmbannführer?*"

"Why us?" Petersdorf flipped the letter around.

"*Herr Sturmbannführer?*"

"I don't understand what they expect us to do. About this man Chelzak. Ask them, please."

TALL PLANTS WITH BROAD leaves blocked all but a few rays of the morning light. Strauss leaned back in his office chair, a handsome leather piece Gretty brought from Vienna. He picked up a microphone on his desk. He pressed a switch on a voice recorder. A reel-to-reel tape turned.

"*Guten tag. Guten morgan. Auf wiedersehn.*"

He played back the recording. The voice he heard grated. He brought the microphone to his mouth. "Dearest Gretty: I am trying something diff—"

The machine stopped. Strauss tapped it. Nothing. He switched it off and turned the reel. He switched it back on and watched the reel turn, then stop. He switched it off, threaded the tape, and switched it on again. He watched the reel turn and leaned back with the microphone.

"I'm trying something different I hope you will like. This is a voice recorder used by the *Luftwaffe*. It's called a magnetophon. It's the very latest. Farben makes it and we swung it with a large order. You won't believe how music sounds on it. You can take the reel to Ribaldi's, the shop in the square. There's a fat Italian man there who can play it for you."

Strauss heard a motor outside and stopped the tape. A road went past his house around an electrified fence that created a perimeter like a moat. He waited for the muffled noise to pass and clicked on the tape again.

"I can't talk long. I am sorry about our argument before you left for Vienna. I was wrong. You were right to be angry. It's only that I didn't choose this and I miss you terribly and I wish you could bring yourself to overlook these temporary circumstances and be at my side. But I do understand—Vienna is Heaven by comparison."

Strauss heard the train now. The whistle, the grinding metal on the track.

"I bought a new whisk broom today, and a scrub brush for the toilet—the gypsy girl who cleans was complaining and a traveling salesman visits the camp every few weeks."

Strauss paused when he heard another motor. He stopped the tape. He listened to gears grind as a truck mounted a shallow hill past the metal moat. He heard men bleating and carping, the motor growling and fighting. Strauss put down the microphone and stood and turned to the window. He spread the plant's leaves apart. He saw a flat bed truck staked on its sides piled high with white naked bodies. He saw guards yelling at kapos and the driver waving his arms from the cab window. He watched the driver floor the pedal and the engine scream and the truck lurch forward, then stop. He watched the guard order the driver, Number 108679, out of the cab. The driver stepped down and stood. The guard yelled and un-strapped his sidearm. The driver saw the gun and dropped to his knees. The guard pointed to the engine with the gun. He pointed to the cab with the gun. Strauss let the leaves close. He went back to the microphone and started recording again. He heard a sidearm's sudden clap and a familiar soaring echo.

Twenty Eight

I n 1066 at Hastings, England, William of Normandy murdered Harold, son of Godwin, the earl of Wessex. Crowned King of the English by a saint—the dying and pious King Edward the Confessor—William the Norman became William the First, King and Conqueror, who terrorized his subjects into submission and imposed the Norman feudalism that had its origins two hundred years earlier, in the harsh governance of the Vikings.

In 1067, an outpost on the road from Kiev to Polotsk in Belarus became a town called *Menesk*, likely named for a heroic giant who used his superhuman strength to repel invaders. War and ruin were woven into the town's subconscious fabric. The unknown author of the Russian epic, The Lay of Igor's Host, described a battle in 1067 on the banks of the Nemiga River as "a vicious and senseless massacre after which Menesk was destroyed, its men murdered, and its women and children enslaved." Like the Jewish Golem, the legend of the hero Menesk comforted the psyche of an exhausted and embittered people.

The conquering hordes brought a babble of languages that turned Menesk into Minsk. By the end of the 15th century, Minsk became a craft and trade hub that joined Poland as one of the largest Jewish centers of Eastern Europe. Two centuries later, Minsk passed to Russia in the second partition of Poland. The

Nazi invasion drove a third partition of Poland that delivered Minsk into German hands.

On July 3, 1941, Minsk became the administrative center of *Reichskommissariat Ostland. Generalreichskommissar* Wilhelm Kube ruled the German-occupied Baltic States (Estonia, Latvia and Lithuania), Belarus, and eastern Poland. *Operation Barbarossa* dismantled a Jewish community that comprised almost forty percent of the city's population. The rape of Minsk was complete with the creation of a Jewish ghetto that with one hundred thousand persons rivaled any in Europe.

SS-Obersturmbannführer Franz Strauss was transferred from Berlin to Minsk on July 4, 1941—the day after Germany took formal control of the city. He arrived to oversee the removal of the largest art collection in Eastern Europe.

"I find it ironic that we have invaded and conquered this city, which found its existence in the first year after the Norman Conquest at Hastings," Strauss wrote to his wife Greta. "Himmler, after all, considers himself a direct descendant of the original Norsemen."

The sun was bright and bare on Rakovskaya Street, where Strauss sat on the steps of a cathedral while his men gathered and mulled before roll call and inspection and the daily duty assignment. He opened a notebook and drew a pierced heart in the Russian Orthodox style. He daydreamed. London, London, oh London—how wonderful she was in the summer, and how he missed her. He met his wife there, fell in love there, and became a scholar in an enclave of learning under melancholy skies that settled his soul. He set aside his daydream and wrote in script *My Separation* and in flowing longhand, started the letter.

"Gretty, I am charged for the next weeks with reopening the Cathedral of St. Peter and Paul. Himmler insists it be reopened because the Bolsheviks closed it in 1917."

A bona fide member of the *Schutzstaffel*, Strauss was careful and thankful—all he did was inspect museums and synagogues while grunts loaded paintings and statues into gray trucks. When he felt like it, Strauss decided which art stayed and which art—always the worst examples of a particular form—would be relocated for the pleasure of *Reichsführer* Himmler or Field Marshal Goering. He made these decisions on days that were too muggy to stand in the sun, or too soggy to stand in the rain.

"You're a goddamn luckful bastard." A shadow engulfed Strauss. He looked up at the eclipsing form—Wölke, a giant with a crooked face and perfect teeth. "Himmler's having lunch with you."

"Dear God."

"What's Dear God? He likes you."

Wölke slipped his fingers together and cracked his knuckles. The pop was loud and Strauss looked at the giant's hands, thick and doughy like his face, almost leprous, as though he were stuck together hastily with the clay left over at the end of a batch —not enough for two men, but too much for just one. Wölke was born in Munich and raised in the Bronx. When their good German son was offered the part of Golem in a school play, Wölke's parents took it as a sign that their gilded age was over and left the States a few months before the October crash of 1929. They settled in Berlin. Now, Wölke was Himmler's security chief in Minsk. Himmler's entourage had been "in country" for a week but no one else had seen the *Reichsführer*.

"I'm not ready." Strauss stood and emerged from the giant's shadow. Wölke looked at the cathedral. The sun peered over the spires.

"It won't be bad. He just wants you to tell him about this place." Wölke said.

"It puts a new wrinkle in my misery." Strauss walked toward the front steps of the cathedral. "When do I meet him? Where?"

"The hotel. He always eats right at eleven," Wölke said. "You've never met him?"

"Why would I meet him? He doesn't have time for people like me."

"He not only has time for people like you—he has plans for people like you."

ATTENTION TO THE MINUTIAE of history had elevated the great nephew of the famous waltz king, Johann Baptist Strauss the Younger, to a position of esteem in Heinrich Himmler's court. Himmler became enamored of Franz Baptist Strauss and his pedigree: an Oxford-educated historian who resembled his Austrian uncle in his love of music and his serious features. He did not, however, wear a mustache. Strauss was one of only three Austrians at Oxford during a time of tension between the U.K.

and Germanic civilization. But he fit in, partly because he laughed at the follies of the "dumb gangsters" who had overrun the German Motherland since the Beer Hall Putsch and Hitler's twisted creep onto the world stage.

Strauss' post-doctoral career began with a spurious bet: Would he or would he not publish a faux treatise entitled *Juden Nibelungen: Teutonic Myth and Modern Judaism in the Last Reich*. Strauss had no money to pay a lost bet to his post-doc friends, nor they to him. So they made the amount uncollectable: a million pounds sterling if the editors at the Journal of Germanic History or the Journal of the Society of Contemporary German Historians accepted his paper, an examination, Strauss wrote, of the "historo-psychological" roots of anti-Semitism in 20th century Germany. The abstract described this high-brow joke on the academic establishment as a "substantive" comparison of Jews to the Nibelungen, a race of evil dwarves that dwelled in Nibelheim, a dark, mythological place immortalized by the subject of Strauss' doctoral thesis, German composer Richard Wagner.

Contemporary Jews, Strauss' fake theory asserted, descended from the Old Testament's King Solomon, from whom they inherited their great wealth. "The king made silver as common in Jerusalem as stones, and cedar as plentiful as sycamore-fig trees in the foothills." (I Kings 10:27)

Likewise, the Nibelungen descended from another legendary king, the Scandinavian Nibelung, who, like Solomon, amassed an enormous treasury of gold, silver, diamonds, and jewels called the "Nibelung Hord." Nibelungen legend said "twelve wagons at the rate of three journeys a day could not carry the treasure off in twelve days."

Strauss made academic-sounding comparisons between Jews and Nibelungs. Buried in the subconscious German mind, he proclaimed, was the idea that present-day Jewish wealth resembled the ancient Nibelung hoard. He wrote that the God of the Israelites commanded Solomon to build a palatial temple in his honor. "Solomon selected seventy thousand men to bear burdens, eighty thousand to quarry stone in the mountains, and three thousand six hundred to oversee the labor," Strauss quoted from the Old Testament. "Solomon overlaid the inside of the house with pure gold, and he drew chains of gold across, in front of the inner sanctuary, and overlaid it with gold. And he overlaid the whole house with gold, until all the house was finished. Also the whole altar that belonged to the inner sanctuary he overlaid with gold."

Likewise, Odin, a God of Nibelungen, commanded the giants Fafnir and Fasolt to build Valhalla, the great hall of the Norse Gods, where golden battle shields adorned the roof.

Greed destroyed King Solomon and King Nibelung. The German warrior Siegfried stole King Nibelung's treasure while the maidens of the Rhine distracted him. Solomon's seven hundred wives and three hundred concubines similarly distracted him, despite this warning in Deuteronomy 17:16-20: "The king...must not take many wives, or his heart will be led astray. He must not accumulate large amounts of silver and gold."

"As Solomon grew old," Strauss quoted, "his wives turned his heart after other gods, and his heart was not fully devoted to the Lord his God, as the heart of David his father had been." (I Kings 11:3-4)

Strauss compared the Old Testament Song of Solomon to the Nibelungenlied—the Song of the Nibelungen—a Middle High German epic by an early 13th-century German poet that tells of the Diaspora of the Nibelung and the slaughter that follows, all inspired by the German warrior Siegfried.

"The *Song of Solomon* and the *Nibelungenlied* are both songs of love—one brutal, one poetic," Strauss wrote. "Their protagonists have the stature of myth—Solomon, David, and Bathsheba; Nibelung, Siegfried, and Brunhild. Each describes a compelling symbol of Diaspora: the loss of a great treasure. Both are stories of synthesis and antithesis—destruction and reconstruction, marathon acquisition and devastating loss."

Wagner, Strauss wrote, "immortalized the fall of the house of Nibelung with *Der Ring des Nibelungen*—the four operas *Das Rheingold*, *Die Walküre*, *Siegfried*, and *Götterdämmerung*—the Twilight of the Gods."

Likewise, "the authors of the Old Testament immortalized the fall of the house of Solomon in the *Book of Kings*. The two epics represent a cross-cultural continuum, a collective subconscious that repeats an essential legend at various historical intervals."

Both journals accepted the paper, leaving Strauss in an embarrassing predicament. He had violated an academic taboo —simultaneous submission of a paper to two or more publications. He had to choose, and in so doing, harm his reputation among journal editors. He chose the more prestigious Journal of the Society of Contemporary German Historians.

After the paper appeared, several European newspapers interviewed him about his "keen insights into history and myth." The Chronicle of London called the work a "groundbreaking analysis of the roots of German anti-Semitism, as recounted in legend. Dr. Strauss' comparison of the Nibelungs and the Jews— the first, a race of dark dwarves and the second, a race similarly caricatured by anti-Semites—posits a subconscious trail that may have led peoples of Teutonic ancestry to their current predicament."

That the paper was published surprised Strauss. That it received any attention beyond the dusty shelves of academe encouraged him to pursue a more serious approach to a similar topic—one that had fascinated him from his first days in Gymnasium: Richard Wagner, a study, Strauss wrote, "in beauty and ugliness of sweeping dimension."

Three years later, Strauss adapted his doctoral thesis into a seven hundred-page history of the legendary operatic genius, for which the media bestowed upon him the title "Wagnerian Scholar." *Wagner: Myth and Man* was the only book Adolf Hitler ever referenced by name in a speech, which brought reviews from the New York Times and every newspaper William

Randolph Hearst published. The Wagner biography became a worldwide sensation because influential pundits repeated a ridiculous thing about it: the book "shed light on the mind of the *Führer*." Hitler considered this "insight" a great international compliment, though he never read more than excerpts from the book.

In an interview with the St. Louis Post-Dispatch, General Patton said he had read *Wagner: Myth and Man* and agreed that the two men shared a personality trait. "Wagner was a terrible businessman. So is Hitler. That penny-comb mustachioed gas bag would be bankrupt by now if he wasn't stealing from the Jews."

Strauss considered his biography a scholarly study few people outside academe would ever read. When the book became a popular success, Strauss went along with "the biggest joke of these idiots' careers and the biggest boon to mine," though he kept his cynicism between friends.

As a citizen of a land conquered by thieves, Strauss was conscripted into an endeavor he labeled "heinously drafted and hopelessly doomed." He had thought about coming to America or trying to disappear, but notoriety coupled with modest means made such choices difficult. Despite his book's bestseller status, academic publishing contracts didn't yield high royalties. Strauss returned to Germany hoping for a desk job where he could wait out the war in relative peace. His low-level fame did afford him a choice: battle or support. He considered support opportunities in every branch: the *Luftwaffe*; the *Wehrmacht*; the *Waffen-SS*.

He selected a division of the *SS*—the *RSHA* or *Reichssicherheitshauptamt*. In 1939, Himmler merged the Nazi secret police—the *Gestapo*—and the Reich's central intelligence office—the *Sicherheitsdienst* or *SD*—into the *RSHA*.

Strauss requested and received assignment to *RSHA Amter* III or Department Three, which replaced the old section C of the *SD*. Section C had been divided into three subsections, each of which appealed to Strauss:

C2—Educational and religious life

C3—Folk culture and art

C4—Press, literature, and radio

Section C's new incarnation—*Amter III*—took charge of cultural matters in German occupied territories. The RSHA gave Strauss the unusually high rank of *Obersturmbannführer*, or lieutenant colonel, and shipped him to Minsk.

THE BALCONY OF THE Hotel Svisloch overlooked a green field that sloped toward the Svisloch River, where a mist hovered white in the early morning and cleared by noon. Strauss heard jackboots clicking in reserved haste on the tile floor beyond the balcony entrance and he stood when the four-man front team walked in, Wölke at the rear. Himmler came a few paces back and alone. Strauss felt unsteady.

"*Herr Reichsführer*," he said.

"*Herr* Strauss."

324   The Fires of Lilliput

Himmler slipped his gloved fingers into Strauss' waiting palm and grasped his shoulder.

"It does me good to finally, at last, meet you." Himmler watched Strauss as the two men sat. There were no others in the room. The security men watched the fields and the river from every side of the balcony.

"This cathedral we are renovating." Himmler leaned forward. "Are we engaged in a fool's errand?"

"Not at all, *Reichsführer*."

"What can you tell me about it?"

"*Reichsführer*, they call it the 'yellow church.'"

"The yellow church?"

"Yes. I don't know why. I'm looking into that."

Himmler raised his hand and rubbed a small scab on the underside of his left cheek. Strauss saw the glove in the warm room. He caught a sweet and pungent smell—perfume over body odor, maybe.

"And?" Himmler asked.

"And—it was built in 1613," Strauss said. "It's the oldest church in Minsk. Cossacks looted it in 1707."

"Cossacks? Under whose orders?"

"Peter the Great."

"Oh!" Himmler nodded.

"I won't know much more until we start cataloging."

Himmler settled back. Strauss saw perspiration around his forehead.

"I read your book," Himmler said.

"You did, *Herr Reichsführer*?"

"You know I did. In fact, you've given me two of the best reads I've ever had."

"I'm faltered—flattered, *Reichsführer*," Strauss said. "What, pray tell, was the other?"

"The other what?"

"The other read, sir. You said two—two reads."

"The thing about the Jews and the little people—the Nibblers."

"Oh, oh—you mean Nibelung. Juden Nib-ay-lung."

"I love that fucking name. Did you make it up?"

"Oh no—no, the Nibelung are real, at least in legend."

"It's brilliant to hear that," Himmler said. "You've helped me put some things in perspective."

"May I ask how? You've piqued me, *Reichsführer*."

An old woman set tea and bread with cheese before them on a tarnished silver tray.

"Tea. It's hot for tea," Himmler said. He leaned back suggestively. Wölke appeared noiselessly. He slipped off the *Reichsführer's* jacket. Perspiration pasted Himmler's long-sleeved shirt to his chest and underarms. He tugged the front and peeled it forward and the shirt burped and billowed.

"We have in our midst the Nibelungen," Himmler said. "Juden Nibelungen. That's what I mean."

"Ah," Strauss said.

"I am Siegfried. And so are you. And you. And you." Himmler pointed to his guards. "We are all Siegfried, in the end."

Strauss tried to smile. He raised a cup to his lips. Himmler took off a glove. He leaned forward and pursed his eyes.

"You," he said to Strauss "fascinate me." He encircled Strauss' fingers and the teacup in his soft, white hand.

"You flatter again, *Reichsführer*," Strauss said. "But I think I see—isn't your daughter called Gudrun?"

Himmler withdrew his hand. He looked around at his men. Wölke walked over and took up the jacket. The men moved to new positions near the double glass doors that opened onto the balcony. Himmler went to stand and Wölke motioned with his eyes to Strauss, who stood first.

"Time to relax," Himmler said. "I have a diversion—perhaps you can join us."

Wölke made with his eyes again.

"Certainly, *Reichsführer*," Strauss said. The sweet and sour smell wafted over him—he thought of something dead covered up. "When and where? I mean, should I arrive."

"Well—you've already arrived it seems," Himmler said.

"No, I mean—*Herr Reichsführer*—for the diversion," Strauss said.

"Yes, the diversion. The diversion."

Wölke made a face over Himmler's head. Strauss restrained a grin.

"Tomorrow—in the morning. I'll send a car for you," Himmler said.

"I'll be waiting, *Reichsführer*," Strauss said. Himmler stepped toward the lobby, before his men. "What time, *Herr Reichsführer*?" Strauss asked.

But the *Reichsführer* didn't hear him and was gone.

STRAUSS SUFFOCATED THE NIGHT with a laudanum-like mixture. Without the drug, dreams woke him that recalled better places. London was all horizon and no landfall, Gretty, the romance of plying his intellect to win a woman and the admiration of his peers. He was clean and clear and smug, a man who held a hidden vassal of truth behind a facade of playing along and getting ahead. Were Strauss the rebellious intellectual he admired in Wagner and Nietzsche, he might have become a nihilist. But he was not a true rebel. As he lay engulfed in a haze of alcohol and opium, he was a pretender under a setting sun watching the horizon recede.

AT 0700 HOURS ON 15 August 1941, Himmler and his adjutants —*Einsatzgruppe B* leader Artur Nebe; and Erich von dem Bach-Zelewski, police leader Russia center group—stood in their pressed uniforms at the edge of a long pit. Trucks drove up and parked. Soldiers herded Jews, a few Russians, and some patients from a local asylum.

"*Reichsführer*," Bach-Zelewski said. "So pleased you could join us."

Himmler smiled. "What are they doing there?" He pointed with his riding crop at a line of people entering the pit.

"*Sardinenpackung*," Bach-Zelewski said.

Himmler watched the pit fill. "They're lying down?" he said.

"For convenience," Nebe said.

"Raise arms," they heard.

Shooters on the side of the pit raised their rifles. Himmler turned to his photographer, Walter Frentz. "No pictures," he said.

"Fire!" The guns echoed and smoke filled the air and anyone still standing in the pit fell. Himmler looked confused.

"Walk, *Reichsführer*?" Nebe, Bach-Zelewski and Himmler walked along the edge of the pit. Himmler looked down at the dead. Their faces were unrecognizable. More filed in front of the fallen.

"Raise arms."   Rifles up again. "Fire!" The air cracked. A shooter dropped his rifle. He turned his head and ran toward Frentz, who was wearing a *Luftwaffe* uniform.

"I can't do this anymore," the gunner said. His face was red. "I need to get posted somewhere else."

Frentz looked at Bach-Zelewski.

"Fall out," Bach-Zelewski told the shooter.

Himmler's entourage stood close to the pit as twenty-five more civilians marched in and lined up.

"Raise arms."

Himmler perspired. He wiped his head. He watched the gunners and the people in the pit. Nebe poked Bach-Zelewski and nodded toward the *Reichsführer*.

"Fire!"

Himmler felt something hit his shoe. He looked down. Only one shoe glistened in the rising sun. He breathed rapidly and looked at Nebe.

"*Reichsführer*?" Nebe said.

Himmler bent and braced himself. "*Reichsführer*!" His men surrounded him. They bent down to him. Himmler huffed and panted. His glasses slid down his nose and fell. Bach-Zelewski caught them.

"*Reichsführer*—are you all right? Can we do anything?"

"Yes," he said. He was breathless. "This must be more humane."

"Humane, *Reichsführer*?" Nebe said.

"Yes," he said.

"They don't suffer," Nebe said. "It's quick and painless."

"Quick and painless for *them*," Himmler said.

SNEEZING WOKE STRAUSS LATE that same August 15th morning. His room was dark but he could see light at the periphery of drawn window shades. Gunk from allergies coated his eyes and his head throbbed. He lifted a shade. The sun seemed high for early morning. He showered in cold water.

He unlocked the rear door of the cathedral and entered through the sacristy. He was surprised to find a soul-less place. He thought the men would be at work. Dust fluoresced in the stained glass-colored sun. The place smelled musty and old. Columns of paintings propped six and seven deep lined the east wall along the floor. Strauss' face reddened at the sight of an unprotected Titian that Venetian traders left centuries ago. He covered it with an old altar cloth. Outside, he heard motors and voices. He unlatched the double wooden doors and saw Wölke walking alongside Himmler's car. The car and the soldiers beside it disappeared around a corner toward the Hotel Europe. Soldiers joined Strauss about an hour later. He outranked them so they spoke only necessities. They worked in the placid half-light of the muggy afternoon.

"Where were you?" Wölke stood at the church entrance.

"What?" Strauss' shirt and hair were wet with perspiration.

"Where were you?" Wölke walked over to Strauss. "We missed you. Himmler's diversion. Remember?"

Recognition dawned on Strauss. "Himmler's men never showed up."

"Yes they did," Wölke said. "They said they pounded on your door and almost broke it down."

"I didn't hear anything," Strauss said.

"You were fucked up."

Strauss flushed. He turned away. "Did Himmler say anything?"

"He doesn't *say*—he *does*. Did he say anything to you? Did he come by here today to find out how you were doing, if you were sick, whether or not you were feeling all right?"

"It wasn't an order," Strauss said.

"It was an order. Yes it was."

"So I fucked up. What did I miss?"

"Everything," Wölke said. "You missed history. They shot a hundred. Himmler got brains on one of his fancy-ass shoes."

Strauss smirked. "Are you serious? Why was he standing that close?"

"It doesn't matter," Wölke said. "It happened and because of it, the Third Reich will no longer engage firing squads for the execution of persons numbering over ten."

"So where did they find a hundred criminals to execute?"

This time Wölke smirked. He shuffled up to Strauss and took his shoulders. "These weren't criminals—well, I mean—they weren't *all* criminals. The brains came from a boy who couldn't have been more than six."

Strauss pushed Wölke away. "And they don't want us fucked up?"

"Only Himmler was sober," Wölke said. "Why the fuck else would he care about brains on his shoes?"

"Six years old?" Strauss said.

"You have a problem with that?"

"Yes. Don't you?"

"I fucking hate it," Wölke said. "But he was the enemy."

"A PAINTING."

Standartenführer (Colonel) Fritz Hösselman sat legs crossed facing the Alps from a porch-top perch on a high hotel with the sun on his face and a crystal glass of champagne in his hand.

"I can't think of anything else that could better describe it," he said.

"If I may propose a toast," *Sturmbannführer* Stephan Bunger said. Hösselman turned to the six people around the table. Franz Strauss shifted his gaze from the Austrian peaks to the mountains of food spread across a white cloth. A pained look crept into his eyes. Greta was oblivious.

Bunger raised his glass. "*Zum Leben!*" he said. "To Life!" He smiled and his white teeth caught the light.

A mumbled chorus followed and glasses clinked. Strauss was late raising his glass. Greta swept the table with her eyes.

"So—duty is upon you." Hösselman looked at Strauss. "Selecting out the bad grapes so fine wines may emerge."

"Fine." Greta raised her glass and sipped.

"I understand Melinka is a pretty place," Bunger said. He sipped.

"Beautiful," Hösselman said. He sipped and choked. "I've skied around there. Near Zakopane."

"It sounds special," Frau Hösselman—the Colonel's wife—said to Strauss.

"It's not," Strauss said.

"Is so," Greta said. "Franny's just angry he doesn't get to play bachelor anymore. We've been separated for a year."

"It hasn't been a year."

"Virtually."

"At least you're getting a promotion out of it," Hösselman said.

"What a joke," Strauss said.

"You shouldn't have pissed off Himmler," Bunger said.

"He didn't piss off anyone," Greta said. "He just overslept."

"He wanted you there," Major Bunger said. "He wanted witnesses."

"He didn't make a big deal of it," Strauss said. "It was no more nor less than a cordial invitation to a 'diversion.'"

"It was a command," Bunger said. "And you shouldn't have mentioned his daughter. You never discuss his family."

"How was I supposed to know?"

"Every good soldier knows the peccadilloes of his commandant," said the major's wife, Frau Bunger.

"Franny is a fine soldier," Greta said. "Himmler needs to communicate better."

"I'm not a soldier." Strauss said.

"Don't say that," Greta said. "You're an officer."

The conversation paused. "I told them I'd never kill anybody," Strauss said.

"You said what?" Hösselman almost spit.

"I said I would never kill anyone," Strauss said.

"Who did you say this to?"

"I've said it to several people."

"To Himmler?"

"Not directly."

"What does that mean—'not directly?'"

"I might have said it to one of his aides."

"Well," Bunger said. He slapped his knee. "Then it is a cruel joke." He leaned forward and looked at Strauss. "Why on Earth did you join the *Schutz*?"

"They had desk jobs," Strauss said.

"You haven't been behind a desk yet," Greta said. "You've been in the field leading men. Just like you." She looked at Major Bunger. "And you." She looked at Colonel Hösselman. "You want to know something else?" Greta smiled peevishly through her champagne glass and moved her eyes from her husband to the group. "Franny is an outstanding fuck." She looked at her husband. "Aren't you, darling?"

"Really," Frau Bunger said.

"Outstanding," Greta repeated.

Everyone but Strauss laughed.

"I say that because I was told that once Franny joined the *Schutz*, our sex life would be over." Greta sipped. Major Bunger changed the subject.

"I hear you're having a greenhouse built."

"For me," Greta said.

"It's a good idea," Bunger said. "I've heard of another commandant who did that. It kept the smell down and he had all the fertilizer he could ever want."

Frau Hösselman looked perplexed. "How so?"

"How so what?" the Major asked.

"How so fertilizer."

"*Muselmänner,*" her husband said.

"Muscle manor?" Greta said.

"Human skeletons," Hösselman said. "A unique feature of those facilities."

"What's so unique about a human skeleton?" Frau Hösselman asked. "I saw one in a hospital once."

"These skeletons are alive, *liebchen,*" her husband said.

"Isn't anything else more fascinating to talk about than this?" Strauss asked.

"Don't concern yourself, darling," Greta laughed. "With all your flowers, you won't ever have to look at or smell one ugly *Muselmänner.*"

"Will I have to look at you?" he said. She was drunk and Strauss hated her indignity.

Greta glared at her husband and tossed her champagne at his face but it landed across his shoulder. She giggled and poured another glass.

Twenty Nine

"Schütze."

Private Höfstaller marched into the major's office. Petersdorf sat at his desk and held up the letter about Chelzak.

"Have you heard anything back about this?" he asked.

"Which, sir?"

"This letter—about the man from Warsaw?"

"May I, sir?"

The major turned the letter and Höfstaller approached. He bent down to look, then stood straight.

"I don't know, sir."

"You don't know?"

"No, sir."

"What did I tell you to do?"

"I contacted them, *Herr Sturmbannführer*. By telephone and letter."

"And you don't know if they've responded?"

"I haven't had time to go through the mail, *Herr Sturmbannführer*. Not for three days."

"What did they say on the phone?"

"That my message would be left and someone would get back to me."

"Call them again. And go through the mail. Get back to me today."

"*Ja, Herr Sturmbannführer.*"

"And bring this Chelzak fellow."

THE INFIRMARY AND THE crematoria were the only prisoner-occupied buildings that had real floors—in both cases, cement. Distinct from the hospital blocks, where hopelessly-sick prisoners were left to die, the infirmary offered limited medical help to kapos, valued laborers, and medical experiment subjects who invariably ended up in the hospital block. Jakub Chelzak walked the floor of the infirmary with a bucket, ladling rust-tainted water to the lips of the infirm, who lay, not in beds, but on the concrete, many naked, without padding, pillows, or covers of any kind.

"Over here, over here." A man leaning on his elbow pointed to another man in the next row. "Over here—quick."

Jakub came to the two men.

"He needs water," the pointing man said. "Give him mine— he needs it worse than me."

Jakub knelt next to the other man, who was mumbling and turning his head.

"He's feverish," his neighbor explained. "Feel his forehead."

Jakub put his hand on the feverish man's head. He ladled water and placed it near the man's lips, but the man moved his head away.

Jakub dipped his sleeve into the water and brought it to the man's forehead. He felt the heat through the damp cloth and let it rest there.

"Typhus," the other man said. "That's why he's here."

"Typhus?" Jakub said. "Everyone will get it."

"That's right," the man said.

But it wasn't typhus. It was tick fever and no one could get it from this man.

"Where are the doctors?" Jakub asked.

"Doctors? No such thing."

The feverish man turned finally to Jakub and looked at him. Recognition shaped his eyes.

"You're Chelzak," he said softly.

"Don't talk," Jakub said.

"Did they bring you here?" the man croaked. Jakub brought the man's head up and let him sip from the ladle. "It's a good thing," he said. "They're short on doctors."

Jakub lay the man's head down. Footsteps approached—two sets, one set stepping evenly, the second unevenly and slower, with one foot hitting the floor harder than the other. Four black shoes stopped—two on either side of Jakub Chelzak.

"166097," Lieutenant von Kempt said. Sergeant Schmidt stood with him.

MAJOR PETERSDORF LOOKED AT Jakub in his office. "Where do I know this face?" the major said. "Where?"

"He has a common face," von Kempt said. "I myself thought I recognized him."

"No—I've seen you before," the major said.

Sergeant Schmidt, who knew good Polish, translated.

"You aren't familiar to me," Jakub said.

"What were you doing in Warsaw?" Petersdorf asked. "This letter tells me you had phony papers and no identity card."

"The papers came from a priest," Jakub said.

"A priest?" Petersdorf said.

"They were not mine."

"How did you come to get papers from a priest?"

"He gave them to me."

"No one wanders freely in Warsaw without papers," von Kempt said.

"I'm aware of that, *Leutnant*." Petersdorf studied Jakub's face. "Yes," he said. "I know you but I can't place you. You're from Warsaw?"

"Yes," Jakub lied.

"He talks like a peasant," von Kempt said. "Not like a city boy."

"Warsaw," the major said. "Yes—that's what it said. Let me see." The major rummaged through the papers on his desk. He found the letter from Warsaw and picked it up. "You claim to be a permanent resident. You have family there?"

Jakub said nothing.

"You have family?"

"I live alone," Jakub said.

"You don't look like much of an insurgent," Petersdorf said. "And you don't look like much of a Jew."

"I'm not a Jew," Jakub said. "I'm Catholic."

"Catholic," Petersdorf repeated. He had been a Roman Catholic seminarian for three years. "Where did they put you?"

"The infirmary," von Kempt said.

Petersdorf looked at the lieutenant, who hadn't shaved.

"Take this man back to the infirmary until further notice," Petersdorf said.

"When will I be released?" Jakub asked. "I've committed no crime."

"That's not for you to ask," von Kempt said.

"I don't make that decision," Petersdorf said. "The paperwork will take time."

Schmidt took Jakub's arm as von Kempt turned to the door.

"*Leutnant.*"

"Ja, *Sturmbannführer.*"

"The next time you present yourself to a superior officer, shave your face."

Thirty

Heinrich Wilhelm Petersdorf entered the seminary at fifteen, a pubescent boy full of fire from his mother's unflinching interpretation of the Lord's call. He dropped out at nineteen, confused, ashamed, and uncertain about the future his mother had seen so neatly before him. The major's father had been a high ranking general under the Kaiser. After Germany's defeat during the Great War, his mother had grown to dislike the sacrifice, the blind obedience, and the bland bureaucracy of military life.

But Petersdorf, like his father and his grandfather, loved the order, the discipline, and the call to higher purpose. He loved the hegemony that man asserted over man, environment, governance, and state. To serve both masters—mother and father—he would be a soldier, but for the Lord. At the end of his first year, he was top seminarian. The bishop sent a letter of congratulations to his parents and his father was happy—his son was excelling—and his mother was happy—Heinrich Petersdorf would be a man of God, specifically ordained.

He worked and studied constantly. He rarely played and never drank. He skipped meals. He came home on holiday pale and exhausted. His papers came back with high marks, streaked with comments about his promise from lay and clerical teachers. They saw his interpretations of Thomas Aquinas, the Gospel of

John, and the perpetual clash between science and faith as prescient, indicative of future scholarship. There was talk of sending him to Paris and the Jesuits, where he could sate his hunger for knowledge.

In Petersdorf's fourth year, he wrote a term paper exploring the changing dynamics of discovery and discipleship. Could the new physics, Petersdorf asked in his paper, be an attempt to dethrone the Almighty by explaining away the mysteries of Creation, replacing faith with fact? Could Relativity coexist with Christianity? Could a man be both academic and apostle?

Petersdorf followed the frontiersmen of physics—Planck, Heisenberg, Bohr, Schrödinger, and most of all, Einstein. He read about the conflict between Heisenberg's uncertainty and Einstein's gravity. He tried to understand how light—at one level, a corpuscular sea of probabilistic uncertainty—always moved, no matter what, at a certain constant speed. He saw photos of Einstein, with his white hair and rumpled sweatshirts, pontificating on the designs of a dice-averse deity and explaining that famous equation to one packed lecture hall after the next. This *was* God's work, Petersdorf concluded, this bringing together of a pantheon of minds to reconcile mystery and reality. It was as though God wanted these questions asked and answered at this particular moment, for how else to explain such a confluence of brainpower, unprecedented in scope and uncanny in timing? Discovery and discipleship were inseparable, Petersdorf decided, looking at history for examples: Gregor Mendel, the Austrian monk who demystified heredity; Berthold

Schwartz, the German monk who invented gunpowder; and Roger Bacon, Petersdorf's personal hero.

In Bacon's footsteps, Petersdorf studied geometry, arithmetic, music and astronomy. Bacon received a degree from the University of Paris around 1241. Petersdorf's professors suggested that he too attend that institution. Petersdorf embraced the idea that, as Bacon had famously said, "Mathematics is the door and the key to the sciences." Mathematics was not Petersdorf's best subject, but the one at which he worked the hardest.

In 1257, after a long stint at Oxford, Bacon entered the Order of Friars Minor, the Franciscans. Petersdorf would enter the Jesuit Order, the Society of Jesus. Unlike Bacon, however, Petersdorf's peers and superiors encouraged him. Communicating his interest in the sciences, first with the Holy Pontiff in Rome, and second to his students, Bacon upset his Franciscan superiors, who imprisoned him for heresy. Science and religion were then a new and uncomfortable alliance.

When Petersdorf read this part of Bacon's story, he decided he could better the great man because times today were different. In modern religions, heresies no longer existed. Modern universities encouraged freedom of thought. Germany herself had benefited greatly from science and though she had lost the war, she would always be remembered for producing many of the twentieth century's finest scientific minds. Look at Einstein, Petersdorf argued in his fourth year term paper. For those who understood tensor calculus, the mathematics behind the equations of General Relativity, beholding Einstein's miraculous feat—a description of gravity as a kind of geometry—was to behold a work of art, a masterpiece of mathematical logic. One could actually see the hand of God writing Einstein's equations across the heavens. Faith and science could not be more perfectly united.

The modern seminary greeted Petersdorf's term paper with a barely passing grade, a few non-committal comments, and nary a word about his future in the Society of Jesus. What on Earth had happened? Stymied and confused, Petersdorf took the case and his paper to his father, preferring not to disturb his mother's comfortable preconceptions.

"It's an excellent piece of work," his father told him, flipping through the pages. "Well argued, reasoned, very detailed. Especially for nineteen."

The son looked at his father quizzically.

"Looking past, of course, the real problem."

Petersdorf felt a knot in his stomach.

"Einstein is a Jew," his father said. "But it's only one paper." He handed back the tainted treatise. "All you can do is soldier on."

FOURTEEN YEARS LATER, HITLER had harnessed German anti-Semitism into a bitter enterprise. Here was Petersdorf, confronting the same issue as second in command of a facility dedicated to the ultimate expression of Jewish antipathy.

"Einstein is a Jew," his father had said, and now the question of who was or was not a Jew had become the soul of a soul-less directive, a single-minded pursuit mindless in its destructive intent.

Petersdorf opened a desk drawer and took out a stained rag. He slipped off his brass belt buckle and sat behind his desk. He opened his mouth and breathed on the buckle and polished it with the rag.

"*Schütze!*" he called between breaths.

Private Höfstaller entered.

"*Ja, Herr Sturmbannführer.*"

"What's for lunch today?"

"They've shipped us Spam, *Herr Sturmbannführer.*"

"Roosevelt Sausage?"

"Three pallets."

"Yum."

Heinrich Petersdorf had soldiered on.

Thirty One

Fog squatted over Camp Melinka. Strauss gazed out a window, lit a cigar. He drew on the cigar and turned to the visiting Major Bunger and his other guests.

"Well?" Bunger asked.

"I'm not really a cigar smoker," Strauss said.

"You will be," Bunger said. He drew on his own cigar. "In time you'll be a connoisseur."

A kapo laid a tray with a brandy decanter and five glasses on a low table centered in a circle of plush chairs.

"Gentlemen." Strauss indicated the chairs. Chief physician Joachim Hehl joined Bunger, Petersdorf, and von Kempt as they sat. The servant poured each man a brandy with a shaky hand. She stood.

"*Danke*," Strauss said and waved her off.

Bunger sipped. "You thank these miserable creatures."

"I have no quarrel with them," Strauss said.

"I wasn't suggesting you did," the major said. "Only that thanking them seems a waste."

"I agree," von Kempt said.

"Have you heard from Gretty?" Petersdorf said.

"As a matter of fact," Strauss said, "No."

"Really?" Major Bunger said. "Trouble?"

"No trouble," Strauss said. "Just busy. We visited last month."

"She likes Vienna?" Bunger asked.

"Very much. No way she's coming to live here."

"My wife was the same way," Bunger said. "We made it work, but she hated every minute of it."

"What about you?" Hehl asked. "Did you hate it?"

Bunger thought. He puffed his cigar. "I did. Until I discovered these." He looked at the cigar.

"I don't understand what's to hate," Hehl said. "You keep order, you keep it sanitary, organized. Everything runs smoothly."

Bunger chuckled. "You wait," he said.

Petersdorf looked at him quizzically.

"They start you out slow—they do that with every camp," Bunger said. "First year, maybe year and a half, steady work load, nothing too overwhelming. Then." He puffed his cigar.

"More work?" Hehl said. He leaned back. "We can handle it."

Bunger smiled, the cigar between his teeth.

"We have capacity," Strauss said.

"*Nein*," Bunger said. "I'm talking about boxcars crammed so goddamned full you have to pull the fucking doors off with a truck. I'm talking about something so foul, so fucking foul you can't get near enough to it to kill it. I'm talking about a fucking tidal wave, and not only one, but one after the other after the other, day in, day out. You think you're ready, you're never ready. Not for anything like that."

The officers tried not to look at one another. No one spoke for a while.

Then Hehl: "They increase our workload, they have to increase our supplies and manpower."

"Have to?" Bunger said. "*They* don't have to do shit. You, on the other hand, have to do the work. You, on the other hand, have to understand that you don't mean a fucking thing to them. You're just here to clean up a mess."

Petersdorf drew on his cigar. "Who made that mess, as you see it, *Sturmbannführer*?"

Bunger sipped his brandy and leaned forward. He lowered his voice. "A bunch of thugs."

Von Kempt cleared his throat. "Thugs?"

"Thugs. They've fucking destroyed Germany."

Von Kempt stood awkwardly and rubbed his bad leg. "Sorry —it gets numb when I sit."

"You make an interesting point," Petersdorf told Bunger. "My father has said something along the same lines."

"A retired general, right?"

"*Ja*," Petersdorf said.

"A general ought to know," Bunger said. "They all hate Hitler."

"Capone robs banks and Hitler robs states—that's what my father said."

"The biggest heist of all," Bunger said. "And we're the ones holding the guns."

"And taking the hostages."

"I'm not helping any crooks," Hehl said. "I did that once. I'll never do it again."

"Of course you will and of course you are," Bunger said. "Rounding up all these Jews, separating them from their money."

"They're the enemy," Petersdorf said. "We're at war."

"It's an interesting theory," Strauss said. "And we could be shot for talking about it."

"Hitler's too busy planning his end game to bother with us," Bunger said. He looked at the others. "Stalin," he said.

"The *Führer* has games on several fronts," Petersdorf said.

"Games he has played half-heartedly at best, pathetically at worst," Bunger said. "Look at England—a few quick bombing raids, some saber rattling, and game what? Over? On hold? Lost?" Bunger drew on his cigar. He blew smoke into the air. "He won't get away with it in Russia."

"Why does he care about Russia?" Petersdorf said. "It's cold. It has Siberia."

"What does a thug hate more than anything else?" Bunger asked.

"The police," Strauss said.

"A rival thug," Bunger said. "They obsess about each other. Hitler and Stalin. Al Capone and Bugs Moran. Always preparing for the final turf war that decides who takes all."

Von Kempt set down his drink and grimaced.

"Wage—you all right?" Hehl asked.

"My leg is killing me," von Kempt said. "I'm afraid I have to ask my leave."

"Of course," Strauss said. "By all means, go take care of yourself."

Von Kempt gathered his hat and coat. "Gentlemen," he said. "Good evening." The lieutenant brought his leg around and unsteadily departed.

"I hope I didn't offend him," Major Bunger said.

AFTER MAJOR BUNGER FORECAST the camp's fate, Dr. Hehl became obsessed with order. Wherever he—as the camp's chief sanitary and hygiene officer—had kept one page of records, he now kept two. Ledgers that detailed the height, approximate weight, age, and sex of the inmates now documented tattoos, scars, birthmarks, deformities, moles, baldness, sexual orientation (where it could be reasonably ascertained), education, ethnicity (Jew, non-Jew, gypsy) and religion (Jew, non-Jew).

One page supply requisitions became three pages of justifications following two pages of over ordering. The camp's fifty-page directive governing sanitation and hygiene became Joachim Hehl's one hundred and thirteen-page preparation bible detailing every way he could think of to minimize waste and maximize value to Berlin.

If the Reich needed money for the war effort, Joachim Hehl would provide it. First, he made inquiries of markets around the world, typing the name "Hehl and Co., Exporters" with an address in Melinka at the top of his letterhead. He wrote to wig and toupee makers; leather exporters; cloth and rag dealers; gold and silver smiths; dental laboratories; opticians; and medical schools. To the promising replies, Hehl responded with entrepreneurial gusto, reorganizing the camp's resources and profiting from a pillage of the mundane.

He ordered the pile of red, brown, blond, gray, white, and sandy-colored hair standing forty-two feet high burned. Complaints about the horrific smell continued, but in the pile's place Hehl erected an enclosed warehouse with bins organized by hair color and sex. Women's black hair for black wigs; women's red hair for red wigs; men's brown hair for toupees. Curly hair, white hair, gray hair, hair of mixed colors and children's hair, Hehl ordered to the incinerator (not enough demand).

Also replaced—the tower of shoes that sat in rain one minute, sun the next, snow in winter, and in summer housed bugs that ate holes in cloth and spiders that nested in dark leather toes. Hehl constructed a second warehouse, then agonized over how to divide the shoes. By size? By sex? By type? Women's size three, high-heel dress shoes. Men's size seven loafers. Boots, sandals, galoshes. What about color? Brown, black, red, gold, silver. Material? Soft leather, patent leather, calfskin, alligator, cloth. Tassels, laces, slip on, buckles, straps. And so many. So many, many, shoes. Hehl decided he needed more market research.

Other clients had simpler needs. Gold and silver fillings went into gold and silver bins under 24-hour armed guard for dental labs and assayers. Eyeglasses, divided by sex, went to German charities. Coats, shirts, trousers, and underwear Hehl ordered piled in boxcars and shipped out. Cloth went to rag merchants. Leather, fur, diamonds, watches, and precious jewelry went to the Reich's Central Supply after the bureaucrats sent Hehl a letter warning him not to resell these items lest they end up back in the hands of Jews. He wondered if the Reich stored the loot, or if senior officers gave it to their wives or girls, a practice he thought atrocious yet likely, especially for the larger diamonds, which he was tempted to pocket himself.

On the side of disorder stood Klaus von Kempt, with his over-large face and his thick, coarse bush of a head. He was Beethoven, without music. Loopy from morphine when he stood with Dr. Fiddler at the ramp, von Kempt selected four pregnant women with promises of care and midwifery, and lined them up a few buildings away. Then he ordered them to the infirmary. They walked, but he yelled "run." The women looked puzzled but thinking the lieutenant drunk and seeing the sidearm in his hand, they ran. "Faster," he cried. "*Raus!*" One woman fell. The lieutenant shot her. The other women froze until the lieutenant walked up to their fallen companion and rolled her with his foot. One of the women fainted, the second threw up, and the third cried and crumpled.

The lieutenant played another game at the infirmary. He sent kapos in to announce the village needed seamstresses and tailors. Hands went up across the floor.

"Line up, line up," the kapos said. But to a few people who began to stand, Jakub Chelzak crawled and pulled them back down. Other people who started to stand saw him and stayed down. The white van with a red cross outside the infirmary, rigged with tubes from the carbon monoxide exhaust for death before cremation, went empty to the crematoria, where the lieutenant waited.

Von Kempt limped up to the driver. "What's this?"

The driver shrugged.

Two days later, Hehl received word of the lieutenant's antics. "Wage—you have to quit this shit."

"It's the morphine," von Kempt said.

"You want I should cut you back?"

"It's all in fun."

"You won't be thinking it's fun when they kick your ass."

"No one gives a shit," von Kempt said.

Hehl told Major Petersdorf unofficially, and the major filed an official report with the Commandant, accusing von Kempt of behavior unbecoming an officer and failure to follow orders.

"Why do they call him 'Wage'?" Strauss asked.

Wage means "dare" in German.

"I don't know," Petersdorf said.

Thirty Two

Five years earlier, when Joachim Hehl was a 21-year-old medical student at the Medical University of Vienna, he heard this speech from the Dean.

"Knowledge, which in the past was pursued mainly for the sake of pure, theoretical science, will now find application in matters of daily life, particularly in those pertaining to sports, occupation, marriage counseling, family origin, proof of marital status and paternity. We physicians are called upon here and now to join in the decision-making process."

Applause. Rousing applause! Hehl looked across the crowd. The day was perfect—dry, clear, cool. Summer's wane had parted the August haze for the clarity of a September afternoon.

"That exam was awful," said Fritzie Heiderich. "Where the fuck does he get off asking about the hyeloid meniscus?"

"Shh."

Hehl's closest friend, Fritzie was a tall German boy from a farming town near Stuttgart.

"You'll get the highest score," Hehl told him. "Stop complaining." They stood in the grass.

"Even if many errors were committed in the past, the new state hands us the tools with which to correct those mistakes in the years before us, to pursue in our own interest that which is desirable for each one of us. For the first time ever, we have the possibility of bringing the ancient Greek injunctions to their fullest realization."

"Ancient Greek injunctions?" Fritzie whispered. "What the fuck's he talking about?"

"How should I know?" Hehl said. "I only just got here."

"Slept late, eh?" Fritzie rubbed his stubble. "Nah. Such a clean boy." He grabbed Hehl's cheek and mussed his hair. Hehl waved him off.

"The purpose of caring for the individual is to sustain the people as a whole," the speaker said. The microphone whined and he stopped and tapped it. It screeched. A collective cringe seized the audience. The speaker tapped again. Another man approached the podium.

"Can you all hear me?" the speaker asked.

"They should fix that fucking thing," Fritzie said. "What's the great state good for if nothing works?"

"I think—I think we've chased it out," the speaker said. "Let's see." He tapped the microphone. "Good. Yes. With this goal before us, our social awareness and the legal guidelines will enable us physicians to treat the body politic, both in the positive sense of supporting the able-bodied but also in eradicating worthlessness and decay."

"Eh?" Fritzie said.

"Jesus," Hehl said.

"You assume the medical care—with all your professional skill—of the body of the people which has been entrusted to you, not only in the positive sense of furthering the propagation of the fit, but also in the negative sense of eliminating the unfit and defective."

"Am I hearing right?" Fritzie giggled nervously.

"Shh," Hehl said. "I want to hear if you're on the list."

"What list?" Fritzie asked.

"Of the unfit and defective," Hehl said.

The methods by which racial hygiene proceeds are well known to you.

"Who do you consider defective?" Hehl yelled to the speaker.

At least one hundred turned.

"Ouch," Fritzie said.

The control of marriage, propagation of the genetically fit—

"Who's defective?" Hehl yelled again. "What are you saying?"

Two men walked down the small stairs on the side of the stage. Fritzie grabbed Hehl.

"Time to go."

"I want to know who he's talking about," Hehl said.

"You have a big mouth. You should shut up sometimes." Fritzie saw the two men round the audience. "They're fat assholes. They'll never catch us if we leave—now!" He grabbed Hehl. He was taller and they moved together. "I just hope no one recognized us."

The speaker's remarks echoed with them, reverberating on the tall brick walls of the admin office and the anatomy lab.

—whose genetic, biologic constitution promises healthy descendants; discouragement of breeding by individuals who do not belong together properly, whose races clash; finally, the

exclusion of the genetically inferior from future generations by sterilization and other means.

They lost the two men through an alley that opened to a pathway that led down and around a lake.

"He's the new dean." Fritzie was breathless and had his hands on his knees.

"He's fucking crazy," Hehl said.

"Crazy—but distinguished," Fritzie said. "He wrote the Topography."

Hehl looked at his friend. "Pernkopf?"

"Yes. You used it night before last if you studied, as I know you did," Fritzie said.

The old buildings distorted Pernkopf's echo. Hehl stood erect and gathered his breath. He stretched.

"I'm going," Fritzie said. "I'll see you in class—maybe."

"They didn't see us. We were in the shadows."

"They recognized your voice." Fritzie jogged away.

"I keep quiet in class. You're the big mouth."

"Not any more," Fritzie called back. "I now bestow that title on you."

EDUARD PERNKOPF. DEAN OF Medical Education. Describer of a rare congenital deformity of the heart "in which the aorta arises from the right ventricle and the pulmonary artery arises from both ventricles." Hehl read the announcement and the short biography.

Eduard Pernkopf.

Son of a practicing physician and youngest of three children. Great interest in music since a child, but his father died when he was fifteen and to help support his family, Eduard entered medicine. Enrolled in the Vienna Medical School at age 19. Long active in *Die Akademische Burschenschaft Allemania*, an old student fraternity for Germans. Graduated in 1912 at age 24. Assistant in the Anatomical Institute of Vienna. Taught anatomy for fourteen years throughout Austria. Served as a physician for one year during World War I. Became professor of anatomy at the University of Vienna and succeeded the venerable Ferdinand Hochstetter as director of the anatomical institute.

Big deal.

An underground student newspaper supplanted the official line: "Pernkopf joined the National Socialist German Worker's Party—now the Nazi Party—in 1933 and the *Sturmabteilung, SA*, or Brown Shirts in 1934."

"He's dean because of Hitler," Hehl told Fritzie.

JOACHIM HEHL FIRST HEARD about the Medical University of Vienna when he was a teenager in gymnasium. The University was a glorious, far-away place that infused him with a scholarly peace and the calm of knowing upon what road your future lies. With an unequaled reputation and four Nobel laureates— Robert Barany, Julius Wagner-Jauregg, Karl Landsteiner, and Otto Loewi—the Viennese school of medicine celebrated achievement and encouraged freedom of thought and expression—an excellent place for a young, forward-thinking mind. The Austrian university rejected native son Hitler's ill disposition toward intellectual Europe and the Jews who made up much of its center.

Hehl was raised—like many peers—in a German family that despised discrimination and embraced their Jewish neighbors. "Without the Jews," his father had told him, "the engine of the world would stop." Jews powered the engine of Austrian medicine, largely because it was the only professional field historically open to them. Jews had done the dirty and dangerous work of caring for the ill during the great plagues of the Middle Ages and now, in 1938, 3,200 of 4,900 Viennese physicians were of Jewish descent. In Germany, a lesser twenty percent of physicians were Jews.

Attitudes toward Jews in the European heartland corroded the engine of their industry. Strident political forces elevated Nazi sympathizers to the top ranks of the social and academic hierarchy. Anti-Semitic propaganda bombarded the common person. Jews began to lose gains that were centuries coming. The Medical University of Vienna was not spared. Many students harbored a quiet cynicism that questioned this course. Sometimes their cynicism crested in open bitterness. But mostly, they kept their impassioned discourses about the "new world order" among themselves.

In three weeks, Hehl lost most of his favorite professors. Each day brought another dismissal notice that named Jews, and the three men everyone knew were not right sexually, but didn't speak of it because one of these men had won the Nobel. Pernkopf reduced his administrative load with remarkable speed. When he started his new job, the University—still Europe's premier medical school—had one hundred ninety seven faculty. Three weeks later, the school had forty-four.

FRITZIE RECEIVED INTERESTING NEWS on a Monday in his mailbox, attached to his grade on the anatomy examination.

"What's wrong with you?" Hehl said. "You look sick. You only get ninety nine instead of one hundred?"

"He wants me to help on his next topography," Fritzie said.

"Who? What's that?"

"Pernkopf congratulates me for being the top student in the class. He says his next topography will be world-renowned."

The first edition of the *Topographische Anatomie des Menschen*—Atlas of Topographical and Applied Human Anatomy—didn't receive wide distribution despite its astounding anatomical maps. Pernkopf blamed the Jews for this slight and grew bitter. Jews, after all, controlled most publishing both inside Germany before the Reich, and outside Germany, especially in America, where all the medical schools used inferior atlases, what Pernkopf called "a disgrace to the grace of the human form."

American schools had money, and represented the biggest market for Pernkopf's genius. When America shut him out, he vowed to develop an atlas that would have no historic equal and could not be ignored.

"My new edition will be the most important portrait of the human body since Vesalius," Pernkopf told the excited members of his much-reduced anatomy department.

Pernkopf came to his new position at in 1938 with monographs, photos, and illustrations. He began work on the atlas in 1933 when he signed a contract with Vienna's Urban & Schwarzenberg (a Jew). He hired only the most talented Viennese artists, who rendered his finely-dissected corpses in exquisite detail. Most of the artists were Nazi party members. Erich Lepier even signed his paintings with a swastika.

"Fucking bastard," Fritzie told Hehl one night over a beer. "Fucking amazing bastard."

"He's a Wagner," Hehl said.

"Definitely," Fritzie said. *Wagners* were in all the universities now. Geniuses without morals. Students invented the term. These days, you were either a *Wagner* or a nobody.

"Why did he have to be so fucking brilliant?" Fritzie said.

Pernkopf timed his revolutionary atlas to coincide with newly-developed four-color printing, a technique that reproduced all eight hundred watercolor paintings he commissioned. Like Wagner's music, Pernkopf's pictures mesmerized the senses. During their first meeting, he showed dozens of page proofs to Fritzie, the best student in anatomy and probably the best anatomist at Vienna since Pernkopf himself.

Fritzie couldn't speak, couldn't move. Each new figure overwhelmed him.

"Everything about Pernkopf amazed me," Fritzie wrote in his journal. "His eye, his colors, his details, and especially, his access to the material of our study." The bodies arrived naked, without identity. "We dissected several dozen, and I was well-paid," Fritzie wrote. "Money was never an issue."

Fritzie might have forgotten his repulsion for Pernkopf had not a live specimen arrived at the lab one evening stacked among the dead.

"We need help." Breathless men stood at the anatomy building's back door.

"Shit—now?" Pernkopf looked up from the open throat of a cadaver on a dissecting table. He looked over at Fritzie, who set his scalpel aside, wiped his hands, and followed the two men.

The hallway was long and cavernous and Fritzie heard something—a voice, a cry. The hallway ended in two open delivery doors. The voice was loudest there. The men were working at the rear of a van and Fritzie saw movement in a stack of burlap-wrapped corpses. They stepped into the van and slid aside the dead and pulled out a fighting, wiggling heap screaming through a gag.

"He wanted a live one," the shorter man said.

Fritzie stared and something sharp jolted his gut and his mouth dried. "Pernkopf?" he said.

"Who else? Look—grab her feet. There—grab them and let's get her up."

Fritzie stood.

"Come on."

"No." Fritzie said.

"You want to see a real beating heart?"

"Only way to do it," the other man said.

"You're completely fucked," Fritzie said. "I'm not helping with this."

The woman jerked and tried to throw herself out of their grip and screamed words either too muffled or foreign for Fritzie to understand. She was wrapped completely, head, face, arms, legs, and waist gripped burlap-tight.

"No way Pernkopf ordered this," Fritzie said. "He must have been talking about a dog."

"She's a retard—what's the difference?"

Fritzie was young, his blood pressure strong, his legs muscular and his head clear. But he felt faint and woozy.

"Shut the fuck up." The man slammed his fist on the woman's head.

"Don't do that shit—he wants her unhurt."

She wheezed and croaked through foamy saliva that wet the burlap around her mouth and chin.

"Here." Pernkopf pushed the men aside and bent over and grappled the girl's arm and thrust a needle in. She jerked and spit and the wrapping around her mouth seeped blood. When they unwrapped her later, they saw she had bitten her tongue nearly off. The shot calmed her.

"Think you can handle her now?"

Fritzie slammed Pernkopf into the wall. He tried to punch but he felt both arms seized from behind. The men pulled Fritzie back and Pernkopf wiped his bloody lip.

"Get back to work," he said.

Fritzie left school for three days. On the first day, he lay in his room and stared at the ceiling and watched the shadows of the sun rise and move and settle into darkness.

On the second day, he grabbed his best friend Joachim Hehl in the Bierhaus and hugged him and kissed his face. Hehl hugged him back awkwardly.

"I had such high hopes," Fritzie said. He could taste the salt from his tears.

On the third day, Hehl found a note. "I don't want that son-of-a-bitch dissecting me," Fritzie wrote.

Pernkopf became the *Rektor Magnificus*, president of the University. But Fritz Heiderich left other notes that stained Pernkopf's reputation. A half-century later—after controversy about Pernkopf's legacy—the Office of the Rector at the University of Vienna provided all libraries with an insert titled *Information for Users of Pernkopf's Atlas*.

"Currently, it cannot be excluded that certain preparations used for the illustrations in this atlas were obtained from (political) victims of the National Socialist regime. Furthermore, it is unclear whether cadavers were at that time supplied to the Institute of Anatomy at the University of Vienna not only from the Vienna district court but also from concentration camps. Pending the results of the investigation, it is therefore within the individual user's ethical responsibility to decide whether and in which way he wishes to use this book."

The investigation—by a commission at the University—concluded with an October 1, 1998 final report, which said that Pernkopf's Institute of Anatomy received "at least 1,377 bodies of executed persons, including eight victims of Jewish origin. On the basis of a general decree of February 18th, 1939, the bodies of persons executed were assigned to the Department of Anatomy of the nearest university for the purposes of research and teaching...no proof could be found that bodies had been brought to the Vienna Department of Anatomy from the Mauthausen camp complex.

"The presumption and suspicions that some of the illustrations might be of prisoners of war or Jewish victims are based predominantly on impressions which strike the critical observer. In these cases, however, the investigation was able neither to prove nor to disprove the suspicions. Because of the systematic practice of making specimens anonymous, it seems likely that a final clarification of such suspicions will not now be possible."

Three of the school's Nobel laureates—including Karl Landsteiner, who discovered O, A, and the other blood types—died outside their homelands. For permission to emigrate, Otto Loewi turned his prize money over to the Reich. A stroke claimed Pernkopf—a free man after the war—while he was at the University working on the first book of the fourth volume of his atlas. No one heard from Fritzie Heiderich again.

Thirty Three

nother letter about Jakub Chelzak arrived on Major Petersdorf's desk a few weeks after the first.

1943/10/23

Forward Command
Warsaw District
Office of *SS-Brigadeführer* Franz Kutschera
Division of Inquiry and Logistics

Kommandant Franz Strauss
Melinka Resettlement Facility
Melinka, Poland

A man previously forwarded to your charge going by the name "Jakub Chelzak" has been discovered by our offices to have been a guest of Jews in our district. We have enclosed a brief dossier about Chelzak you may wish to review.

Heil Hitler!
Beruge Stain
Chief

For Heaven's sake, Petersdorf thought. Four months later they send this information. Nothing about the previous inquiry, nothing about how this man ended up here, not a word of instruction or command. He faulted the new commander, Franz Kutschera. Thirty-something years old, Petersdorf had read. Young, overwhelmed, trying to make a name for himself. Jürgen Stroop would be a tough act to follow, so Kutschera was busy proving he was no pushover. He ordered mass Jewish liquidations shortly after his arrival. Stroop had a reputation as a great warrior. Sammern-Frankenegg before him was a yes man to Himmler. Kutschera was building a reputation out of neither soldierly diligence nor obsequiousness, but rather, out of blood.

Petersdorf dumped the dossier's contents on his desk. Black and white photos of Chelzak talking with a rabbi; standing by a wall; eating a piece of bread; speaking with a young woman.

Petersdorf looked for a date stamp on the photographs, wondering at what late date a rabbi was walking around freely in Warsaw. He saw memos signed by members of Sammern-Frankenegg's staff, and other memos under Stroop. No wonder Kutschera couldn't care less.

A memo Sammern-Frankenegg signed—in a pile of memos and letters his underlings signed—caught Petersdorf's eye.

1943/4/15

From: Forward Command
Warsaw District

Office of *SS-Oberführer*

To: Field Commanders and Staff
Warsaw District

This office has received several inquiries about the status of
Jakub Chelzak, a reported stigmatic who appears to be visiting a
family in the Jewish district. The Reich's official position on the
stigmata is that it is a form of hysteria and not miraculous.
However, this office is sensitive to the concerns of staff and field
personnel and so it is hereby ORDERED that no members of
Command Staff nor their subordinates shall harm or cause to be
harmed Jakub Chelzak.

Signed,
Ferdinand von Sammern-Frankenegg
Oberführer
Forward Command
Warsaw District

cc: Jürgen Stroop

Stigmatic? The image conjured Saint Francis in Petersdorf's
Catholic   mind.   Sammern-Frankenegg—the   outgoing
commander—writing a letter about what should have been
Stroop's concern as the incoming commander also struck
Petersdorf as unusual. The major set the letter aside and looked

at a photo out of place with the others. This photo showed Chelzak, not in a city, but near a farm or in the country. People stood near a house: villagers, a woman, and in the center next to Chelzak, a priest with a big floppy hat. Petersdorf held the picture up to the light from the window.

THE NAZI PARTY'S OBSESSION with mysticism helped drive the Reich's concerns about Jakub Chelzak. Prominent among Hitler's cronies was the *Thule Society*, a pro-Aryan fraternal organization that borrowed heavily from middle-Eastern mysticism.

"Thule members were the people to whom Hitler first turned and who first allied themselves with Hitler," wrote the society's founder, Rudolf von Sebottendorf, a student of *Sufi* meditation and astrology. The Thule Society claimed several top Nazis, including Rudolf Hess and the dentist Friedrich Krohn, who converted a symbol of middle-Eastern spirituality, the swastika, into the Nazi Party's guiding insignia. A great Thule influence on Hitler was the man to whom he dedicated *Mein Kampf*, Dietrich Eckart. A wealthy newspaper publisher and occult aficionado, Eckart supposedly taught the future *Führer* public speaking techniques that involved voodoo-like methods of persuasion.

Heinrich Himmler founded the *Ahnenerbe Society*, dedicated to the study of Aryan heritage through occult-oriented treks such as the search for Atlantis and the Holy Grail. The society organized costly expeditions to Tibet, Nepal, Greece, and

370 The Fires of Lilliput

the Arctic to find remnants of *Hyperborea*, a mythical Aryan
nation, and its capital, *Ultima Thule*. Himmler embraced the
legend extraterrestrial beings from the star Aldebaran had
founded *Hyperborea*, becoming otherworldly Aryan ancestors
set apart from the rest of humanity.

The Reich leadership's occult fascination no doubt helped
motivate Adolf Cardinal Bertram's inquiry into Chelzak's
otherworldly qualities.

AFTER INSURGENTS TRIED TO kill Franz Kutschera, Warsaw
command stepped up retaliations against Jews and Poles. The
Gestapo sent a letter to every resettlement facility demanding
renewed interrogations of all former Warsovians, which
Heinrich Petersdorf carried as he crossed the camp in a light
morning rain. He found the Commandant typing in his office.
Strauss looked at the letter.

"So?" Strauss said.

"They're implying we torture him if we don't get 'good'
information."

"Did they define 'good'?"

"No."

"Then what should it matter?"

Petersdorf thought. "In my opinion Franz, we should release
him."

"And tell Warsaw what?"

"That he escaped. That we let him go before we got the directive. Whatever."

"No," Strauss said.

"I'm uncomfortable," Petersdorf said. "You know that."

"The stigmata is Catholic nonsense—no offense to you. It's never been verified by any real science."

"Not true. The Church has taken great pains to verify these wounds in dozens of people, including Chelzak."

"Have you seen any wounds?"

Petersdorf hesitated. "No," he finally said.

"When you do, let me know." Strauss continued typing.

IN HIS OFFICE THAT afternoon, Strauss had two magnetophons. On one, he listened to music; on the other, he spoke into a microphone.

"Dearest Gretty. Today we have background music—one of your favorite pieces. Dr. Hehl wrangled the other magnetophon out of *Farben* for an extra large order." He inhaled and sighed. "I miss you very, very much. I so enjoyed our short visit. Without you, where is my strength?"

Strauss paused and held the microphone toward the music.

"I haven't time for a long letter today. Himmler sent out a district-wide memo stepping up the destruction of Warsaw. We both know what that means. More inmates, more drunkenness, more problems, and less leave time for Vienna evenings. So I want you to visit me. I have a beautiful present for you that I bought in the village. I know you will like it." He held the microphone to the music again. "PS. How do you like the tapes? And the music? I'll send another shortly. PSS. I've made all the arrangements. I can't wait to see you. With more love than your heart could ever hold, your loving husband, Franny."

He leaned back and let the music play.

RAIN FELL IN THE evening. In Melinka village, a man wrapped in a black raincoat ran toward the rear of a small building. He knocked. He stood. He knocked again. Then he pounded on the narrow door. Another man unlocked the door and opened it barely. He was a silhouette in the light of a fire. He saw a rare visitor with a familiar face. Major Petersdorf peered back at him from beneath his hood.

"I'm here to see Father," Petersdorf said.

The man hesitated. He saw the major's sidearm.

"*Bitte*," Petersdorf said.

"It's okay," Father Waleska spoke in Polish from behind.

The man stepped aside. Petersdorf entered. A smoldering fire lighted the room.

"What brings you here on such a night?" the priest asked the major in German.

Petersdorf stepped closer. Fr. Waleska signaled to his servant.

"The führer's coat, please."

Petersdorf slipped his coat into the manservant's hands.

"I'm not the *Führer*," he said.

The priest showed the major into the living area. Petersdorf hesitated.

"Please."

The major sat. "I couldn't sleep," he said.

"Couldn't sleep?"

"I haven't slept in a few nights."

"I'm surprised you ever do."

"I didn't come here for criticism," Petersdorf said.

"What then?" Waleska stood.

Petersdorf looked at the fire. "I wanted to be a priest once," he said.

Rain blew against the window. Waleska stoked the fire. He looked up and saw the door to the upstairs ajar. He moved and it closed. He walked to it and opened it and saw a squat little woman walking up the stairs.

"Meara," he said in Polish. "Some coffee, please."

She kept walking.

"Meara."

She stopped and turned. As she emerged from the stairway door, she eyed Major Petersdorf and went into the kitchen.

"I want you to do something for me," Petersdorf said to the priest.

"What?"

"Hear my confession."

Waleska looked at the rain out the window. "What good would it do?"

The major felt a chill. "That's a thing to say."

Meara returned with a tray and two cups of coffee. She set it down on a table before the two men.

"Thank you," Waleska said.

She stared at Petersdorf.

"Meara—good night," Waleska said.

She turned and went through the door to the second story, her footsteps on the hardwood stairs.

"You want absolution," Waleska said to Petersdorf. "It's not in my power."

"Whatever you loose is loosed."

Waleska sipped his coffee. "I can't absolve you."

Petersdorf picked up his coffee cup then set it down. "I could leave the Reich," he said.

"You've said that before. You haven't yet."

"You think I'm a coward?" The major took the Father's arm. "You want me to beg?" he said.

Waleska looked at the fire, and the light from it. "It would be a sham."

Petersdorf knelt with his hands on the Father's arm. "Bless me Father, for I have sinned," he said.

Thirty Four

German words on the loudspeaker, then a second voice translating—Czech, English, Polish: "Guests: It is my pleasure to welcome you to the Melinka Resettlement Facility."

In the crowd of "guests," some were talking, ignoring the *Arbeitsführer* as he blathered on about this or that rule, this or that directive from the podium that overlooked the ramp.

"Over there," a man near the ramp said. "He was killed over there. They tell me by a doctor."

"A doctor?" asked a woman.

"He was killed by a doctor?" someone choked.

"With an injection."

The chatter rose, until it became an audible din begging for reproach.

"And our *Führer* has decided," the *Arbeitsführer* was saying. "No talking. No talking in ranks."

The *Arbeitsführer* motioned to the guards with his head. They moved into the crowd.

"No talking," they said. "No talking."

Someone shouted from the ranks.

"No talking. Shut up!"

A guard hit a man with the end of his rifle. Another guard pushed toward some hecklers. Pandemonium advanced. Chaos moved from one person to the next, like a wave. Then part of the crowd fell silent. The wave flattened. A truck came into view, overflowing with suitcases and purses and wallets and bags. The truck approached the railroad track and struggled to get over it. The engine wheezed and the driver floored the gas pedal. The truck lurched back and forth. It bounced and bucked and crept onto the tracks. A thin wail rose from the crowd. With a desperate lurch, the old lorry cleared the tracks. The inmates started to flee. Guards fired into the crowd. Nimble "guests" slid under the rail cars. Others stormed the ramps. The *Arbeitsführer* jumped from the podium and ran. A pregnant woman pressed through the rioting crowd. She made her way around the selections ramp and through an opening in a low wire fence. She was a thin woman and she tried to run down a narrow alley behind the barracks. She almost stumbled twice. She emerged where soldiers were heading toward the Commandant's quarters.

AT THE COMMANDANT'S QUARTERS, a soldier opened a staff car door. Greta Strauss stepped out. Her husband was at his desk when he saw his wife for the first time in months.

"Gretty!" He stood and took her reserved arms into his and kissed her.

She doled out a kiss. "Where's the lovely gift you promised me?" she asked.

Strauss led his wife to the back entrance and out. They walked toward the stables and heard voices on the camp loudspeaker. They went into a barn. Sunlight streaked between the planks. Hay and dust floated in the air.

"Close your eyes," Strauss said.

"Close my eyes?"

"Close them." Strauss put his hands around her eyes. "Closed?"

"Yes, Goofo."

He took his hands away. He took her hand and led her to the front of a stall.

"Open your eyes."

Greta saw a stallion swiping flies with his tail. "Franny—he's beautiful." She threw her arms around her husband's neck and kissed him. "When can I ride him?"

"Now, if you like."

Strauss opened the stall and a voice intruded.

"*Kommandant*." Von Kempt stood near the entrance of the stables. "I'm sorry to intrude, *Kommandant*, but we have a situation."

"So—handle it. I'm busy."

"We may not be able to, *Kommandant*."

"You want to saddle him?" Strauss said to his wife.

"No—just bareback."

Strauss helped his wife onto the horse.

"*Kommandant*," von Kempt said.

"What, goddamn it?"

Greta Strauss lay forward and hugged the horse. She set her head on its mane and looked down at the lieutenant.

"Well, *Leutnant*?" Strauss said.

Von Kempt regained his stiff poise. "We'll handle it, *Herr Kommandant*." He turned and limped out.

Frau Strauss looked at her husband. "*Herr Kommandant*," she purred.

THE SOLDIERS IN FRONT of the Commandant's quarters saw the pregnant woman. She turned and tried to run. Von Kempt yelled at them and they took her by both arms and walked toward the house.

"What is this?" von Kempt said. "*Kommandant's* coming."

Strauss walked with his wife on the horse. The woman looked at Strauss and thought his face gentle.

"*Kommandant*," she said. "*Herr Kommandant*."

But Strauss didn't look at the woman and kept walking. At the front of the house, Greta started to slip down from the horse. A guard released the woman and ran to help the Commandant's wife. The woman broke free from the other guard and ran to Strauss.

"*Bitte, Herr Kommandant. Bitte!*" She grabbed his arm, but before he could act, Greta drew his pistol from its holster, undid the safety, and shot the woman. Strauss grabbed his wife's arm.

"My God!" Strauss said. He shook the gun out of her hands. "What are you doing?"

"She was trying to attack you." Greta stiffened. A pathetic pucker gripped her face from forehead to chin. She buried her face in Strauss' jacket. "I'm sorry," she choked. She moved back and looked at Strauss with a reddened, scrunched-up face. She raised her hands to his cheeks and pressed her palms against him. "You have to forgive me," she said.

The guards held the dying woman.

"She's pregnant," Strauss said to Greta. "How could you?" He looked at his men. "Take her to the infirmary."

Von Kempt picked up the gun and handed it to Strauss. But Greta intercepted it.

"You need to get me one of these," she said to her husband. "It isn't safe here."

IN THE COMMANDANT'S OFFICE, Lieutenant von Kempt read his end-of-week report. Petersdorf stood. Strauss sat while a kapo shaved his face through a thick layer of foam, and a prisoner shined his shoes.

"This week, despite the uprising," von Kempt noted, "one thousand seven hundred and thirty six Jews, seven hundred and fifty two gypsies, two hundred and seventy three mental deficients, one hundred and sixteen deviant homosexuals and seventy three miscellaneous undesirables were gassed."

"How many casualties did we take?" Strauss asked.

"Final count—four, *Kommandant*."

Petersdorf interrupted. "I warned you, Franz. I warned you this could happen."

"You did."

"What happened couldn't be helped," von Kempt said.

"It couldn't?" Petersdorf said. "Why not?"

Sergeant Schmidt tapped on the door.

"Come," Strauss said.

"*Herr Kommandant.*" Schmidt nodded to someone in the hall.

Private Höfstaller entered with Jakub Chelzak. His head was shaved and he had lost weight. Strauss eyed him through a cloud of shaving cream.

"What's this?" Petersdorf asked.

"*Herr Leutnant,*" Schmidt said.

"I ordered it," von Kempt said.

"Franz," Petersdorf said.

"*Ja—bitte. Leutnant*—what are you intending here?"

"An interrogation," von Kempt said. "If *Herr Sturmbannführer* would like to ask the questions."

"We've already been through this," Petersdorf said.

Von Kempt turned to Jakub. "Are you a spy?" he asked. Schmidt translated in Polish.

"No."

"Do you work for the Resistance?"

"No."

"Are you with the allied forces?"

Jakub turned a sallow face on von Kempt. "No."

"Have you ever bled here?" Petersdorf interjected. Jakub looked at him. Petersdorf took Jakub's hand. "I can see the scar, here. See."

He held up Jakub's hand. Strauss leaned forward for a look. Von Kempt stood fast. Schmidt translated back and forth.

"How do you explain this?" Petersdorf said.

"I can't," Jakub said.

"That's a stupid question. There's nothing to explain," von Kempt said.

"*Leutnant*," Strauss said.

"Take him back," Petersdorf said.

"Now?"

"Take him back!"

Von Kempt looked at Strauss.

"Do it," Strauss said.

They opened the door and led Chelzak back to the yard. The heavy air came into the room. Strauss lit his pipe and puffed on it as the kapo wiped foam from his face.

"God it stinks out there," Strauss said.

CITY

Thirty Five

Karl Chelzak played his harmonica on the porch.

"Can you smell it?"

He jumped. "I didn't see you," Karl said to his mother. "Don't sneak up on me like that."

Mia stood with her son and looked across the field, under clouds streaked with moonlight.

"What could possibly be burning, day and night?"

"You know what they say," Karl said. "You've heard."

"I've heard a lot of things. Like your brother is doing fine and coming home. Like they're just burning rubbish."

"They *call* it rubbish." Karl put the harmonica to his lips.

"I miss Jakub," Mia said. "The rabbi used to write so often."

"They were leaving Warsaw," Karl said. "They're busy."

"I don't know why he's stayed so long," Mia said.

"Money."

"We don't need money that badly."

"Not anymore," Karl said. "Because of Jakub."

"Monsignor Starska says I'm right to be worried. He says we should never have let him go."

"Jakub said he'd be home after the family was settled," Karl said. "Give it time."

They heard spring thunder crash across the sky. "If he isn't here soon," Mia said, "I'm going to find him."

Karl stopped playing.

"What?"

"You heard me."

"You don't know anything about Warsaw."

"I've been," Mia said. "I know it's different now, but I'll go back if I have to."

"The rabbi said they were leaving. If you go, they won't be there."

"Who's to say they make it out okay?"

"They have their ways," Karl said.

"And I have mine."

"It's too dangerous."

"I don't care."

Karl started playing again. Then he stopped. "How do we pay for it?"

"It would take time to get the money together," Mia sighed. "The rabbi tells me he sends money in the last letter, but I don't always get the last letter."

"He sends cash. People steal it. What else can he do?"

Mia thought. "So the getting of the money will be up to us," she said.

"It won't be cheap, mama. It might take a while."

Karl started playing again. He felt temporarily relieved.

MIA CHELZAK RECEIVED A letter from the rabbi with American dollars, much favored over devalued zlotys. He was careful—as he was in every letter—not to mention his exact whereabouts. The rabbi explained that Jakub did not join the Mordechai family when they crossed the Wisła into Praga.

"I urged your son to go home," the rabbi said. "I wanted him to return to his family."

But the letter was over a month old. Jakub had been gone seven months, and if he was on his way home, it was five weeks now. He was not on his way home at all, Mia decided.

"I realize Warsaw, like all of Poland, is in a state of flux. But your son was beheld with some fear," the rabbi wrote. "Many soldiers knew him by reputation. Jakub was never molested and I suspect he is or will be shortly returning to Marienburg. Jakub Chelzak was a great friend to us and will forever be remembered as a hero of both the Jewish and Polish peoples."

Mia flushed when she read the last sentence. She went out the front door to walk and think. Karl came back late from town late and joined his mother on the porch, eating his dinner on a plate.

"You never told me how your day went," he said. He looked at her trembling hands. "What's wrong?"

"The rabbi says Jakub is not with them."

"Where is he?" Karl said.

"Coming home."

"That's good news," Karl said. "He's on his way?"

"The rabbi didn't say. He only said not to worry and that Jakub was a good friend."

"See—he's coming home."

"Maybe," Mia said. She stood and thought. Karl said something else but she didn't hear him.

"Where's the letter?" he said.

She went into the house. She returned and handed Karl the letter.

"It had money in it," she said.

"That's good." Karl read the letter. "But it's from a month ago, mama."

"I know." Mia went toward the door.

"Where are you going?" Karl asked.

"I've decided," she said.

"Decided what?"

"I'm going to Warsaw."

Karl went to her. "That's crazy."

"I'm going."

Karl took her arm. "You're not going to Warsaw."

"I am. Your brother may need me and how would I know?" Mia pulled away and opened the door.

Karl stopped her. "I'll go," he said. "If anyone goes, I'm the one should go."

"I'm not letting both my boys go," Mia said. "What if you're both killed?"

Karl looked at his mother. "We won't both be killed."

Mia took Karl's hand. "I don't want to think what life would be like."

Karl kissed his mother's head. "It's much better if I go. I'm strong and I can fight."

"You wouldn't be going to fight. Don't say that." She pulled her son close. "Why did we let Jakub go in the first place?" Mia said. "To help a bunch of Jews."

"The woman died, mama. Remember. He didn't help much."

"Poor girl. She sounded like a real fighter."

"Like us, mama."

"They kill the real fighters," Mia said.

"Not us," Karl said. "They won't kill us." He looked at the field, dry and white. "How much money was with the letter?"

"I didn't count it," Mia said. She went back into the house and returned with an envelope she handed to Karl. He pulled out a wad of currency.

"There should be enough here," he said. "With what we already have."

"Your brother left me to make this money, and now you use it to leave me, too."

Karl looked at his mother, then bent and kissed her forehead.

WITH MONEY SAVED AND help from friends, the Chelzaks decided Karl would leave for Warsaw in November to find his brother, before winter.

"I have friends there," Monsignor Starska told Karl and Mia. "They can get you into the city." Mia hugged the priest and he squirmed. "That's not necessary," he said. "You won't have any trouble finding people who want to help. They all know of Jakub."

Karl spent an hour consoling his mother and promising her he would return with his brother. He left for Warsaw on the back of a wagon filled with hay.

After three days on wagons, horses, a bicycle, and his own feet, Karl saw the city under a thin cloud of smoke that turned the sun orange. Monsignor Starska's friends lived in the Aryan section but knew about the rabbi. They found it hard to believe he had escaped "that, over there," on the other side of the wall. There was nothing left of the Jewish quarter.

"Jakub was there?" Karl asked one of the Monsignor's friends.

"If he was with the Mordechais. They lived there for years."

"We heard they went across the river, to Praga," Karl said. He showed around some of the letters.

"It's a wonder," people on the Aryan side said. "But anyone rich enough might have made it there. It's possible, what you say. But we have not seen your brother."

THE RABBI SAT ON the edge of a bed holding Rebekah Mordechai. Shosha was gone over a month now. They had heard twice from her that she made it back to Warsaw and was staying with members of the Underground. She said it was not safe for her to cross to Praga and that she couldn't communicate well or often.

The rabbi couldn't help much. He had lost most of his contacts on the left bank, central Warsaw. The suburb had become isolated from the city as Soviet forces closed around it. Rebekah often felt nauseous and a chill nagged her, though the days were warm and muggy now and the air hung in a fog off the Wisła, which stood almost still.

"She'll die and her death will be for nothing," Rebekah said.

"You can't say that," the rabbi said. He brought his hand to her cheek.

"Just like Lev," Rebekah said. "Just like her father."

The rabbi was silent.

"I don't want my baby to die," Rebekah said.

"She won't."

"My Lev is dead and for what? Things are only worse now." Her voice trembled. "I hope," Rebekah said. "I look at the door every day. I look up and down the street. I wake at night and open my eyes. I feel around beside me."

The rabbi drew her face toward his chest.

"He's not coming back," she said. "If he's not dead, he'll die in a camp."

"He won't," the rabbi said.

Rebekah took a deep, distressed breath.

"You don't know," she said. "You can't be sure. It's what's so awful about war."

"He won't die in a camp," the rabbi said. He paused. With her head against his chest, Rebekah could hear his breathing. She looked at the window, at the hazy light outside. She thought about what he said and the way he said it. Then she looked at him.

"How do you know?" She moved. "How?"

"Lev won't die in a camp," the rabbi said.

The tone of his voice struck Rebekah. "You sound sure." The rabbi went to stand but Rebekah held him. "How do you know?" she said.

He hesitated.

"Tell me."

"We were by the river," the rabbi said.

"Oh G-d."

He stared out the window. "I heard yelling. Lev was marking a map. There was a small group of us. Nobody thought about it."

"About it? About what?"

"There was yelling all the time," the rabbi said. "Somebody was always yelling something. This time, something about we're all dead anyway. I heard a loud pop, like a rifle. I woke in an infirmary."

"Soldiers? A soldier killed Lev?"

"Not their soldier."

"What are you saying?"

"Some kid," the rabbi said. "Just a kid."

Rebekah was shaking. "What?" she said. Her voice sounded like it was falling apart.

The rabbi took her wrist. "Lev pushed me out of the way," he said.

"Of what?" Rebekah breathed fast and light. She moved. "Why didn't you...why dint you—" She gathered herself. She brought herself together. She breathed and she stood. "Why didn't you tell me, why didn't you tell us. You son, you, you— Why didn't you tell us? Why?" She stood and breathed, fast and shallow.

"He talked about you all the time," the rabbi said. "He told me all about you."

"Why didn't you tell me?" Rebekah said. "Shosha, Leia, me?"

For a long time, it seemed, the rabbi sat and stared. Then, his lips parted.

"I couldn't," he said. "I couldn't." He waited while she cried in little, exhausted gasps. "You needed him alive."

Thirty Six

Karl Chelzak got a job working for a family who owned a store on the southern outskirts of Warsaw. He sent his mother enough money to hire help some days. Men needed work around Marienburg, especially gypsies and Red Army deserters who wandered in from the Eastern Front.

Karl also wrote to Mia. He described Warsaw and how the people were coping. He told her they were kind to him, once they found out he was not a Jew nor a German. He said he had enough to eat most days and learned to avoid the soldiers. He never mentioned the Ghetto, nor how it looked over the wall. He wrote that he asked every person he met about Jakub, and that many people had heard of him. People told him they would spread the word, keep their eyes open, and pray. He was planning a trip to Praga, he explained to his mother, after the Red Army made it safe. The Red Army, everyone said, was very close now.

CONSPIRATORS TRIED TO ASSASSINATE Hitler with a bomb on July 20, 1944. But a heavy oak table protected him, and he was only wounded. Fear of reprisals spread across Europe and an ominous quiet settled on Warsaw. Shutters were battened, doors and gates chained, streets emptied. The attempt on

Hitler's life portended. One word dominated the Underground papers and notes and whispers that carried news around Warsaw's central district—UPRISING. The word flew from face to face, followed feet up steps, entered houses and sallied from room to room, upstairs and down, from the lowest basement to the highest attic perch. Aryan Warsaw would follow Jewish Warsaw and fight.

Insurgents—ragged and ready—sprouted everywhere. They were civilians in regular clothes and the only way you could tell their allegiance was to see the armband each fastened around his or her sleeve. These warriors wore helmets and hats, railway and tram caps and caps with school insignia. Shopkeepers, street sweepers and bus drivers carried machine guns and knives and bullet-laden belts that sagged with hand grenades. Men took up positions in attics, near windows, at the entrances to basements and underground hideaways. Women organized first aid stations. To one basement laundry, they brought cots and tables, medicines, and bandages. They hung a sign on the door: *First Aid*. They lined the walls with stretchers. Three nurses—ages 17, 18 and 23—stood ready.

When darkness fell on July's last day, artillery throttled the air. Bullets broke plaster and windows and pitted bricks. The sky was so clear you could see the constellations. Underground fighters evaded searchlights single file, rushing tight against walls along empty streets to storm arms depots for more weapons.

Skyward cannons shook the nearby fields of Mokotów next morning. Recoiling gunstocks jarred Shosha Mordechai, who stood near a window a few streets from the field. Reunited with the AK, she was a guest at the home of Stazek Pszenny, a Roman Catholic cousin of Jozef Pszenny, aka "Chwacki," the AK captain who led the failed effort to blast through the Jewish Ghetto wall at Bonifraterska Street with a land mine.

Shosha could not get word of her whereabouts to her mother and the rabbi, and she could not use the most important means of communication—rumor. Rumors about Jews often reached gendarmes, so she kept quiet.

Karl Chelzak stood on a balcony a few blocks away and saw people in houses, standing at windows and pointing toward the sky. Planes passed between the clouds.

"Let's go—time to go."

Karl and a few others went down to a basement. Numbered doors lined a long, narrow brick corridor. People sat on suitcases and chairs and boxes and trunks.

"Chelzak! You should have stayed in Marienburg."

Karl made good money in Warsaw, good compared to selling produce back home, but now he was a bona fide fighter. He realized that finding his brother in a city this size would be difficult, and he thought his chances improved if he joined the revolt. All he heard about Jakub was what a hero he had been to the Underground and that he was last seen alive.

"Jakub could be anywhere. Warsaw is a big place," Karl wrote his mother. "It seems even bigger now."

A mix of hopeful rumor and vague despair circulated in catacombs beneath streets and buildings. A few facts trickled in, but generally, the central district was cut off from hard news. Radios were few, telephones were down, and newspapers were local. Real news came from London or the U.S., often in papers with outdated stories people updated with their own retellings. Reading last week that the Red Army was twenty miles from Praga today became: "The Reds are in Praga!"

"Hear that. The Germans should give up."

"Our fighters already have Stare Miasto."

Rooftop lookouts climbed down to say the planes were gone. People left basements. They heard shooting, but not as bad. The streets were empty but adults came into their yards and children played, with sticks and what they could find. Karl joined a group of men who gathered with "news."

"Are the Russians here yet?"

"It doesn't matter. Our fighters have the city. Scouts are reporting our red and white banner flying over Town Hall."

"The Russians have Praga."

"Hey Chelzak—the rabbi's over there."

"What?" Karl said.

"The rabbi who was with your brother—he's in Praga with a family."

"I heard that, but how can I find them?"

"I don't know. You can't get there now. We'll have to keep our ears open."

Karl shook for the rest of the day and with shaking hands wrote his mother the night of August 2. He couldn't sleep. He finally collapsed around four in the morning. He woke at dawn to planes circling high. Some men were outside sharing binoculars.

"Reds. Told you they're here."

"Those are Krauts."

An old woman came up from a cellar.

"It doesn't matter whose planes those are," she said. "Each of them is here to bomb Warsaw. The Germans will bomb the Poles. The Brits will bomb the Germans. The Reds will bomb everyone. Get in here and keep the doors shut."

In the basement, they heard shots, hollow like kettledrums up and down the street. The basement walls shook. Someone at a dirty window cried, "Tanks!" Karl and others gathered at the window and saw steel treads breaking across brick pavers.

"They look like Soviets."

"Here?" said a woman with a child in her arms. Her face was long and tired and she had heavy bags under her eyes. The child grabbed her neck and pressed his body against her. "Finally?"

BUT SOVIET TANKS WERE not in Warsaw and Europe's other crime boss, Joseph Stalin, didn't intend to send them anytime soon. The Soviet armies were approaching Praga to establish a bridgehead on the left bank of the Wisła. They would eventually move into Warsaw, but under Stalin's plan, they would commit the most sinister act of negligence in history—they would sit across the river and watch Hitler's forces reduce the central city to embers and kill almost every person in it.

Stalin had a history of conflict with Poland. The Red Army had marched on the nation four times during the 20th century— in 1918, 1920, 1939, and 1944—with mixed success and one stunning failure. In the first 20th-century Battle of Warsaw, the Poles, under General Pilsudski, decimated Stalin's Bolshevik army, ending a two-year battle that once heard Soviet Marshal Tukhachevsky declaring he would march over the corpse of Poland on the road to world revolution. Instead, Poland marched over Stalin and his marshal. The Polish victory was so complete and so humiliating that the Soviet government tried to erase it from the nation's memory. Now, in 1944, Poland was again threatening Stalin's ambitions.

With three hundred thousand insurgents and AK soldiers and the support of Great Britain and the United States, Poland's Leader-in-Exile—Stanislaw Mikolajczyk—wanted to rebuild an independent Polish Republic. Stalin wanted a Communist regime that devout Polish Catholics bitterly opposed. He believed the Soviet Union had a claim on Poland, and with the Hitler–Stalin Pact, he divided the country with Germany. To stake his claim and complete the division, Stalin proceeded with wicked craft.

SHOSHA MORDECHAI HEARD ALL about these conflicting political ambitions.

"The Polish Communists have a representative in Moscow," Stazek Pszenny said. They were eating a soup of crushed tomatoes, potatoes, and warm water. "Bierut." Bolesław Bierut, future communist dictator of Poland.

"You know what they say about the Home Army?" his son Eugeniusz (Gene) said. "That we're cowards. That we can't take care of ourselves. Poles. Saying this about other Poles."

"You see the dilemma," Stazek said to Shosha. "We fight the Germans and we open the big Red door."

"Poland can go to Hell as far as the Reds are concerned," Eugeniusz said.

"So why help them?" Shosha said.

"To kill the Krauts."

"Let them destroy each other," Gene said. "That's the real hope."

German troops visited the Pszennys earlier that day. Stazek and his son hid Shosha in the attic, presented their permanent resident documents, and lived to eat the evening meal. The occupiers were going from house to house, pulling people out of basements and shooting them—papers or not. Presence in a basement meant subterfuge. Not as many homes had attics large enough to live or plot in. The Pszennys set up the attic as a guestroom. In case of a surprise German invasion, Shosha could leave by the roof exit and go across to the vacant building next door, slip in through a broken grate on the roof, and hide until the Germans left. She was on the roof now, standing alone, looking at the fires across the sky. She didn't hear Stazek as he came alongside her.

He lit his pipe.

"You missing your mama?" he asked. He drew on the pipe and she saw tobacco embers glowing in the bowl.

"Yes," she said. "I wish I knew why it had to be this way."

"It's easy to ask why," Stazek said. "In all this."

"How long before they destroy what's left?"

"They can't destroy everything," Stazek said. "They can't kill all of us."

"Where can we run?"

"I don't know. But the uncertainty, at least, gives hope."

Shosha ran her hand through her hair. "I wish Jakub were here," she said.

"Chelzak?"

"Yes."

"My nephew spoke of him. He helped rescue an entire squadron of fighters."

"The Germans wouldn't touch him," Shosha said. "They knew better."

"Was it true about his wounds?"

"Yes."

"Did you see them?"

"Yes."

"Like the Crucifixion?"

"I haven't studied it, but I'd say so—yes."

"What did the rabbi think?"

Shosha thought for a moment. "One holy man to another, I suppose. I don't know. In the end, he let the Germans take Jakub."

"What a terrible thing. Why?"

"To save us, though I hated him for it."

"I've heard that about the rabbi," Stazek said. "A pragmatist. A strategist."

"He betrayed a friend," Shosha said.

"If he hadn't, what would the Germans have done?"

Shosha thought. "Killed us," she said. "Maybe."

"Then the rabbi chose life," Stazek said. "What other choice is there?"

Thirty Seven

A Nazi officer and a few soldiers came to the housing block where Karl lived and ordered all gates locked and the appointment of a "block commandant" to oversee compliance with every German whim.

"If even one shot is fired from this block," the officer said in German, "every person in the block will be brought to this yard and immediately"—he raised his revolver, aimed at the wall, and pretended to squeeze the trigger.

"What did he say?" asked a man who spoke only Polish.

"This Babel could be the death of us all," a woman said.

Karl understood some German. "Anyone shoots," Karl said, "anyone at all, for any reason, and they shoot us."

"How do they think we can prevent someone from shooting?"

"Confiscate all the guns—that's what they want. That's the only way."

"Fuck 'em. I say fuck 'em."

People went back to their daily lives until the afternoon, when someone somewhere fired three shots out a window. Three shots, into the air. Minutes later, buildings shook and things started crashing to the ground. Karl looked out from the balcony and saw smoke rising. People ran to basements. He heard a new and strange sound—an awful sound, like a wounded cow. The sound was so loud and grating Karl covered his ears. More bricks and plaster hit the ground.

In a basement corridor, after the explosions stopped, Karl thought about food. At home, he had food. Now, it was a luxury. He had seen men stripping a dead cavalry horse in the street. They offered him some meat but he turned it away. The idea of eating an animal whose sole function on a farm was helping the farmer repelled him. Speaking of the farm, how about getting the fuck out of here and going home? Leaving may have been doable a few weeks ago, but how would he get out of the city now? It wasn't the Ghetto, but it was almost as isolated. And if he left now, would he be abandoning his brother, the fight, his people? He sat in the corridor thinking amid cots and chairs and suitcases. Candles glowed low. People spoke in hushed tones. Cannons and rifles roared outside.

"Fuckers," said a man next to Karl. "I need some sleep."

In the early cold hours of the morning, someone pounded on the door. Karl heard footsteps and a woman's voice down the corridor.

"Who is it?" the woman said. "Who's there?"

"*Aufmachen*."

Karl heard locks opening and men speaking Polish with heavy German accents.

"Where are the men?"

"There are none," the woman said.

"Don't piss with us. Where are the men?"

"Only women here. You mean boys?"

They pushed her aside. Karl heard them coming down the steps to the basement. Almost in unison, every mother with a child in the corridor grabbed her child.

"*Kennkarte, Kennkarte!*" the German soldier yelled. They came around to Karl.

"No men, huh?" said the soldier. He eyed Karl's identification card and him over. "Do I know you?"

"No," Karl said.

"Chelzak. Your name is familiar," the German said.

"We've never met," Karl said.

"Good thing. Then it's okay if I shoot you."

"You wouldn't want to do that," said a Polish man.

"Who says this?" The squad leader came to the little man, squatting against the wall. "Well—what do you know?" The squad leader wheeled around and announced, "Another man. Not just boys after all."

"Karl Chelzak is not a man to be toyed with," said a woman standing nearby.

"He has God on his side."

"Didn't you know—all the Yappers were afraid of his brother."

"All the Krauts."

"Jakub Chelzak. Surely you've heard of him."

The voices rose.

"You shoot Karl Chelzak and you shoot the wrong man," said the nearby woman.

The squad leader reached for his sidearm, but in the shadows of the corridor, he heard click, click, click. Safeties off, hammers cocked. The squad leader looked again at Karl's identification card. "Who am I to argue with God?" he said. The three soldiers turned and headed back up the stairs and out into the dawn air.

PLANES CIRCLED IN THE midday sun, so high they were lost in the light. People in the street heard the planes but no one paid much attention until children started calling out. "Papers, papers." Leaflets fell from the sky. A paper landed near Karl. He picked it up.

"He's got one!"

A crowd surrounded him. Up the street, Shosha Mordechai saw the crowd and walked toward them.

"What's it say?" someone asked. "Can you read it?"

Karl looked at the leaflet. "Soldiers," he read.

"That's all?"

"Soldiers of the," he continued.

"Can't read," someone called.

"Come on—read it or give it to someone else."

Karl looked down at the leaflet again. "I can read it."

The crowd turned. Shosha pushed through and took the leaflet from Karl.

"Soldiers of the National Army," she began. "Our Government from London announces that Prime Minister Mikolajczyk's position in Moscow is such that he is unable to reach a free decision and to have freedom of speech.

"I HEREBY ORDER a stop to all acts of hostility against occupational German authorities. Anyone disregarding this order will be shot immediately.

"Long live Poland! Chief Commander of Polish National Armed Forces."

"It is signed: Bor. Warsaw, 2nd August 1944," Shosha concluded.

"Bor signed that?"

"I don't believe it."

"It has to be a lie, something the Krauts cooked up."

"Absolutely."

"Chelzak—what do you think?" said one of the men.

Karl looked up. Shosha looked at him.

"A lie," he said. "Obviously."

"Chelzak?" Shosha said.

"Yes—my name is Chelzak," Karl said.

"Brother of the great Saint Jakub," someone in the crowd said.

Shosha's knees almost fell out from under her. Karl grabbed her. "Steady," he said.

"You're Jakub's brother," she said.

"Yes," Karl said. "You know him?"

"Yes! Yes, I know him," Shosha gathered her breath. She was light-headed and had trouble standing straight. "Forgive me a second," she said. She took a deep breath. "Yes I know him. He came here to help my family."

"Shosha," Karl said. "My God," he said. "I came here to find you."

The crowd was dispersing.

"We shouldn't stand here," Karl said. He led Shosha to a brick planter near a wall.

"You're looking for him, aren't you?" she said.

"Yes. We heard he was coming home."

"Not unless the Germans were taking him home."

"What?"

"They took him months ago. I don't know where."

Karl felt his own legs weaken but he stood and walked around. He grabbed his head and covered his face with his hands. He sighed and Shosha heard a little grunt.

"You didn't know," she said.

"The rabbi sends money and writes," Karl said. "He said Jakub was on his way home."

Shosha thought for a moment. "He shouldn't have told you that," Shosha said.

"Oh God," Karl said. "Oh God."

Shosha put her arm around him. "Where you staying?" Shosha asked.

Karl gazed across the street. They heard cannon fire in the distance.

"You can stay with me for a while," Shosha said.

"I have friends here," Karl said. "It's not necessary."

"It is," Shosha said. "For me, anyway. Please."

They stood for a time while Karl thought.

"We'll send word to your friends—tell them you're okay,"
Shosha said.

Karl was tired and Shosha took him back with her to the
Pszenny house.

STAZEK PSZENNY WELCOMED KARL like a brother. He
opened his best whiskey, in a dusty bottle hidden in a bricked-up
cubby in the basement. He kissed Karl on both cheeks, pulled
him close, and spent an evening drinking whiskey, eating hors
d'oeuvres made with salt and cooked potatoes, and extolling the
virtues of Brother Jakub.

"But you haven't heard from your mother?" Stazek said.
"Don't be too worried—the mail hardly gets through anymore."

"She's alone," Karl said.

"Nothing you can do about it," Stazek said. "Not right now.
I'm sure your mother's fine. She probably writes and it doesn't
get through. By now, she probably knows our situation. Everyone
in Poland does."

SHOSHA AND KARL SPENT time in four places—the Pszenny
basement when bombs fell close; on the main floor of Pszenny's
house when bombs sounded blocks away; on the street when
they could only hear gunfire; and on the roof when everything
was quiet. They saw the city burning from up here. They saw the
cannons and the soldiers smoking above the trenches in the

Mokotów field. They watched planes come in and with binoculars could tell which planes dropped steel bombs (meaning a trip to the basement); and which dropped paper bombs, meaning they might have news.

"How did you know about the Germans taking my brother?"

It was late and the night was humid, so Shosha and Karl didn't sleep.

"I saw it," Shosha said. Karl looked at her.

"Why did they take *him*? Why didn't they take you? You're a Jew."

Shosha looked at her hands. She rubbed her fingers. She thought she felt a tear.

"I know," Karl said. "It's not a fair question."

"It is fair," Shosha said. "I just don't know how to answer it."

PLANES SCATTERED THE SKY with thousands of delicate white petals that looked like manna. The airborne propaganda turned people into cynics, but they still ran in the streets to retrieve the fliers and crowds still gathered to read them.

Shosha read today's announcement.

CITIZEN!

The time of freedom is approaching. The Polish People's Army, with self-sacrificing battles, paved the way for victory. The Russian allies have broken the yoke of the Fascist occupation. The Polish Government in London acknowledged that the Red

Army and the Polish People's Army carried on their shoulders the weight of the battles for freedom. Marshal Stalin has guaranteed wide boundaries for Poland.

"Stalin is about as good a friend to Poles as Hitler," someone said.

CITIZEN!

Reborn Poland is a Poland of the people. Everyone must add their efforts to rebuild the country. All kinds of Fascist elements will be crushed. Every Pole, every organization has to cooperate with us. The Free People's Poland is calling you. The new vigorous state organization will guarantee your freedom and prosperity. The Polish People's Army is defending our Poland.

Death to the Fascists!

Long live the Polish People's Republic!

Signed: General Berling, Commander of the Polish Army in Russia

"A lot of talk," a woman said. "So what? When will we start seeing the benefits of all this cooperation?"

Karl picked up a smaller flier. "Did you see two planes up there?"

"No," Shosha said.

"This one looks different."

Shosha read it to herself.: Stop! The Uprising Is Our Death!

"What does that one say?" a man asked. "What's it say? Read, please."

"Now the Communists have achieved their aim," Shosha read. "We ourselves are destroying Poland. The Polish underground is getting weaker in her fight with Hitlerism; later the Bolsheviks will come and crush her.

"NEVER Will We Give Our Country To The Communists!

"Keep cool, remember our fallen heroes. They sacrificed their life for free Poland, never for the support of Communists."

"What to believe, eh?" Karl said.

Shosha looked up and down the street where groups in different spots read the fliers. She circled her mouth with her hands. "The Uprising is our Life!" Shosha called out. People turned around. Some smiled. Some waved. "Our Life!" Shosha cried.

"Our Life," someone cried back.

"Life," Shosha said.

"L'Chaim!" This was a Jewish term and as soon as Karl heard it, he put his hand on Shosha's shoulder.

"Don't respond," he said.

She didn't look at him before she hollered "L'Chaim" in return.

THE BLOCK COMMITTEE CALLED a meeting about a pressing problem—a garbage heap that stunk but couldn't be moved as everyone on the block was a prisoner of the block.

Everyone attended the meeting—Karl, Shosha, the Pszennys and a few dozen others, minus those who couldn't get around well. Stazek Pszenny insisted on burning the garbage. Mila Gorcewicz insisted on burying it.

"Burning is quick and effective," Pszenny argued.

"Burning will bring unnecessary attention to this block," Gorcewicz countered.

"It'll cause a mighty stink, too," someone else said.

"What do you think Chelzak?" the block commander said.

"Why do you ask me?"

"You seem like a wise fellow."

"I don't know anything about burning trash."

"Chelzak doesn't know."

"Shall we put it to a vote?"

"Burning may not be that effective," Karl pointed out. People lowered their voices and listened. "Half the trash may be tin or things that won't burn."

"We can bury that."

"If we're going to bury half, why not bury all?"

"Chelzak—what about that?"

"Well—how many shovels have we got?" Karl asked.

They counted two dozen shovels and plenty of hands.

"I move we bury the trash," Gorcewicz said. "Not half, but all."

"I second. All in favor, say 'aye.'"

The "ayes" carried. The block dug a hole in back of the row of houses facing Mokotów. The Germans stood in trenches and sat on tanks and smoked. They saw the people digging and yelled a few things, but the words were German and didn't mean much. Everybody was so busy digging that at first they didn't notice the latest fliers. Karl and Shosha stopped digging as a young woman read the "news."

CITIZEN!

"Prime Minister Mikolajczyk held a conference with Stalin and pledged mutual co-operation with the Red Army. The same Red Army which murdered the soldiers of the National Army in Wilno.

"The Russian Government has clearly shown its treacherous plans by setting up a Bolshevik government in Chelm. The hostile reaction by the Polish people taught Stalin a lesson. Now he has returned to the way of deceitful treachery.

"Prime Minister Mikolajczyk let himself be used for the ignoble plans, probably being afraid of losing his position.

"Prime Minister Mikolajczyk stained the honor of the Polish soldier who fought for five years and never gave up. Poland's enemies, heavily armed, can occupy our soil but cannot conquer the Polish people. To pave the way, they are now using treachery.

"The German occupier is fighting with his last breath. In the West, the Americans and the English have broken through the Front and are streaking forward quick as lightning.

"Russia is also at the end of her possibilities. Great and independent Poland will soon appear at the side of our allies,

America and England, but never under the German yoke, nor the Soviet whip.

"I hereby announce the following Order of the Day. The Bolsheviks are near Warsaw and proclaim that they are friends of the Polish nation. This is a treacherous lie.

"The commanders of the Polish National Army must stop all acts which are trying to help the Soviets. The Germans are fleeing. On with the battle with the Soviets.

"Long live free-fighting Poland!

"BOR, Chief Commander of the Armed Forces in Poland."

"Poorly fucking written," Stazek Pszenny said. "I don't believe it's him. Bor is much more eloquent."

Three shifts had the trash buried by next morning.

THE FAMILIAR ACRID SMELL of fire woke Shosha in the dark. It was close. She sat up and put on her shoes and walked downstairs to the first floor. She looked out the window and saw smoke. She opened the front door. She felt heat and heard fire barking and cracking. Then she saw flames flipping and twirling above stone and brick up the street.

"Oh dear God," Stazek said. He stood with her. "It's the Jesuit monastery."

"We should look," Shosha said. "We should help them."

"Absolutely not. The fire's done burning. See the smoke. It's turning white. There's no one left to help."

Shosha looked at him.

"I'm sure they all got out," Stazek said.

Soldiers came in from the trenches that afternoon for rest and recreation. They stood on the streets and talked to people they had been shooting at the day before. The talk was friendly. The soldiers showed photographs of their families. The children pretended they were soldiers. Women gave the soldiers food. In exchange, the soldiers told them which windows to avoid and which streets to stay off. This queer detente lasted a day and kept a few people alive.

Two subjects dominated the conversations of the women on the block: the Jesuit monastery and the potatoes that were growing in the Mokotów field. No one had the courage to ask the soldiers about digging up the potatoes, so Shosha did.

"I make the best potato soup you've ever had," she told the soldiers. "But I need potatoes."

The soldiers talked among themselves.

"Come with us," one of them said. "We'll have to take you over."

When the soldiers were outside the gate and it was clear they planned no trickery, Shosha, Karl, Stazek, Gene, and four other women and one other man followed them into the field. From there, they could see smoke still rising from the Jesuit monastery and chapel. Bricks and stained glass littered the lawn around the buildings.

Stazek approached one of the soldiers. "How did that happen?" He pointed toward the chapel. "Do you know?"

"Weapons search," the soldier said.

"There?" Stazek asked.

"We found rifles, bullets, some incendiaries."

"So you attacked the fathers?"

"Not me," the soldier said.

"Anyone hurt?" someone else asked.

"If anyone was in there," the soldier said.

"There were people in there?" asked one of the women. "How many?"

"I don't know."

"Jesus," Stazek said.

"Was it during services?"

"I wasn't there," the soldier said. "I don't know."

"Is the old Father dead? Did they kill the old Father?"

"Father Philip," Stazek said.

"I don't know who they killed," the soldier said. "I wasn't there."

They came in from the fields with dozens of potatoes expecting an excited welcome. Instead, the streets were bare.

"One of the Jesuits is in Mirim's cellar," someone whispered after nightfall.

A FEW WOMEN MADE enough potato soup to feed the block. The Jesuit priest came into the yard after midnight for air and a smoke. He had a bandage around his hand and neck. When he lit the priest's cigarette, Karl held his hand around the match so no one would see the flame. Shosha joined some other people who gathered around the priest. Stazek stayed home with his son.

"Your brother's Jakub," the Jesuit, Father Peter, said to Karl.

"You know him?"

"I know about him."

"Have you seen him?" Karl said. "Do you know where they took him?"

"No," the Jesuit said. He drew on his cigarette.

"What happened?" Shosha said, indicating the chapel.

The Jesuit folded his arms and held the cigarette between his fingers. He shook.

"They came in," he said. "They wanted to search. They said we had weapons."

"What kind of weapons?" said a man standing there.

"Did they kill Father Philip?" someone else asked.

"Rifles, grenades—I don't know. They pushed us into the basement and next thing we know there's a loud blast in the chapel. Just deafening." The priest's lips quivered. "People were praying," he said. "People in the chapel. They didn't see the soldiers. The soldiers came through the sacristy."

"Surely they heard them."

"The people there that time of day are old, slow and deaf," Fr. Peter said.

"Did Father Philip make it out? Is he alive?"

Father Peter lowered his head.

"How did you get out?" Karl asked.

The priest drew on his cigarette as he sat on a stone bench against a wall in the yard. He looked at the people. "The SS came down to the basement and shot everybody," he said. "Father Edward, our superior. Father Francis. Father Władysław." His face was hot. "I don't know how they missed me." He lowered his head. Shosha sat next to him.

"Did anyone else make it out?" someone asked.

Shosha put her arms around Fr. Peter. She could feel him tremble. "I'm the only one," he said. He rubbed his forehead and his eyes.

Shosha took the priest's head onto her shoulder. The crowd started to break up.

"You'll be all right here?" Karl asked.

Shosha nodded. She stayed with the priest until his composure returned. Three days later, she stood with the others when Father Peter celebrated Catholic mass in Stazek Pszenny's living room.

Thirty Eight

After Resistance attacks on Rakowiecka Street and the Avenue of Independence, Niepodleglosc, exhausted German soldiers offered a short, self-serving truce on orders of Warsaw Command. To assure people still felt punished and no men would fight on the Polish side, the Germans restricted the truce to women. To assure only Poles felt and appeared "in retreat," the occupiers insisted Poles wear white handkerchiefs. The truce was such a relief that any man who didn't go along risked severe consequences from the woman or women in his life.

Women—and a few men—came from several blocks to dig potatoes and socialize with people on the Pszenny's block, which was close to the Mokotów field. They came pushing carts with children. Men just in from the fighting were wounded and dirty. People kissed and hugged and exchanged small gifts.

Darkness ended the truce. Two German officers ran into the yard and shooed everyone into basements. The soldiers looked after these women, who fed them, talked to them, listened to their complaining, and tended their wounds.

FROM PSZENNY'S BASEMENT WINDOW, Shosha watched the occupiers pull a cannon up the street, moving close along the walls. She no longer felt safe in the attic. Basement purges had given way to artillery shelling.

"Get away from there," Karl said.

"They aren't shooting yet," Shosha said.

"So?" He walked to her. "You want to risk it?"

The cow bellowed again and Shosha cringed. They covered their ears. She looked at Karl. After the noise stopped, she took his palms away from his ears.

"Stay with me," she said.

The shooting started an hour later and continued all night. Shosha lay on a mattress in the dark and kept her eyes open and watched the basement window, where flames and shadows danced by. Karl lay next to her. Stazek and Gene Pszenny were upstairs.

"We men should be out there," Karl said.

"And leave me with a bunch of women?" Shosha said. "We need you here."

"I can't move here," Karl said. "I can't find Jakub. I can't ask anyone about him."

After a while: "You want to know about him?" Shosha said. She looked up at the ceiling. "I can tell you about him."

She turned to Karl. He looked at her like he was going to speak. "He helped me bury my best friend," she said. "He said Kaddish with me. He helped keep us safe because the soldiers were afraid of him and because he had an uplifting way." She paused. "Do you know what Kaddish is?"

"I've heard of it," Karl said. "Some kind of prayer."

"It's *the* prayer," Shosha said. "It's the final prayer, the goodbye of goodbyes. What you say to the L-rd about the person you love before they see Him."

"That's a strange thought," Karl said.

"What's strange about it?"

"Talking to God, here."

"Your brother did."

"Jakub talk to God? Only when he's drunk."

Shosha turned away. "He seemed devout to me."

"In his own way. But he doesn't pray much."

"He prayed with me. I heard all stigmatics pray."

"Not Jakub," Karl said. "Well, sometimes, but not every day."

They let some silence pass between them.

"Your best friend is the one Jakub came to help," Karl said.

"He carried her body a mile," Shosha said. She lay on her back in the darkness and saw light from the corner of her eye. She left her eyes open until they pooled with moisture and the light from the corner went away.

PEOPLE EMERGED FROM THEIR cubbies in the morning. Near first aid posts, soldiers lay in cots—German and Polish fighters, side by side. Polish nurses tended them and smiled and spoke to each one the same. Toward midnight, a young doctor and several nurses wearing white handkerchiefs came to the yard with a horse-drawn wagon. Karl helped unload stretchers with wounded fighters. The medical team was from one of the suburbs and everybody who was outside surrounded them for news.

"There's so much fighting there," a nurse said. "The hospital's too full, we have no painkillers, no anesthetics. We can't get to the wounded with all the fighting."

"What do you do?" someone asked.

"They lie for days," the nurse said. "Too many times we have to amputate."

"You can't believe all the fighting," another nurse said.

Two German soldiers—the same boys who had dined on Shosha's potato soup—ordered everyone out of Pszenny's block the following morning.

"They're burning the houses," one of them said. "It has to be done."

"Burning houses?" Shosha said. "Why? No one is fighting here."

"Orders," the boy said.

"This is crazy," someone said. "It's insane—you can't just burn our houses."

"We're giving you fair warning," the other boy said. "Get out or get burned."

"Let me see your orders," Shosha said.

"Orders?" the boy said. "We don't have those."

"Well—then how do you know what you're supposed to do?"

"Our commanders tell us. Listen, you shouldn't be questioning."

These boys had begged to defend Germany against her bitter, hateful, imperialist enemies. Now they were arguing with a bunch of skinny women.

"If your commanders have the orders, let's see them," Shosha said.

"That won't happen," the other boy said. "They won't show you anything."

"Then we won't leave," Shosha said.

"You sure you know what you're saying?"

"She knows what she's saying." Karl stood in the little group. "We need official signed orders, just like you."

"I'm not so sure about this," said another man. "They can shoot us any time.

"It only makes sense," a woman said. "It's only fair."

"It's not fair," the soldier said. "We don't carry around written orders."

"Why should we listen to mere boys?" Shosha said. "How old are you?"

"I'm twenty," one said.

"You're not twenty," Shosha said. "You're sixteen maybe. What if I tell your commander he has a child for a soldier?"

"I'd shoot you before you could," the boy said.

"Then you'd have to shoot everybody here," Shosha said. "They all know now."

The other boy took his friend's arm. "Let's go."

EVERYONE ON THE BLOCK packed. They bundled sheets, emptied wardrobes and drawers, carried trunks and suitcases down from attics and boxes up from basements. They dug holes in the ground and buried their valuables. They took food and essential things. Some praised Shosha for her courage; others condemned her stupidity. Arguing with the boy soldiers would only make things worse, they said. They complained about other things, too.

After dinner, Karl helped fold up the first aid station. Shosha was in the yard with the other women and Stazek. She felt someone behind her. Her heart jumped. It was the boy soldier, with papers in his hand.

"Here," he said. He handed the orders to Shosha.

She took them and her hands shook when she tried to read. "I can't read them," she said. "I can't read German," she lied.

The boy took the papers and read them. The houses would be burned tomorrow, September 9, 1944. The orders were signed: *Korpsgruppe* Erich von dem Bach-Zelewski.

SS-Obergruppenführer Bach-Zelewski was now a battle-fatigued fat man who recovered from a nervous breakdown two years earlier. He commanded all German troops in the area. He was assigning the job of burning the houses to a man whose name Shosha had heard.

Oskar Dirlewanger.

Her heart leapt again. "Of the soap?" she asked.

The boy looked at her. He hadn't heard the rumors: that this Dirlewanger character made soap from people his brigade murdered. He injected his victims with poison the tales went, then cut them into small pieces, mixed the pieces with horse meat and boiled the fatty mess into soap.

"They never let photographers travel with this man," Shosha told the boy. "Even Stroop had photographers."

"Well, I didn't choose him," the boy said. "I hope you leave. I like you. All us guys do."

Shosha walked away from the soldier and picked up her pace. By the time she was at Pszenny's, she was running.

"Oh L-rd, Oh L-rd," she thought. "Please forgive me for taking thy name in vain. Oh L-rd, Oh G-d."

She told Karl.

"Oh fuck," he said.

WORD SPREAD DIRLEWANGER WOULD start burning houses the next day.

"*Sonderkommando*? Good God. They kill anything that moves."

People grabbed belongings and went into the street despite cannons and gunfire. They looked up the streets and crossed one at a time. On the other side, they started down alleys and went through open doors—laundries, basements, boiler rooms, kitchens, bombed-out shells—as shortcuts to adjacent streets. The Germans marked block after block for burning and people filled yards and streets with their belongings.

Karl and Shosha moved down the street with Stazek and his son. "They're going to burn the whole fucking city," Stazek said. "A bunch of women and children—they're insane. If I needed proof, I have it. They're insane, this war's insane. I may go insane if I live long enough."

German soldiers came out of empty buildings waving guns. Planes would be dropping bombs in only a few minutes, they yelled.

"*Sich verschanzen!*"

Someone came out of another building yelling and pointing downward.

The crush began toward a basement. People tripped over bags and suitcases. They swore and prayed and pushed their crying children. The first explosion shook the walls. *Luftwaffe* bombers circled in the sky. Karl and Shosha saw the bombs falling and dust clouds rising above the houses. The people heard tanks and the swoosh of flamethrowers and fire crackling.

The bombing slowed by dusk and they moved toward a pristine park near the German officers' recreation center. It had big, old trees, green shrubs and a thick green lawn. They found lawn chairs and benches. Shosha and her men set down their sacks and suitcases. They lowered themselves to the cool green grass. Dozens of refugees spent the night on the lawn, covered with coats, blankets, and rags.

Cooking smells woke Shosha in the morning. Women were using pots and the few utensils they managed to save. Men were showering in a hydrant, and though the morning was chilly, children ran through the spray.

Shosha saw an *SS* officer among the evacuees. "Can we go home?" she asked. "They aren't burning the houses."

"They will," the soldier said. His voice shook. "The order was only postponed."

"Why?"

"They need more petrol."

"Do we have time to get a few more things?" Eugeniusz Pszenny asked. "Our houses are near." Stazek took his son by the shoulder.

"I don't think so," the soldier said.

Shosha noticed his hands shaking. "We have vodka at home," she said. "Everyone does."

The soldier thought. "*Nein*," he said again.

"Too bad," Shosha said. "It's Red. The best."

The soldier raised a trembling hand to his face. "All right," he said. "But stay with me."

Eugeniusz started to walk with them, but Stazek held him back. The soldier led Shosha and two women wearing white handkerchiefs tied around their sleeves. Karl ran and caught up with them.

"Where are you going?" He was out of breath.

"Back," Shosha said. "We could use more food."

"He's taking you?" Karl asked, indicating the soldier.

"For vodka."

They walked over bricks and glass and metal rubble and arrived back at the row of flats, empty save for a few people who would not leave. The women went into their houses and gathered food and Shosha brought the soldier a half-bottle of vodka. He sat on a bench in the courtyard and drank. He closed his eyes. When it was time to return, Shosha went to rouse the soldier. She shook him.

"Do we need him?" Karl said. "We can get back on our own."

"It's a good idea if he took us back," a woman said. "They won't shoot at him."

Shosha patted his cheeks. She shook him again and he slumped. Shosha—the former infirmary attendant—felt his neck and wrist for a pulse. "I think he's dead," she said.

"Dead drunk," Karl said.

"No—really—dead."

Karl and the women came over to the soldier. "From one drink?"

Shosha stood back and saw a small envelope sticking out of his coat pocket. She bent and picked it up. Something inside felt like sand.

"What is that?" Karl asked.

She opened it and looked inside. "It's white," she said.

"Smells like almonds," said another woman. "I can smell it from here."

Karl looked at the vodka bottle. "Poor man's Amaretto," he said.

"He killed himself," Shosha said.

"Good," one of the women said. "One less killing us."

Karl looked around. He reached down and took the soldier's handgun and tucked it away. He went through the soldier's pockets. He took money, tobacco, some coins.

"What about the rifle?" Shosha said.

Karl picked it up. "The soldiers will see us with it," he said. He threw it over a high brick wall.

WHEN THEY RETURNED TO the park with food and supplies, more refugees had flooded in. Their clothes were dirty and torn, and bones shown in their cheeks. Down the long stretch of lawn toward the street, *SS* stood or sat with rifles.

Soldiers and inmates from the *Stauferkaserne* barracks *SS* troops converted into a prison pulled carts piled with flock—a mixture of rags, wool, and oil-soaked paper. Other carts carried barrels of gasoline. The work was methodical. First, soldiers threw grenades through windows. Next, a blast scattered glass and debris. Finally, inmates lit flock and threw it through broken panes. Flames exploded and the refugees heard the whoosh and hiss from the park as the fire fought to breathe.

The fires burned methodically. First they consumed lightweight furniture and drapes and then moved along wallpaper, to pictures and books. The flames became brighter and spread, creeping upstairs and piercing roofs. From as far as the park, people felt heat on their faces. Clouds of black smoke rose in the sky and billowed in the street.

Some people watched from the park and broke from the crowd as the Germans moved up the street. They jumped over fences and ran toward their burning homes. When the first people returned with belongings on their backs, Eugeniusz Pszenny broke away.

"Gene," his father called. Stazek started after his son but Karl caught him.

"I'll go," Karl said.

"He's *my* son," Stazek said.

"I'm younger and faster," Karl called back. He chased Gene across the lawn.

Karl ran and saw people throwing furniture and clothes and boxes from burning buildings. Soldiers continued up the street, breaking and burning, one by one. The fires burned higher and Karl dodged falling glass. The heat was so intense he couldn't come near the sidewalk, so he stayed in the center of the street. He saw a man spraying himself with a hose. The man dropped the hose and ran into his house. Karl kept running. He stopped to catch his breath and turned and saw the man come out the front door with a stack of books. His shirttail was on fire. He set the books down. He lay and rolled on the wet grass, then picked up the hose and aimed it at the house.

Karl ran again amid gunfire. He turned and saw the man lying next to his books. He still had the hose in his hand, but he was not moving. In another block, Karl arrived at the Pszenny's. The house was engulfed and he couldn't stand near it so he stayed in the street.

"Gene," he called. "Eugeniusz!" Sunlight drifted in and out and shadows passed over the flames. Bricks crumbled and glass fell on both sides of the street. "Gene!" Clouds moved together. The sky darkened and Karl stood, calling to Eugeniusz. The light from the fires kept the street bright, even as rain fell.

Karl waited out the rain in a vacant house. He walked back toward the park after midnight. He heard thunder, but not from the sky. Through alleys in the dark, he saw faint shadows of tanks moving on neighboring streets. When the tanks fired in just the right place, Karl saw yellow and orange sparks rising over buildings and scattering along rooftops. He heard the bellowing cow three times and had to stop and cover his ears. The moaning made his eyes tear. He heard it came from a thing called a *Nebelwerfer* (smoke launcher) that fired six missiles at once. Karl heard the impacts and bricks falling and he smelled particularly pungent smoke. He crossed the lawn at the park. Stazek ran up to him.

"Where's my Eugeniusz?"

Karl looked at him. Stazek grabbed his hand. "Don't tell me this—where's my baby, my Gene?"

Shosha put her hand on Stazek's shoulders. He crumpled. He wrapped his arms around Karl's leg and pressed his head against it.

"It can't be," he cried, and his voice fell. "Don't tell me this. Don't tell me this."

Karl knelt on the grass and held Stazek's head to his chest.

They heard gunfire and artillery blasts. Shosha saw ash and dust and fires glowing in the buildings across the street and she saw smoke rising to meet clouds that grayed the night over the burning city. She felt heat on her face.

"Did you see Gene?" Stazek asked. "Did you ever see him?"

"No," Karl said.

"So you don't know if he's dead—you don't know. You didn't actually see."

"I didn't see him," Karl said. "I called for a long time."

Stazek stood.

"What are you doing?" Shosha asked.

"I can't accept this," he said.

"You can't go back," Karl said.

"You're saying give up—give in?"

"Please don't," Shosha said.

"What if he's alive?" Stazek said.

He picked up a bag with some food and water. Karl stood in his way.

"Move," Stazek said.

Karl stood firm.

"We don't know that he's dead. What if he's hurt and he needs me?"

Shosha took Karl's arm. Stazek walked around them and they watched Gene's father cross the lawn toward the street. They saw nothing in the darkness and then they saw the shadow of a man moving toward the flames.

Thirty Nine

A sh covered everything in the morning. Leaves hung gray with it and people stood where they had slept on the lawn and brushed it out of their hair and clothes. Children cried with it in their eyes. Men spit it out, especially the ones who snored with their mouths open. No one could hear any birds, not even the morning doves that cooed the arrival of light.

Shosha opened her eyes and saw a paper draped across her leg. She sat up and saw leaflets littering the lawn, white on gray. She opened one and saw a crude illustration of a black eagle standing on a broken cross. Shosha (**S**) read the flier and interpreted it in her mind.

ULTIMATUM

To the people of Warsaw:

The German High Command wants to avoid unnecessary bloodshed, which will mainly affect innocent women and children, and therefore has issued the following appeal:

1. The population should leave Warsaw in a western direction, carrying white kerchiefs in their hands.

2. The German High Command guarantees that no one who leaves Warsaw of his or her own free will, will come to harm.

2S. Bullshit. The German High Command guarantees nothing.

3.   All men and women who are able to work will receive work and bread.

3S. See 2S.

4.   People unable to work will be accommodated in the western district of Warsaw's province. Food will be supplied.

4S. People unable to work will be starved or shot. Jews —who we all know aren't people—will be deported for extra cruelty to one of the camps.

5. All who are ill as well as old people, women, and children needing care will receive accommodation and medical treatment.

5S. See 4S.

6. The Polish people know that the German Army is fighting Bolshevism only. Anyone who continues to be used as a

Bolshevik's tool, irrespective of which slogan he might follow, will be held responsible and prosecuted without scruples.

6S. Bolsheviks? Scruples? Where?

7. This ultimatum is for a limited time only.

7S. Ultimatum! Then what—what more can they do to us? Fuckers.

Signed this 11th Day of September, 1944

ERICH VON DEM BACH
COMMANDER IN CHIEF
WARSAW DISTRICT

S. FUCKER.

Karl walked up with a plate of cooked potatoes and apples. "I think we should leave," he said. "Word has it they're breaking up families and taking the men to labor camps."

They ate as evacuees from other neighborhoods moved up the street. The people were dirty, bent and covered with soot. In their arms and on their shoulders, backs, and heads they carried packs of last things. Their eyes were dull and they walked with heavy, tired steps, wiping perspiration from their faces and foreheads and looking at the ash on their handkerchiefs.

Karl and Shosha gathered their things.

"What do you think happened to Stazek?" Karl asked.

"I thought all night about him," Shosha said.

"I tried to make him stay," Karl said.

"Maybe he found his son," Shosha said. "He knows the town well as anyone, better than any German. He can probably hide for a long time."

"We may see him again," Karl said.

"No," she said. "We won't see him again."

KARL AND SHOSHA CROSSED several streets with soldiers nearby.

"I don't want to risk it," Karl said. He motioned Shosha toward a building. "Let's go through here."

The building was partly collapsed and smoldering but passing through it would lead to a different street. They stepped inside, over bricks and heaps. Heat from rocks and mortar made it hard to breathe. They started to sweat and their dirty clothing clung to their skin.

"Don't touch anything," Shosha said.

They got through the building and stopped and gasped for air on the street. Karl bent down. Shosha leaned against a light pole.

"Look at this." Karl pulled his wet shirt away from his chest and it made a sucking noise as it separated from his skin. He did it again. He made the shirt breathe in and out like a makeshift accordion. Shosha smiled and giggled.

"I can't believe I'm laughing," she said.

They walked through clouds of dust and smoke, the smell of fire, the sound of rumbling between buildings. A tank came around the corner behind them.

"*Halten!*" A soldier on the beast fired his rifle. Karl froze.

"*Hände hoch! Hände hoch!*"

They raised their hands. Karl held the white handkerchief high.

"What do they want with us?" Karl said. "We were free to leave."

The tank pulled beside them. The soldier aimed his sidearm at Shosha.

"You—up here. Up here!"

She looked at Karl.

"Up here," the soldier screamed in uncertain Polish.

She started to move and lowered her hands.

"Hands up. Up!"

Shosha climbed onto the tank. She slipped. The soldier reached down and yanked her by the arm. He pressed her against the turret. He pressed his sidearm into her bony back.

"Hands up." He stuck a white handkerchief in her hand. He called to Karl and waved the rifle toward him.

"You—in front. In front."

Karl stepped in front of the tank.

"You're not going to run over him," Shosha said.

"Walk."

Karl started to walk.

"Hands up!"

The soldier hollered down to the driver.

"Alle! Vorwärts!"

The tank lurched and trundled. Karl walked holding his hands and the handkerchief high. Each time he slowed, the tank commander yelled down and the tank sped within a meter of crushing him. The tank crew marched him from deserted, hollowed-out buildings to occupied houses still in Underground hands. Other combatants joined the tank along the street. They came from no place in particular. They were not dressed like the German soldiers. They were Ukrainian Trawniki men.

Shosha saw resistance fighters in windows and holes blasted in walls overlooking the street. They held fire, and a few withdrew their arms. Each time Shosha's shoulder tired of holding the white kerchief and her arm faltered, the soldier rammed the sidearm into her back.

The occupiers fanned out and ran into each building, forcing stragglers to the street and lining them up in front of the tank. They dragged a woman clutching a newborn wrapped in rags. Shosha saw the infant's flush, wrinkled face, still mottled with blood and afterbirth. There was little water to drink, and no water to wash. The woman with the baby slowed and fell behind and a Ukrainian soldier tried to take the infant. She screamed and the child screamed. The soldier hit the woman with his rifle and tore away the child. He smashed the newborn's head into a pile of bricks and threw it into the ruins of a cellar.

Karl felt sick and almost fell. But he gathered himself and kept his eyes straight. He trod over craters and rubble, tangled barbed wire, twisted rebar and pipes, and corpses that, with the guns and the smoke, filled the air with a burning putrescence.

The tank stopped amid the rubble. The turret commander spoke to his driver. Shosha felt the pistol barrel. She heard shots. She was surprised to see a Ukrainian fall in the street ahead of them. The turret commander screamed obscenities toward the bombed out windows and wrapped his hand around Shosha's face. He stuck the gun hard into her back. She looked up and saw shadows in the windows. She smelled hot, dirty fingers. They heard another shot and another Ukrainian fell.

When another shot echoed, Shosha felt something swipe against her back and then nothing. She didn't turn but looked up, toward the windows. In the darkness, she thought she saw a familiar face, thinner and older, but unmistakable.

"Antek," she whispered.

She turned and saw the dead turret commander, slumped and bleeding around his collar.

The tank kept moving and the people marched and a Ukrainian fighter in the street pointed to Shosha but before he could do anything, a bullet popped his gut. Resistance fighters ran out of buildings and rushed the tank. They pushed the line of people out of the tank's way and came alongside and motioned Shosha down. The turret began to turn. A Polish resistance fighter grabbed Shosha's hand and helped her down. He pulled her toward a hole near the street. They ducked and the tank fired, blasting bricks in a crumbling building.

"Shit." The fighter pushed Shosha toward the hole. "Take this toward the river—that way," he pointed.

"A tunnel?" she asked.

"Kind of," he said.

She looked for Karl. He was with resistance fighters stuffing incendiaries into the tank. The tank fired at abandoned buildings and swerved and the turret swung but couldn't shake the fighters.

"Karl," Shosha called.

He didn't hear her.

"Karl!"

He looked around and saw her, standing near the hole. She waved him over.

"Karl. Hurry!"

He waved at her. He jumped off the tank and stumbled in the rubble and ran toward her. They went through the hole toward darkness and a terrible smell. They were in the sewers.

"I can't breathe," Karl said.

"It's not poison," Shosha said. "You can breathe. You have to."

"I'll hold my breath."

The tank exploded above ground, knocking them into the walls and causing Shosha to stumble. She took Karl's wrist. "You can't hold your breath," she said. "You'll faint, and if you faint, you die."

They walked in darkness over wet bricks. There wasn't much water now so the way was dry. They passed sunlit spots that went a few feet then became darkness again. They said almost nothing —each word encouraged breathing. Shosha guessed the way toward the river. She heard people above them and figured they were going out of the city along a street near the bank. They climbed up rusty steps toward an open manhole and the sun. Karl emerged first. He helped Shosha. They stopped and breathed.

Women, children, and men flowed like lava out of the burning city. Some people carried clothes, books, and food. Others dragged their things with slender ropes, stopping every few meters to rest. Some people were burned, others wounded and bleeding, walking around bodies to the left and the right— Germans and Poles and Ukrainians, fallen in battle or to stray bullets that screeched everywhere in the air like angry birds.

"Where from here?" Karl asked.

Shosha walked up to a woman. "This is an evacuation?" she asked.

"Yes," the woman said.

"To where?"

"They haven't told us yet, but no one's been shot."

Shosha motioned to Karl. They walked in the procession.

"Run," someone yelled. "They're shooting!"

People heard screaming in Ukrainian. "Himmler's Hounds," someone cried. The crowd ran across the highway and up an embankment, but the Trawniki men shot them like fleeing

game. The Ukrainians ran up the hill and pulled the women
down and the children, the easy ones. They beat them in the
head with rifles and sticks and anything else they had. Karl and
Shosha crawled up the embankment. Karl looked toward the
top.

"Come on." He turned to reach for Shosha but she wasn't
there. He looked down. Two men were dragging her feet. Karl
went after them and remembered. He pulled the revolver he had
confiscated from his belt and undid the safety and aimed. They
had Shosha at the bottom of the hill and the first man stopped
and stood back. Karl fired and hit him in the neck and he
grabbed himself and fell. The other man looked up. Karl fired
again. The bullet missed but the man turned and ran. Karl slid
down the hill.

"Your hand," Shosha said.

"What?" Karl looked at his hand, then her. "Are you all
right?"

Shosha took up her skirt and tore it. She wrapped Karl's
bleeding hand. "What happened to you?" she asked.

"Me? I wasn't the one almost killed."

"Did you take a bullet? I didn't see anything."

Karl looked up the hill. "Maybe glass. Something in the dirt."

The dead Ukrainian lay nearby. "We have to keep going,"
Shosha said.

They started up the hill again and Karl took her hand. At the
top, Shosha stood and turned and saw before her the Wisła and
Praga across the water.

Forty

Shosha and Karl spent a mid-September night under stars and trees near the river. They heard guns and shelling into the early morning hours. Across the Wisła, in the low exploding lights that reflected off the water, Shosha saw Soviet tanks and Red Army soldiers, walking, standing, and talking, knights leaning against muzzled dragons.

"Why do they sit?" she asked. "Why don't they do something?"

"It's a complicated situation," Karl said. "That's what they said in the city."

More than any other, one man complicated the situation. When the British parliament protested to the world press that Joseph Stalin was being grossly unfair in his dealings with Poland—a fellow ally—the Soviet dictator decided on a course of duplicitous assistance designed to calm the international uproar. On September 9, 1944, Stalin ordered his planes to drop arms and ammunition to the insurgents—but at night without parachutes. The crates smashed on the ground and the supplies were ruined or confiscated by the Germans. In mid-September, the situation started to look more hopeful. Stalin ordered Praga subdued—a process that took only four days.

Liberation for Warsaw seemed just across the river.

But across the river is where the liberators stayed. Marshal Konstantin Rokossovsky stopped the Red Army in Praga. Sometimes known as "the son of a Warsaw railwayman" the Soviet commander attended a Gymnasium in Warsaw, worked in Warsaw as a young man, and spent time in the Pawiak prison. He wrote in his memoirs that his former home was in the "throes of its death. The city was covered in clouds of smoke. Here and there houses were burning. Bombs and shells were exploding. Everything indicated that a battle was in progress." A battle Rokossovsky—on orders from Stalin—would not engage. With little explanation, he maintained his armies "would not be able at the present time to liberate Warsaw," and so they sat across the river.

Logs captured from the German 9th Army, meanwhile, cast the matter this way:

"...as long as the fighting in Warsaw went on, it constituted a harassment of the Germans that could not but be welcomed by the Soviet command. A successful outcome of the uprising was not in the interest of Moscow, because it was bound to bring demands totally incompatible with Moscow's intended course of action."

"I BROUGHT FOOD," SHOSHA said. She descended the narrow embankment with a bucket. Karl was sitting under trees near the river.

"Oh," he said. He rubbed his neck. "I'm stiff."

She looked at him and set down the bucket with two sprouting potatoes, a half sausage looking dry, and a tin can filled with clean water.

"Where did you get it?"

"In a flat," Shosha said. "No one was there."

She knelt down and put her hand on his forehead.

"You're hot," she said.

"Head aches, too."

"You've been keeping your hand clean—right?"

"It's fine—much better." He pulled back the cloth dressing.

"It doesn't look bad," Shosha said. She felt around the edges. "Sturdy and pink—it's healing." She took the tin of water from the bucket and handed it to Karl. "Drink a little," she said.

He sipped the water. "I was thinking about getting into the river," he said.

Shosha looked across the mid-day haze that lay atop the water. She saw tanks on the Praga side. She saw children there, and Reds—soldiers, sitting and smoking.

"Let's get in," she said. "Take your clothes off." She started unbuttoning her blouse.

"Here?" Karl said.

"Certainly here. We need a bath. We stink."

Shosha slipped off her blouse and Karl turned away. She laughed. "To see or not to see," she said. He didn't look at her. "We're already naked," she said. She undressed the rest of the way and stepped into the water. Her skin wrapped her bones. "Ahh—it feels wonderful," she said.

"It's clean?"

"Cleaner than we are," Shosha said. "I'm not planning to drink it."

She bent down and submerged herself to her neck. Karl looked at her.

"Get in," she said. "It'll cool you."

He hesitated and dabbed his forehead with his shirt.

"Come on."

Karl pulled his shirt over his head. He slipped his shoes off, stood, and walked behind a tree.

"Shy?" Shosha said.

"You should turn your head," Karl said. "It's only fair."

"Fair has nothing to do with us," Shosha said. "Come in."

"Turn your head."

"No. Then I have to look at that tragedy across the river and worry about my mother and the rabbi."

"They're safer than we are."

"Who says?"

"Cover your eyes, then."

Shosha brought her hand up to her eyes. "Chicken," she said.

"Yes, if you have some. I'm very hungry." Karl walked naked into the river. He lowered himself. Shosha watched him.

"Handsome boy," she said.

"You cheated."

"No."

"Ahh—you were right. This is wonderful."

They stood a few feet apart with the water up to their necks. Karl looked at the Praga shore. "Think they can see us?"

"Fuck them if they can." Then Shosha yelled toward the Russians: "*Jeszcze Polska nie zginiela bugy my zyjemy!*" Poland is not dead whilst we live!

"I've heard that. Who said it?"

"Kosciuszko," Shosha said. "He was here before us."

After Russia invaded Poland in 1792, Tadeusz Kosciuszko led several battles to liberate his country. He routed the Russian Army more than once, most notably as commander of the Polish rebellion named for him, the Kosciuszko Uprising. He earlier fought in the American Revolution and returned to his native Poland an American hero. Thomas Jefferson said of Kosciuszko, "He was as pure a son of liberty as I have ever known."

KARL WAS HOT WITH fever in the night. He tossed and woke and kept his eyes open. He looked at the stars through the glow of fires in Warsaw and listened to the guns. He tried to turn his head but his neck was too stiff. He tried to open his wounded hand but it was cramped and he had to raise it and pry it open with his other hand. When he woke in the morning, he could turn his neck enough to see the sun casting shadows across the Praga shore.

"I can barely move," he told Shosha.

She felt his head. "You're burning," she said. "I need to get help."

"It's too dangerous," he said. "Besides, where would you find someone?"

"I can try," she said. "I know where they might have a doctor."

Karl turned toward the shore. "I'm thirsty," he said. "I'd rather have water."

"How does your jaw feel?"

"Stiff. Like my neck."

"Open your mouth."

Karl opened it a little ways.

"Is that all?"

"Yes," he said.

She took his wounded hand. She stared at him.

"What?"

"Can you move your fingers?"

He tried. She looked at him.

"What?" he said.

She stroked his cheek and took his good hand and squeezed.

"I think you have tetanus," she said.

"Tetanus?"

"Lockjaw."

"God," he said.

"You got it through the dirt."

"I cleaned my hand."

"It doesn't matter," she said. "Have you had the vaccine?"

"I don't know."

She looked up at the bluffs. "There's no antibiotics," she said. "Not up there."

Karl breathed and held her hand. "Where did you get that water?" he asked. "Yesterday."

"From a broken pipe. I can get more."

"Is it safe?"

"I didn't see anybody. The soldiers have moved."

She took off her blouse and went down to the river and soaked it. She brought it back and pressed it to Karl's cheeks and forehead. He saw her bones through her skin and the small, starved curvature of her breasts. She took his good hand and with it held her blouse against his face. He raised his other hand, curled and cramped, and smoothed the back of his palm against her cheek. She looked at his eyes. "I'll get the water," she said.

DURING THE NIGHT, RAIN drizzled and Karl felt coolness and relief. At dawn, Shosha saw him lying next to the river. His hands were in the water.

"I wouldn't drink that," she called to him.

"I'm not drinking."

She walked to him with a worn gray blanket around her shoulders. Karl was wiping his face with her damp blouse.

"I can barely swallow," he said.

She took the blouse from his cramped hands and submerged it in the water and brought it to his brow.

"Take me into the river," he said.

"You'll drown." She patted his forehead and cheeks with the blouse.

A spasm ripped across his stomach and side. He clenched his teeth and winced. "I'm cramped," he said. "But the heat is worse."

"I should have gone," Shosha said. "I should have found a doctor."

"Where?"

Shosha looked at the river.

"Take me in," he said.

"I'm too weak," she said. "I couldn't move you."

"Put your arms around my chest and we'll push off together."

"How did you get down here?" she asked.

"Crawled. But that was last night, when I could." He seized and cringed. "Come on," he said. "Before I can't move at all."

Shosha crept over to him. "Can you lean forward?" She slipped her hands underneath his arms and wrapped her fingers around his chest. "Ready—push," she said. "Push." They pushed their feet forward, together on the muddy bank. They turned toward the water.

"I have to rest," she said.

"We're almost there."

"Why didn't you do this last night?" she said. "When you could?"

"I didn't think it would get this bad."

They pushed again and together they slipped into the water. They moved out, into the river.

"Can you stand?" she said.

"Here in the water."

He felt chills and cramps. "Can you hold me?" he said.

Shosha slipped behind him and stood with her arms around his chest. She tucked her head next to his, set her chin on his shoulder. Karl closed his eyes and his head fell forward. He laughed.

"Look at us," he said. "If my brother could see us. If my mother could see us."

Shosha smiled.

"My mother would like you," Karl said.

"I'll meet her someday," Shosha said. "I'm sure I'll like her too."

Karl was silent for a moment. "I think she's dead," he said.

"Don't say that."

"It's a feeling."

"Why aren't you crying then?"

"I don't have it in me."

Shosha looked at the sky, where a lone cloud shadowed the river. She sang softly and slowly, about wishing on stars, waking up to cloudless skies, and troubles melting like lemon drops. Karl turned and looked at her, her soft brown eyes and her hair, wet along the edges.

"That's beautiful," he said.

"The Wizard of Oz," she said. "Did you see it?"

"Me?" He laughed and a spasm bent him. "I have to stop laughing." He took a breath and straightened and looked across the water. "Is that all?" he said.

"What?"

"Do you know the whole song?"

"I heard it in Warsaw when I was a girl," she said. "You expect me to remember?"

"It's about a rainbow," Karl said.

"I thought you didn't see it?"

Karl looked at the cloud. It was single and peculiar. "I'm feeling tired," he said. "You can't hold me forever."

Shosha pulled them toward the shore. "Let's rest," she said. "You can stay where it's shallow."

Karl set his head against a rock. Shosha got out of the river and brought fresh water in a can to his lips. He sipped and looked at her. "Tell my brother I loved him," he said.

"You can tell him yourself."

"No."

"You need to drink," she said. "You have to stay hydrated."

"That sounds hard," Karl said. "I'm tired."

Shosha smoothed her hand along his face. "Rest," she said.

"Will you sing to me? You have a beautiful voice."

"Close your eyes," she said.

She watched him. His hands slipped from his chest and the water lapped his side. When his breathing was rhythmical, she knew he was asleep. She went ashore and rested against a tree. She looked at Karl. He was turned toward the river and Praga across it. She thought about her mother and the rabbi, and for a moment considered swimming across. She fell asleep thinking about the last time she had sucked a lemon drop.

THE SKY WAS CLOUDY, the air muggy and thick. Shosha woke and didn't remember where she was. She heard voices and looked toward the river and saw Karl, lying on his back. The water was higher than before and almost covered his chest. She felt faint in the heat and hungry but the voices roused her. She looked around first and then went down to Karl. A thin white crust glazed his lips. She saw a blister. She knelt down to him and patted his face.

"Karl—we have to go. Wake up." She flicked water on his cheek. "Wake up."

The voices were closer and she saw a slender line of soldier boys coming over a distant knoll toward the shore. She took Karl's hands and tugged him. "You have to stand," she said. "We have to move."

He didn't open his eyes and she placed her ear against his chest. She thought she heard his heart but couldn't be sure through the water.

"Help me. Stand. Stand up."

She straddled his body and put her arms under his shoulders and tried to lift him. She stopped and considered the water. She slipped him away from the rock and tugged him out until they floated together. She saw his eyes open.

"You're awake," she said. "Try to stand. Help me."

She thought they could move down river, away from the soldiers, in the water. She pushed them with her legs and kept her head close to his cheek. She heard him breathing softly. The water around them was still, but Shosha saw the river moving faster toward the center. Tree limbs and war waste floated by, submerging in the chop, then surfacing in little eddies.

She grew up warned about the undertow here and when she felt her legs pulled from beneath her, she was frightened and angry. She held Karl but felt the river tugging him. She kicked her legs and moved to the side of the current. She rested and moved her legs again, keeping her feet on smooth rocks along the hard pebbled bottom. She looked at the tanks on the Praga shore. They moved several more meters when the undertow pulled Karl out of her hands. She was weaker now but she grabbed his shirt and pulled herself forward and got her arms around his neck. She moved to get a better grip on him but the current slammed against her legs. She struggled to hold Karl and swallowed water and choked.

Her feet were on a stand of large rocks. She stepped off the rocks and kicked through the water and turned the two of them toward the shore. The water became murky and when she lowered her feet to walk, she felt nothing. She struggled to keep them afloat and moved a little farther and lowered her feet again, and again felt no bottom.

"Shit," she said.

She moved them back to where she knew the rocks made a solid footing. She saw the rocks through the water and lowered her feet and stood, supporting Karl in about five feet of water. She saw his eyes open and close.

"Can you stand? Try to stand."

She was weakening and having trouble keeping him afloat. She felt him support himself barely. She looked up, at clouds trying to close the sky. She looked at Karl. She rested. Then she began pulling them toward the shore. In a few meters, the current grabbed her and pulled her under. She fought and tried to touch bottom but the water was deeper. She panicked. She couldn't see Karl but she didn't remember losing him. She stretched her arms and swam, toward the Sun, where she saw it penetrating the water's surface. The current pulled her down again and she felt faint and breathless. Her arms flailed and her legs felt numb.

"I'm going to die," she thought. She panicked and fought her way toward the surface but the current pulled her back. She thought about Karl. She prayed. "We can't die. Please, don't let us die."

She saw the surface recede and she felt helpless in the river's grip and she thought against all good sense to let the current carry her. It would swirl and sweep and carry her down and drown her and take everything away. It would bring the end and the cloudless sky and the rainbow after the storm. She let the river carry her and it carried her, to three feet of water over smooth gray pebbles, about two meters out from the shore.

VILLAGE

Forty One

Frau Strauss stood by the window in her bedroom on the second story of the Commandant's quarters, looking toward the Dolina Koscieliska. She saw the reflection of the moon on the greenhouse glass.

"Come back to bed."

"Why?"

"I want to hold you," her husband said.

She looked outside, at the grounds. "No one cares what you do here, do they?"

Strauss slipped out of bed.

"It's pathetic," she said.

He took his wife's shoulders. "Is that why you shot that woman? Because no one would care?"

Greta turned to her husband. "Why did she come to you? Were you in love with her? Did *you* get her pregnant?"

"Gretty. That's absurd."

She looked away.

"Why did you come here?" Strauss asked.

"To be near you," she said. She wriggled away and went to the door. "I hate this," she said. "We had a *life*."

Before he could say anything, she slipped out the door. He heard her step down the stairs and then he heard nothing.

MORE ARRIVALS THAN USUAL detrained at Camp Melinka. Boy soldiers with rucksacks slung over their shoulders or hanging at their sides stepped off a rail car just inside the main gate. They slept as the train entered the camp and now they rubbed their eyes and looked around. They covered their noses and some laughed uncomfortably. One boy dropped his hand from his nose and took a deep breath.

"Pussies," he coughed to the others.

"New personnel—over here. Line up," barked an SS *Blockführer,* corporal or *Unterscharführer* rank, near the gate.

The recruits hefted their bags and fell in.

"Follow me," the *Blockführer* said. He was a big man but walked quickly. The boys slowed and looked around. The boy who breathed deeply felt his knees give out and he toppled. The others stopped and ran to him.

"Leave him," the *Blockführer* yelled.

"Leave him, *Herr Unterscharführer*?"

"He'll come around."

They turned a corner and almost stumbled into a pile of corpses. Two more collapsed.

"Tough lot," the *Blockführer* said.

They started to walk and one boy felt something grab his pant leg. He stumbled. He saw an arm, outstretched from the corpses, and a head, eyes barely open. The woman's grip had surprising strength.

"Please," she said.

The boy stared at her.

"Pull me out," the woman said. "Just pull me out." She struggled to breathe. She gathered more of the boy's pant leg and held it. "Please," she said.

The boy reached down but the *Blockführer* grabbed his arm and pushed him back. The *Blockführer* raised his rifle and thrust it butt-down toward the woman's head. The boy yelped. The *Blockführer* missed and raised the rifle again but something stopped him.

Jakub Chelzak held the *Blockführer's* arm in a wicked grip.

"What?" The *Blockführer* tried to pull back. Chelzak was thin. His arms were thin and his hands were big and bony. The *Blockführer* was used to tossing these people aside—they never weighed much, they were weak. But he couldn't retrieve his arm.

"You want to die?" the *Blockführer* asked. He tried to bring his arm to the rifle, but Jakub tightened his grip.

"Pull her out," Jakub said.

The *Blockführer* hesitated. He yanked on his arm, but Jakub squeezed.

"Pull her out!" Jakub said.

"Pole—I can't understand you."

"*Ziehen Sie sie heraus!*" Jakub said.

"You're crazy," the *Blockführer* said. Jakub tightened his grip and the *Blockführer* winced.

"*Unterscharführer.*"

The *Blockführer* turned. He clenched his teeth. Petersdorf came up to them. "What are you doing?"

"Dealing with a situation, *Herr Stürmbannführer*," the *Blockführer* said.

"Where are your men?"

"The men are here."

"Give me the gun," Petersdorf said. "What is this prisoner doing here?"

"She needs water," Jakub said in broken German. "We were taking her to the infirmary."

Petersdorf looked at the *Blockführer*. "*Ja*, it's true," he said.

The young recruit nodded.

Petersdorf whistled at two passing guards. When they came up, he pointed at the woman.

"Pull it out. Take it to the infirmary," Petersdorf said. To Jakub: "I have a job for you." To the *Blockführer*: "Get back to your men."

Jakub and the major walked across the camp together. They came around to the stables, where one horse lived. They went into the stable to the stall.

"*Kommandant's* horse," Petersdorf said in German. "I want you to feed him, brush him, keep him clean. It's a better job than the infirmary."

Jakub understood generally what the major was asking. Petersdorf looked at him in the shadows and picked up a brush.

He approached the horse and ran the brush over the long hair along the side of its neck. Jakub watched the major's slender, delicate hands. Petersdorf handed the brush to Jakub and straightened his jacket.

"If it were up to me, you wouldn't be here," he said. He looked down at his boots. "I can't help any of this. No one can, especially not a Lilliputian like me."

Jakub looked at the hay and dust streaming in the sun.

PETERSDORF CROSSED THE GROUNDS to a large yard surrounded by barbed wire. Warehouses bordered the yard on three sides. The major turned and walked past three mountains. On a mountain of trunks, suitcases, purses, kit bags, and parcels, stagnant water shimmered in oily pools. A thousand blankets molted on the second mountain. Full size blankets formed an organized bottom. Couch and divan blankets and blankets for legs near a warm autumn fire girdled the heap. Baby blankets— pink and blue, quilted and woolen, softer and rougher, wound round and round to the summit. A treacherous pass marked the third mountain—of baby carriages, wagons, and other wheeled things that periodically broke loose and plummeted, causing assorted injuries, including a broken shinbone and two broken fingers. Petersdorf entered an office where clean young women with red, healthy cheeks sat reading lists to Dr. Hehl.

"*Neunzig und sieben* thousand sets of men's clothing; *siebenzig und sechts tausend* sets of women's undergarments; *neun tausend* girl's dresses; *drei tausend* kilograms women's hair."

With each entry, Hehl banged the keys of a khaki-colored Burroughs service-issue adding machine. Petersdorf looked at it.

"How did you manage that?" he said.

Hehl looked up. "*Stürmbannführer*—I didn't even hear you."

The physician started to stand. He looked old in his bifocals, but he was only twenty-seven.

"Don't get up," the major said. He looked at the inventory lists. "What are you intending for this stuff?"

"What I can't sell, I trade."

"For what?"

"This adding machine," Hehl said.

"How did you get an American machine?"

"Soldiers need socks," Hehl said. "And blankets."

"Since when did our soldiers start carrying American adding machines?"

"Not our soldiers, Major."

"What?"

"*Kommandant* likes caviar," Hehl said. "You like vodka. That smelt from the other night—you think the Reich provided it?"

"I didn't think about it," Petersdorf said. "Now that I am, I don't like what I'm hearing."

"The Reich takes all the metal, all the tin, all the leather, all the rubber."

"Trading with the enemy is treason."

"Treason?" Hehl stood up. "You're going to tell *Kommandant* and his lovely wife no more Belgian chocolates, no more English kippers, no more Russian caviar, and no more American books?"

"Who has time to read?"

"*Kommandant* reads two books a week. He just finished A Farewell to Arms—in English."

"A farewell to arms," Petersdorf said. He looked at the inventory lists again. "These women?"

"From the village, major."

Petersdorf looked at the teenagers. They smiled and blushed.

Hehl sat. He started punching numbers again. "What about the stigmatic?" he said.

The major looked at Hehl.

"What can I trade for him?"

The major smirked and shook his head.

"I have some interest from the Commissariat of Research," Hehl said. "They could get us things here."

"I've seen no evidence of any stigmata," Petersdorf said. "Only hearsay and a few church records."

"That's enough," Hehl said. "They're interested."

"Get rid of the carriages," Petersdorf said. "That pile is a danger."

Hehl kept typing.

"Did you hear me?"

"*Ja, Stürmbannführer*. I heard."

Forty Two

I n November of 1002, Emperor Henry II donated sixteen thousand square kilometers of land to the ruling house of Austria called the *Wienerwald*, or "Vienna Woods." Its low trees and gentle hills wrap Vienna in a forest five times larger than the combined boroughs of New York City.

"A culture is no better than its woods," the poet W. H. Auden wrote, and eight hundred years after Henry's donation, the Vienna Woods—where Auden spent the last part of his life—became a centerpiece of imagination for the lights of western culture. In the Woods, Beethoven composed his later symphonies; Schubert wrote sonatas and his famous Lindentree; Mozart composed The Magic Flute; and Johann Strauss immortalized the forest in Tales from the Vienna Woods.

Legends grew with the trees. Here, the tales tell, Beethoven realized he was going deaf when, on one of his frequent walks, he could no longer hear the birds. Franz Kafka, scholars say, spent his only happy time with a woman in the Woods—perhaps his only happy time ever—four days with Milena Polak.

Emperor Franz Joseph tried to lure back his wayward wife Elizabeth with Mayerling, a magnificent Wienerwald hunting lodge. If that legend is true, it is one of the bitterest ironies in European history. At Mayerling, Crown Prince Rudolph—the Emperor's depression-prone son—shot himself and his

462   The Fires of Lilliput

seventeen-year-old mistress, Baroness Marie Vetsera. The crown prince committed this murder-suicide at the end of a singular year: 1888-1889. That year, Strauss wrote his Emperor Waltz; Sigmund Freud coined the term "subconscious"; and Clara Hitler gave birth to Adolf.

Joachim Hehl leaned against a spruce on a hill in the Woods, reading the Physician's Prayer by the 12th century Jewish scholar Maimonides:

Almighty God, Thou hast created the human body with infinite wisdom. Ten thousand times ten thousand organs hast Thou combined in that act, unceasingly and harmoniously, to preserve the whole in all its beauty...

A young man with small spectacles, a woman thin to emaciation, and two nondescript children walked by, chattering down a path snugged against the hillside. They distracted Hehl and he looked away from the prayer and considered, for the seventh time that day, the role into which he would soon be forced: conscript. His stomach gnawed. A doctor in the Reich became *"Herr Doktor,"* a title bestowed most often by a subordinate—an enlistee, a nurse, or a prisoner. More doctors went to the camps than to the front or anywhere else.

The Nazi master plan sold the camps as medical research facilities where physicians were caretakers of the German gene pool. The Nuremberg Public Health Laws enacted for the "Protection of German Blood and German Honor" gave doctors control over marriage, birth, education, employment, Nazi party membership, and professional status. Doctors enforced eugenics laws that mandated sterilization of some 350,000 people with inherited disorders. They classified individuals with physical handicaps, mental disorders, and chronic illnesses as *Lebensunwertes Leben*—unworthy of life—and referred them for *Sonderbehandlung*, or special treatment—a euphemism for euthanasia at the end of a phenol-filled syringe plunged into the heart.

Hehl put in for service to the dismal science, where he could paper-push economic regulations based on studies of how "racial hygiene" influenced labor costs and productivity. But he had little likelihood of landing such a coveted desk job, usually reserved for conscripts with political connections.

Hehl first read the Physician's Prayer in his Philosophy of Medicine class during the second year of medical school.

Yet, when the frailty of matter or the unbridling of passions deranges this order or interrupts this accord, then forces clash and the body crumbles into the primal dust from which it came.

"The 'frailty of matter.' The 'unbridling of passions.' The 'derangement of order.' What an apropos description of—our own age." Naturally the instructor, Professor Dr. Auster, a Jew, would see things in this way at this time, Hehl thought. "Will forces clash?" he asked the class. "Will bodies crumble into the primal dust?"

Was National Socialism the natural order or a derangement of it?

"A derangement, of course." Auster sat with his lunch on the lawn next to Hehl and Fritzie Heiderich. "But I'd never say that in public." The day was bright and blue in May. "National Socialism is a disease and war is the sickness it will spread," he said between bites.

"Interesting," Fritzie said. He sipped a beer. "Hitler, then, is a bug?"

"More hideous than Gregor Samsa," Auster said.

"I'm immune," Fritzie said. He chewed, swallowed, and looked at Hehl.

"Him, too."

"No one is immune," Auster said. "You have to vaccinate yourself."

Hehl, lying on the grass, shaded his eyes from the Sun.

Fritzie had to chew before he could speak. "How does one self-vaccinate?" he asked.

Auster considered. "If I knew that," he said, "I doubt I would still be here."

Thou hast blest Thine earth, Thy rivers and Thy mountains with healing substances... Thou hast endowed man with the wisdom to relieve the suffering of his brother...

"So who was this Maimonides, who dared suggest man was endowed with the wisdom to relieve suffering?" Auster scratched the name "Maimonides" with a stubby chalk on a black board. He followed with "12th Century. Scholar. Physician to the Sultan of Egypt. Wrote numerous books on medicine. JEW."

"First and foremost, Maimonides was a Jew," Auster said. "That means *all of you* who do not wish to hear about the wisdom of a Jew are permitted to leave this classroom with no penalty whatsoever. Remember, though, that you've been listening to the wisdom of a Jew for the past three months."

That none of forty students left—or even stood—was a testament to the times. National Socialism had not yet conquered Viennese academe, and Theodore Auster's popularity among his students was undeniable. He considered nothing too sacrosanct or above challenge—including his own ethnicity (he did not, however, practice a word or a wit of the Jewish faith).

"Why do I say Maimonides was, above all, a Jew?" Auster paused. "Because he was *steeped* in Judaism." He waved his hands. "*It* was him and he was *it*." He stalked across the room. "Judaism was what *he was about*." He handed a stack of papers to the first student. "Pass this around, please." He spoke to the rest. "Maimonides' biography and his famous Physician's Prayer— sometimes attributed to Marcus Herz, a German-Jewish physician, but I don't believe that for a minute. Maimonides wrote it and I expect you to read it and comprehend it for tomorrow's discussion."

Hehl read the assignment in bed next to a low light that evening.

Support me, Almighty God, in these great labors that they may benefit humankind... Inspire me with love for my art...Do not allow thirst for profit, ambition for renown and admiration, to interfere with my profession...

Hehl thought about Maimonides at the gates of Melinka, in the shadow of a guard tower, where he stood with a small brown suitcase and a plastic bag with two pairs of shoes. Low clouds nestled overhead, suffocating and cottony.

Illumine my mind that it recognize what presents itself and that it may comprehend what is absent or hidden. Let it not fail to see what is visible...Should those who are wiser than I wish to improve and instruct me, let my soul gratefully follow their guidance; for vast is the extent of our art.

"*Herr Doktor* Hehl." Major Petersdorf extended both his hands. "I've arranged a rather hasty orientation and I do have a book for you."

The Practice of Medicine in the Resettlement Facility. Hehl lay the manual on his thin mattress in the officers quarters. "The physician in service to the Reich remembers his first duty," the book began. "To the Reich. And in that duty, to the public good."

Grant that my patients have confidence in me and my art and follow my directions and my counsel. Remove from their midst all charlatans and...cruel people who arrogantly frustrate the wisest purposes of our art and often lead Thy creatures to their death.

Hehl's orientation began over brandy and talk of the "groundbreaking" work of Dr. Josef Mengele on twins and genetics. The other camp doctor, Fiddler, bragged about retiring and how his approach to "patient care" required alcohol.

Should conceited fools, however, censure me, then let love for my profession steel me against them...because surrender would bring to Thy creatures sickness and death...Imbue my soul with gentleness and calmness when older colleagues, proud of their age, wish to displace me or to scorn me or disdainfully to teach me.

"Thrust it in—thrust it right in." Dr. Fiddler stepped back and waved a syringe like a fencer with a foil. "In God We Thrust. Then—drink!" Which he did, from a silver pocket flask. "You'll never be able to do this shit sober."

Hehl read up on wound management and emergency medicine. He assumed he would handle gunshot wounds and other battlefield accidents. He also assumed he would not be here long, but would move to the front. One look at Fiddler told him this was where burnouts ended, here was where they sent medicine's sorry cases: the quacks, the incompetents, and in his own case, the young and poorly connected.

Dr. Fiddler saw the triage textbook in Hehl's hands. "Don't be fucking naive," Fiddler said.

The night before he took selections duty for the first time, Hehl reread Maimonides' Prayer and parts of *Triage Procedures in War*. The ramps, he thought, would be a first line of triage, a place where the sick were separated for treatment, the healthy assigned to work details, and the acutely ill provided emergency care. The manual emphasized *special treatment*, giving *Herr Doktor* Hehl, twenty-seven years old, a measure of Hippocratic comfort. Maimonides' Prayer provided guidance, though here he kept it hidden.

Almighty God! Thou hast chosen me in Thy mercy to watch over the life and death of Thy creatures. Support me in this great task...

The skies were blue and warm the day Hehl walked onto the ramp for the first time, after the train had stopped and the new arrivals gathered in a stretched, confluent mass. He looked over heads and heard Sergeant Schmidt give the welcome over the loudspeaker.

"For those who need treatment, we have doctors," Schmidt said.

Dr. Hehl stepped forward.

I am now about to apply myself to the duties of my profession.

And the selections began.

Forty Three

Strauss ordered Jakub to saddle his wife's horse. He had the house kapos prepare a picnic—wine, cheese, caviar, chocolates, and two kinds of bread. He took a book and Gretty. They went out the rear gates toward the Dolina Koscieliska. Jakub carried food and blankets a few paces behind the horse. Strauss did not wear his uniform. They walked about three kilometers (two miles), to an open area near a stand of pines.

"This is good?" Strauss asked.

"*Sehr gut*," Gretty said. "This was a nice idea."

Jakub spread the blanket on the grass. He set out the food and Strauss opened the wine. He gave some bread and cheese to Jakub.

"Eat," Strauss said in uncertain Polish. "Over there."

Strauss and Gretty sat together on the blanket. Jakub went a ways off, to a fallen log where he sat and ate and drank water from a canteen he shared with the horse. He watched the Commandant and his wife and thought about killing them and running. But soldiers would follow. They would come to his house and burn it. They would kill his mother and brother. And if he killed the Commandant and his wife, would he be saving anyone? They would only be replaced. But he would still feel better if he killed them.

"This reminds me of Green Park," Greta said to her husband. "Do you remember?"

"In the spring," Strauss said.

Greta sidled up to her husband's ear. "You fucked me there, in the grass," she said.

Strauss choked and smiled.

Greta leaned back and sipped her wine. She looked at the sky. "How did we end up here?" she asked.

"We couldn't stay in London," Strauss said.

"Look at you—out of uniform," she said. "Couldn't they shoot you for that?"

"You said they don't care what we do."

Greta looked in the direction of Jakub. "What's this I hear about him?" she said. "Saint or something."

"A saint here?"

"He's not a Jew?"

"No," Strauss said.

Greta's gaze became a stare. "How many have you killed?"

Her husband looked at her. "None," Strauss said. He chewed his food. "Dessert?" he asked.

"*Ja. Danke*. Why not?"

Strauss cut a piece of sweet bread and handed it to his wife on a silver platter.

"Why haven't you killed anyone?"

"Because I can't," Strauss said. "It's not in me."

"Yes it is." She bit the bread. "Speaking of dessert, why don't we?"

"That's funny," Strauss said.

"Why stay?" his wife asked. "Why don't we keep on walking?"

"We'd have to run," Strauss said. "That's not in me, either."

"Well—it's in me." Greta sipped her wine. "How did we end up in this god-awful place? You never answered me."

"I want more than this," Strauss said. "You know that. When it's over, we'll get our life back."

"Why don't I believe you?" she said.

THE FIRST DAY AFTER Greta Strauss expected her period, she didn't think about missing it. She was always regular, but with all the commotion and stress, a day or two late might be normal. But after a week, a knot tied in her stomach. She tried not to think about it, but when she did, it was in little dire bursts: "God —a child here!" Prancing on her horse in a makeshift equestrian yard beyond the camp gates, she did not seem a woman for children.

"Dr. Hehl." She whispered his name loudly as he walked in the front door of his office.

Hehl turned. "*Frau* Strauss?"

She never spoke to the men. If she had something to say, even to Petersdorf who was second in command, she told her husband. She never looked at the prisoners. When Jakub escorted her horse, he had prior instructions. She never had to ask or order anything. She approached the doctor.

"Keep going please," she said. "I need you to look at me."

Hehl stopped but she prodded him through the door. Inside, she shut the window curtains.

"I need you to look at me," she said.

"Are you sick?"

"I think I'm pregnant."

"Have you—?"

"Told the *Kommandant*? No."

"Well—come in here." He led her to a side room set up as a clinic for officers and their families. He took a stethoscope from a drawer. "Sit on that table," he said. He fumbled with the stethoscope and placed its cup on her chest. He moved it around uncertainly.

"It doesn't seem like you use that very much," she said.

"Shh," he said. "I can't hear if you talk."

He went around her with the scope—chest, stomach, back. "Deep breath."

She took several deep breaths.

"Any nausea?" he asked.

"No," she said. "Unless you mean the nausea that comes with being here."

"Anything else?" Hehl said.

"I missed my period."

"Are you tired much?"

"No more than usual," she said.

Hehl looked her over. "I don't see pregnant women," he said. "I don't know if I'm the right person for this."

"There's no one in the village," Greta said. "I have to know."

"I'd have to read up," Hehl said. "It's been a while." He took a book down from a shelf and opened it.

"Do you know what to look for?" Greta asked.

"Generally," the doctor said.

"And where to look?"

"Generally," the doctor said.

"Well?"

Hehl took a deep breath. "Take off your shirt."

"*Sehr gut.*" Greta slipped off her shirt.

Hehl put thin rubber gloves over his hands. "And brassiere," he said.

She slipped that off too. He looked at her hesitantly.

"Be a doctor," she said.

Hehl placed his trembling hand on her breast. "Is it tender?" he asked. "Does it hurt?"

"No," she said. He gently palpated. She watched his face.

"How do you stand it here?" she asked.

"*Frau* Strauss?"

"A doctor. How do you stand it?"

"I don't know what you mean."

"Franny tells me you graduated top of your class in Vienna."

"Yes."

"Then you're here. You must have had such aspirations."

"I'm not here by choice," he said.

"What did you want to do with that fine education?"

Hehl pressed the underside of Greta's breast. "Any tenderness?" he asked.

"No." She looked at his hand. "Well?" she said. "What did you dream of being?"

"Me?" Hehl said. "A healer."

"*Mein Beileid*," Greta said. "So?"

Hehl looked at her.

"How on Earth did you end up here?" she said.

"Lunatic family, crazy professors," Hehl said. "I joined the Reich for a compass."

"Hah! You joined voluntarily?"

"*Ja*," he said. "*Dumm*."

"But—you didn't think so at the time."

"I never dreamed they would send me to a place like this," he said.

"What was it like," Greta asked, "when you killed for the first time?"

Hehl lowered his eyes.

"If you don't want to talk about it," she said.

"I was drunk for a week," he said.

"You felt terribly."

Hehl said nothing.

"I understand," she said.

"How can you?" he said.

"Maybe I can't."

"I didn't just kill one," Hehl said. "I killed dozens with a needle. I killed hundreds more with a twitch of my thumb."

In her left breast, Hehl felt something solid. "Have you noticed this?" he asked.

"What?"

He took her hand. "This."

She felt cold the moment she touched it. "No," she said. "What is it?"

"It should be checked," he said. "But I can't do it here."

"You can't tell Franny," Greta said.

"I have to," Hehl said. "You need to go to a doctor with a proper setup."

"I'll tell him," Greta said. "What about the baby?"

"For me here, it's too early to tell."

TWO *SS* OFFICERS STOOD with Lieutenant von Kempt in Hehl's office. On seeing their attire and demeanor, Hehl rose behind his desk.

"*Herr Doktor*," the lieutenant said. "May I present *Standartenführer* Sievers and *Frau Doktor* Oberheuser."

"Oberheuser is a woman!" Hehl thought. He extended his hand as he walked from around his desk. "*Standartenführer, Frau Doktor*."

"*Herr Doktor* Hehl," Sievers said. Wolfram Sievers directed the Military Research Institute, under the Reich Commissioner for Health and Sanitation. "The office received your letter. *Frau Doktor* Oberheuser is an expert on wounds."

Herta Oberheuser was, in fact, establishing a name for herself as the Reich's premier wound researcher. At camp Auschwitz-Birkenau, she simulated combat casualties by wounding prisoners and rubbing foreign objects—wood, nails, glass, dirt or sawdust—into their wounds. Rumors said she removed the limbs of younger and younger children to observe at what age the missing parts might grow back. Regeneration, after all, was a common feature of lesser animals—planaria, skinks, lizards—so maybe even the creatures in these camps. Harvesting the mechanism of resurrection would be of obvious and immeasurable benefit to the Reich, so Oberheuser—a grim-faced woman with short black hair—was amply supported. Hehl knew little about her research. He was almost shaking with excitement.

"Might we see the stigmatic?" Sievers said.

"Certainly," Hehl said. "*Leutnant?*"

"He's in the stable," von Kempt said.

"Stable?" Oberheuser asked.

"He cares for *Kommandant's* horse," Hehl explained.

They crossed the grounds. Sievers kept a handkerchief to his nose. His tightly-groomed mustache twitched. Von Kempt went ahead of them. He saw Jakub combing the horse and made a show of taking him roughly by the arm to the visitors, who stood at the other end of the stable.

"Beautiful horse," *Doktor* Oberheuser said. She saw Jakub. "Careful now—don't injure him," she told von Kempt. Oberheuser took Jakub's hands. He stood. He was surprised how soft her hands were—softer than Shosha's hands.

"Where do the wounds normally appear?" Oberheuser asked.

"Well—they've never appeared," Hehl said. "But his stigmata is well-documented."

"By whom?" Sievers asked.

"By the Catholic Church, by many noted experts. By Szarzynski."

"*Ja*," Oberheuser said. "I saw that. Very impressive."

"I also sent pictures to your office."

"We got them. *Doktor* Oberheuser?"

"If he bleeds," she said, "he heals remarkably. But one can't ascertain for certain unless one actually witnesses the event." She looked at the horse again. "Beautiful horse," Oberheuser repeated. "You know Buchenwald Zoo?"

"Buchenwald has a zoo?" von Kempt said.

"Their *Kommandant* loves animals."

"We're building a cinema," von Kempt said.

"Auschwitz has a new pool," Oberheuser said. "Heated during winter."

"The Reich takes this stigmata report very seriously," Sievers interrupted. "But we have to observe the wounds. Without that, your research proposal isn't much good."

"Could the wounds be induced, brought on somehow?" Oberheuser asked.

"I don't know," Hehl said. He turned to Jakub and tried to ask the question in Polish. Jakub looked at him. "He's reported to be a healer," Hehl said. "Perhaps that would be of greater interest."

"We aren't interested in healing," Oberheuser said.

"I would be eager to approve your proposal, but I have to see something to support my recommendation," Sievers said. He touched his mustache in a way Hehl found annoying.

"A NEW POOL IS bullshit," von Kempt told Hehl after Sievers and Oberheuser departed. "What about us? I'd love to swim. It's the only exercise I can do."

That evening, von Kempt drank himself drunk, pouted, and shot a woman in the yard. On hearing of this wholly unnecessary act—a violation of *SS* protocol for the behavior of officers—Petersdorf insisted the Commandant take action.

"That people have to die over such a trivial matter as a swimming pool," Strauss acknowledged.

"They're people are they, now?" Strauss said.

"It's more than that, Franz," Petersdorf said. "It's a breach of the highest order, typical of the low depths to which the *leutnant* so frequently sinks."

"I want to be absolutely clear," Strauss told both men. "Absolutely, crystal clear. I will requisition a pool. But you both need to know—I can promise nothing. Is that clear?"

Petersdorf choked. "Franz."

"*Leutnant*?"

"*Ja*," von Kempt said. He smirked at Petersdorf. "Will it be heated, *Herr Kommandant*?"

GRETA STRAUSS THOUGHT OF nothing but her body. She lay awake at night waiting for her husband to sleep, then rose and stood at the upstairs window gazing toward the valley. She lost her appetite for sex and her interest in things that previously sustained her—shopping in a town; walks in the valley; her horse. She daydreamed about the day it—and this, this awful place—would be over.

Strauss meanwhile confronted news from his Viennese friends that the Reich had discovered the Strauss Jewish ancestry. How much Jewish-ness was allowed? he wondered. Who, among his staff, would share the discovery? What would be its impact on morale? Would he be relieved of his command? Imprisoned? Executed? He thought about telling his wife, but while they walked together and dined together, they rarely talked of anything important anymore.

"A sore throat, *Kommandant*? That's an odd complaint for this time of year." Hehl pressed a stick on the Commandant's tongue. "Say 'ahh.'"

"Ahh."

"It's not red."

"It's almost autumn," Strauss said. "My allergies usually kick in."

"It's not like you to complain about a common malady."

Hehl felt the Commandant's throat.

"You took the training at the Hygiene Department?" Strauss asked.

"Which part?"

"Racial purity," Strauss said. "From the *Reichssippenamt*." Reich Office of Genealogical Research.

"The subject came up, but it was not emphasized."

"No?"

"It made people uncomfortable," Hehl said. "They left it as a given. A Jew is a Jew, an Aryan is an Aryan."

"Did they define *Aryan*?" Strauss asked.

"In what way?" Hehl said.

"Well—by percent purity. Did they ever mention how much Pole or Negro, or even Jew a person could have before they considered that person a non-Aryan?"

"Race mixing was not expressly discussed. But it troubled the Reich."

"How?" Strauss asked.

"A half-Jew could never serve," Hehl said.

"What about a quarter Jew?"

"Probably not."

"A tenth Jew?"

"How could you ascertain who was or was not one-tenth a Jew?" Hehl asked.

"That's what I want to know," Strauss said. "Didn't they teach you?"

"No."

Strauss sat on the exam table staring at his feet. Hehl wrote notes in the Commandant's medical file.

"You know Vienna," Strauss asked.

"Do I know Vienna," Hehl said.

"You loved her."

"Yes."

"I loved her too. My family is from there."

"I knew that," Hehl said. "What an honor to be part of such a family."

Strauss hesitated. "Perhaps not," he said. He hesitated again. "Some discoveries have been made—some skeletons have come tumbling out of our closets."

Hehl kept writing. "Anything titillating?"

"You can't say anything to anyone. It has to remain between us."

"Always."

"It seems we have some Jews in our bloodline."

Hehl didn't look up. "Jews?"

"Yes. Distant relations on my father's side."

Hehl stared down at the paper in front of him. "How distant?"

"I don't have all the information, but it looks like Strauss Senior's grandfather."

Hehl looked at his watch. He wrote.

"All those notes for a sore throat?" Strauss said.

"*Ja*," Hehl said. He noted the day, time, and precise wording of the Commandant's confession. "What was his name?"

"Whose name?"

"The Jew in your bloodline."

"Johann Michael Strauss." He stood. "From Hungary. I believe he converted, but to Catholicism." At the door, Strauss turned to the doctor. "What do you think?"

"You'll be fine. Just allergies."

"About my family," Strauss said.

"Trivia," Hehl said. "No one will care."

"It makes my heart sick to think about Vienna," Strauss said.

"Mine too," Hehl said. "But I know I will return."

The doctor took the Commandant's medical file back to his office and wrote "Johann Michael Strauss, Hungary" in it.

AFTER TWO MORE VISITS with his secretive patient, Hehl was not sure a child was growing in Greta Strauss' belly. But he was sure she had a lump growing in her breast.

"You need to go to Berlin," he told her one bright October morning.

"What will they do there?"

"Operate, probably."

"Probably?"

"I can't be sure—I'm not a surgeon. It's most likely benign, but surgery is the only way to tell."

"What do I tell Franny?"

"The truth."

"I can't."

"I can tell him if you want me to."

"No," she said. "What about the baby?"

"This early an operation shouldn't affect a baby. But stay off the horse," Hehl said. "You don't want to fall. You don't want a miscarriage."

"You're not even sure I'm pregnant."

"Just to be safe," Hehl said.

Greta left the doctor and went to the stables. She saw Jakub brushing the horse. "Saddle him," she said. She mounted the horse and they went outside the camp, through a back way toward the valley. Jakub walked beside the horse holding the reins.

"You're looking well fed," Greta said to Jakub.

He looked at her, above him on the horse. She had dark hair in a nation of the fair. She looked ahead, at the sun on the hills.

"I've heard about you," she said. "But I don't believe in that."

They walked past some tall plants with broad, dying leaves along the road. The leaves were gray with ash. Jakub slowed. Greta saw him looking at the leaves. They walked ahead, to a shady clearing beneath some trees. Greta lay forward and turned her head and rested it on the horse's mane.

"What am I going to do?" she said.

Jakub sat on a rock and looked past her, toward the hills that rose from the valley. Greta sat up. She swept her hair back and turned away. She spoke to the hills.

"I've always been in control," she said. She turned toward Jakub. "Why is this happening? We were so happy before."

She slipped over and took Jakub's hand. She was shaking. She looked down at him and parted her hair with her other hand.

She felt warm. Her neck flushed and her face felt hot and she thought it was from tears.

"Go on back, huh?" she said. "Go on back now. I want to be alone for awhile."

Forty Four

O n June 6, 1944, the D-Day invasion at Normandy Beach landed Americans on the European front. From Normandy, under the command of Dwight Eisenhower and George Patton, allied troops spread across the western part of the continent. By July, Hitler's high command was in enough disarray that senior officers including Colonel Claus von Stauffenberg and General Henning von Tresckow tried to assassinate him at Wolf's Lair, the *Führer's* secret Eastern Front headquarters. By August, allied forces had retaken most of France, liberating Paris on August 24th with the help of the French Underground.

The Germans were in retreat on several western fronts by September, but in the east, at 8:00 p.m. on October 2, Germany declared victory over Warsaw with the "capitulation declaration" signed by General Erich von dem Bach-Zelewski and emissaries of General Bor. The Germans evacuated Warsaw, sending fifteen thousand fighters, five thousand wounded, fifty thousand "dangerous elements," and one hundred fifty thousand innocents to any camps that still had space.

AN ENGINE PULLING TWELVE decrepit passenger cars rounded the knoll that opened the panorama of the Koscieliska on the outskirts of Melinka. The cars carried survivors of the latter days, people who had eluded capture until this late in the war. In the fall of 1944, these survivors included members of underground groups who spent days and nights in hollows and tunnels and bunkers, drinking dirty water and eating rodents and mangy cats. Latter day survivors also included "enemies of the Fatherland." These were political dissidents; Catholics; Communists; Red Army POW's; gypsies; and people with chronic or debilitating diseases such as multiple sclerosis or Crohn's colitis.

Stragglers from the failed rebellion in Warsaw were survivors of the latter days. Mostly Jewish or Polish women, conventional wisdom labeled them whores. Whores were likely to survive. Soldiers needed whores. Rebels needed whores. Whores would be fed, sheltered, fucked and protected.

The train slowed and the people aboard looked through dirty, scratched windows. They saw delicate Melinka village nestled in the valley Scott Fitzgerald made famous with boozy letters to his editor and a few movie producers (some even visited the Koscieliska to scout locations). The unmolested village idyll provided soldiers at the camp a nearby place for rest and recreation. On those rare visits from spouses and girlfriends, they were able to treat their girls to the wonderful surroundings, rather than the woeful center, of their daily awful lives.

Himmler ordered *Organisation Todt* to place a "resettlement camp" near Melinka in a nod to the success of *Theresienstadt*, an *SS*-run Czech ghetto with a happy face—well-stocked dummy stores, cafes, schools, gardens, even healthy-looking people—designed to deceive Red Cross ambassadors and newspaper reporters. After all, look what the British press had stirred up in Parliament about Britain's dreadful neglect of the Poles in Warsaw. Bad press, Hitler knew, could force otherwise circumspect leaders to act. The *Führer* also knew that one front alone does not win a war. The propaganda front had always been a fundamental component of the Nazi strategy and Hitler waged a public relations *blitzkrieg*.

During the so-called Great Terezin Embellishment, Theresienstadt "guests" enjoyed a children's opera, *Brundibar*, while the SS filmed *The Führer Gives a Village to the Jews*, a propaganda pastiche that showed ghetto Jews living well under Hitler's benevolent protection. The film's director, Kurt Gerron, was a cabaret performer and actor who appeared with Marlene Dietrich in *The Blue Angel*. After filming wrapped and the ruse ran its course, the Nazis sent cast and crew to Auschwitz, where they executed Gerron and his wife on October 28, 1944. The film was posthumously edited into short propaganda "bites."

To maintain the Melinka ruse, Himmler ordered a "don't shit where you work" policy that was more pragmatism than propaganda. Heinrich Petersdorf had been brilliant in its implementation, helping make camp Melinka a model of death by design. To make the villagers more accommodating, Petersdorf immediately squelched or assuaged any outbursts there by his staff. He sometimes attended Fr. Waleska's Catholic mass, especially on holidays. He ordered community involvement. Guards and kapos helped villagers fight fires or dig drainage canals after spring floods. To prevent messes on the tracks, Petersdorf stationed guards along the railroad before, within, and after the village. These "trackers" kept constant watch on the trains. Where before they shot anyone jumping from windows or cattle doors, now they sent a special team of kapos to track the fleeing escapees and bring them back, dead or alive, but quietly. They scooped up anyone who landed beneath a locomotive's steel wheels, loaded the body aboard an unmarked van, carried it into the camp, and burned it.

On the issue of cattle cars—a death camp cliché—Petersdorf ordered that no livestock vehicle ever enter camp Melinka. Designed for life, not death, livestock cars provided opportunities for escape and created a circus-like atmosphere. Hands, feet, heads, hair, faces, even whole bodies dangled between the planks in these cars. Asses stuck out and people shit and pissed their way through the village. Crowds of adults and children cheered, watched, jeered, and helped—by throwing food, running alongside and grabbing hands, taking valuables for "safe keeping," and sometimes dying themselves. Instead of livestock cars, Petersdorf used Hehl's requisition skills to arrange that only passenger cars or solid boxcars with no windows or openings made inmate deliveries to the Melinka Resettlement Facility.

The major's public relations proved effective. The villagers remained, if not warm to his men, at least tolerant. Merchants didn't close shop and vanish when they saw soldiers coming.

Whores were available. Complaints from local *gmina* councils and *powiat men* by way of the Reich to the desk of Franz Strauss were rare.

"PULL. PULL. PULL. PULL." Naked men yelled from an outdoor concrete swimming pool littered with fallen leaves. They drank beer and laughed on this warm October afternoon. The pool sat a few meters from a closed metal door, where Corporal Walkenburg and other guards tugged on large handles. Von Kempt supervised.

"You packed it too full," one of the men in the pool yelled. "Dumb fucks."

"You packed it too full," von Kempt repeated sarcastically. He pointed with his riding crop. "Get your boot up there and push off the wall."

Walkenburg stuck one foot against the wall and wrapped his slender hands on the handle.

"You other men—hold onto him."

One man wrapped his arms around Walkenburg's waist. The other man wrapped his arms around the waist of the first man.

"Ready, children," they heard from the pool.

"Can I tell them to shut the fuck up?" Walkenburg said.

"Shut the fuck up," von Kempt yelled back. "Now open this son of a bitch."

"You girls need help?"

Von Kempt turned and saw two of the men from the pool standing wet and naked on the concrete. "Get your fucking clothes on."

"*Ja wohl!*" The men in the pool saluted and laughed.

The door moved.

"It's coming, lieutenant."

"About time. The next moron who overloads this will be inside it."

The door groaned backward and an arm flopped out.

"Get a grip around the sides—over here, over here."

Three men gripped the side of the door and pulled. One of the naked men stepped up and grabbed the top edge.

"You stink."

"Me?"

"Drunk fuck."

They pulled the door back and bodies tumbled out. They were naked and the women had no hair. Shit smeared their skin and blood caked their ears and eyes and the hollow spots around their noses. Bruises and vomit covered their cheeks and lips. There were children with their skulls pushed in and fingers with hair and blood and bits of mortar embedded under the nails.

Von Kempt stepped away. "Bring the trucks around."

AFTER SELECTIONS, A LINE of shivering people crammed an outdoor tunnel with brick walls covered with an arched barbed-wire trellis woven with pine branches and leafy camouflage from the forest beyond the valley. Some people cried and talked; trembled or knelt; prayed. Others stood motionless, staring blankly at sparse strokes of sunlight through the branches and the leaves.

Kapos with shears went from woman to woman, cutting hair and saving it in baskets. One barber—a thin, nervous woman—came to a red-haired beauty with locks to her ass.

"What are you doing?" the beauty said.

"You won't be needing it," the barber said.

"What? Of course I'll need it!"

The barber's hands shook as she raised the shears. "No."

"I'm going to have a shower. I'll have it all clean."

The barber took the beauty's hair and she kicked and fought. The barber stepped back. "Stop it!" the barber said. "You're all fools. Stop fighting before it goes worse for you." She raised her hand to the red head again.

"Don't touch me, bitch!"

The barber whistled. Two guards pushed into the line. They grabbed the red head and took her away from the others. They smashed her head three times hard into a wall of stone.

"Give me the scissors," one of the guards screamed.

The barber hesitated.

"Give them to me!"

She handed them over. They grabbed the beauty's hair and cut it. The guard gave the hair and scissors to the barber.

"No one wants a bloody wig," the barber said.

"It's red," the guard said. "Who'll notice?" They dragged the beauty away.

The line moved. People in the back saw those in front enter a cavernous chamber with a single light. They heard guards calling back and forth.

"Can we get everyone in?"

"Everyone?"

"Everyone—can we get everyone in?"

"Tightly."

"*Sardinenpackung*?"

"*Nein!*"

"Okay. That's fine."

The chamber swallowed the line.

"We'll have the showers on momentarily."

All this business about hair: there were lice and the first thing they would smell when the doors closed was a de-licing compound, the kapos explained. Everyone knows lice live in hair. The guards closed the doors. A private carried a canister of *Zyklon-B* crystals up a ladder. He walked across the roof of the chamber and gave the canister to Corporal Walkenburg. The corporal whacked the canister with the sharp end of a hammer. He slid open a slot on the roof and poured the crystals through.

Against the light in the chamber, people saw the crystals fall, like sleet, clear and clean. They smelled the odor and though they were packed tight, they knew they would be clean. The lights went out and gas rose from the floor. The men on the roof heard the first cries as death entered the room. They heard the struggle, the strong trying to climb over the weak, hands pounding and digging the walls with screams and anger or angry resignation. The men on the roof checked their watches and did what they always did at this time—they opened a second slot in the roof and yelled down encouraging words.

"Up here. Fresh air. Up here."

"Breathe," a private said. "Disinfect your lungs."

They watched faces appear near the opening. They saw eyes and noses, mouths and cheeks; the top of a head and a brow; the veins in a passing neck. They saw hands and shirtsleeves, collars and buttons. Teeth. If they saw a gold filling, they would make a mental note and complain it had been missed. They heard coughing become choking and choking become retching.

But through the sour little opening, they couldn't see a father crush his son, or an old woman pinned to the floor and trampled. They couldn't see people clawing the walls, embedding their nails until their fingers bled. They couldn't see a mother using her mouth to give her daughter air. They laughed at the ones they did see and shoved them back with the butts of their rifles.

"Breathe," the guards said. "Breathe. It will all be over soon."

The guards emptied the chambers and hauled the corpses away. They crammed in the next group, packed them like sardines. They shut and latched the big heavy doors. The light in the chamber went out.

"*Halten.*"

The light came on again. The door opened. Sergeant Schmidt and another guard pushed through, forcing people aside. They came to a woman with an unshaven head. Her hair was dirty. Her clothing was shabby. Schmidt took her by the shoulder. He whisked her around.

"This one still has hair," he yelled back.

Shosha Mordechai stepped into the light. They dragged her out and away.

Forty Five

At dusk, when Greta Strauss didn't return from her ride, her husband ordered Lieutenant von Kempt to conduct a search. Sergeant Schmidt assembled a detail. "Get Hehl in case she's hurt," Strauss said.

The Commandant led the men outside the camp, into the valley. About an hour later, "Gretty!" Her husband ran to her. She lay still on the ground. The horse was gone. Strauss lifted her head and saw blood in her hair. Hehl listened to her chest.

"Is she breathing?" her husband asked.

"Yes."

They put cold cloths on her face and smelling salts to her nostrils. She stayed asleep.

"She's unconscious," Hehl said. "We'll take her back and get her to a proper hospital."

Strauss tucked his wife's head under his chin and kissed her hair. He stroked her face. Hehl put a stethoscope to her chest.

"Heart's beating. Nice and strong." He put the stethoscope near her stomach, listening for an infant.

"What can you hear there?" Strauss asked.

"Nothing," Hehl said.

They took Greta Strauss back to the camp in the only vehicle long enough to accommodate a stretcher—a gas van. They kept her body straight with splints.

GRETA LAY UNCONSCIOUS IN the officer's infirmary with a bandage around her head. Her husband stood with her. Hehl felt around her neck.

"It doesn't feel broken," he said.

Her husband sighed.

"She may have a concussion," Hehl said.

"Is she comfortable? Can you tell?"

"I'd say. But we need to get her to Munich or Berlin."

"I'm working on it," Strauss said. "It's not so easy—the hospitals are over flowing."

Hehl sat next to his patient. He placed his hand on the underside of her right breast and palpated it.

"What are you doing?"

"You need to know some things," Hehl said. "Your wife may be pregnant."

"What did you say?"

"I said your wife may have a baby."

Strauss felt his knees weaken. His mouth went dry. He took the doctor's arm.

"She said nothing."

"Go sit," Hehl said. "There's more."

The doctor led Strauss to a chair.

"What else could there be?" Strauss said.

Hehl pulled up a chair and sat beside Strauss. "She didn't tell you anything?"

"Nothing," Strauss said.

The doctor placed his palm over his commander's hand. "She has a growth in her breast," he said.

Strauss looked up. "A growth? Like a cancer?"

"May be," Hehl said.

"I don't believe it," Strauss said. "Why didn't she say anything?"

"She didn't know how to tell you," Hehl said.

"I don't believe this. I can't believe it."

Hehl looked at Strauss. "I can show you." They walked to her together. "Give me your hand," the doctor said. Hehl placed Strauss' fingers on the underside of his wife's left breast. "They can grow faster with the hormones of pregnancy," he said.

Strauss felt around. "I don't feel anything," he said. "What should I feel?"

"A hard lump."

"It's all soft. A little bumpy, maybe."

Hehl stepped in and Strauss pulled his hand away. The doctor palpated the familiar area of Greta's breast. He felt above, below, around. "I'm certain it was her left breast," Hehl said. He looked at his bedside notes. "Yes—left breast. There—see for yourself." He palpated her right breast to be sure.

Strauss looked at the doctor's notes. He saw a sketch of the breast and the approximate location of the mass. He saw his wife's name. "When were you planning to tell me?" Strauss said.

"She would have had my head," Hehl said. "I planned to leave the telling to her."

Strauss went back and palpated his wife's breasts again. "I don't feel any hard lump anywhere," he said. "Maybe you were wrong."

FROM HIS DESK, MAJOR Petersdorf heard a gentle knock at his open door. "Come."

Newly-promoted Corporal Höfstaller stuck his head in. "The *Leutnant* and *Unterfeldwebel* Schmidt to see you, *Herr Stürmbannführer*."

Petersdorf nodded without looking up from his papers. He heard the studied footsteps of a familiar limp.

"*Stürmbannführer*," von Kempt said.

Petersdorf mumbled.

"Schmidt has information."

"Hmm."

Schmidt hovered at near attention over the major's desk. Von Kempt just stood.

"*Herr Stürmbannführer*," Schmidt said. "The peasant Chelzak was with the *Kommandant's* wife before her accident."

"Really?" Petersdorf said.

"He tells me he left her alive and conscious."

"That's not the point of interest," von Kempt said. "He told us *Frau* Strauss was ill."

"Ill? How so?"

"He didn't say, *Herr Stürmbannführer*."

"How would he know such a thing?" Petersdorf said.

"We have no idea," Schmidt said.

"*Frau* Strauss would not have told him anything like this. Or anything at all," Petersdorf said. He rubbed his hand through his hair. "Anything else?"

"We thought you'd want to know," Schmidt said.

"*Ja,*" Petersdorf said. "It is interesting."

STRAUSS DINED WITH HIS senior officers at least once a month and after an early supper, all but Strauss stood on his balcony smoking Cuban cigars overlooking the dusky Koscieliska. They sipped cognac, commented about the valley's scenery, and tried to disguise and ignore the stench of the camp. They continued their dinner conversation without their Commandant. He had begged out early to visit his wife in the infirmary.

"It's absolutely true," Dr. Hehl reiterated. "She had a lump. I felt it. I examined her."

"It's unbelievable," Dr. Fiddler said. "Imagine if we could bottle that."

"It is unbelievable," Petersdorf said. "And I don't believe it."

"I've checked and re-checked," Hehl said. "Now, nothing."

"Toast," Fiddler said. Everyone toasted.

Petersdorf went inside and sat in a plush red chair. The other officers—von Kempt and the two doctors—trickled in behind him.

"Perhaps Chelzak healed her," Petersdorf said. "He knew she was ill, apparently."

"Nonsense," Fiddler said.

"If not, perhaps our doctor should concede a mistake," Petersdorf said.

"I wouldn't make a mistake like that," Hehl said. "If anything, I would give Greta Strauss a higher standard of care. I wouldn't deliver such a diagnosis lightly and if I were in any way uncertain, I would have told her immediately. Instead, I reconfirmed it myself on three separate occasions. The lump was evident."

Petersdorf sipped his drink.

"Shall I tell you what else?" Hehl said. "Greta Strauss may be pregnant."

"Toast to *that*," Fiddler said. Glasses clinked.

"I had no idea," Petersdorf said.

"What a thing to have happen," von Kempt said. "How is she?"

"Resting," Hehl said. "Her breathing is regular, her heartbeat is normal."

"Rest is the best thing," Fiddler said.

"Did they figure out what happened?"

"She had contusions on her head."

"Sounds serious," von Kempt said.

"Bruises," Hehl said. "A bump. She fell off the horse. I told her not to ride."

"Maybe it bucked her."

"That wouldn't happen," Petersdorf said. "Greta was an equestrian."

"Chelzak was with her."

"For a short time," Petersdorf said.

"How did he know she was sick?" Fiddler asked. "Could he have done this?"

"A strong woman," Petersdorf said. "Versus a man, weak and hungry?"

"He could have scared the horse. Deliberately."

"Even if he did, Greta could have subdued the animal."

"You'd think she'd be careful," von Kempt said.

"Here, here," Fiddler said. He raised his glass and his stogie. "A cigar for the good father." He looked around. "Wherever he may be."

STRAUSS STOOD NEXT TO his unconscious wife in the officer's infirmary. He held her hand and sang softly.

Der Vollmond strahlt auf Bergeshöhn
Wie hab ich dich vermißt!
Du süßes Herz! Es ist so schön.

The full moon shines on mountaintops
How badly I missed you!
Oh, heart, so sweet! How lovely it is.

He heard Hehl enter. "How is she?" Strauss said.

"She breathes fine and her heart is well," Hehl said.

"The baby?"

"I don't know. Alive, if there is a baby."

Strauss looked at his wife. He sighed in a low way. "What about Berlin?"

"I've been trying," Hehl said. "The hospitals are a mess."

"Munich? Frankfurt? Dresden?"

"Same," Hehl said. "Though I don't know anyone in Dresden."

"What about Vienna?" Strauss said.

"Impossible."

"Why?"

"No doctors. They were mostly Jews."

Strauss squeezed his wife's hand. "Still no lump?" he said.

"I stopped checking. It may have been a cyst."

"A tense muscle that has since relaxed."

"I don't think so," Hehl said.

"Maybe cancer."

"No," Hehl said. "I don't see how."

"But you told her it was."

"Yes."

"It must have depressed her."

Hehl said nothing.

"She was depressed. I could tell."

"She did seem sad," Hehl said.

"She talked to you. What did she say?"

"I've told you enough," Hehl said.

"I could order you," Strauss said. He looked at his wife. "Did she say she wanted to die?"

"No," Hehl said.

"But how do we know?" Strauss said. "Could the diagnosis have depressed her to the point of taking her own life?"

"Not *her* life," Hehl said.

Strauss looked at his wife. "What?"

"I told her to stay off the horse," Hehl said. "If she was pregnant."

Forty Six

D
r. Fiddler saw a familiar *Kriegslokomotive* creeping toward the camp on October 13. "God damn," he said. Major Petersdorf walked toward the selections ramps. "No cattle cars," he yelled. "We don't take cattle cars."

But a long line of cattle cars with people crammed inside trundled into the camp and went a ways beyond it. The engine stopped and steamed and the boxcars slowed and settled. Petersdorf and Fiddler stood motionless and watched. The air was cool and still. The people, by the hundreds up and down the track, were quiet but for whispers. Arms and legs and coats and pants rustled like leaves in a breeze. Boilers sighed and brakes relaxed and wisps of steam slipped away. The people looked out, with hollow eyes. The boxcars creaked and stirred. Someone coughed and someone sneezed. A baby cried. Someone hushed a child.

"We can't handle this many," Fiddler told the major. "How do they expect us to?"

"I don't know," Petersdorf said.

SERGEANT SCHMIDT CAME INTO the Commandant's stable with a private and a corporal. "Chelzak," he called. He moved around the room. "Jakub Chelzak." He saw Jakub sleeping in a hay pile. "On your feet," Schmidt said.

Jakub tried to stand.

"I said on your feet." The two guards grabbed his arms and pulled him up. They hauled him into the sun. He winced and closed his eyes. They dragged him to the officer's infirmary.

"You didn't rough him up, did you?" Hehl asked.

"*Nein.*"

"Take him in there," Hehl said. They took Jakub into an empty exam room. "Put him on the bed. Let him get his wits about him."

Jakub opened his eyes in the soft October light. The room was dark except for a window with parted shades. He felt a man standing over him and saw a face after his eyes adjusted.

"*Herr* Chelzak," Strauss said. "Are you feeling rested?"

Schmidt interpreted the words in Polish. Jakub mumbled something.

"You must be hungry," Strauss said. Jakub said nothing.

"Fine," Strauss said. "I've asked our doctor to let you clean up and bring you some clean clothes. *Unterfeldwebel* Schmidt will bring you around to my quarters."

Jakub sat where no other prisoner would ever sit—in the Commandant's private dining room. Strauss sat across from him —not at the head of the table, but at the side. Schmidt sat next to Jakub. Hehl sat beside Strauss. Kapos brought plates of food and bottles of wine and brandy. Rain pattered the windows. Strauss cut a tender lamb.

"Can you tell me, *Herr* Chelzak, what happened that day?"

Schmidt translated from German to Polish and vice versa.

"We went out on the horse," Jakub said. He drank the brandy.

"And how many times had you done this before?"

Jakub thought. "A few," he said.

"How was my wife?"

On hearing the translated question, Jakub shrugged.

"He's not sure what you mean," Schmidt said.

"Was Gretty angry?" Strauss said. "Sad? How did she behave?"

Jakub thought. "She didn't want the child."

Schmidt looked at Jakub and struggled with the translation.

Strauss choked. "What?" he said.

"She did not want the child."

Strauss put his knife down. "He said it again. Did he say Gretty doesn't want our child?"

"*Didn't* want, *Herr Kommandant*."

"She said nothing of the kind to me," Hehl said.

Strauss looked at Jakub. "Did she tell you this? Did she confide this to *you*?"

"I knew it," Jakub said.

"How?" Strauss said. "How could you know this? Is it possible you had too much to drink that day?"

"I'm barely given water to drink," Jakub said.

"My wife didn't pack anything? No wine, no brandy? She didn't offer you anything to drink?"

"No," Jakub said.

Strauss leaned back in his chair and swept his head around the room. "My God," he said.

"If Frau Strauss didn't want the child, I think she would have confided that," Hehl said. "She seemed...anticipatory, at least."

"Anticipatory," Strauss repeated. He looked at Jakub. "You were not there when she fell off the horse?"

"She asked me to leave," Jakub said. "She was sitting on the horse when I left her."

Strauss sighed. "Well," he said. Strauss contemplated the man.

Jakub whispered to Schmidt.

"Did you want to know anything else, *Herr Kommandant*?" Schmidt asked.

Strauss considered the question, then leaned forward and picked up his knife. "No," he said. Schmidt went to take Jakub out. "Leave him," Strauss said. "Let him eat."

After dinner, Strauss gave Jakub the leftover food. He gave him the leftover wine and some brandy. Hehl returned to his quarters. Schmidt led Jakub past a kapo who held the front door of the Commandant's house.

"*Herr* Chelzak," Strauss said. They turned to see Strauss on his porch in the light from the open door. "I appreciate your candor."

JAKUB SLEPT ON A hard plank bunk in the stable. He used hay to make it softer. He lay on the bunk and looked at the ceiling and thought about time. How much longer before he would be free? He thought about his mother. He saw his house in his mind and it looked clean. He thought she must be worried. What could he do? What power did one man have against all this? He thought Karl would reassure her. Karl knew him better than his mother did, and Karl would know that he was not dead.

He heard footsteps. He never heard anyone here at night so he swung his legs over and stood. He saw Klaus von Kempt and Sergeant Schmidt.

"*Herr* Chelzak," Schmidt said in Polish. "Good evening."

They came to him.

"Remember we spoke to you about *Kommandant's* wife?"

"Yes," Jakub said.

"Did you touch her?" Schmidt asked in Polish.

Jakub said nothing.

"Did you touch her?"

"No," Jakub said. "She touched me."

Schmidt and von Kempt looked at each other. The lieutenant prodded the sergeant.

"*Herr Leutnant* was wondering." The sergeant stammered. Von Kempt prodded him again. "*Herr Leutnant* was wondering if you could touch his leg."

Jakub looked at them.

"Maybe you should show him," Schmidt said to von Kempt.

The lieutenant stood on one foot and pointed at his left leg, which was shorter than his right and scarred from failed surgeries.

"Well?" Schmidt said to Jakub.

"He would be better off dead," Jakub said.

"What's that?"

"He would be better off dead," Jakub said again.

"What's he saying?" von Kempt asked.

"You shouldn't say that," Schmidt said to Jakub.

"Tell me what he's saying."

"The lieutenant is not a bad man," Schmidt said.

"It doesn't matter," Jakub said.

"What the fuck is he saying?"

The sergeant leaned over and whispered the answer. Von Kempt gazed at Jakub. "You fuck." The lieutenant lunged at him. They fell against the bunk. Jakub pushed von Kempt back. Schmidt grabbed Jakub and pulled him off. Von Kempt lay against the bunk.

"You want to die?" Jakub screamed. "You want to die?"

"What's he saying?"

"He asked if you wanted to die."

"What the fuck. He's threatening me?"

Von Kempt grabbed the sides of the bunk and fought to stand. He slipped in the hay. He struggled. "Put him in the H-block," the hospital block, he yelled. He was finally able to stand and grasped the sides of the bunk. He perspired around his brow. "Pampered son-of-a-bitch," he said. "Mother fucker."

Schmidt took hold of the lieutenant.

"I want him in the fucking H-block. You make sure of that."

"*Kommandant* won't like it."

"Fuck him! Put a kapo in here to watch the fucking horse. If the *Kommandant* says anything, I'll tell him Chelzak admitted trying to kill his wife."

Schmidt led von Kempt out.

COOL FALL AIR SETTLED on the valley next morning. Jakub still slept in the bunk in the stable. Von Kempt shook him. "Chelzak. *Herr* Chelzak. Wake up."

Jakub stirred.

Von Kempt patted his face. "*Herr* Chelzak."

Jakub's eyes opened. The site of von Kempt startled him. He sat up and moved away.

"Don't worry," the lieutenant said. He smiled. "I have something I want to read to you." The lieutenant took a folded piece of paper out of his jacket. "I know you don't speak German but you'll understand."

Von Kempt lit a lantern that hung from the side of the bunk. The flame rose and filled the cramped space with soft light. He moved the paper into the light and read. "My Dearest Klaus: I don't know how to tell you this in a way that will not wound you." He took a deep breath. "I cannot...continue...us—" Von Kempt stopped. "I hesitated when you decided to join the *Wehrmacht*, but you were so excited—what could I do? You began to think only of your service and, I think, you began to forget about me."

Von Kempt paused and looked at Jakub. "She's been here three times this year," he said. "Three times! Most guys only get to see their girl once in a year."

Jakub looked down at the lieutenant's side arm and kept his eyes there. Von Kempt continued.

"I might be able to better deal with it if you were in Berlin, but you're not and that's the way it is. You are smart and able, and loyal—so why do they put you in a filthy resettlement camp? You know what they say here. They say the camps are not where the best officers go. I've asked, Klaus. I've asked wives and girlfriends. I've asked husbands of women who serve on Himmler's personal detail. They all say the same thing. The Reich doesn't send its best men to the camps. We both know why they sent you."

The lieutenant shook his head. "Fucking bitch," he said. He looked at Jakub. "You know what she's talking about. I can't march as well as the rest, so I get sent here. I'm not good enough. Just like Strauss. And Fiddler. And that prick Petersdorf. But they're *Schutz* and I'm *Wehrmacht*." He rose and approached Jakub. "Heal my leg," he said. He moved closer, obscuring the light. "I don't belong here. Maybe some people do—but not me. I don't deserve to be here."

Jakub looked at him.

"I don't just kill, you know, like some of the guys. There's some real freaks here."

Von Kempt looked at Jakub intently. Then he reached over and touched Jakub's hand. Jakub hesitated, but von Kempt held him. He took the hand and moved it to his left leg. He placed his palm over the crested top of Jakub's hand and delicately pressed. Jakub felt familiar quills rise on the back of his neck, penning his discomfort with a hundred little points.

"If you heal me," von Kempt said, "I'll get you out."

VON KEMPT REPEALED HIS demand Jakub be taken to the hospital block, which was not a hospital at all, but a warehouse-sized barracks with dirt floors and wood bunks. To an airborne observer, hospital blocks looked like Noah's Arks run aground. The Reich mandated each camp have such a block. The only quality a hospital block shared with a hospital was that it housed the sick. No one in the block received care, and no doctors visited. Instead, the sickest inmates—those who couldn't work, or stand in line long enough to be gassed—came here to die.

Lice, rats, and other vermin ravaged skin-and-bones inmates who lay immobile and covered with bedsores on straw mats, wood bunks, or dirt. Filthy water ran through rusty pipes and dysentery spread. Death rattles in the lungs and hacking from emphysema and tuberculosis kept anyone from sleeping much. In winter, the ground froze, the pipes burst, and hundreds died of exposure or lost limbs to gangrene and frostbite. In summer, the heat killed almost as many, and bugs—mosquitoes, flies, biting chiggers, and stinging ants—crawled and gnawed. In the hottest, wettest months, maggots nested in the dead.

Clipboard and smoldering cigars in hand, Schmidt and Corporal Walkenburg stood outside the main door of the block. Schmidt fumbled with some keys. They heard moaning and coughing inside.

"Fucking *Stinksaal*," Schmidt said. "I never go in here."

They opened the door. "Oh," Walkenburg yelped. He squeezed his nose shut.

The sun jumped in and glared at a few ghastly souls leaning against the wooden plank wall. The rest of the place was dark except where light peered in from a few windows high up, near the roof. Schmidt plugged his nose and looked down the corridor. He saw the dead and dying, three and four to a bunk. He stared for a few minutes while his eyes adjusted. He handed the clipboard to Walkenburg.

"Remember—everyone counted once. Even dead."

He didn't recognize the woman from the gas chamber whose hair had not been shorn. Shosha Mordechai looked at him as he passed. She wanted to spit at him, but she was barely strong enough to breathe.

THREE PEOPLE CROWDED EACH two-person bunk in the hospital block. People sat on the ground. They lay against the walls. They slept next to latrines. They kept each other warm.

Shosha lay on her back on the hard wood of a bunk staring at her face in a jagged mirror fragment. She fogged the mirror when she breathed. She touched her cheeks.

A woman who told everyone to call her Julia sat with her bony legs crossed on the edge of the same bunk drawing on the butt of a dead cigar.

"Why are you puffing that cold stogie?" Shosha asked.

"I can taste the tobacco," Julia said.

The door at the far end of the block opened and light came in and struck the face of the woman in the next bunk.

"Let me see the mirror—quick," she said.

"You don't want to see your face," Julia said.

Cold air swept in.

"Close the fucking door."

"Shh!"

"Stupid—what are you saying?"

"It's fucking cold."

Everybody waited for the guards to storm the aisle. They watched in the direction of the door. They saw shadows. Then the door pulled back the light.

"Why do I keep thinking they don't care about us anymore?" Julia said.

"They don't have time for torture," said a voice nearby. "This place is overrun."

"Under run is more like it," Julia said. She drew on the lifeless butt.

They heard low voices and watched shadowed shapeless forms move. They heard greetings.

"Not here."

"No, you can't sit here."

"Keep going."

"Fuck off!"

"Watch your step."

"There's no room at the inn."

"This village is under quarantine."

"Go away!"

Someone chuckled hoarsely. The shadows moved down the aisle.

"We have a space," Shosha said. "We can get one more in at least."

Julia whistled toward the newcomers. She waved them over. "Down here."

A girl arrived first. Shosha looked up at her. "There's room for one," Shosha said. "We'll have to draw straws."

"You are so fucking nice," Julia said. "How'd you get to be so nice?"

"You're nice too," Shosha said. "You let me borrow your mirror."

"If they catch me with that mirror, I'm a goner," Julia said.

"See—you take such risks for your friends."

"I want you all to see how ugly you are," Julia said. "And how beautiful I am." She made a mock gesture.

The other two newcomers arrived—a man and another girl. "Is this where?" the man said.

Shosha recognized the voice. She turned her head. "Come here," she said.

The man stepped forward. She couldn't at first remember his face. His cheeks sat higher on his bones. His lips were lines and his eyes recessed. His hair was thin. His skin looked worn and old. He had creases and cracks where stress had fractured him.

Shosha remembered him by looking at his hands. "Oh!" she said. Her lips quivered. She turned and when she was on her stomach, she pushed herself forward. Julia stood and moved away. Shosha pushed herself out of the bunk and stood on her thin, shaky legs. She took the hands and turned them and looked at them. She looked into the man's eyes. "Janusz Jerczek," she said.

"Yes," he said. "Yes I am."

SHOSHA GATHERED HERSELF. "I told the rabbi. I told him what a mistake it was," she said to Jerczek. "He wouldn't listen. He told me I was mistaken—that I was meddling."

"He couldn't have known," Dr. Jerczek said. "None of us knew."

"How could you be so stupid, I said. How could you trust them?" Shosha said. "Rebbe said it was all right. He said everything was arranged. He said you were going to a new orphanage, outside Vienna."

Jerczek took a deep breath. "We went to Stutthof."

"From Vienna to Stutthof," Julia said. "Tell me your travel agent."

"Shh."

Shosha forced herself to ask the next question. Her lips didn't merely quiver—her entire mouth shook. She could barely speak and her face felt hot. A new pit opened in her empty stomach. "The children?" she asked.

Jerczek brought his hand to his mouth. He clenched his fingers around his chin. Then he spread them across his cheeks. His eyes looked moist in the dim light. Shosha saw a fine crack across one of his eyeglass lenses.

Julia put both her arms around him. "It's cold in here," she said. "Someone hand me my blanket."

Forty Seven

I n July 1944, Soviet troops marching from the East reached the Polish border. On July 19, they liberated Majdanek outside Lublin, where one million three hundred and eighty thousand human beings lost their lives to the Final Solution, second only to the one million five hundred thousand human beings murdered at Auschwitz. At Majdanek, the Red Army found thousands of *Muselmänner*, skeletal witnesses. The camp itself—and its evidence—was intact.

How to kill the hundreds of thousands of prisoners in the Polish camps—and destroy the incriminating remains—before the allies arrived perplexed the Reich. Only so many people could be killed at one time. Even mass murder had limitations. To address this dilemma, Himmler created a counterpart to mass extermination—mass evacuation. Pressed for time, the Nazis were only able to evacuate one thousand of the quarter million or so prisoners at Majdanek before the Red Army liberated it.

But those numbers improved. On July 20th, twelve hundred Jews marched from Lipcani, Moldavia. On September 17, five thousand Jews began a six-week march from the Bor labor camp in Hungary. Only nine survived to the end of the war. Seventy six thousand Jews marched from Budapest in the direction of the Austrian border on November 8. Only a few hundred survived.

ON OCTOBER 26, 1944, Himmler ended the Final Solution of the Jewish Question with a one-sentence command: *I forbid any further annihilation of Jews.*

The order arrived at Auschwitz on October 27.

The order arrived at Melinka with the first frost, on November 3. On November 5th, evacuation orders arrived at Camp Melinka marked for Franz Strauss—*Offizier in Das Kommando.* Heinrich Petersdorf opened them. His hands trembled as he read.

A mandatory march of resettled persons and camp personnel to Oswiecim, near the Wisła River, for relocation to the facility there.

Auschwitz.

"Every piece of this plan has been mad and this is the maddest piece," Strauss told Petersdorf later that day. "Why march? Why not evacuate with trucks and trains?"

"Not enough fuel," Petersdorf said. "They're using it all at the Front."

"Fronts," Strauss said.

"They want a man in charge," Petersdorf said. "I say von Kempt."

Strauss looked at him. "He can barely walk. How can he be expected to march that far?"

"He walks fine."

"Be serious."

"I am being serious. He's the best man for the job."

"He's not going," Strauss said. "Get someone else."

"YOU SENT FOR ME, *Sturmbannführer*?"

Petersdorf stood by the fireplace in his office. He took a leg from a broken wooden chair and fed it to the fire. He went to his desk and picked up the orders. He looked at von Kempt and handed him the orders. "Some are fortunate enough to be reassigned away from here," Petersdorf said.

Von Kempt read the directive. "*Herr Sturmbannführer!*"

Petersdorf said nothing.

"This isn't fair. How can I march?"

Petersdorf went behind his desk.

"I won't go," von Kempt said. "I refuse."

"You have no say in the matter."

"I refuse. I refuse it."

"You have no say. There's nothing anyone can do about it."

"I'll take this up with the *Kommandant*."

"By all means," Petersdorf said.

The lieutenant limped out.

VON KEMPT WORRIED ABOUT the march. He thought about ways he could avoid it. He would put in for a disability waiver. Who would question him? He was a cripple. They could test him and confirm it, but they already knew it. Dr. Hehl had a file full of X-rays and medical information confirming a congenital malformation, a dwarf leg, and attempts to correct it that only made it worse. No one ever made von Kempt march, at least not far. That's why he was here at Melinka, a stinking hellhole. He was not fit for duty elsewhere. He had sacrificed to be here. There would be no glory for him in this war. There would be no medals, no homecoming parades. He would learn no skills that he could transfer to a new job after the war. His girl was leaving him. His future was a cloud. He was 25 years old and he creaked like a bitter old man, a cynical executioner tired of the smell. He had given up enough for the Reich; he would not participate in some insane travail designed only to set the mass murder in motion, to scatter the mayhem into the wider abyss like so many leaves in a storm.

Lieutenant von Kempt woke abruptly in the cold early morning hours of November 7. His hair and face were wet with perspiration. He felt his heart beating. He brought his hand to his chest and breathed. He looked down at his feet and saw the rise in the blanket. It looked different. He threw off the sheet and looked at his legs. He swung his legs around and looked at his bare feet. He wiggled his toes on the floor and put pressure on his bad leg. It felt different. He pressed down on his good leg.

Then he stood, on both legs, evenly.

JAKUB FELT ROUGH HANDS on his face. The hands dragged him out of his bunk and yanked him to his feet in front of von Kempt.

"Is this a joke?" von Kempt said. "You think this is funny?"

Jakub looked at him. Von Kempt pulled up his pants legs.

"I have one question for you," he said. "Why now?"

Jakub looked bewildered. Von Kempt motioned to the guards. They dragged Jakub toward a line five columns deep. Prisoners from across the camp streamed toward it.

STRAUSS SAW THE PRISONERS from a window in the officer's infirmary. He set a vase of flowers from his hothouse next to his wife's bed. He caressed her cheek and watched her chest rise and fall.

"You going to wake?" He leaned down and kissed her forehead. He spoke into her ear. "You going to wake for me?"

A CORPORAL AND A KAPO crossed the yard toward the hospital block. They saw kapos and guards throwing piles of paper into burning death pits. They came to the hospital block. The kapo opened the door. "Careful," he said. "Don't step in any shit."

The corporal waved a cigar. "Phew. They stink more alive than dead."

"The *Kommandant* wants it cleaned."

The corporal unclipped his revolver. He aimed toward the ceiling and fired. "Time to clean up. You hear!"

They walked among the bunks. People turned their eyes. The two men stopped near Shosha's bunk. She looked at their legs and feet. They looked in at Janusz Jerczek, sandwiched between Julia and Shosha.

"What are you doing?" Shosha said.

The guard and the kapo dragged Jerczek out of the bunk. The corporal dropped his cigar.

"What are you doing?" another voice said. "What do you want with him?"

"Where are you taking him?" Shosha asked. Jerczek looked at her sternly but knowingly.

"Shut up or I'll shut you up," the corporal said.

They dragged Jerczek out of the hospital block.

"Where are they taking him?" Shosha said. "Are they going to kill him?" Julia took Shosha's wrist and squeezed. "Are they going to kill him?" Shosha asked. "Why did they take him?" Shosha lay in the bunk. She stared at the floor. Her eyes moved to the corporal's cigar butt. She stared at it. Then she extended her hand toward it.

"Leave it," Julia said.

Shosha picked it up.

"It's mine," Julia said. "You don't smoke."

"You can have it when I'm done."

She tore a piece of her dress and set the lit end to it. Soon she had a flame.

"You have a fire."

"Dear God—a fire."

Shosha sat next to her bunk, peeling thin slivers of wood from planks and posts. Other prisoners crawled over. They handed her papers and rags and pieces of wood.

"We ought to burn this fucker down," Julia said.

"Yes!"

The man from the bunk over Shosha watched the fire grow. "You have a fire," he said. "That means you can eat a warm meal."

"With what?" Julia asked.

"With this." The man held out his bony hand.

"Go away," Shosha said.

"You think I'm crazy."

Shosha wouldn't look at him.

"I'm not living long," he said. "Why should my death be meaningless?" The other prisoners looked at Shosha. The man lowered his hand. He started to withdraw it when Shosha reached up and grabbed it. She looked up at him. He could see her eyes, purple-blue and clear in the flame.

"You won't die," she said.

"Wanna bet?" Julia said.

Shosha looked around at the others. She licked her dry lips and took a deep breath. "L'Chaim," she said. Then louder, "L'Chaim!"

No one responded.

"L'Chaim," Shosha yelled again.

Silence. No one spoke. Julia looked at Shosha.

"Okay," Julia said. "L'Chaim!"

"L'Chaim," someone else finally responded.

"L'Chaim," from a little farther down. "L'Chaim."

"L'Chaim!"

"L'Chaim!"

"You Jews stop saying that. You'll get us all killed."

But the echo kept traveling.

"L'Chaim."

"L'Chaim! L'Chaim! L'Chaim!"

"I'm not a Jew, but L'Chaim!"

"Make that a double! L'Chaim! L'Chaim!"

"Ah what the hell," another woman said. "L'Chaim!"

Shosha looked up at the man with the bony hand. "We live," she said.

LEBENSRAUM

Forty Eight

Sergeant Schmidt spoke to long lines of male prisoners through a bullhorn. "You have all been fortunate enough to be selected as the first *Kommando* of laborers from our facility to serve the needs of the Third Reich."

"Cut the shit," von Kempt told him.

Schmidt lowered the bullhorn.

"Go on," von Kempt said.

Schmidt raised the bullhorn again. "You will march," he said. "North and east, toward Oswiecim."

The whistles blew and five columns of fifty men each marched through the main gates with *SS* guards at their sides and chief kapos at the front. Von Kempt, the *Lagerelder* or march commander, rode in a motorcycle sidecar. Janusz Jerczek marched in the third column, Jakub in the first.

They marched through Melinka village in the first hour. Some villagers stared. What they saw defied the comforting expectations Heinrich Petersdorf created with his public relations campaigns: men who were sick, frail, thin, starving.

The guards yelled and acted like asses. It was cold, but only the guards wore coats.

The marchers made eleven kilometers (seven miles) the first day. Trucks pulled alongside around dusk. The guards at the front motioned with their hands. They blew whistles and the march stopped near an open field.

"Line up," the kapos yelled. "Line up. Time to eat." They gave each man one piece of stale bread and a lukewarm liquid that smelled like coffee but tasted like muddy water.

"They want us well fed," Jerczek said. "So we won't drop." He devoured his bread.

"I wouldn't do that," said another man.

"What?" Jerczek said.

"Eat so fast."

"I'm hungry," Jerczek said.

"All the more reason not to eat fast."

"I always eat fast when I'm hungry."

"This is it," the man said. "They told me. Until same time tomorrow."

"Here," Jakub said. He handed Jerczek his bread. "Take it."

"I can't do that," Jerczek said.

"I'll take it," said the other man.

"Me too," said another.

"Take it," Jakub said.

"You don't want it?" Jerczek said. "You're not hungry?"

"You should eat, even if you're not hungry," the other man told Jakub.

But Jakub kept the bread extended in his hand. Jerczek hesitantly took it.

"You should divide that," said another man. "You might make the others angry."

"Divide this a hundred ways?" Jerczek said. "Each man gets a crumb?"

"I'm not being absurd," said the man. "I meant for the few of us standing here."

Jerczek started to break the bread but Jakub took his wrist. "You have some," Jakub said to the other man. He pointed to the ground. "You must have dropped it."

The man looked down and saw a piece of stale bread near his feet. "I didn't drop it," he said. "Someone else—" He looked around. Men were bending over, picking up bread on the ground. He looked at the bread at his own feet and then at Jakub. The man picked up the bread and put it to his lips.

"It's not very good," Jerczek said. "But it is bread."

They slept on the cold ground in the field that night, under a clear sky with stars.

THE MARCHERS CAME TO a village late the second day. Drizzle misted the air and the men shook in the damp cold. They talked among themselves. They kept their heads down. They had lost three men—one to the cold, one to a beating, and one to the dogs.

The guards and kapos heard grumbling. The refrain was a variation of "this is insane. We should go back, turn back. We'll starve out here. We'll freeze out here. We were better off at the camp." The supply trucks passed and slowed ahead. A man fell. Jakub turned and helped him to his feet. A kapo ran up and whacked Jakub's arm with a stick.

"You don't help," the kapo screamed. "You don't help." He looked at the marchers. "Forget going back," he yelled. "Forget it! The camp is being burned as we speak and will be gone in a few days."

THE THIRD DAY STARTED with sun, then the sky grew overcast and rain fell. The marchers made four miles (six kilometers) on a cup of cold water and a piece of hard bread. They walked in the rain, some with blankets on their shoulders, ragged clothes stuck to their flesh. Their eyes were red and faces dirty with stubble and grime.

They rounded a shallow curve in the road. Ahead, they saw other soldiers and a tank listing to one side. Jakub could see where the roadside had flooded and the earth had given way under the tank's heavy tread. Soldiers were leaning against the tank, smoking and pointing through the rain. The marchers heard von Kempt yelling orders and they stopped. The lieutenant strutted toward the tank commander. They both wore the *Wehrmacht* uniform.

"Stuck?" Von Kempt asked.

"What's it look like?"

"We can get you out."

"With them?" The tank commander smirked. "*Müselmanner*?"

Von Kempt signaled toward his men and raised the whistle to his lips. The tank commander caught his arm. "Don't waste our time."

"You'd rather stand in the rain?"

"What would you know about it?"

Von Kempt turned and blew his whistle. He waved to his men. The camp guards herded a group of marchers around the tank. They yelled the order. "Dig. Dig."

The marchers shoved their hands into the mud. The tank commander looked bemused.

"No shovels?" he asked. "Is that your way?"

"You have shovels for them?" von Kempt said.

The tank commander drew on his cigarette. He blew out the smoke. "Which camp?" he asked.

"Melinka."

"Never heard of it."

"Near the village."

"What a waste." The tank commander watched the digging. "We're losing the war for this."

The earth sunk and the tank slipped. The commander threw down his cigarette and walked over. "All right—all right," he said. "Get away. Get the fuck away. Fucking morons. Get the fuck away. Get back. Get away." He pulled his sidearm. The guards and marchers fell back. "I'll shoot the next mother fucker gets near this."

Schmidt and the other camp guards looked at von Kempt. His cheeks were red in the rain. He felt wobbly on his new leg.

"You heard him," von Kempt said finally. "Back in line. Time to go!"

The tank commander held his sidearm and watched the marchers pass. "Fucking morons," he said. His men laughed and stood in the rain.

Forty Nine

Franz Strauss was a fastidious man, but to Heinrich Petersdorf he looked weary and unshaven today.

"Franz?"

"What is it? More good news?"

"Word from Berlin has the Red Army moving toward us at a rate of seven kilometers per day."

Strauss looked down at his desk. "Seven kilometers. Where were they last?"

"Jaroslaw."

"That close?"

"*Ja.*"

"How big a detachment?"

"Brigade."

"Whose command?"

"I don't know." Petersdorf looked out the window. "You're following commanders now?"

"It's important," Strauss said. "It adds or subtracts to our time." He looked at the major. "What are our numbers?"

"Three thousand before the march," Petersdorf said. "They took two hundred fifty. Another group leaves tomorrow. Down to two hundred a day in the gas."

"Two hundred?"

"Berlin told us to stop. We dismantled six and seven."

"I don't see that as particularly humane "

"Agreed."

"We have food enough for our men. Anyone else will starve."

"Winter's coming."

"Starve and freeze then," Strauss said.

FOR OVER A WEEK after Himmler ended the Final Solution, no trains came to the camp. Fiddler celebrated the end of selections duty by drinking for three days. Hehl said there was nothing to celebrate but he felt the knot in his stomach loosen. Strauss ordered the ramp dismantled. With regular marches, an increased rate of three hundred killings per day, and no new inmates, the camp population fell.

From his perch in the far guard tower, Corporal Walkenburg was the first person to hear the whistle and the grinding wheels of the *Kriegslokomotive* that now approached. He didn't believe it at first, and had to confirm what he heard through binoculars.

PEOPLE IN THE HOSPITAL Block tried to peer through knotholes in the pine walls for the same reason.

"What do you see?"

"It's a train all right," Shosha said.

"Maybe it's the allies."

"Don't be stupid."

"Supply cars, probably," Julia said.

They saw Petersdorf and Fiddler hurry by. The engine pulled a long line of cars, but no one could yet tell what kind.

"WHEN WAS THE LAST time supplies came by train?" Petersdorf asked.

"Hardly ever," Fiddler said. "They never bring enough to fill a boxcar."

Hehl joined them.

"You know?" Petersdorf asked him.

"What?"

"When did we last get supplies by train?"

"I can't remember," Hehl said. "It's usually by truck through Krakow."

The train slowed through the gates and cars packed with evacuees rocked by.

"Shit," Fiddler said.

Petersdorf jogged to the engine. Two *SS* guards stepped down. "What's this?" Petersdorf asked.

"Orders," said one of the guards. He handed Petersdorf a sheet of paper. The major looked it over and handed it back.

"We can't take them," Petersdorf said. "We're shutting down."

"Well—we can't take them back."

"Why not?"

"You ask that?"

Petersdorf surveyed the train. He heard people yelling, questioning, moaning, sobbing, and talking.

"You'll have to take them back or somewhere else."

"It's not possible," the guard said.

"You have to take them back." Petersdorf raised his sidearm.

"*Herr Stürmbannführer.*" The engineer leaned out of the locomotive. "This is not our doing."

"I don't care," Petersdorf said. "We're shutting down. We can't take them."

The guards looked at each other. The engineer stepped out and pushed past them. "Then shoot me," he told Petersdorf. He took a hammer in his gloved hand and rapped a releasing screw on the heavy chain that coupled engine to cars. "You won't shoot me." He pounded the screw and pulled up on it. Petersdorf fired into the air. People in the cars screamed and made other noises. Both train guards drew their weapons.

"Don't be stupid *Herr Stürmbannführer*," said one of the guards. "If you shoot us, you'll hang."

The engineer undid the couplings and with a wrench released the brake lines. He climbed back into his cabin. Strauss ran up behind them as the engine fired. He was breathing hard. He climbed the steps to the engineer's cabin.

"You can't leave these people here," Strauss said.

"Orders," the engineer droned.

"There's to be no more killing," Strauss said.

"So don't kill them."

"We can't take them."

"Leave them, then." The engine started to move forward. "*Herr Standartenführer*—step off."

"You can't leave these people here," Strauss gasped.

"We're not arguing with you." One of the guards pushed Strauss off the train. He fell and hit the ground. Petersdorf and Hehl helped him stand. The engine moved away.

"We can't handle this many," Hehl said.

Strauss looked at the solid boxcars and slatted stockcars that stretched so far he couldn't see the end.

"Hehl's right," Fiddler said. "They'll run us over."

Petersdorf watched the engine moving away. "Don't open any doors," Petersdorf said.

"What else can we do?" Hehl asked.

"What would we do with them if we opened the doors?" Petersdorf asked.

"You know what we'd do," Hehl said.

"We can do the same thing, doors closed."

"I'm sorry," Fiddler said, "but I cannot administer injections behind closed doors. I cannot make assignments behind closed doors. I cannot order duties behind closed doors."

"Administer injections?" Petersdorf said. "You shoot them in the heart with poison."

"You know what I mean," Fiddler said.

"I know you make assignments for people to dig their own graves," Petersdorf said. "I know you make assignments for people to go to the gas. I know you make assignments to carry dead bodies to the fire. I'm suggesting cutting all the bullshit and getting to the end right now."

"Burn them?" Hehl said.

Strauss staggered back. He started to laugh. "You mean it?" he said. Strauss placed his hands on the major's shoulders. He looked his friend in the eyes. "Have you lost your fucking mind?"

Petersdorf looked at Hehl. "Get the petrol."

The doctor looked at him. "I won't, *Stürmbannführer*."

"Then I'll do it."

"You will not," Strauss said. "I order you not to."

"Do you know what you're ordering?" Petersdorf said.

"Yes," Strauss said.

"Ordering that these people stay here and starve?" Petersdorf said. "Stay here and die in the cold and spread disease to the rest of us?"

"So burn them after they die," Fiddler said.

Petersdorf pulled his sidearm and turned to Hehl. "Get the petrol," he said. He raised the weapon.

"Shoot me," the doctor said. "I won't do it."

"*Stürmbannführer*." Fiddler put his hand on Petersdorf's arm.

"Get the petrol."

"I won't do it," Hehl screamed. "I won't do it. You shoot me. Shoot me!"

Petersdorf aimed at Hehl's head. The doctor closed his eyes.

"Heinrich," Strauss said.

Petersdorf pressed the barrel hard into the side of Hehl's head. They heard sobbing and talking on the train.

"Heinrich!"

Petersdorf lowered his sidearm. Hehl stood motionless. Petersdorf looked at Strauss, then turned and walked away. Hehl raised his hands to his face.

Fifty

The kapos kicked the marchers awake before sunrise. They slept in an open field on the cold November ground. By this seventh day of the march, they had lost eighty seven men. Two *SS* guards went into the forest to shit and never returned. The guards beat over a dozen marchers to death. They shot dozens more. Exhaustion and starvation brought down the rest.

Von Kempt stood in the field with Schmidt, unfolding a map. "Where do we go?" the lieutenant asked.

"We're supposed to follow the Wisła."

"The Wisła is a river. Where is it?"

"Here, *Herr Leutnant*." Schmidt pointed to a place on the map.

"And where are we?"

"We"—Schmidt bent his head closer to the map—"we should be here." He pointed.

"Should be?"

"We're here, *Herr Leutnant*." Schmidt pointed on the map again. "Here."

A FEW HOURS LATER, the marchers moved up a gravel road.

"Should be lunch time soon." Jerczek said.

"You're hungry?" Jakub said.

"You're not?"

The marchers saw civilians coming from the other direction, pushing carts and wheelbarrows and leading horses that pulled wagons piled with furniture, clothes, books, pots, pans, and food. The civilians passed the marchers. They were women, men, children, and wounded. Their eyes were tired and they moved without life. They looked forward or down or away.

"Could they be more miserable than we are?" asked the man behind Jakub.

Two miles up, they entered a village.

"*Herr Leutnant*—where is the supply truck?" Schmidt asked.

"You think I know?"

"They should have been here with food an hour ago."

"Stop complaining."

Von Kempt looked around the village. All the shops were closed but the buildings looked intact. "You want food?" von Kempt said to Schmidt. He pointed to a bakery. "Go get it."

"Break in?"

"Or wait for the truck."

Schmidt whistled at a few guards. They walked to the bakery and kicked in the door. Villagers—a few remained—watched. Children came into the street and threw stones, but adults ran after them and pulled them back. Von Kempt's men brought out bread and pastries and liquor for drinking and baking.

"Set it down," von Kempt said. "Here in the street."

They hauled out bags of flour and seeds and metal canisters filled with milk and clean water. Some prisoners moved toward the food. The guards saw them and shoved them back.

"Let them eat," von Kempt said. He looked at his men. He looked at their eyes. These were young men, younger than he was, but they looked worn. "Everyone eats," von Kempt said.

Jakub took two small loaves and hid them in his shirt. The other marchers broke the bread and passed it around. The guards sat in the street and ate. They talked.

"Ask him," said one of the guards.

"He had a surgery."

"When? He's been in camp the whole time."

"Ask him."

"I won't. You do it."

"I'll do it," said a corporal. "*Herr Leutnant.*"

Von Kempt and Schmidt ate together, away from the others.

"*Herr Leutnant.*"

"What is it?"

"Some of us were wondering."

"*Ja*—what?"

"Well, we were wondering, *Herr Leutnant*, what happened to your gimp?"

Von Kempt looked at them. "What?" he said. He stood up and walked to them.

"We were wondering—you used to limp."

"Why ask such a thing?"

"It's only—"

Von Kempt pulled back his leg and kicked the corporal. "Time to go," he said.

"But *Herr Leutnant!*"

"Time to go," he repeated. "Time to go, all of you!" He kicked over a milk canister. He kicked over a water canister. The milk and the water ran into the street. Marchers fell to their knees and lapped the running streams. One by one, Von Kempt kicked over every other canister. "Now," he yelled. "Are we ready to go?"

THE MARCHERS SLEPT IN the open along a road and when they woke, they had frost in their hair and on their beards. A new routine had everyone walk out of the field and line up on the road. Schmidt counted those left lying in the field and marked them as dead and the rest marched away. To pass the time one afternoon, Schmidt drew a graph that plotted number of days on the march versus number of men left for dead in the fields. The line sloped upward without end. This morning they marched for five kilometers and one of the soldiers fell.

"Get up." His compatriots tried to rouse him. "We have to stay on our feet."

But he didn't move.

"*Herr Unterfeldwebel*—we have a man down here."

Schmidt walked back to them. When he saw the soldier, he whistled at the car carrying von Kempt. Schmidt bent down and examined the man, eighteen-year-old *Schütze* (Private) Heerensburg from a farming community outside Munich. He placed his fingers on the man's neck. Von Kempt appeared at his side.

"What's wrong with him?" von Kempt said.

"He's dead, *Herr Leutnant*."

"Pull him aside. We have to keep moving."

Schmidt looked at his men. He saw how their uniforms sagged. He saw the darkness around their eyes. He saw the hollow spots in their unshaven cheeks.

"*Herr Leutnant*—I don't think we should go any farther today."

"What? Why not?"

"We have to bury him."

"You have the energy to bury him? What will you be left to walk with?"

"We shouldn't leave until the food truck comes," Schmidt said. "Then we'll have the energy."

"The food truck hasn't come for three days," von Kempt said. "It's not coming."

Schmidt looked at his men and the prisoners.

"We need food, *Herr Leutnant*."

Von Kempt looked at the men. He spit and rubbed his dirty face. "Goddamn it!" He walked away and looked up the road. "God *fucking* damn it!" Then he walked back. "You need food?"

"Yes," Schmidt said.

"How hungry are you?"

"We'll die out here without food."

One of the marchers wavered. The men around him propped him up. Von Kempt looked in their direction, but they closed in and he saw only men standing.

JAKUB PULLED AN APPLE from his pocket. Keeping it down, he handed it to Jerczek. "Split it," he said. "Tell everyone to split it. A little piece for each." Jakub pulled another apple from his pocket, and a piece of cheese.

"Where did you get all that?" Jerczek asked.

"From the village. A woman slipped them in my pockets."

Jerczek looked at Jakub's pockets. "Where have you been keeping it? I haven't seen anything." Jerczek split the apple with his fingers four ways. He took one piece and handed three others around. He looked at the soldiers up the road. "They're arguing about food," Jerczek said to Jakub. "*Their* food. Doesn't that take it!"

VON KEMPT STARED AT the private, lying in the road. He stared and he thought. He lifted his knife out of its sheath and bent down toward the dead man.

"*Herr Leutnant?*"

Von Kempt cut the buttons along the man's coat. He pulled the dog tags from the man's neck and put them in his pocket. His men watched. Von Kempt moved the knife down to the private's boots and cut through the laces.

"*Herr Leutnant*—what are you doing?"

Von Kempt looked at Schmidt and the other men.

"You eat what you have, Schmidt."

A pang shot through Schmidt's stomach. He tried to open his mouth.

"Build a fire," von Kempt said. "You men—get some wood. Start a fire. *Jetzt!*"

"I—" Schmidt grabbed the lieutenant's arm. "What are you doing?"

"Start a fire." Von Kempt looked at his men. "Build a fucking fire."

Schmidt pulled the lieutenant back. "Why not one of them?" The sergeant looked at the marchers. "One of the dead ones."

"Eat that filth? Who knows what diseases they have."

Schmidt looked at Private Heerensburg. Von Kempt stood and lifted the young man and dragged him off the road. Schmidt rushed forward and grabbed the body around the legs.

"You can't," the sergeant said. "We can't do this."

Von Kempt dropped the corpse and drew his Luger.

"Let go."

Schmidt was whimpering.

"Let go *now!*" Von Kempt said.

"I can't, *Herr Leutnant*. I can't. I can't." Schmidt weakened and relaxed his grip. Finally, he slumped.

"The wood's wet," a soldier yelled back.

"There's petrol in the sidecar trunk," von Kempt said. "Only use a little."

The soldier brought a gas can from the trunk. In a moment, von Kempt heard fire crackling and felt heat on his back. He heard Schmidt whimpering. He saw the marchers a little ways off, grabbing their sides and lifting their feet in the cold. Von Kempt stripped Private Heerensburg naked and lifted his body under the shoulders. He didn't ask for help and he dragged it toward the flames.

Fifty One

A boy inside a slatted cattle car at Camp Melinka saw soldiers splashing yellow liquid from large cans. He saw people grabbing their eyes and crying. The liquid splashed next to the boy. He looked at his father. "What are they doing?" the boy asked.

His father swabbed the liquid with his fingers and held it to his nose.

"They're going to burn us," a woman screamed.

The father moved his son away and covered the boy with his body.

The guards threw matches into the cars but the prisoners stomped them or kicked them back out. "We need rags," one of the guards yelled. "Someone get rags."

"Go to Hehl," another guard screamed. "He has all that."

Hehl refused to open the stores. He told the soldiers if they needed rags, they could strip. He said he would shoot the first man who tried to open any storehouse doors.

"*Herr Stürmbannführer*," Corporal Walkenburg complained to Petersdorf in his office. "We can't simply stand outside the cars holding matches until the wood takes."

"Use a flamethrower," Petersdorf said.

"They're dead—none of them work."

"How did that happen?"

"Rusted."

"They were never kept clean," another guard said. "Some were left out."

Petersdorf looked out the window at a pit full of naked bodies. "Forget it," he said.

"*Herr Stürmbannführer*?"

"Forget it. Just forget it."

The day passed. The fuel on the boxcars evaporated. The soldiers could try again, but petrol was running short and the whole issue seemed to lose momentum.

MAJOR PETERSDORF WALKED ACROSS the camp toward Strauss' office. He heard something smash in the greenhouse. He went around to that entrance and went inside. He saw Strauss on his hands and knees, sweeping up a broken flowerpot and puffing a pipe.

"Franz?"

"Did you shut the door?"

Petersdorf approached.

"I hope you shut the door, Heinrich." Strauss stood and walked to the major. The Commandant took his pipe out of his mouth and whispered. "That goddamned stench out there—I can't even go out in my own yard anymore."

"It doesn't matter," Petersdorf said. "It's time."

"Time for what?" Strauss cut roses. Petersdorf saw his hands shaking.

"We have to evacuate."

"Evacuate? Where?" Strauss said.

"Across the border. Germany."

"Do you realize it's been over four months since anyone from the camp directorate has inspected us?"

"We have to evacuate," Petersdorf said.

"Why in hell should we? What will we be going to?"

"Any place is better than here."

"What about Gretty? What do I do with her?"

"We can move her."

Strauss waved off the suggestion. "I'm seeing her later," he said. "I'll ask her."

Fifty Two

Snow fell the morning of the tenth day of the march and Jakub awoke to bleeding wrists and feet. He was not in pain lying still. But when he tried to roll over and press his hand on the ground, pain shot through his arm. He couldn't stand. He couldn't march. A fearful pang made him feel sick. He felt sicker than he had in the Ghetto or in the camp. He knew they would shoot him.

"*Raus! Raus! Aufstehen!*"

The soldiers started morning wake up and they walked along the bodies lying in the open field. "Get up. Get the fuck up. Get out! Time to go. Time to go!"

Jerczek saw Jakub lying still. He watched the soldiers and waited for them to turn away. Then he crawled to Jakub and lay beside him. "Jakub," he whispered. "What's going on?"

Jakub turned his red eyes to Jerczek.

"You're always the first up."

Jakub held up his hand.

"Shit," Jerczek said. "How did that happen?"

Jakub pulled up his pant leg. He slipped off a clog.

"Foot too?"

"Feet and ankles," Jakub said. "I can't walk."

"You look like you've been shot."

"No," Jakub said. "It's a condition."

"What can I do?" Jerczek asked.

"I'm thirsty," Jakub said.

Jerczek looked up at the snow. "Catch the flakes on your tongue." Jerczek opened his mouth and stuck out his tongue. He looked at Jakub. He looked at the soldiers. He looked at the gray sky and the snow. Jakub moved his arm.

"Be still," Jerczek said. "Don't move and don't talk."

The soldiers were getting closer.

"Right before they get here, open your eyes and don't blink," Jerczek said. He put his arm over Jakub and pressed his face into Jakub's shoulder. "Remember," Jerczek said. "Don't blink."

Jakub felt the hard kick first on his left leg.

"Up. Stupid fuck. Stand up."

He felt the second kick in his groin. He wanted to breathe. He wanted to jump up and grab the soldier by the neck and strangle him until he was dead. But he lay still with his eyes open. He saw the soldier standing over him. The soldier spit in his face and used his foot to roll Jerczek away from Jakub. Jerczek flopped back. He was still. The soldier stepped on his stomach. He pressed. The soldier took his foot off and walked to the next line of bodies.

"Stay still." Jerczek gasped under his breath. "Wait till they leave."

"You're staying?" Jakub said.

"Escaping," Jerczek said. "You and me."

The marchers and the soldiers moved toward the road. Jerczek raised his head a little and saw von Kempt walking toward his men. The ground was muddy dark and mottled with snow. Jerczek watched them move away.

"How long before your condition clears up?" Jerczek asked.

"Usually a few hours."

"Then you can walk?"

"Yes. But it depends. Sometimes it can take a day."

Jerczek looked at the other bodies. "We need to stay warm," he said. When he no longer saw any soldiers or marchers, he stood.

"Where are you going?" Jakub said.

"Not far."

Jerczek went from body to body. He undressed them. Some clothes came off easily. Others he left because the cloth was frozen to the flesh or the ground. He rolled a few bodies off blankets. He found stale biscuits and hard candy in pockets. He gathered these things and brought them to Jakub. They lay under a pile of filthy blankets beneath a cloudy sky sucking lemon drops speckled with lint and saving the bread.

JAKUB RAISED HIS ARM. He watched the snowflakes land, one by one on his woolen shirt. He sucked the moisture on his sleeve. He looked at the sky and opened his mouth and felt the cold sensation of the fall. He saw Jerczek coming out from the trees with an armful of sticks.

"You won't believe what I found," Jerczek said. He dropped the sticks. He took a military issue flint from his pocket and showed Jakub. "That Kraut they ate—they left his clothes. It was in his pants."

"Leftovers," Jakub said.

Jerczek looked at him. Then he laughed. He stopped and laughed. "That's very funny," Jerczek said. "It's good to have humor in times like these." He arranged the sticks for the fire. "So where do you think they went?" he said.

"They were lost," Jakub said.

Jerczek peeled thin scraps of bark into a pile. "Laughing at such tragedy," he said. "I should be ashamed. But I don't feel a bit sorry." He looked around at the bodies in the field. "I used to laugh so often," he said. "I used to joke and laugh." He looked at his hands. He scraped the flint against the bark scraps. "How you feeling?"

"Better," Jakub said. "I should walk by tonight."

"We won't be walking at night," Jerczek said. "We'll start in the morning." He kept scraping the flint but he couldn't rouse a spark.

"Let me," Jakub said.

"With those hands?"

Jakub motioned for the flint and Jerczek handed it to him. In a few minutes, Jakub had sparks and smoke and embers he finessed into flames.

"Bravo!" Jerczek said. "Where did you learn that?"

"My father," Jakub said.

"He must have been an outdoorsman."

"He spent a lot of time outside."

"Yes?"

"He was in the Resistance."

"Ahh. Where is he now?"

"Dead."

Jerczek hesitated. "I'm sorry," he said. "You have other family?"

"Mother and brother."

"Are they in the Resistance?"

"In ways," Jakub said.

"Where from?"

"Marienburg."

"Marienburg? Ahh. Near the castle?"

"A few kilometers from it."

"I visited there once," Jerczek said. "Amazing place. I love the history of it. It makes me think about all the pretenders around us." Jerczek added some dry twigs to the fire.

"What about your family?" Jakub asked.

"Scattered," Jerczek said. "My father's side went to America. My mother stayed in Warsaw."

"Did she get out?"

"In a manner of speaking," Jerczek said. "She died."

"I'm sorry," Jakub said.

Jerczek sighed. "They say a long life is a good thing, but death can be a good thing too. Think of all the bad things you miss when you die."

"You could have gone to America?" Jakub said.

"They argued about it," Jerczek said. "My father wanted us all to go. My mother thought it was treasonous, like desertion. It broke them."

"You lived in Warsaw?" Jakub asked.

"I ran an orphanage," Jerczek said. He looked around. He didn't speak for a while. "Until I had to close it."

"I know Warsaw," Jakub said. "I was captured there."

Jerczek looked at him. "*You* were captured in Warsaw? What were you doing?"

"Helping a family."

"So."

"A Jewish family."

"Which family?"

"Mordechai."

"I know them! And I saw the Mordechai girl at the camp."

Jerczek suddenly felt Jakub's hands on both his shoulders.

"Shosha?"

"Yes," Jerczek said. "Yes. You knew her?"

Jakub tried to get up.

"What are you doing?" Jerczek asked. He placed his hand on Jakub's arm. "What are you doing?"

Jakub looked at Jerczek. His face was a contorted mass of conflicted emotions.

"She's gone," Jerczek said. Jakub froze. "They were either marching us or killing us in the H-block, and now they're burning the place." Jakub was shaking now. "I should have listened to her," Jerczek said. He pulled his knees up. "She told me to stay in Warsaw, me and the children." He looked toward the woods, across the field. "But we were damned either way." He looked at the road and the falling snow. "There is nothing but damnation here," Jerczek said. "Damnation all around."

Fifty Three

Commandant Strauss walked past Corporal Höfstaller and another man. They stood at attention but the Commandant didn't acknowledge them. He was in full dress uniform, shaved clean and his hair was combed and his hands were full with a magnum of red wine, a bouquet of flowers from his greenhouse, and the magnetophon. The corporal and the other man watched Strauss turn a corner. They continued walking toward the hospital block. Another group of *SS* waited there.

At the hospital block entrance, Höfstaller looked at the four men and the image of the Commandant flashed in his mind. Here were these men instead, dirty and unshaven. Dust and mud streaked their boots. Wrinkles marred their uniforms. Their belt buckles didn't align with their gig lines. Under their covers, Höfstaller could see who had washed his hair and who had not. He could also smell someone, maybe more than one.

"Nobody's bathing anymore?" he asked.

"This is dirty work, *Rottenführer*. Why be clean to do it?"

Höfstaller had always worked in Petersdorf's office. Now he was reassigned. He reached down with a key and opened the big door to the hospital block. The men gasped and stood back.

"Get used to it," a private said. "You can't be holding your nose."

Three guards went in. One leaned against the outside wall. Höfstaller stood in the doorway marking a ledger on a clipboard. "First five," he said. "Out."

The guards heard praying, pieces here and there of Kaddish and Our Father and a Hail Mary from a rosary bead. They heard a prayer to Allah from an Albanian gypsy. They heard crying and singing and a low, sad wail that seemed to hover over the words. They heard a truck drive up outside. The guards reached down and took the inmates under their shoulders. Who could not stand they dragged outside to an empty flatbed truck. Inside the hospital block, the prisoners heard how each person answered death.

One man cried and begged for his life.

Another man cursed the guards. He told them what hideous human beings they were, what terrible things they had done. He spit at them, but he was not strong enough and the spittle only dribbled down his chin. He told them they were all going to Hell. He told them they would hang.

One woman said nothing. She weighed seventy-two pounds and was too weak to speak.

Shosha heard "it's about time," in her native Polish from someone else.

One prisoner vomited, but only bile and acid came up.

The block inmates heard three gunshots outside—*pop, pop, pop.*

"Shit—fucker's jammed."

More gunshots: *Pop. Pop. Pop.* One to the head. One grazed a head and another sent to the heart landed above it, near the throat. They loaded this man on the truck with the rest and threw him into the pit, where under a heap of bodies he would bleed to death before he burned.

"Second five," Höfstaller said. His voice sounded strained. "Bring them out."

The guards moved toward Shosha. She looked like a lifeless skeleton now, and one could see no life when she closed her eyes. She looked across at Julia, who had not moved for days. Shosha tried to talk to Julia and wanted very much to touch her. But she was too weak to pull herself out of the bunk and crawl across to Julia's bunk, so instead she prayed but she would not say Kaddish because she didn't want to think that Julia had simply lain there and died.

Shosha told Julia about Jakub and his brother Karl. She told Julia who these men were, how in all this darkness she had found them. She told Julia about her mother and the rabbi. She explained that her mother was the strongest woman she had ever known. She explained how without the rabbi, she would never have lived long enough to love, not one man, but two.

When Julia didn't say anything, Shosha felt awkward. "I loved the rabbi too," she explained. "But in a different way. I loved them each in a different way."

"Did they love you?" Shosha heard this question from a few bunks down. She couldn't tell whether the quiet voice came from a man or a woman.

"Yes," Shosha said. "They did."

The guards dragged five more people out. Two were already dead. Shosha heard the pleas and the gunshots again.

"Third five—out."

The guards pulled out others around Shosha. She watched them with one eye partly open as they reached in and tugged on Julia. Her bones and limp flesh flopped out of the bunk and hit the floor. Shosha felt tears coming and she held them in.

"Watch the sores." One of the guards looked at Julia's arms and legs. "Don't touch her there. She's covered. Take her by wrists."

"We have gloves."

"One pair. You don't want to have to burn them."

They dragged Julia out by one arm.

"Why do we have to drag out the dead ones?"

Shosha heard the guards conferring outside. She couldn't make out what they were saying.

"Next five—out." Then someone blew a whistle. "Leave the dead ones."

SOMEWHERE IN THE HOLLOW, Shosha heard a woman begin a prayer in a foreign tongue. Shosha didn't recognize the prayer, but it was beautiful, the way it settled the void.

"Bismillaah ah-Rahman ar-Raheem
In the name of God, Most Gracious, Most Merciful

"Al hamdu lillaahi rabbil 'alameen
Praise be to God, the Cherisher and Sustainer of the world

"Ar-Rahman ar-Raheem
Most Gracious, Most Merciful

"Maaliki yaumid Deen.
Master of the Day of Judgment.

"Iyyaaka na'abudu wa iy yaaka nasta'een."
Thee do we worship, and Thine aid we seek.

Shosha heard the guards enter again.
"He should be helping."
"He's in charge."
"He's a pussy."
They came to Shosha. She could feel their breath as they bent down to look at her. She could feel their shadows. She knew a hand was reaching out to touch her face.
"She's got sores. Don't touch."
"Sorry."
"You want to get sick?"
"I'm not touching it."
"Unless you want to burn your gloves, don't touch them. We don't have any other gloves."

The guard craned his head around to see Shosha's face. She kept her eyes open in a dead stare. She felt sick—sicker than she thought she had ever been—when the guard's eyes met hers. She couldn't look away, couldn't blink, couldn't cry, couldn't close her eyes.

The guard pulled back. "This one's gone."

"Leave it."

When the guards moved away, Shosha let her eyes close. She didn't know whether to thank G-d or cry out for them to take her and get it over with. She wondered why she didn't blink and let them take her. Why should she lie here when there was no hope? Why should she lie here and die?

But even if she had wanted to call out, she could barely raise the strength to speak. So she would lie here and wait. She would live a little longer, another hour or maybe another day. Maybe she would live a few days. She would live here alone among the dead they had left, but she would live and they would not kill her directly, with their own hands. She would starve to death but she would die on her time. The pain of starvation was terrible but she was more used to it now and at least there would be meaning. She heard the prayer again.

"Ihdinas siraatal mustaqeem Siraatal ladheena an 'amta' alaihim

Show us the straight way

"Ghairil maghduubi' alaihim, waladaalee.

The way of those on whom Thou hast bestowed Thy Grace
Those whose portion is not wrath, and who go not astray.

"Aameen."

It sounded like "Amein" to Shosha and she was surprised. It was almost a reflex when she said it in her mind. She heard shots again. Only three this time. The living were getting fewer and harder to find.

STRAUSS ARRANGED THE BOUQUET next to his wife's bed. He poured two glasses of wine. He set the magnetophon to play, but did not turn it on.

Dr. Hehl came into the room. "*Kommandant.*"

Strauss said nothing until Hehl came to his side. "*Doktor.*"

Hehl lifted Greta's thin white wrist and counted her pulse against his wristwatch. "Strong," he said. "She baffles me. She should be awake." He checked her IV, a simple contraption designed to keep her alive with a crude cocktail of nutrients, vitamins, and electrolytes.

Strauss moved his wife's catheter bag with his foot. It was half full and her urine was light in color. "She took a terrible fall," he said.

"She's healed from her fall," Hehl said. "If Berlin had taken her, she'd be up and around by now."

"Berlin doesn't care," Strauss said. He paused and caressed his wife's cheek. "What if she did awaken? What then?"

"I don't know," Hehl said.

Strauss stared at his wife. "You'll be evacuated tomorrow," he told Hehl. "You best be getting your things together."

"I have duties here," Hehl said. "I still have one patient."

"We'll be fine," Strauss said. He caressed his wife's forehead. He watched her breathing, her chest rising and falling.

"Will I see you again?" Hehl said.

"I don't know," Strauss said. "My ambition is to put this behind me."

Hehl sat for a moment. Then he stood and walked toward the door. At the door, he turned to Franz Strauss. "I had such high hopes," the doctor said. He stepped out and closed the door.

Strauss raised his glass to his wife. He looked at her. He gulped the wine. He replaced the glass on the little side table. He turned on the magnetophon. He walked over to the other bed and took the pillow and went to his wife's side. He bent down and kissed her and whispered.

"Without you, where is my strength?"

He raised the pillow and his hands shook but he gathered himself. He took the pillow in both hands and brought it over his wife's face. He watched her breathing, her chest rising and falling. He thought about how she would fight when her unconscious mind woke in a breathless torment. He thought about how he might lose his resolve and botch the job and instead of killing her mercifully, leave her brain starved for oxygen and only that part of her dead. He was a careful man and he considered these things. He lowered the pillow.

He looked at the closed door. The blinds were down but he drew them tighter. He turned up the volume on the magnetophon. He turned out the lamp in the room. He let a pale sun guide his hands as he pressed the pillow against his wife's head and drew his sidearm and pressed it into the pillow and fired one bullet. He looked at his wife's chest. It rose and fell no more.

SHOSHA WAS ALONE. THEY had left only the dead with her. She was cold and she covered herself with a blanket and wrapped her feet in a pair of pants so filthy and smelly she could hardly bear them.

She crawled on the straw-covered dirt to a water pipe that had dripped for a month. It wasn't freezing inside the block yet and she knew that unless they shut off the water, the pipe would freeze and burst. She planned to be far from it when she felt the temperature fall. For now, she lay beneath it with her mouth open, catching the drops.

She thought about thirst and hunger and which was worse. Both burned. Both were painful. Both were tragic, maybe more than sickness or disease because hunger and thirst caught early were easily cured. The rabbi had warned her not to eat too much after an intense bout of hunger. She had learned to eat slowly back in the Ghetto—to savor food and avoid the fatal consequence of hunger after starvation. She lay under the pipe now, watching each droplet form. First a bud, then a swell, then a clear, clean drop that caught enough light to distort a tiny portion of space Shosha could see from where she rested her head.

STRAUSS LOCKED THE DOOR to his wife's room in the infirmary. He went into the dispensary and looked through the glass shelves. He saw aspirin; bandages; candy pills for hypochondriacs; liquid for stomach flu; liquid for diarrhea; and laxatives. He saw a locked cabinet. He rummaged in the drawers, found a stainless-steel speculum, and used it to pry open the cabinet. He found painkillers: four bottles of Pethidine, better known as Demerol; and two bottles of Amidon, an opium-like pill later called methadone.

Strauss had argued with Hehl about this requisition, insisting the doctor push for it. Supplies of morphine and other pain killing drugs were running low, and Hitler wanted to reduce Germany's dependence on drug imports. The *Führer* turned to the firm that brought Zyklon gas and pain and death to so many —I.G. Farben, whose chemists discovered Pethidine and synthesized Amidon.

The Commandant took bottles of both.

GUARDS BURNED BUILDINGS THROUGHOUT the camp. They worked in darkness piling bodies into graves. Petersdorf went to his quarters after two in the morning. He had three days to complete the evacuation. He would spend two days destroying evidence. The last day they would leave. He lay on his bed. He went over the things left to do in his mind: burn the hospital block; burn the boxcars on the track; burn the enlisted barracks and the officer's quarters; burn the warehouses. He closed his eyes and slept in his uniform.

In his quarters, Dr. Hehl looked at clothes laid out on his bed —a shirt and hat, pants and socks and suspenders, plain and pedestrian. He had chosen each piece from the warehouse stores for their blandness. He took off the uniform jacket and began the exchange.

When he finished dressing, he slipped on a pair of scuffed brown shoes. He went to the mirror and combed his hair in a new way. He tried on a pair of weak eyeglasses that were tight around his temples. He slipped the eyeglasses into a case. He slipped the sidearm out of its holster and into his belt and covered it with a plain dark jacket. He slipped a wallet full of cash into his vest pocket with the eyeglass case. He was not *Herr Doktor* anymore.

Hehl stepped outside and walked across the yard. The guard towers were empty. He walked toward the boxcars left on the tracks that entered the camp.

"Hey mister—where you going?" A man spoke German under his breath from one of the cars. Other hushed and whispered voices followed, in Polish and other eastern European dialects.

"Mister—you have any food?"

"How did you get out? Aren't you afraid?"

"Where are the guards? Where did you come from?"

Hehl saw lights come on near the front gates. He moved closer to the cars.

"Don't get too close to this—there's shit all along here."

"Don't step in shit—you're going to step in shit."

"Those are guards over there. If they see you." The man who was speaking drew his finger across his throat.

"There's a trap door under the car," someone said. "You should get in here with us."

Hehl saw more lights. He knew if they caught him, they would shoot him for deserting. "Where's this door?" he said.

"Underneath. Through the bottom. They sweep cow shit through it."

Hehl bent and looked beneath the car. He saw a latch. He thought about slipping under the boxcar to the other side, but it was too close to the fence. He would have no room between the cars and the fence. He heard voices behind him and saw more lights.

"Hurry—you don't have much time."

Hehl slipped under the car. He took a rock that lay against the track and slammed it against the latch. The thick, rusty metal rod moved. He whacked it again on both sides. The rod slipped back and forth. Finally, it slipped out. He lowered the trap door. Two men in the car looked down. They didn't see Hehl but they knew he was there.

"Come up. We'll help you." They lowered their hands.

"No," Hehl said.

"What?"

"They will burn these cars," Hehl said.

"No—they tried that."

Hehl raised the rock through the trap door. "For the other latches," he said.

"Get in before they see you. We can get out later."

"The lights go out at three," Hehl whispered. "They're trying to save power. You can get out then."

"Well—thanks mister."

"You're crazy—out of your head. But thank you."

"Be careful."

"Danke!"

"Good luck," Hehl said. He stayed low and crawled beneath the boxcars. He went out the railway gate. He crossed the fields and without looking back, headed toward the village.

Fifty Four

"Listen." Jerczek stood. "Planes."

It was the first sound they heard in a day and a half and the first time they heard airplanes during the march.

"They're flying low," Jerczek said. He looked into the sky. They heard bombs and shelling. "We need to get into the trees."

He tried to help Jakub stand. "You can do it," Jerczek said. "Walk on the sides of your feet. Only a few hundred meters."

Jakub tried to stand but the pain overwhelmed him.

"I can't move," he said. "Go ahead."

"You can do it. Can you crawl?"

"My hands won't bear it."

"Then I'll drag you."

"Leave me. Go without me."

"I won't do that," Jerczek said. "We don't know who they are."

The planes came in low in the distance.

"Go on—get out of here."

Jerczek went behind Jakub.

"I'm going to lift you under the shoulders and pull. You kick with your heels. Can you do that?"

"You need to go," Jakub said. "I'll be okay."

"We have to get into the trees," Jerczek said. "If it snows hard, we'll have shelter, too." Jerczek lifted Jakub under his shoulders. "Push while I pull."

Together the men moved toward the trees. They rested twice. They were in the woods in about ten minutes. Jerczek went back for the blankets. He could hear the airplanes in the field. He returned with as much as he could carry.

"How far do you think those planes are?"

"I don't know," Jakub said. "Maybe a couple kilometers."

"Russians—or looking for Russians?" Jerczek looked through the woods. "Maybe foot soldiers are near. I could make a few kilometers today. Maybe find them."

"If you wait, I'll go with you."

"We don't have time. They may be gone by then and we may be frozen." Jerczek looked at the ground before him, covered with pine needles. He took Jakub's hand. "Pray for me," he said. He bundled himself and stood and headed into the woods.

THE GRAY SKY BECAME black without moonlight. Jakub fell asleep in the cold under blankets and pants. Late in the night, a light in his face woke him. Then he heard voices in a language he had heard before but didn't understand.

"He's alive."

The lights separated and he saw two lanterns and a flashlight. A man squatted down to him. The man tried speaking German first.

"Hey. Wake up!"

Jakub could make out the man's uniform. It was not German. "You're safe," the man said.

"You're safe now," said another man who was standing.

Their voices were clear and calm.

"Did Jerczek bring you?" Jakub asked. "Is he with you?"

One of the Russian soldiers recognized Polish and he came forward and spoke in that language.

"Jerczek?"

"Did Jerczek bring you? He left here to get help."

"There's no one but us," the soldier said.

"What about the other marchers?" Jakub said. "We heard planes. There were bombs."

"You mean the bodies in the field?"

"They were part of our group," Jakub said. "The rest went on, toward the river."

"We're armored," the Polish-speaking soldier said. "There have been air strikes around here, but that's not our group. We're reconnaissance."

The soldier saw blood on Jakub's hand and on the edge of the blanket by Jakub's feet. "Are you injured?" he asked.

"Not from bullets," Jakub said.

"Can you walk?" Two Red Army soldiers came forward to help Jakub stand. He brought his legs up and pressed down on his hands. The pain was gone. Jakub stood.

"The rest of us are across the field," a soldier said.

Jakub put on his clogs. They threw a heavy wool shawl around him and the four men walked out of the trees. "Be careful where you step," another soldier said.

Jakub heard them talking in their language. He followed the light cast on the ground from the lanterns. They came to the first body. He watched light pass over the man's face. They walked between other men. Some lay naked. Jakub could see their bones in their cheeks and chests. He could see their legs, like sticks. Then he tripped and one of the soldiers grabbed him and he gasped. He stood over a fully-clothed man who lay dead with the rest. Jakub felt a terrible urgency. He tightened his grip on the soldier.

"We have to go back," he said. "We have to go back now!"

The Russian didn't understand him. He whistled for his mates, who had walked ahead. They ran back.

"What's wrong?" said the Polish speaker.

Jakub looked at him. "We have to go back," he said.

"Back where?"

"Melinka. To Melinka."

"That's a day from here. Why?"

"That's where we came from."

"Who?"

"All of us. All of us here." Jakub looked at the man on the ground. "All of us came from Melinka."

"There's nothing in Melinka," one of the soldiers said in Russian. "It's just a village."

"Why were you in Melinka?" the Polish speaker said.

"There's a camp," Jakub said.

The Polish speaker translated. "He says there's a camp."

The other soldier scoffed. "There's no camp there."

"The closest resettlement camp is at Oswiecim."

"We were being evacuated from there," Jakub said. "From the camp at Melinka."

"There's no camp at Melinka. We would know."

"Not necessarily," the Polish speaker said. "There may be camps around we would not know about."

"We have orders," said the third soldier.

"We're reconnoitering," said the Polish speaker. "We have some latitude."

"Not that much."

"Who's to say? No one's here to say different except me."

Jakub knelt before the dead man and looked at him. A spotlight shined on the four men from the woods on the other side of the field. One of the soldiers shaded his eyes and looked in the direction of the light. Jakub looked up and heard "it's okay," in Polish.

Toward the light, they heard a diesel engine roar. White exhaust burst through the trees. They heard creaking and screeching and the ground vibrated under their feet and a large thing came through the trees. One of the soldiers motioned with his lantern and the tank followed the light like a trained beast and came alongside them, away from the bodies. The engine idled and the soldier at the turret looked down at them. They spoke in Russian. They raised their voices and Jakub knew they were arguing and he stood up and grabbed the one who spoke Polish.

"We have to go to Melinka," Jakub said. "There are more like us and they are still alive." He looked down at the stiff, cold body of Janusz Jerczek, whose face looked up with open eyes. "We have to go back to Melinka."

THE RUSSIAN PLATOON TRAVELED in two tanks and three trucks during the night and the men slept two hours. The Polish speaker was the platoon commander—a Red Army lieutenant named Kirlinovsky. The platoon was a reconnaissance arm of a western-moving division traveling across the extreme southern part of Poland.

Jakub rode in the back of a canvas-covered truck. One of the soldiers handed him a bar of chocolate but before he could take it, Kirlinovsky grabbed it away.

"You could kill him with that," the lieutenant said. He looked around the group in the truck. "You men—don't give anyone food."

"Not even the Krauts?"

The men laughed.

"How can chocolate kill me if nothing else has?" Jakub said.

Kirlinovsky smiled. "Maybe it wouldn't, but I've seen this before. Here." Kirlinosky broke off a small piece of the bar and handed it to Jakub. "That's enough for now."

They joined a Red Army squad rooting out German bunkers, but no one in the squad knew about the camp at Melinka. The two groups of Red Army soldiers came down roads and through trees. They crossed streams and fields where the soil was hard enough for armor. A few miles outside Melinka, the trucks stopped and soldiers stepped off and spread out.

"Do you have masks?" Jakub asked Kirlinovsky.

"You think they'll use gas?"

"No. For the smell," Jakub said.

"If we need them."

"You will."

Fifty Five

A voice from a bullhorn roused Shosha. She lay beneath as many blankets as she could salvage. She didn't sleep but stayed on the verge of sleep and tried to fight bad thoughts.

"*Niederbrennen! Niederbrennen!*"

She had heard this word before but she did not know it. She knew conversational German but this word was not conversational.

"*Niederbrennen!*"

Major Petersdorf walked between the buildings with the bullhorn. His face was dirty. He had not ironed or starched his uniform for two weeks. He had not shaved in days. He shouted the command.

"*Niederbrennen!*"

Petersdorf earlier ordered Hehl to open the warehouses and when Hehl refused, the major ordered him held at gunpoint while the guards opened the stores.

"I don't know what you hope to accomplish except to get us all hung," Petersdorf said to Hehl.

Under Corporal Walkenburg's watch, the guards hauled out all the cloth. They soaked shirts and pants, skirts and socks, long johns and soft hats in gasoline and piled it on flatbeds with wheels. Now they walked from building to building, splashing wooden walls with fuel. They lit rags and threw them against the walls. They stripped the crematoria and left brick shells behind.

When Shosha smelled smoke, she remembered where she had heard the word *Niederbrennen*. In Warsaw, during the Uprising, *SS* officers yelled it to the men on the carts who went from building to building with flamethrowers and burning dross.

Shosha raised her head. She looked around the hospital block. She heard the wood creak and saw bat guano trickle from the rafters. The bats had come in through knotholes in the pine as the weather cooled. Shosha saw an empty bird's nest teetering overhead. A mama had raised her babies there and left the spring before. The bats left every night, but it was cold now and she hadn't seen them.

She smelled smoke but it was outside, in other buildings.

IN THE LOW LIGHT of flames from his bedroom fireplace, Franz Strauss unbuttoned his uniform jacket and looked out the window. He slipped off the jacket and set it on the bed with the cover. He untied the necktie and laid it on the jacket. He slipped off the shirt and undid the belt and placed them both on the bed. He slipped off the pants. He went to the fire and stoked the flames. He slipped off his socks and underwear and gathered the uniform and the cover and his underclothes and pulled the grate away from the fire. He threw everything into the flames but belt and boots, leather that would stink if it burned.

He was naked and he watched the fire consume it all and he heard yelling and gunshots in the yard. He looked out the window and saw mud on the ground. He looked at the fire and saw metal things in the ash.

Strauss walked to the bathroom. He filled a glass of water and took Amidon and Pethidine. He didn't empty the bottles. He didn't take enough to overdose, only dull the pain. He went to the bathtub and turned on the spigots and tested the water with his hands. He put the stopper in the drain and went back to the mirror, where he shaved his face and nicked himself twice.

PETERSDORF WOKE BEFORE DAWN. He combed his hair, shaved, and washed his face and hands. He went outside. He saw smoldering barracks. He turned and in the early morning shadows, saw the upstairs light through the second story window of Strauss' quarters.

"*Stürmbannführer!*" Dr. Fiddler saluted him. "The men need rest."

"We can't rest," Petersdorf said.

"Some deserted."

"What?"

"Walked away in the night."

"What time? Why weren't they caught?"

"No one cares."

"You will care when you're staring through a noose."

"Hehl left too."

"Fuck him. That's no loss. Who's caring for the *Kommandant's* wife?"

"*Kommandant.*"

"How do you know? I haven't heard this."

"Hehl said you knew."

Petersdorf ran his hand through his hair. "How many men are still here?"

"There's a few."

"Get Höfstaller and burn the other buildings today," Petersdorf said. He looked up at the Commandant's window. "I will shoot any man who tries to desert."

The major walked away from the doctor. He ran up the stairs to the Commandant's house. The guard there saluted him.

"When did you get here?" Petersdorf asked.

"I relieved Beckar at five."

"Did either of you see the *Kommandant*?"

"I haven't," the guard said. "I didn't ask Beckar."

Petersdorf went into the house. The front office was empty. "Franz," he called. He went into the library. He looked in the study. He went into the drawing room and the kitchen and back to the greenhouse. "We're evacuating! *Evakuieren!*" He went upstairs. The bed in the master was neatly made. He saw embers glowing in the fireplace. He saw the Commandant's polished shoes, together on the floor. He saw a typewritten note on a writing desk. He picked it up and recognized Hemingway again, writing about how the world kills the good, the gentle, the brave, and the courageous, and how if you are "none of these," it will kill you, too, but with "no special hurry."

None of these was underlined.

Petersdorf felt his mouth go dry. He went out of the room and down the hall. He saw the closed door to the bathroom. The door was not locked. He opened it.

"Franz?"

Strauss lay in the bathtub. His eyes were open, toward the window. The water was red. Petersdorf went to his friend and lifted his wrist. He set down the lifeless hand and saw blood on his fingers. He turned the wrist over. Strauss had cut himself, but he didn't penetrate the artery. He bled, but not enough to die. His other hand lay in the water.

Petersdorf shook. He lifted Strauss' hand to his quivering lips where a high-pitched sigh escaped. He saw the razor blade and the empty pill bottles. He heard a commotion in the yard. The burning had started for another day.

THE RED ARMY TROOPS passed through Melinka village. Curious villagers followed them. Father Waleska stood at his gate and watched the tanks creeping and trucks rolling and the soldiers walking in the cold. In the last truck, he thought he saw a familiar face in the early light peaking over the mountains. He opened the gate.

The smell hit the soldiers. "What is it?" They winced and gagged. "What is that?" Several troops bent over and heaved.

They covered their faces with their gas masks. "I haven't *ever* smelled anything like this. Ever!"

Jakub looked at the men through his mask. They halted, then moved again. A rumbling, persistent, slow-treaded slog moved toward the camp. Bullhorns demanded surrender. Guards left their posts. The Russians pressed down the gate. The stragglers watched safely from behind.

Corpses lay piled and scattered and *Muselmänner* stood dying. Some prisoners had escaped the boxcars, except those who were too weak. Guards lay down their arms and raised their hands.

"Stop the fires," Kirlinovsky ordered.

His troops fanned out. They drew water in buckets and threw it on the burning buildings. They went to the infirmary and kicked in the door to Greta Strauss' room and found her where and how her husband had left her.

The Russian troops came to one building that wasn't burning —the Commandant's quarters. The entrance guard had left his post and out of respect for the Commandant and in the hope that he would turn the camp over with no violence, Kirlinovsky didn't storm the house but stood in front of it with his troops, demanding surrender through a bullhorn.

Major Petersdorf walked out the front door, tall and stiff, into the sunlight. Father Waleska walked up behind the troops. One of them gave the priest a gas mask.

"*Herr Kommandant*," Kirlinovsky said through the bullhorn. "We are asking for you to surrender."

"This priest has something to say," one of the men told Kirlinovsky.

"That's not the Commandant," the Father said. "I know him."

"Where is your commandant?" Kirlinovsky said to the major.

Petersdorf stared. Father Waleska took the bullhorn. "Heinrich," he said. "It's time to lay down your arms."

The major's hands trembled. He didn't speak or move.

"You protected our village," Waleska told him. "The allies will know of this, I assure you."

With his shaking right hand, Petersdorf blessed himself—in the name of the Father, the Son, and the Holy Ghost. He lowered his hand toward his sidearm. Kirlinovksy's men raised their rifles.

"Take it out and put it on the ground," Kirlinovsky said.

Major Petersdorf lifted the gun from its holster. Then he turned it toward himself and raised it and the soldiers fired. He fell on the steps.

ON THE OTHER SIDE of the camp, the hospital block burned. Shosha saw flames and heard voices outside. She had crawled away from the walls. She reached up to one of the bunks. She pulled herself up, along jagged boards, slipping her frail fingers between nails and knots. She pulled and her feet slipped in the mess but she kept her grip and tightened her fingers and with the emaciated muscles in her wrists and arms, pulled herself to her feet.

She stood on her legs for the first time in days. She breathed and coughed through the smoke. In front of her, she did not see fire and she moved. She moved and shook. She was unsteady but she kept moving, toward foreign voices that seemed close and the sound of water sizzling on fire. She saw sunlight and steam. She kept moving.

The Russian troops used a hose from a camp truck to douse the fire. They didn't at first see the emaciated figure who stepped around the falling walls and away from the flames. Her eyes were so used to dark that Shosha raised her hand to block the sun. On her trembling, skinny legs, she walked awkwardly forward, placing her sore-covered feet one in front of the other, one foot in front of the other, until she stood, away from the building. Shosha breathed as deeply as she could. Her knees shook. She looked beyond the smoke and called out in her native tongue.

"I am here. I am here!" Tears and smoke clouded her eyes.

The Russian soldiers heard her. They pressed through the smoke and saw her. They went to her and took her and she walked with them. Villagers who had made their way into the camp saw her and ran to help.

"She is very weak," one of the soldiers said. "Very weak and very sick."

"Did they bring a doctor? They must have brought a doctor?"

"These people need doctors!"

"Where is Chelzak?" asked one of the villagers. "Bring him. I saw him. Jakub Chelzak."

"Is he a doctor?"

"No, but some say just as good."

Shosha's legs gave way and the soldiers and the villagers lowered her to a blanket on the ground. A woman knelt beside her and took her hand.

Jakub couldn't walk well so some villagers and a Russian soldier lifted him in a litter and carried him through the haze. They set him next to Shosha. She looked at him and blinked her eyes.

"Jakub?" She touched his arm. "Is that you?" she said.

"Yes," he said.

She licked her dry lips. "I can't believe it." She drew in a deep breath. "I can't believe it." She smiled and her cheeks felt it.

"Janusz brought me," Jakub said.

"Janusz? Janusz Jerczek? Is he with you?"

"No," Jakub said.

"Is he all right?"

"Yes."

Jakub took her hand and pressed it to his cheek. Shosha looked up through the smoke at the sky. Then she looked at Jakub and closed her fingers around his hand.

"L'Chaim!" she said, as loudly as she could. "L'Chaim, Jakub!"

Jakub bent and kissed her forehead.

"L'Chaim, Shosha," he said. "L'Chaim!"

CITY-STATE

Fifty Six

"In March of the following year, Rabbi Azar Gimelman crossed the Wisła River into Warsaw and stood alone. He tried to find places he knew and streets he had walked on, and he walked over piles of bricks and heaps of cinders and he bent down many times and had to use his hands and knees to cross from one place to the next.

"The rabbi saw Soviet soldiers pulling stragglers from burned-out buildings and dragging men by the hair from underground bunkers. The Polish fighters had dirty faces and dusty clothes that hung limply from their starved bodies. The Red Army soldiers lined them up and yelled at them. From living for months around the Soviets in Praga, the rabbi understood that the soldiers would shoot the men if they wavered or fell.

"Several times, soldiers approached the rabbi and demanded his papers. Many of the soldiers had red faces and they stunk with vodka and cologne. They were young, young as the occupiers. They acted tough. They carried guns. They could beat or shoot any woman, man, or child without consequence.

"Before, the rabbi had watched from Praga. He watched the Germans raze and burn the city. He watched the fires and felt the heat from across the water. He watched the Soviets. He saw their tanks along the river and their men, drunk and smoking and growing lazy in the warm glow and the river breeze. He screamed at them in Polish but they didn't understand and told him to 'fuck off' in their own language.

"When the fighting was over and the rabbi made the crossing into Warsaw, an anxious knot in his stomach replaced his chronic hunger. He spent a day without food.

"It was the year 1945, the year of the great liberation. When the rabbi returned to Praga, he brought all that was left of the Warsaw he remembered—the gray and white dust that covered his shoes."

CARDINAL JOSEPH BERNARDI LOOKED up from the papers in front of him. He peered over his reading glasses. He sat at a conference table in a decorous Vatican chamber with other Church prelates—archbishops and cardinals in the Congregation of Saints.

"How can you be certain that what you've just read is an accurate portrayal?" he said. He spoke in Italian and a translator repeated in both Polish and English.

The canon lawyer assigned to Jakub Chelzak's case, Francisco Darrelli, looked at Shosha Mordechai. Her cheeks were red and her eyes were drawn.

588   The Fires of Lilliput

"It is, Your Eminence," Darelli said. "It comes from the best testimony we have about Rabbi Gimelman at that time. An eyewitness, a soldier who met and remembered him."

"A soldier in which army?"

Darelli looked at his notes. He looked up at the Cardinal. "The Red Army, Your Eminence."

"Hardly a reliable source." The Promoter of the Faith, the "Advocatus Diaboli" or "Devil's Advocate," Monsignor Zyporszka from Warsaw, faced the Congregation.

"The soldier saw the rabbi several times that day," Darelli explained. "He can't be precise about the date, but he does remember it was early spring."

"Who was this soldier? We have a name but nothing else?"

Darelli looked at his notes. "I'd say the soldier was an excellent source. He was an aide de camp to Marshal Rokossovsky, the commander of Soviet Forces."

The Devil's Advocate cleared his throat.

ADVOCATUS DIABOLI. THE DEVIL'S Advocate. It may be apropos that so sinister a name described the contentious center of the most labyrinthine legal endeavor ever devised— canonization. Between the beginning and end of the road to sainthood in the Roman Catholic Church, centuries have often intervened. To become a saint, a person must live an exemplary —and more importantly—a *verifiable* life of witnessed and recorded deeds. Indisputable miracles a Vatican scientific panel documents and verifies must follow after death.

During the "Prejuridical Phase," Jakub Chelzak's supporters verified his life with photographs, narratives, and a Super 8 film. They petitioned Lazslo Jocie-Wudl, Bishop of the diocese that included Malbork, formerly Marienburg, to initiate the "Ordinary Process," which begins after the candidate has been dead at least five years.

Bishop Jocie-Wudl established a tribunal during the "Informative Phase" to determine whether anyone prayed to or otherwise venerated Chelzak after his death. People all over Poland came forward.

Church officials scrutinized everything written to and from Chelzak during the "Judgment of Orthodoxy" phase. Though literate, Jakub left few writings, so the Church instead reviewed letters from his brother Karl; his priest, Monsignor Jaruslaw Starska; journalists; and a biographer writing a book about mystics, stigmatics, and faith healers. Written materials such as letters, diaries, journal entries, and biographies often include evidence of heresy or thinking at odds with Church doctrine. But Chelzak left nothing of this sort.

Bishop Jocie-Wudl forwarded these findings to the Vatican at a time of keen interest in potential Holocaust saints. Accused of ignoring Jewish suffering and enabling Hitler, church officials sought amends. Sainthood candidates like Maximilian Kolbe, a Franciscan friar from Warsaw who gave his life to save a Polish army sergeant at Auschwitz; and the Capuchin monk Anicet

Koplinski, nee Koplin, killed at Auschwitz after weeks in the hospital block, were among exemplary individual Catholics the Church was eager to recognize.

Church officials declared Chelzak a "Servant of God" and appointed a Postulator to launch an exhaustive final investigation during the aptly titled "Roman Phase." The Postulator argued Jakub Chelzak's candidacy before the Vatican's Congregation for the Causes of Saints opposite the Devil's Advocate.

Chelzak's Roman Phase began with the solution of a mystery that had stalled his petition. The one person still living who could most intimately bear witness to his life—a former Warsaw resident named Shosha Mordechai—had left Poland after the war. She had lived for a time in London, but Vatican investigators couldn't establish her whereabouts after 1957. Sixteen years later, the Church Postulator assigned to Chelzak's case, Monsignor Jaruslaw Bachleda, located Shosha Mordechai living in an apartment in Brooklyn, New York.

"I CALL SHOSHA MORDECHAI Price to the witness table," the Devil's Advocate, Monsignor Zyporszka said.

Cardinal Bernardi looked at Father Darelli.

"Any objections?"

"No, Your Eminence."

Shosha walked to the stand.

"Please remember that you are under oath during these proceedings," the Cardinal told Shosha.

"Signora," the monsignor began. "This is the first we've heard of the rabbi's fate during these proceedings. Did you ever see him after December of 1944—after the liberation of Melinka?"

"No," Shosha said. "I didn't see him after I left Praga."

"Other than the subject of this inquiry, Jakub Chelzak, did you see anyone you had previously known from Warsaw?"

"No," Shosha said.

"Not your madre or padre?"

"No."

"And when did you last see Signor Chelzak?"

"In 1947."

"The year before his death."

"Yes."

"How many times had you seen him after Melinka?"

Shosha looked at Fr. Darelli. He nodded.

"Several times right after," Shosha told the monsignor. "They took us to the same hospital—in Krakow. After that, I wrote to him. I moved to London for a time and then to the States."

"Did Jakub Chelzak ever discover what happened to his own family?" the monsignor asked.

"I told him about his brother. I told his mother as well," Shosha said. "Jakub went back to live with his mother in Malbork until he died."

"She outlived him by twenty years, did she not?"

"I don't know the exact number, but it was several years."

"So, as close as he supposedly was to Our Lord, Jakub Chelzak died in ill health, a young man."

"I object to the inference," Darelli said. "The Promoter may make such a statement during his summation, but it is not appropriate here."

Cardinal Bernardi looked at a woman transcribing the proceedings. "You will strike that last remark," the Cardinal instructed. He looked at the monsignor, who turned again to Shosha. Darelli interrupted.

"What did Signor Chelzak do when you told him about his brother?" he asked. "How did he take it?"

Shosha looked stricken. Her face was red and pained. She was trying hard not to cry or appear weak. "Terribly," she said.

The Cardinals conferred. Then the room returned to a hush.

"Is that what occasioned your seeing Signor Chelzak?" Darelli asked. "To tell him about his brother?"

Shosha was silent for at least a minute. "One reason, yes," she said. "I had kept it from him. We were not well enough to discuss it for a long time. I wanted to tell him in person." Shosha paused. Her voice was unsteady. "When he died the following year, I was not there. He was better and then he died and that was not expected."

"You were married by this time?" the monsignor interjected.

"In 1948."

"And your husband died in," he looked through his notes, "1967?"

"Yes," Shosha said. "Nine years ago next month."

"He was ill?"

"Yes," Shosha said. "He had cancer."

"I'm sorry to hear that." The Devil's Advocate paused. "Let me ask you, Signora Price—did you have occasion to pray to Jakub Chelzak to heal your husband?"

"I object to that question," Darelli said. "Signora Price is not here to provide witness to Signor Chelzak's posthumous demeanor."

"I will allow that Signora Price can answer the question or not, according to her own wishes," Cardinal Bernardi said.

Monsignor Zyporszka looked at Shosha.

"I don't pray to saints," Shosha said. "I'm a Jew."

"Indeed," the monsignor said. "Then why are you here, Signora Price? What would motivate you to bear witness in this forum on this man's behalf as—a Jew?"

"Again, an objection Your Eminence," Darelli said. "Whether or not Signora Price is a Jew is not at issue here."

Cardinal Bernardi looked at the men at his table. "Again," he said, "I will allow that Signora Price answers the question only if she so desires."

Shosha looked at the Devil's Advocate.

"I asked," said the monsignor, "why you were here—why are you bearing witness at a hearing about Christian sainthood, since you yourself are a Jew?"

Shosha thought about this question. She thought about it long enough that in the quiet of the room, you could hear fidgeting and papers rustling, and coughing, here and there.

"I'm not here as a Jew," Shosha said finally. "Just a person. From where we were, the name Jew or Christian only mattered to the enemy. We were just people, trying to survive."

"But still, you don't believe in saints?" the monsignor said. "Why help someone become something that you yourself do not believe in?"

Shosha looked at Fr. Darelli as he had coached her to do when questions arose that might be objectionable.

"Must she answer that, Your Eminence?" Darelli said.

The Cardinal conferred with the others on his panel. He looked at Fr. Darelli and Shosha.

"We believe in light of her previous answer to the first part of the question that she must also now answer the second part," the Cardinal said.

Darelli looked at Shosha.

"Again," the monsignor said. "Why help—"

"I remember the question," Shosha interrupted. She thought. She looked at the frescoes on the walls and the ornate furnishings. The afternoon sun peaked through velvety drapes. The room felt hollow.

"You're asking me how can a Jew vouch for a saint and I would say that I can vouch for a good man. Jakub and his brother Karl were good men—two of the best men I ever knew. The rabbi was a good man. My father was a good man. Janusz Jerczek was a good man. My husband was a wonderful man and he was not a Jew."

"Why did you marry him?" the monsignor asked.

"Because I loved him," Shosha said.

Father Darelli stood and looked at her. "You knew many saints during the war, didn't you, Signora Price?"

Shosha took a deep breath. "Yes," she said.

The room was silent. Darelli smiled. The Devil's Advocate circled and looked at Shosha.

"You must not be observant," the monsignor said to Shosha. She stiffened.

"I am," she said.

"You married a Gentile."

"My husband converted."

"Converted?" the monsignor asked. "From what faith?"

"Michael was Catholic," Shosha said. The monsignor winced.

"He did this for you?"

"For both of us," Shosha said. "For our children. But mostly, for himself. We raised our daughter in the faith—she had bat mitzvah at twelve and we have shared Torah ever since she was little. We are not strict Orthodox, but we observe the holidays and go regularly to Synagogue. My faith has sustained me my entire life."

"Your faith," Darelli interjected. He looked at Shosha. "Your faith sustained you! But tell this proceeding, Signora, per favore, tell this proceeding: how did *you* sustain your faith?"

The question hit Shosha, and she thought. Her face felt hot. She tried to answer but couldn't find the words.

"How did you sustain your faith?"

"I never forgot who I was," she said.

"Not for one moment?" Darelli said.

"No."

Monsignor Zyporszka looked up from his papers. He cleared his throat. "I still believe it is unprecedented that a Jew would bear witness in a proceeding such as this."

"Not so," Fr. Darelli said. "I refer to the case of Edith Stein, which has been wending its way through these chambers for some years now."

The Congregation looked at the Devil's Advocate. "The case of Edith Stein has not gone forward," Monsignor Zyporszka said. "It has been stalled for years."

"It is moving at the usual rate," Darelli said.

"Edith Stein did not bear witness for a candidate."

"No," Darelli said. "Edith Stein *is* a candidate. She was also a Jew. With her life, she bore witness for herself."

EDITH STEIN WAS BY birth a Jew and by faith an atheist in her younger years and a Carmelite nun thereafter. She was born on Yom Kippur in 1891 in Breslau, Germany, now Wroclaw, Poland. One of the first women admitted to the University of Gottingen, Stein studied under the philosophers Edmund Husserl and Martin Heidegger. Husserl said she was the best doctoral student he ever had, brighter even than Heidegger.

Stein volunteered for duty in military hospitals during the First World War. For her service, the German Army awarded her the medal of valor. After the war, she became Husserl's assistant at the University of Freiburg. One evening in 1921, the twenty-nine year old atheist-philosopher started reading the autobiography of St. Teresa of Avila, founder of the Carmelite Order. She didn't put the book down until she had finished it and at that point, she decided Catholicism was her faith. On New Year's Day 1922, she received Catholic baptism, but continued to attend Synagogue with her aging mother.

By the standards of the day, Stein was a radical feminist. She gave talks around Europe with titles such as The Ethos of Women's Professions; Principles of Women's Education; and The Significance of Woman's Intrinsic Value in National Life.

"There is no profession which cannot be practiced by a woman," she said. "The nation...doesn't simply need what we have. It needs what we are."

"Her best pupil is the Holy Father," said another Jewish convert to Catholicism, Jean-Marie Cardinal Lustiger, the Archbishop of Paris. "Anyone who has read the Pope's encyclical on The Dignity and Vocation of Woman, or his more recent Letter to Women, will see immediately how much they owe to Edith Stein's pioneering work on this subject." The Holy Father to whom Cardinal Lustiger referred was Karol Joseph Wojtyla— Pope John Paul II—many years after Stein's death.

Stein also considered a woman's role as mother and spouse. A woman who gives birth has an innately greater need to nurture life, Stein reasoned. "To cherish, guard, protect, nourish, and advance growth is her natural, maternal yearning," she wrote.

The two world wars Stein witnessed were masculine constructs. Men started and executed the wars. Male despots ruled the Soviet Union and Germany. Men, Stein argued, had a lesser capacity for empathy than women did. The people who knew Edith Stein said she had a tremendous capacity for empathy.

She possessed "a tender, even maternal, solicitude for others," wrote her spiritual director in the late 1920's, Abbot Raphael Walzer. "She was plain and direct with ordinary people, learned with the scholars, a fellow-seeker with those searching for the truth. I could almost say she was a sinner with the sinners."

In 1933, Edith wrote about an insight she had at a Holy Thursday mass she attended at the Carmelite Convent in Cologne. "I told our Lord that I knew it was His cross that was now being placed upon the Jewish people; that most of them didn't understand this, but that those who did would have to take it up willingly in the name of all. I would do that."

After she entered the convent at age 42, Stein's mother and siblings—except her sister Rosa—viewed her as a traitor. "Why did you have to get to know him [Jesus Christ]?" Edith's mother told her. "He was a good man—I'm not saying anything against him. But why did he have to go and make himself God?"

Stein continued her scholarly work with books on Christian philosophy. She formally requested Pope Pius XI write an official defense of the Jewish people. Had he done so, the Church may have been in a better position to defend itself against charges

Church officials turned away from their Jewish brethren in the time of their greatest need.

After the November 8, 1938 Nazi attack known as *Kristallnacht*—the Night of the Broken Glass—the Carmelite Convent Prioress transferred Stein to the Dutch convent at Echt. At the convent, she offered her life to God for the Jewish people, global peace, and her Carmelite family. Her sister Rosa joined Edith in Echt as a Third Order Carmelite nun.

When Holland fell to the Third Reich, Edith and Rosa Stein were in danger again. They applied for Swiss visas so they could transfer to the Carmelite Convent of Le Paquier. The Swiss convent could accept Edith but not her sister, so both remained at Echt.

For four years, Edith and Rosa Stein lived each day knowing that the fatal knock at the door would come. It did, on Sunday, August 2, 1942. Stein had spent the day working on a book about St. John of the Cross. At 5:00 o'clock in the afternoon, *SS* officers came to the Convent and took the sisters away. Edith grasped her frightened sister's hand and reassured her that the two of them were "going for our people."

Eyewitnesses say Edith Stein was a model of composure during the early days of her captivity at the detention camp in Westerbork, Holland. She comforted and consoled the other women and fed the children and washed them and combed their hair.

"Maybe the best way I can explain it is that she carried so much pain that it hurt to see her smile," wrote a female survivor who was with Stein at Westerbork. "In my opinion, she was thinking about the suffering that lay ahead. Not her own suffering—she was far too resigned for that—but the suffering that was in store for the others. Every time I think of her sitting in the barracks, the same picture comes to mind: a Pieta without the Christ."

Five nights later, the Nazis deported the Westerbork captives to death camp Auschwitz. No one from the transport survived. On August 9, 1942, the Nazis gassed Stein. She was fifty years old when she died.

On May 1, 1987, Pope John Paul II beatified Edith Stein together with Father Rupert Mayer, a Jesuit Nazi-resister, at a Mass in Cologne, West Germany. Eleven years later, this same Pope canonized Edith Stein, Saint Edith Stein, philosopher and martyr, Christian and Jew, the patron saint of lost parents, on October 11, 1998 at St. Peter's Square in Vatican City.

SHOSHA MORDECHAI PRICE—WHO never learned the fate of her lost parents—opened a letter at her home in Brooklyn on July 2, 1991. She was sixty nine years old.

My Dearest Shosha:

It is my profound joy to inform you that the Holy Father, John Paul II, will return to his native land to beatify Jakub Chelzak at a Mass at the Church of Our Lady of Perpetual Help in Malbork, Poland on September 17 of this year. We have positive and irrefutable confirmation of the first canonical miracle in his name.

It is my sincere pleasure to invite you and your family to attend this very special occasion in honor of the friend you supported on his long journey to the pinnacle of honor in his Church.

I want to express to you my gratitude for your support and defense of Jakub Chelzak during the proceedings of so many years ago and your patience with this interminable process. His is a remarkable case and a similar one in my lifetime I will almost surely never see.

I recall what our friend and patron Edith Stein said as we walk in her path:

"The darker it becomes around us, the more we ought to open our hearts to the light that comes from on high."

In the darkest moments of your lives, Jakub Chelzak had a remarkable friend in you and you in him.

I sincerely hope to see you at the Mass—it's been some years! My best to your daughter and her family.

I remain,
Yours in the Lord,
Francisco Darelli, S.J., J.C.L, J.C.D.

Shosha's hands shook and she set the letter down and she wept for an hour alone. She didn't pick up the letter again until she was standing at the window on the evening of the 4th of July, watching fireworks across the bridge near the river. She heard the nearby explosions and watched the brilliant rain, the blues and the reds and the yellows. She turned away when she heard voices and the bell at her door—she was going out tonight, grand kids and all, and telling her daughter the news.

She went to answer the door when a bright burst lit up her living room and for a moment reminded her of Warsaw. She stopped short and she was startled until she realized what it was: A light from on high, come to remind her she was not in the dark anymore.

NOTES

About.com. *Death Marches. The Jewish Cemetery in Warsaw. Lebensraum. Tadeusz Kosciuszko.*

Adam Mickiewicz Institute for Polish Culture

Aktion Reinhard Camps Research Group. *Warsaw Ghetto. Warsaw Ghetto Uprising. Warsaw Ghetto Liquidation.*

Atlas, Michel C. *Ethics and access to teaching materials in the medical library: the case of the Pernkopf atlas.* Bulletin of the Medical Library Association. 2001 January, 89(1): 51–58.

Benjamin, Jordan L. *Understanding the Tradition of Shiva.*

Berenbaum, Michael. *Witness to the Holocaust.* New York: HarperCollins, 1997.

Bettelheim, Bruno. *Surviving and Other Essays.* New York: Random House, 1980.

Blessed Anicet Koplinksi, Capuchin Priest and Martyr. *CapDox: Capuchin   history   and   studies.* https://www.capdox.capuchin.org.au

Butovsky, Mervin and Jonassohn, Kurt (ed.). *Memoirs of Holocaust Survivors in Canada.* Concordia University Chair in Canadian Jewish Studies.

Carty, Charles Mortimer. *Padre Pio the Stigmatist.* Tan Books & Publishers, 1989.

Cook,   Stephen.   *Heinrich   Himmler's   Camelot: Pictorial/documentary: The Wewelsburg Ideological Center of the SS, 1934-1945.* Kressmann-Backmeyer, 1999.

Crankshaw, Edward. *The Gestapo: Instrument of Tyranny.* New York and London, 1956.

Davies, Norman. *Rising 44: The Battle for Warsaw.* London: Penguin Books, 2004.

Dornberger, Walter. *V-2: The Nazi Rocket Weapon.* New York: Viking Press 1954.

Ducki, Symforian Feliks, OFM, Cap. *Capuchin Martyr at Auschwitz.*

Edelman, Marek. *The Ghetto Fights*: *Warsaw, 1941-43*. London: Bookmarks Publications, 1990.

Englebert, Omer. *St. Francis of Assisi: A Biography*. Servant Ministries Publishing, 1979.

Ernst, Edzard. *A Leading Medical School Seriously Damaged*: *Vienna 1938*. Ann Intern Med. 15 May 1995, Volume 122, Issue 10, Pages 789-792.

Fest, Joachim C. *The Face Of The Third Reich*

Florida Center for Instructional Technology, College of Education, University of South Florida. *A Teacher's Guide to the Holocaust*. Entries on the Warsaw Ghetto.

Freeman, Joseph and Schwartz, Donald. *The Road to Hell: Recollections of the Nazi Death March*. St. Paul, Minn.: Paragon House, 1998.

Garcia, Max R. Survivor of Auschwitz, Mauthausen, Melk, Ebensee. Oral testimony. *Telling Their Stories: Oral History Archives Project*. The Urban School of San Francisco. May 2002, April 2003.

German Accounts of the Warsaw Uprising: Mathias
Schenk; Lt. Eberhard Schmalz; Lt. Peter Stölten; Lt. Hans
Thieme. http://www.warsawuprising.com/witness.htm

Gilbert, Martin. *The Final Solution: An Essay.* The Oxford
Companion to World War II. Oxford: Oxford University
Press, 1995.

Gilbert, Martin. *The Holocaust: A History of the Jews of
Europe During the Second World War*. New York: Henry
Holt and Company, 1985.

Goodrick-Clarke, Nicholas. *The Occult Roots of Nazism:
Secret Aryan Cults and Their Influence on Nazi Ideology.*
New York: New York University Press, 1994.

Gorcewicz, Halina. *Why, Oh God, Why? A Daily Diary of
Life Inside the Warsaw Ghetto.* Translated by Jerzy Klinger.

Gutman Y. *The Jews of Warsaw 1939-43.* Brighton: The
Harvester Press Ltd., 1982.

Guttman, Jon. *Genocide Delayed.* World War II Magazine,
March 2000.

Hale, Christopher. *Himmler's Crusade: The Nazi Expedition to Find the Origins of the   Aryan Race.* New York: Wiley, 2003.

Hebrew Lord's Prayer from the *Targum Franz Delitsch.*

Hiatt Holocaust Collection of the College of the Holy Cross. *Saint Edith Stein.*

Hilberg, R.; Staron, S.; Kermish J., editors. *The Warsaw Diary of Adam Czerniakow* New York, 1979.

Hitler, Adolf. *Mein Kampf.* Boston: Houghton Mifflin, 1971.

Höfer, Fritz. *Statement of a truck driver in Sonderkommando 4a,* 1959.

Hohne, Heinz. *The Order of the Death's Head: The Story of Hitler's SS.* New York: Penguin, 2000.

Holocaust History Project. *The Stroop Report: The Warsaw Ghetto Is No More*

Höss, Rudolf; Fitzgibbon, Constantine; Neugroschel, Joachim. *Commandant of Auschwitz : The Autobiography of Rudolf Höss.* Vermont: Phoenix Books, 2000.

Internet Sacred Text Archive.

Israel H.A. and Seidelman W.E. *Nazi origins of an anatomy text: the Pernkopf atlas*. Journal of the American Medical Association, 1996 Nov 27; 276(o): 1633.

Jewish Virtual Library. *Heinrich Himmler*.

Judaism 101. *Kashrut: Jewish Dietary Laws.* http://www.jewfaq.org/kashrut.htm

Kazantzakis, Nikos. *Saint Francis*. Touchstone, 1971.

Katz, Robert. *Second Sabbath: the Journey Ends.*

Korbonski, Stefan. The Polish Underground State: A Guide to the Underground, 1939-1945. New York: Hippocene Books, 1981.

The Koscieliska Valley.
http://www.koscieliska.pl/en.html

Levi, Primo. *Survival in Auschwitz*. New York: Simon and Schuster, 1996.

London Branch of the Polish Home Army Ex-Servicemen Association, *Polish Resistance in World War II*.

Lumsden, Robin. *Himmler's Black Order, 1923-45*. New York: Sutton Publishing, 1997.

Nuremberg Testimony of Jurgen Stroop.

New Advent Catholic Encyclopedia. *Mystical Stigmata.*

Nickell, Joe. *Stigmata: In Imitation of Christ*. Skeptical Inquirer, July 2000.

Noakes, Jeremy. *Hitler and Lebensraum in the East*. BBC History, 11-05-2004.

Ozick, Cynthia. *The Shawl*. The New Yorker, March 26, 1980.

Padfield, Peter. *Himmler: Reichsführer-SS*. London: Cassell, 2001.

Pipes, Jason. *Feldgrau: Research on the German armed forces, 1918-1945.*

Pope John Paul II. *Homily from the Canonization Of Edith Stein.*

Potapov, Valeri. *The Russian Battlefield.*
http://www.battlefield.ru

Roberts, Stephen H. *The House That Hitler Built.*
London: Methuen, 1938.

Roth, John K., Rubenstein, Richard L. *Approaches to Auschwitz: The Holocaust and Its Legacy.*   Westminster John Knox Press. August 31, 2003.

Ruffin, Bernard C. *Padre Pio: The True Story.* Our Sunday Visitor Publishing, 1991.

Ringelblum, Emmanuel. *Notes From the Warsaw Ghetto.* New York: Schocken Books, 1974.

Sabatier, Paul. *Life of St. Francis of Assisi.* Hodder and Stoughton, 1902.

Schwarzwaller, Wulf. *The Unknown Hitler: His Private Life and Fortune.* New York: Berkeley Books, 1990.

Shirer, William L. *The Rise and Fall of the Third Reich: A History of Nazi Germany.* New York: Touchstone, 1959.

Shumway, Daniel B., trans. *The Nibelungenlied.* New York: Houghton-Mifflin, 1909.

Simon Wiesenthal Museum of Tolerance, Online Multimedia Learning Center

Skarbek-Kruszewski, Zygmunt. *Bellum Vobiscum: War Memoirs.* Victoria, Australia: Skarbek Consulting Pty. Ltd. 2001.

Soudakoff, Sharon Ann. *Jewish Funeral and Mourning Customs.*

von Chézy, Wilhelmina Christiane. *Der Vollmond strahlt auf Bergeshöhn.*

Tebinka, Jacek. *Policy of the Soviet Union Towards the Warsaw Uprising.*

University of Minnesota Center for Holocaust and Genocide Studies. Histories, Narratives and Documents.

United States Holocaust Memorial Museum. *Holocaust Personal Histories. Trawniki.*

Uris, Leon. *Mila 18.* New York: Bantam, 1983.

W. K. Kellogg Health Sciences Library. *Oath and Prayer of Maimonides.*

Warsaw Uprising—1944: Diary Entries and Personal Accounts. Poland on the Web. University at Buffalo.

Warsaw Uprising of 1944.
http://www.warsawuprising.com

Warsaw Ghetto.
http://www.scrapbookpages.com/Poland/WarsawGhetto/index.html

Weinbaum, Laurence and Libionka, Dariusz. *Heroes, Hucksters, and Storytellers: On the Jewish Military Union (ZZW)*, The Polish Center for Holocaust Research, 2011.

Wikipedia. *Lebensraum; Saint*

Williams, D. J. *The History of Eduard Pernkopf's Topographische Anatomie des Menschen.* Journal of Biocommunication. San Francisco, Spring 1988, 15 (2): 2-12.

Winkelman, Roy, Ph.D. *A Teacher's Guide to the Holocaust: Archival Ghetto and Camp Photographs*

Winnington III, Paul F. *The Road to Sainthood.* Philadelphia: St. Joseph's University Campus Newsletter, 1997.

Wistrich, Robert. *Who's Who in Nazi Germany*, 2nd edition. New York: Routledge, 1995.

Woodward, Kenneth L. *Making Saints.* New York: Simon and Schuster, 1990.

World War II Multimedia Database. *The Polish Home Army Uprising*.

Yad Vashem. The Holocaust Martyrs' and Heroes' Remembrance Authority. *Photographs from the Warsaw Ghetto: The Jurgen Stroop Collection*, 2004.

Ibid. *Another View of the Warsaw Ghetto*

Ibid. *The Auschwitz Album.*

Yehudah Aryeh Leib Alter. *Sefat Emet*

DISCUSSION QUESTIONS

These questions address themes and subject matter in *The Fires of Lilliput*.

Symbolism

1) Which number or numbers recur in the story? How might they relate to the novel's themes?

2) What do you think the title means?

3) What purpose does the river Wisła serve as a recurring motif?

4) What do you think Shosha's visit to the empty orphanage symbolizes?

Relationships

1) Describe the relationship between Shosha, Rebekah, and Leiozia. How do you think it is like friendships between women generally? How is it unique?

2) How does Rabbi Gimelman's relationship with the Mordechai family change him?

3) How would you describe the relationship between Jakub and his brother Karl? Jakub is unique; do you think Karl really understands him?

4) Why do you think the rabbi recites the Lord's Prayer in Hebrew with Jakub?

Love and Friendship

1) Shosha says she loves several men, but differently. What does she mean?

2) Describe the friendship between Rabbi Gimelman and Jakub Chelzak.

3) Describe the friendship between Henryk Wojskowy and Moryc Zydowski. What role do their differing faiths play in their friendship?

4) Do Franny and Greta Strauss love one another? How would you describe his love for her? Her love for him?

Family

1) Who are the married couples in the novel? Describe their marriages and how they evolve.

2) Fathers are a recurring motif in the story. Who are the fathers (or fathers-to-be)? How do they approach fatherhood?

3) Compare and contrast the Mordechai and Chelzak families.

4) What do the officers at Camp Melinka have in common with a dysfunctional family?

Religion and Mysticism

1) In instances of "magical realism," several unexplainable events happen during the story. Describe some of them and what they might represent.

2) Jakub Chelzak has a reputation as a healer of maladies. Does he actually *heal* anyone during the story? How do you think he got this reputation? What happens to the people that he "heals?"

3) If the Dolina Koscieliska is a Garden of Eden, what do you think F. Scott and Zelda Fitzgerald represent? Franz and Greta Strauss?

4) The "Christ Figure" and "Moses Figure" are literary devices. The prisoner Andy in the *Shawshank Redemption* is a

Moses Figure who finds freedom and shows his friend the "promised land." In *One Flew Over the Cuckoo's Nest*, R. P. McMurphy becomes a Christ Figure by sacrificing himself for the freedom of his friends. Who might represent a Christ or Moses Figure in *The Fires of Lilliput*? Why?

Theme

1) How do the thoughts of Jewish philosopher Viktor Frankl mirror those of Christian theologian Langdon Gilkey? How do you think they relate to the story?

2) What do you think the evolving relationship between Shosha and Jakub represents?

3) "Character is Destiny," says an old adage. Who survives in this story? Who perishes? In each case, what kind of people are they?

4) After reading this story, do you see any differences between *religion* and *faith*? Which term would you use to describe Shosha—religious, faithful, or both? Jakub? Rabbi Gimelman? Major Petersdorf?

ABOUT THE AUTHOR

Michael Martin is a science, technology, and social justice journalist. He started his career as a science writer for United Press International and has written articles for The Scientist, MIT's Technology Review, Harvard Magazine, the Journal of the National Cancer Institute, the Epilepsy Foundation, the Association of American Medical Colleges, the US. Department of Energy, and the California, Oregon, and Missouri university systems.

For Science Magazine, Mike broke the story of British Prime Minister Tony Blair's attempt to "gag" his Chief Science Adviser over a climate change controversy. Other UK publications followed the piece, including The Independent and Daily Telegraph.

After Mike profiled her mysterious seven-year disappearance for Psychology Today, famed evolutionary biologist Margie Profet reunited with her family when a reader reported her whereabouts to authorities.

Mike has been a member of the National Press Club, the National Association of Science Writers, and the Local Independent Online News publishers association.

Contact Us

Heart Beat Publications, LLC
POB 125
Columbia, Mo   65205
marketing@heartbeatpublications.com

Thank You!

Thank you so much for reading The Fires of Lilliput. If you are so inclined, we'd greatly appreciate your thoughts on the book as a **rating or review** on its Heart Beat Bookstore customer page or on Goodreads. Reader reviews enhance the reading experience for everyone, and have become the number one way new readers discover new books. But they are also hard to come by, and always an honor to receive. Heart Beat Books and Goodreads offer star ratings and narrative reviews.

Rate and Review The Fires of Lilliput at HeartBeatBookStore.com or on Goodreads, The Fires of Lilliput page.